D0723960

"Well written, aptly conveying a strong sense of family among the sisters, the quartet shows great promise."

—4 stars, *RT Book Reviews* on *Undone by the Duke*

"Using lots of emotion, *Seduced by Her Highland Warrior* is sure to touch your heart and soul with the tenderness and love that shines from the pages. Michelle Willingham has penned another winner."

—4.5 stars, *CataRomance.com*

"Michelle Willingham writes characters that feel all too real to me. The tortured soul that is Kieran really pulled at my heartstrings. And Iseult's unfailing search for her lost child made this book a truly emotional read."

—*Publishers Weekly* on *Her Warrior Slave*

"Willingham successfully draws readers into an emotional and atmospheric new tale of the Clan MacKinloch. Allowing a gentle heroine to tame a hero who has lost his ability to speak draws readers into the story and keeps them enthralled to the very end. Well-crafted, brimming with historical details and romantic from beginning to end, this is Willingham at her best."

—4 stars, *RT Book Reviews* on *Tempted by the Highland Warrior*

"Two wounded souls find hope and redemption in *Surrender to an Irish Warrior*, a richly detailed and emotionally intense medieval romance."

—*Chicago Tribune*

"Willingham neatly folds equal measures of danger and desire into her latest historical, and the snippets from Emily's cookbook that open each chapter add an extra dash of culinary spice to her well-crafted romance."

—*Booklist* on *The Accidental Countess*

Unraveled
by the Rebel

Also by Michelle Willingham

SECRETS IN SILK SERIES (REGENCY SCOTLAND)

Undone by the Duke

MACEGAN BROTHERS SERIES (MEDIEVAL IRELAND)

Her Warrior Slave

"The Viking's Forbidden Love-Slave" in the *Pleasurably Undone* anthology

Her Warrior King

Her Irish Warrior

The Warrior's Touch

Taming Her Irish Warrior

"Voyage of an Irish Warrior"

"The Warrior's Forbidden Virgin"

Surrender to an Irish Warrior

"Pleasured by the Viking" in the *Delectably Undone* anthology

"Lionheart's Bride" in the *Royal Weddings Through the Ages* anthology

Warriors in Winter

Unraveled by the Rebel

A **SECRETS IN SILK** NOVEL

MICHELLE WILLINGHAM

Montlake Romance

Published by Montlake Romance, Seattle

www.apub.com

ISBN-13: 9781477807712
ISBN-10: 1477807713

Library of Congress Control Number: 2013938437

For Frankie—the best brother a girl could have. Thanks for always being there for me and for being such an inspiration.

Prologue

"He killed him." Paul Fraser's voice was flat, holding a lifetime of pain in those three words. "The Sassenach bastard hanged my father."

He looked half-wild with grief and anger, and Juliette Andrews's heart broke for him. Never before had she seen Paul this upset. His cropped black hair was matted, his blue eyes shadowed, as if he hadn't slept in days. Perhaps he hadn't eaten, either.

All the air seemed to leave her lungs, and she demanded, "What do you mean, they hanged him? Why?"

"No' here." Paul took her palm as he guided her across the glen and toward the hillside. A small copse of pine trees would hide them from open view, and she followed him into the shadow of the woods. Juliette held on to her skirts, stepping carefully over fallen logs and past the underbrush. Though her family would be furious with her for stealing away alone with him, she didn't care. In her eyes, there was no harm in it. Paul was seventeen, while she was only fourteen.

From the day she'd arrived in Scotland a few months ago, she'd been fascinated by the handsome Highlander. Paul had taken her out exploring near the foothills of Ben Nevis, showing her the beauty of this wild land. It was a forbidden thrill to take his hand and climb high above the valley, with a boy who made her heartbeat quicken.

And now, her blood ran cold at the thought of something happening to him.

"I swear to you, I didna steal anything. I tried to stop Malcolm from taking a sheep." The story came spilling out—of the raid gone bad and how Paul's friend had defended himself with a blade, only to be shot afterward. "They died, Malcolm and Lord Strathland's factor. I couldna save them, and I—I ran."

His eyes glittered as he tried to hold back the turbulent emotions. "Strathland's men followed me home, saying I'd murdered the factor. Da tried to talk to them, and they took him in my place."

He fell silent for a time, and she knew what he was about to say next.

"They left his body on the noose," he finished. "At Eiloch Hill, as an example to the others." Paul swallowed hard, his eyes filled with fury. "He's dead because of me." His hand tightened into a fist, and before she could stop him, he rammed it into a tree.

When he punched the trunk a second time, he drew back bloody knuckles. He didn't weep, as she would have done. The raw pain in his voice went deeper than any physical pain.

She wanted to say something. Anything to tell him how sorry she was. But words would mean nothing to him. Words wouldn't bring his father back.

Juliette hardly realized she was crying for him until he was in her arms, holding her with a desperate need. Leaning up against the tree, she let him take comfort from the embrace, her tears dampening his cheeks.

This was what he needed from her now. His posture was stiff, his body so tense, he was nearly trembling with rage. And yet, he never let go, as if she were the single strand holding his life together.

"It's not your fault," she whispered, stroking the back of his head. Paul didn't answer, but from his slumped shoulders, she could tell he didn't believe her. The only sign that he'd heard was a tightening of his arms around her.

For long moments, they stood together, their bodies pressed close. Although they had spent countless hours together, this was the first time she'd sensed the ground of friendship shifting between them. Her skin grew more sensitive to him, his body hard and strong against her own softness.

It was wrong to let him hold her like this. He was a poor crofter's son, and she, the daughter of an officer. Her parents expected her to wed a knight or a baronet one day. Perhaps even a peer, since her uncle was a baron. Although a quarrel between her father and his brother had brought them to this small estate in northwest Scotland, she hadn't minded leaving her home in London. Here, she had a freedom she'd never known before.

Her heart was pounding as she closed her eyes, fighting against the unbidden response to his touch.

"I'm leaving Ballaloch," Paul said at last. "My mother is sending me away to Edinburgh, to live with my uncle."

The words sank into her like a blade, though she knew he had to go. They might have hanged Kenneth for the raid, but it was only a matter of time before they came after Paul. "It will be safer for you there."

"My mother doesna wish to look upon my face anymore," he said, his eyes staring off into the distance. "No' after what I did."

His words were laden with grief, and she squeezed his palm, wishing she knew what to say to him. "It will be all right."

"No. No it won't." He let go of her hand, resting his elbows on his knees. "I don't ken when I'll be able to come home again."

Juliette drew up to her knees, reaching to touch his face. "Your mother likely wants to protect you from the men who did this. You're the only son she has left."

"It should've been me swinging on those gallows."

"Don't say it." She touched her forehead to his, and he covered her hands, bringing both her palms to his face. "I know you grieve for him."

"I just . . . canna believe any of it happened. I keep thinking that I'll wake up and he'll be with us again." His midnight-blue eyes grew shadowed, and he closed them as if to push back the grief. In the filtered light of the trees, the outside world slipped away until it was only Paul and her.

Her hands moved up to his shoulders, and in a moment, she was in his arms again.

This is wrong. Move away, her conscience ordered.

He's your closest friend, her heart argued back. Paul needed her, and she felt his pain as if it were her own. If her father had died in such a way, she couldn't imagine the emptiness inside.

"You can't stay in Scotland," she whispered, resting her cheek against his. "It's too dangerous." The scent of his skin reminded her of the wild pine that grew in the Highlands. She inhaled it, trying to make a memory of him.

"I want nothing to happen to you," she insisted. "Promise me that you'll do as your mother bade you and be safe."

"I want justice." He cut her off, closing his eyes. "How can I go to Edinburgh and turn my back on what Lord Strathland did to my father?"

"When you return, perhaps things will change." Juliette touched his cheek, and his hands moved to her waist, absently stroking her spine. A ripple of aching warmth flooded through her, and she shied away from the feelings she wasn't ready to face.

His gaze grew distant, and he shook his head. "The earl should suffer the same fate as my father."

Juliette said nothing, knowing he was speaking words born of suffering and fear. "Let it go, Paul," she murmured. "Lord Strathland is too powerful to fight against."

When he gave no reply, she sensed that if he stayed here, he would do something rash. She didn't doubt that was another reason why his mother was sending him away. "Please," she repeated. "For me."

"For now," he acceded. "But his time will come." From the dark look on his face, she saw the promise of vengeance. "Someone has to hold Strathland to blame for the way he treats the clansmen. He's earned his riches from their blood."

"It doesn't have to be you." She wrapped a handkerchief around his knuckles, raising her eyes to his. "Not now, anyway."

His midnight-blue eyes locked on to hers. "I won't forget, Juliette."

"I hope you don't," she said. "Not everything, anyway." A nervous energy rose up in her stomach from the way he was looking at her now. She let go of his hand, not knowing what to say to him.

His gaze centered on her face. "Some things canna be forgotten."

When his palm touched her cheek, she went utterly still. The look in his eyes was of a haunted man, one who saw her as far more than a friend. Although they were both too young, there was an undeniable bond with Paul Fraser. She couldn't say what it was, but in his eyes, she glimpsed a pathway leading toward a forbidden life.

"Could I kiss you before I go?" he murmured.

Blood rushed to her face, for she'd never been kissed before. He flustered her, and she didn't know what to say. But he took her silence for acquiescence. His mouth poised over hers, and at the touch of his lips, a thread of innocence bound them together. It was the barest whisper of a kiss, only a slight pressure upon her lips.

And yet, it held an unspoken promise. She'd never known that this sort of temptation existed, and without understanding it, she kissed him back. Warnings poured through her as his mouth moved upon hers, the heat awakening a rush of sensation. When his hands moved down her back, she felt a thrill of anticipation. Of wanting him, needing more.

Both of them gave in to the desire, the kiss opening, his tongue sliding within her mouth. She accepted him, her breath seizing in her lungs as she realized that there had always been more than friendship between them.

Juliette clung to him, even knowing that this was wrong. Paul Fraser was a secret desire she could never, ever fulfill.

"I'll write to you," he said against her mouth.

She could hardly catch her breath, for her mind was spinning with the certainty of broken dreams. In her heart, she was afraid she would never see him again.

Chapter One

He'd been waiting two years to see her again.

Dr. Paul Fraser held back from the other wedding guests, searching for a glimpse of the young woman who had haunted him since the day he'd left Ballaloch. Although he'd come back a few times in the past five years, Juliette had been gone during his most recent visits. The last time he'd seen her, he'd asked Juliette to marry him . . . and since that day, all of her letters had stopped. Without a single word of explanation.

He wanted to believe that something had happened to the letters. That she'd never received the dozens of notes he'd sent, and that one conversation would solve the misunderstanding. But a heaviness centered within him as he suspected that it was no misunderstanding at all. She'd made her choice, and it wasn't him.

He wouldn't beg for answers. But neither would he let her disappear among the crowd of guests at her sister's wedding. After all this time, he wanted to look into her eyes and see the truth—no matter how bitter it might be.

The bride and groom stood at the top of the staircase, while the unmarried women gathered below. Paul stood among the men, but his attention was fixed upon Juliette. She had her back to him, but she had grown taller, her waist slim. He yearned to see her face and the green eyes that had held him spellbound all these years.

The voice of reason told him to leave her be and let go of the past. But his stubborn heart wouldn't relent. Not yet.

The bride tossed her ice-blue silk bonnet over the railing, and it landed in Juliette's arms. She stared at the bonnet as if it were a poisonous snake, and the cheers from the wedding guests were deafening.

"You'll be the next to marry!" The housekeeper beamed. "Isn't that wonderful, lass?"

But Juliette did not appear pleased at all. Instead, her face had gone white, as if she'd been chosen for her own execution.

Before Paul realized what was happening, the bridegroom had tossed his hat over the top of the railing. It was about to fall into the hands of one of his kinsmen, and Paul seized it before the man could lay claim to it.

He knew what the token meant, and this was a means of speaking with her, of finally learning why she was refusing to see him. But as he moved through the crowd of people, he stopped before her and saw more than he'd expected.

The young woman standing before him was no longer the same Juliette he'd known. Paul could see it in the way she stared off into the distance, her mind distracted. To a stranger, she might appear like any other woman . . . calm and composed.

And yet . . . he saw through her façade. Her brown hair, once gleaming with gold strands, was now dull and matted, as if she hadn't bothered to do more than pin it up. She was an enigma to him, with her sad green eyes. She'd grown into a slender lady, but there were hollows in her cheeks and shadows beneath her eyes. Almost as if she'd stopped eating.

Juliette shoved the bonnet into her younger sister Amelia's hands and started for the door. It was as if she couldn't bear the thought of being paired with him.

Pride made him hold his ground while she fled. It was clear that she wanted nothing to do with him, and that was the answer he'd expected. Even so, it wasn't like her to run. The young woman he'd known would have blushed and laughed at the good-natured teasing. She wouldn't have fled.

It wasn't safe for her to be outside alone. And while she might not want his company, he intended to ensure that she was all right.

One of his friends, Rory MacKinloch, caught his arm. "She's a bonny lass, but with a tender heart, lad. Mind yourself." Rory tightened his grip, as if he considered himself Juliette's adopted big brother.

Paul shrugged the man's hand away. "I've known her e'er since the day she set foot in Scotland." And he'd easily wager that he knew her better than anyone. She'd opened up her heart to him in dozens of letters.

A knowing smile spread over Rory's face. "She doesna seem to be wanting your attentions, lad. You might set your sights on another."

"She's the one for me. Always has been." He crossed through the crowd of wedding guests, knowing Juliette had slipped away outside. When he reached the front door, he opened it and saw that the clouded sky held the promise of snow. The late January weather had been harsh, the bitter cold making it even more difficult for the crofters.

Juliette had grasped her skirts and was running toward the barn. As he followed her, his gaze passed over the rows of tents housing the refugee crofters. The tents were set up amid the snow, while several outdoor hearth fires had dwindled to ashes.

The crofters had been forced off the land when the Earl of Strathland had refused to renew their leases this past fall—his mother among them. If it weren't for the Duke of Worthingstone, who had agreed to let all of the crofters rebuild their homes on his land, Paul would have brought his mother back to Edinburgh. As it was, Bridget had insisted on remaining among the others, no matter how dismal the living conditions were. She was their only midwife and was stubborn enough to endure the freezing nights.

Others had refused to be displaced. When some of the crofters had tried to return to their homes in secret, Lord Strathland's factor, Mr. Melford, had ordered their homes set on fire.

Sometimes with the crofters still inside.

Paul's jaw tightened at the memory. He'd treated countless burn victims, fighting to save their lives. It only strengthened his need for vengeance against the earl. Not only because of what had happened to his own family, but for all the others as well.

He stopped before the barn, resting his hand against the wooden doorframe. Instinct warned him to leave Juliette alone, but the need to protect her was stronger.

He was here.

Juliette Andrews's heart was beating so fast, she could hardly breathe. The past few years had transformed Dr. Paul Fraser into a fiercely handsome man. His dark hair had a hint of curl to it, and those midnight-blue eyes had turned her knees to uncooked custard. After she'd caught her sister's bonnet, he'd reached for the groom's hat.

Any other woman would have been thrilled that he'd been the one to grasp it, instead of another man. Juliette, on the other hand, was filled with panic. This tall, devastatingly handsome man was not going to listen to her reasons why she intended to remain a spinster for the rest of her life. From the moment Paul had returned to Scotland, she'd been well aware of his pursuit, despite her attempts to avoid him. He wanted answers, and she had no intention of revealing anything to him.

She tried to find her calm, sensible side. It was natural that he should want to speak with her after all this time. They'd been friends, after all.

But he wanted more.

And more wasn't something she could give.

Juliette went to stand by one of the stalls, reciting the multiplication tables in order to calm her disordered mind. If only she could sort her life into neatly ordered columns that added up correctly.

Her brain reminded her that she owed him no explanations at all. Feelings altered, especially when time and distance were involved.

Yes, that would do. She willed the ice around her heart to harden, reminding herself that she could not allow herself to weaken around Paul Fraser. The desires of a young girl had no place in her life now.

Numbers, ink, and paper were her dearest companions now. She would grow old, her fingers stained with the written numbers that accounted for her family's earnings. Her heart was frozen over so that she would never feel the broken edges that remained.

Juliette took comfort from the decisions she'd made. She would not dwell upon the nightmares of the past or the mistakes. Nor would she allow one sinfully handsome Highlander to unravel all of her carefully laid plans.

Her heart had already been broken. And so help her God, she would hold fast to her secrets so that he would turn away from her and find a woman worthy of his love.

For it could never, ever be her.

Paul fingered the hat in his hands and set it down outside the barn door. Juliette had retreated farther inside, her hands resting against one of the stalls as if to steady her thoughts. Though he didn't speak a word to her, she glanced up when he entered.

"You followed me." Her expression held traces of resignation. "I was afraid you would."

It wasn't exactly an encouraging greeting. "I came to watch over you, not to bother you." He studied her, sensing that this would be one of those conversations where not a single word he spoke would be the right one.

"I'm all right, really." She nodded toward the door, as if hoping he'd leave.

Beneath her mask of indifference, he knew there was more to this. For weeks now, he'd tried to see her, and she'd stubbornly refused. Now, she was a stranger to him. In the evening light, she appeared more fragile. Almost as if she'd forgotten how to laugh.

"It was kind of you to watch over me," she said. "But I just needed a moment alone." She tucked a strand of fallen brown hair behind one ear and eyed the door as if she wished he'd walk through it.

But Paul had no intention of leaving. Not yet. He took a step forward and eyed the horse stalls. "I must tell you, this wasna how I imagined seeing you again."

"It's been a long time." Her voice was cool, as if she were anxious for him to go. And damn it all, he couldn't think of why she'd come to dislike him so. All he'd done was ask her to marry him.

"You should go, Dr. Fraser," she advised. "I'm certain your friends will be missing you."

Your friends. As if she weren't one of them? Then, too, she was calling him *Doctor,* instead of using his name. Aye, her desire for distance was perfectly clear, though he didn't know why. He hadn't seen her in years, and he doubted if he'd offended her during the ten minutes he'd been in her presence.

If she were any other woman, he'd think she was playing games. But then, Juliette had never been that sort. She'd always been steadfast and honest.

"*We* were friends once," Paul reminded her. "Or has that changed, since I left to study medicine?" He crossed his arms and waited for an answer. If she didn't want him any longer, then he'd go.

Beneath the guise of indifference, he caught a glimpse of fear. She was trying to remain calm, to behave as if nothing had changed. But there were shadows beneath her eyes, a frailty to her pale skin.

Juliette walked closer to him and stared for a long moment. "I don't know what we are anymore." Her voice held years of regret. "But you shouldn't be here alone with me. It's not proper."

"Now you sound like your sister Margaret. Not the girl who used to climb trees with me." Paul took a step closer, watching to see if she truly meant it.

She didn't retreat but instead stood her ground, repeating, "I said you should go."

"So you did." And he would, as soon as he had the answers he wanted. He'd always trusted his instincts, and there was something about her demeanor that belied her words.

Slowly, he reached out to take her hands, bringing them to rest upon his chest. It was a test to see if she would consider him a threat. Her gloved fingers were small, but when he released them, she didn't pull away. Instead, her palms covered his beating heart. There was heartbreak in her eyes, as if she drew comfort from the touch. It took every ounce of restraint not to pull her into his arms and hold her tight.

After they'd grown so close through years of letters, he'd made his desires known. And although his prospects were uncertain, he wanted her to know that he would take care of her. "You've been avoiding me since I returned to Scotland."

"I was in London," she argued.

"You refused to see me when I paid a call on you."

"That was my mother." She shook her head. "I didn't know you'd come until she'd already turned you away."

"Would you have wanted to see me?"

For a moment, her expression held a yearning that nearly stopped his heart. Her hands moved slightly against his skin, and she closed her eyes. She'd been about to say yes. He was sure of it.

A brittle look flashed over her face before she veiled it. "We hardly know one another anymore. It's been too many years."

"Did you forget what there was between us?" His hand moved to the curve of her cheek, and fear welled up in her green eyes. She looked as if she wanted to flee but didn't. A blush colored her cheeks, and he could see that she hadn't forgotten. It was in her eyes and in the way she wasn't shoving him back, telling him she didn't care a whit.

She *did* care. It was there in her touch, for she wasn't pulling away. She was leaning against him as if she remembered every day they'd spent together when they were young. He relaxed his hands, giving her every opportunity to move away. The fact that she remained in place offered a grain of hope. It was only her words that contradicted her actions.

"There are dozens of women back there who would fall down at your feet, if you would but look at them." Her voice was heavy, and she lowered her gaze.

"It wouldna make a difference," he said quietly. "There is only one woman I want."

"Not me." She took a breath and stepped back from him. In that moment, he saw such a wounded spirit, he wondered what had happened during the last two years. She was behaving older than her nineteen years.

"What changed, Juliette?" He wanted to hear the reasons from her own lips, to understand why she'd been avoiding him.

He thought back to the fires that happened a few months ago during the evictions. Had she somehow been threatened during the violence? He'd believed she was safe in London at the time, but perhaps not. His time had been spent tending the wounded, and he'd lost track of everything except the fight against death.

"We're not children anymore, Dr. Fraser," she reminded him. "Both of us have changed."

"Look in my eyes and tell me you want naught to do with me. Tell me your feelings changed, and I'll walk away this moment. You willna see me again."

When he met her gaze, she only flushed. "It's been a long time." It wasn't the answer he'd been expecting. Something was troubling her, but she would not say what it was.

Paul put his hands on her shoulders, his thumbs caressing her through the wool of her gown. "Aye, it has." With a heavy sigh, he admitted, "I suppose we could start anew, as friends again." He took a step back, trying to grant her distance.

A vulnerability crossed her face, as if she remembered the lost years between them. But she shook her head with regret. "I don't know if that's wise."

"Because I'm poor?"

"Poverty has nothing to do with it." She softened her tone. "You've done well for yourself, Dr. Fraser. I'm happy for you." There was a hint of pride on her face, as if she meant what she'd said.

Her sudden shift confused him, for in her tone, he'd caught a glimpse of the girl who had once been his friend. The one who had answered the early letters, encouraging him through the endless hours of study. The girl who had kissed him, on that day he'd left Ballaloch, so many years ago.

"When I returned to Ballaloch, two years ago, I asked you to wed me." He met her gaze, unflinching. "You said it was too soon, but you didna say no. Then I ne'er heard from you again." It was the silence that bothered him most, more than the secrets she was holding back. "Do you no' think I deserve an explanation, Juliette?"

He refused to call her Miss Andrews, despite what was proper. To him, she would always be Juliette.

She went motionless, as if trying to find the right words. At last, she answered, "I know the sort of life you want. And it's not for me."

Again, she was trying to push him away. But what did she mean, "the sort of life" he wanted?

"I want the life every man wants. I want a wife and bairns. I want to spend my days making you happy." He moved behind her, waiting to see if she would flee. Instead, she remained still. He drew his arms around her, pulling her back against him.

"You can't." But she leaned her head against him, making no move to escape his embrace. He didn't know if he was imagining it, but she seemed to welcome his arms around her. It gave him hope that perhaps there *was* a chance for them.

"Is it all men? Or just me?" He breathed in the scent of her hair, knowing that there would never be another woman for him. Not like her.

She turned around to face him. "All men. And if it's a wife and children you want, you should look elsewhere."

She wasn't saying no to *him*. Only to marriage. He didn't know what to think of that, or why she no longer wanted to marry anyone. But like a stream that could wear down any mountain, he intended to quietly smooth away her reluctance.

"Why did you run from me, back at the house?" he demanded, resting his mouth against her temple. "Have I done something to make you afraid?"

"No." She moved her cheek against his, her breath warming his face. But in her voice, he caught the tremor of nerves.

Paul kept her palm in his, stroking the sensitive flesh with his thumb. Then he drew back to see the play of emotions on her face. "Something happened in the last year, didn't it?"

She paled at his words, and he saw that he'd stumbled upon the truth. "M-my father became a baron and inherited his brother's estates. And his debts."

"No. That isna the reason. You're no' the sort of woman who cares about a title."

She flushed and pulled away from him. "He went to fight in the war, leaving us behind. We had to struggle to survive here, and there's been so much violence between the earl's men and the crofters."

He still sensed that she wasn't giving him the full truth. In her green eyes, he caught a flustered air, as if she didn't want to reveal more.

"What happened to *you*, Juliette?" He deliberately used her first name again, wanting to remind her of the days when they'd been close friends, hardly more than adolescents.

She closed her eyes, crossing her hands around her waist. "You're a good man, Dr. Fraser. And you deserve so much more than a woman like me." Juliette braved a smile before she returned outside, leaving him to wonder about the secrets she held.

Juliette returned to her sister's wedding, feeling as if Dr. Fraser had already guessed her shame. Seeing him there, so handsome and strong, had made her heart weaken. But she was scarred by the past, and if Paul learned of it, he would turn away from her in disgust.

Worse, he wanted children. Her heart bled at the thought, for he would make a wonderful father. She could easily imagine him holding a son's hand, taking him for a walk across the glen or telling him stories before bedtime.

You can never give him children, her conscience warned. *It's best to let him go.*

Inside, she raged at the unfairness of it all. It was as if someone had severed the ribbons that bound up her dreams, letting them spill to the ground.

A thousand if-onlys wouldn't change the past. Nor could she allow the anger to consume her. It would only eat away at her spirit, transforming her into a bitter woman.

No, she would remain strong and steadfast in her vow to remain a spinster. Paul would live his life, and she would remain wedded to numbers and accounts.

Her traitorous, foolish heart thought that was a terrible idea.

What were numbers, compared with a Highlander who took her breath away? Although the years had distanced her from Paul, he'd never faltered in his friendship. But it wasn't friendship he wanted now.

She could see that in the way he'd watched her, as if he could see through her words to the secrets she held inside. He'd grown taller, and his body was lean and muscled. When he'd touched her, the warmth of his palms had made her pulse quicken.

She'd expected it to be awkward and strange, after so many years. Instead, from the moment she'd seen him, Paul Fraser was a threat. Not only because he cared for her . . . but also because he'd conjured up feelings she never wanted to face.

He might have stolen a kiss, if she'd encouraged him. She might have allowed it, if she were still an innocent.

Juliette blinked back the tears, ignoring the ache within her. She leaned back against the wall, wondering what she should do. The wisest move would be to push Paul away, to refuse to see him again, as she'd done already. But seeing him again after so many years had only pried open the door holding back her rage at being ruined.

Another woman might hide the truth, pretending to be a virgin, leading Paul down a path to marriage. But she was irrevocably broken, and it would be unfair to him, leading him to believe in lies.

She exhaled a slow stream of breath, freezing back the dormant feelings. Gathering her control until no one would see her discomposure.

Her older sister Margaret crossed the room to come nearer. "Are you all right? Dr. Fraser didn't do anything to upset you, did he?" Though her sister didn't chastise her, Juliette knew that Margaret disapproved of a woman and a man meeting alone. It wasn't at all proper, even though she'd known Paul since she was fourteen.

"No, I'm fine." Turning her attention back to their eldest sister, she remarked, "Toria looks lovely, doesn't she? I'm happy for her."

The wedding had been simple, a gathering at home while their eldest sister had married the man she had come to love. When the Duke of Worthingstone had gazed at his bride, they'd all seen the appreciation in his eyes.

"A duke." Margaret sighed wistfully. "Can you believe it?"

"I know she'll be happy, but I don't envy her at all," Juliette admitted. The thought of becoming a duchess in London society was impossible to imagine. And for her sister, it would be even more difficult, since Victoria had been too afraid to leave the house for the past five years. When they'd journeyed here, an accident en route had caused her to be inadvertently left behind, leaving her stranded in the Scottish Highlands for days. After that, her anxieties had held her prisoner in the house. It was only with the duke's help that she'd managed to walk past the front door. No one knew how she would manage to travel to London with her new husband.

Juliette moved into the parlor, keeping on the outskirts of the other guests. Her mother, Beatrice, was beaming with joy, thrilled at her daughter's successful match. Soon enough, she would drag the rest of them back to London, in the hopes of securing successful marriages.

The thought was both reassuring and frightening. Juliette had her own reasons for wanting to be away from Ballaloch. Yet, her mother would never understand why she wanted to remain a spinster. At the thought of confessing her nightmare, nausea roiled in her stomach. She intended to put it off for as long as humanly possible.

Victoria crossed the room alone, and Juliette thought it odd that her husband would have left her side on their wedding day. Her sister was twisting her hands, eyeing the door with uncertainty.

A moment later, Dr. Fraser came through the front door. His gaze narrowed upon one of the Highlanders, and he crossed through the crowd, speaking quietly to Mr. Cain Sinclair. There was a sense of urgency in his demeanor, and when Juliette made her way toward them, she caught only Paul's last words: "Get the horses."

For what purpose? Juliette frowned, wondering if there had been another raid or if anyone was hurt. Paul met her gaze for a fraction of a second, inclining his head in a nod. He donned his hat and hurried back outside.

Before Mr. Sinclair could join him, Juliette caught the man's arm, craning her neck to look at him. "What's going on?"

"Let me by," he said. "We heard that Lord Strathland has sent men riding toward this house. We're wanting to know where they are and why they're coming."

Her mind went numb at the thought. Only this past autumn, the Earl of Strathland had evicted the MacKinloch crofters on his land in order to make room for his vast herds of sheep. Her family had given the local clan refuge before the duke had agreed to give them space on his land for permanent homes, but the fighting had continued between the earl's men and the crofters.

Lord Strathland was a threat to all of them. The very thought of the man tightened the fear within her, and she wished he'd go back to England. She couldn't understand why he stayed here, in the midst of thousands of acres of grazing land, when he could live on another estate. For as long as she could remember, he'd lived in this region like a king trying to conquer all the surrounding lands. He'd tried, time and again, to buy her parents' land, only to have her father refuse. It was also the reason why he'd wanted to wed her—in the hopes of winning Ballaloch as a marriage settlement.

Juliette clenched her hands together to stop them from shaking. "Don't let Strathland ruin my sister's wedding."

Sinclair's blue eyes hardened into chips of ice. "None of us will let any harm be done here. No' when we can stop them." Without another word, he pushed past her and opened the door.

Juliette followed him. She caught a glimpse of Dr. Fraser and the duke as they mounted their horses. At the sight of Paul riding away, a pang of worry caught her heart. *Let him be safe,* she prayed. She stood watching them until the three men disappeared into the hills and she closed the door at last.

An iciness threaded through her veins, though she pushed it back. From the window, she saw the sun sinking below the horizon. Her sister Victoria was standing near the edge of the crowd, as if she desperately wanted to escape.

Juliette understood that feeling. She made her way past the wedding guests until she reached her sister's side. Excusing them both from the others, she led Victoria back into the parlor.

"I thought you might want a moment to collect yourself," Juliette offered. "You look a little pale."

"I'm just worried," Victoria admitted. "We heard a rumor from one of the younger boys about Lord Strathland's men approaching the house. It may be nothing, but—"

"But they won't take that chance," she finished. Though she spoke with a reassuring air, her stomach twisted at the news. "I heard about it from Mr. Sinclair," Juliette added. "He and Dr. Fraser have gone to stop them from coming close." And God willing, they would succeed.

Her sister nodded but still appeared frightened. "My husband has gone with them."

Juliette squeezed her hands, murmuring words of reassurance that neither of them really believed. "Why don't you go to your room for a moment?" she suggested. "You look overwhelmed."

Her sister sent her a grateful look. "Thank you."

Though both of them knew that the bride wasn't supposed to abandon her own wedding celebration, Victoria wasn't comfortable around so many people. Her sister hated being the center of attention.

"Do you want me to accompany you?" Juliette offered.

For a moment, her sister faltered, as if considering it. "No, that's all right. I'll just take a moment to catch my breath before I return." Her cheeks flushed, and Victoria added, "So many of the women are teasing me about my wedding night. I'm not afraid at all, to be honest. Well, maybe only a little." There was an unexpected sparkle in her eyes, but Juliette could not imagine anticipating a wedding night with anything except dread. Were she in her sister's place, she'd be terrified.

For she knew exactly what Victoria would face. And though some of the women laughed and made innuendos about making love, it wasn't something Juliette wanted to ever endure.

Not again.

She closed her eyes for a moment and collected herself. Then she walked alongside her sister, until Victoria went upstairs, returning to her room. Juliette's hands were shaking against her own volition, and she returned to the parlor, inwardly repeating the words like a mantra.

It wasn't your fault. You were forced.

The shame coursed through her again, until she felt ill. Her vision blurred, and she gripped the edge of the chaise longue to steady herself.

It wasn't your fault.

Even so, the damage remained. Although at one point she'd dreamed of having a husband and children, she couldn't imagine that now. Never could she relive the pain of lying beneath a man, suffering the degradation of a wedding night. She would embrace spinsterhood wholeheartedly if it meant that she wouldn't have to experience such a nightmare again.

A sudden crash of breaking glass made her jump. Seconds later, Juliette saw that the cause was a flaming brick, wrapped in cloth and soaked with oil. The moment the brick hit the edge of the sofa, the fabric caught fire.

Juliette jerked back in shock, moving instinctively for a pitcher of water or something to smother the fire. The flames were moving far too quickly, and she saw a wet residue along the perimeter of the room.

Oil.

Her mind went numb, for it meant that someone had deliberately planned the fire. Someone who had come to her sister's wedding, possibly one of the crofters. But why? Her family had done nothing except offer sanctuary to them. They'd given the Scots a place to live.

Unless one of the earl's men had disguised himself among the others.

One of the guests spied the flames and cried out a warning. The screams of frightened children mingled with the voices of their mothers trying to shush them. Too many people pushed their way to the door, fighting to get out.

Someone grabbed her hand and pulled hard, dragging her outside with the others. The scent of smoke was acrid, the fire raging faster than it should.

Men were already gathering buckets from the well, forming a line to put out the fire. Juliette searched the crowd until she found her mother. Beatrice hugged her tight, already holding the hand of Amelia. Her sister's eyes were wide, terrified of the fire.

"Where's Margaret?" Beatrice demanded. "And Victoria?"

She let out a shaky breath of air. "Victoria was in her room, the last I saw her. I haven't seen Margaret." Juliette glanced up at the house and saw that the flames were spreading so fast, it was nearly impossible to keep the fire under control. "Do you think they got out?"

An icy coldness gripped her at the thought of losing her sisters.

It couldn't happen—she refused to even think of it. She stared at the flames, a thousand prayers rising up for their safety.

"Stay here while I find out." Beatrice took Juliette's hand and put Amelia in her care. "Watch over your sister."

As soon as their mother left, Amelia started crying. Though her sister was sixteen and prone to dramatics, in this instance, she had reason to fear. "Toria's still in the house. I just know it. I don't want her to die."

"She won't die." Juliette held her sister tight, trying to soothe her, though she silently feared Amelia was right about Victoria. "They'll bring her out, if she's still there. Though I don't think she would stay inside a burning house." Even as she said the words, she wasn't convinced. Her sister's fears were deeply rooted, and Juliette had never once seen Victoria walk outside in the five years they'd been here.

"They'll find her," she promised. But she kept searching for a glimpse of her sister. *Someone find her, please.*

There was an eerie silence, as the crofters passed their buckets down the line to the burning rooms. Though they fought bravely, Juliette suspected it was a losing battle to save the house. The stone exterior might remain, but the inside was crumbling apart.

Horses approached, and at last, the riders returned. The duke wasted no time in dismounting from his horse, racing inside the burning house when he learned that his wife was still inside. Juliette was horror-struck, afraid that both of them would die in the conflagration.

Dr. Fraser pushed his way through the people, his eyes searching until they rested upon her. The remainder of the crowd seemed to disappear until there was only him. His dark hair was rumpled, his eyes drinking in the sight of her. Though he didn't move any closer, she sensed his unspoken words.

You're all right?
Yes, I'm all right.
Thank God.

Juliette forced herself not to move forward, to let the distance remain between them. But she was so glad to see that he'd returned unharmed. It was a visible relief, though she couldn't let go of the worry for her sisters.

Dr. Fraser gave an almost imperceptible nod, fading back among the others until he took his place with the crofters. He rolled up his sleeves and aided them in fighting the fire while Juliette held back, praying that someone would find her sisters.

An invisible weight lifted from her shoulders when Margaret joined them at last. Her sister's hair was rumpled, her face flushed, but in her arms, she held a cloth bundle. Juliette recognized it as the garments Victoria had been sewing—hundreds of pounds' worth of silk and satin. Their eldest sister had taken it upon herself to begin selling corsets and chemises in December, and the profits had been staggering. Though Margaret had balked at the idea, at least she'd had enough sense to salvage their raw materials.

"I'm so glad you're safe," she murmured as Margaret embraced them both. Though her older sister gave no explanations about where she'd been, she pointed off in the distance. "Mr. Sinclair is hitching up the coach for us. He's taking us somewhere safe for the night, since we can't"—her voice broke off as she glanced back at the burning house—"sleep here."

"But what about Toria and Mother?" Amelia looked appalled at the idea of leaving them.

"Mother is safe, and His Grace is bringing Toria out," Margaret said. "We'll wait beside the coach until they're both with us."

Amelia balked. "I don't want to leave until we know she's all right."

Juliette took her sister's hand, guiding her away from the house while Margaret led them toward the waiting coach. "It's safer. The men will put out the fire, you'll see."

Again Amelia hesitated, her eyes upon the conflagration. "I don't want her to die," she whispered. "It's her wedding day, Juliette. It was supposed to be her happiest day."

A lump gathered in Juliette's throat, but she nodded. "Don't be afraid. His Grace will find her. I know he will."

Mr. Sinclair stood near the edge of the glen, helping Margaret inside the coach before he returned to the crofters. On horseback, he urged the women and children to move south, away from the burning house.

The three sisters huddled together in the coach, all of them silent as the waiting dragged onward. Their footman, Mr. MacKinloch, arrived to drive them, and Juliette stared outside as Dr. Fraser continued helping Mr. Sinclair and the other crofters as they fought to put out the fire. The blaze was still going, and at last, the duke appeared. His arm was around Victoria as he guided her outside, away from the fire and toward a snowdrift.

Juliette let out a slow breath of air, so grateful to see her sister alive. Within moments, their mother returned, wiping the tears from her cheeks.

"She's safe," Beatrice pronounced, climbing inside the coach. From the expression on her face, she seemed to have aged ten years in that last hour. "Both of them are unharmed." She pressed her fingers to her temples, as if to steady her nerves.

"Will they go with us?" Amelia ventured.

Beatrice shook her head. "There's not enough room in the coach. His Grace will look after her. We're going to his house at Eiloch Hill. I believe they will meet us there." Their footman closed the door to their coach and began the journey south.

The horses struggled through the drifts, making Juliette wonder if a sleigh would have been easier. Many times, they had to stop along the way, but none of them spoke. It was strange to think that their house was now gone, when only a few hours ago, they had been helping their sister dress for her wedding.

Juliette stared outside the window, worried about Dr. Fraser. He'd taken command, guiding the crofters south to the duke's land. But where was he now? It would be an hour or more before he'd reach Eiloch Hill, especially if he was keeping pace with those who were walking. It was freezing outside, and she couldn't stop thinking of him.

There was no sense to the feelings muddled inside. She shouldn't be letting her mind wander with thoughts of *him*. But when he'd rushed through the crowd of people, he'd been looking for her. She couldn't pretend that she wasn't relieved to see that he was all right.

The sensible side to her brain reminded her that they were only friends. Of course she would be glad that he was unharmed. It was nothing more than that. The pounding of her heart was no more than fear over what had happened.

She took several deep, slow breaths. After all the mistakes she'd made, she had no right to believe she could start again. Her choices had been flawed, and she'd paid the consequences tenfold.

But she had a beautiful son. A child who had utterly captured her heart, whom she loved more than life itself. He had a new family, parents who would give him a title and wealth. He would have everything he ever wanted.

Everything except his true mother.

There was a hole in her heart now, with the realization that Matthew could never know the truth about who his mother was. And because of the difficult birth, another baby would surely kill her. Not only had she bled badly, but she'd nearly died of a fever afterward. The midwife had advised her to never try again.

Which meant that, even if she wanted to, she could not share a man's bed for fear of becoming pregnant. In so many ways, it was a relief. She had no wish to ever be touched in that way, and she had a strong reason for it—it would risk her life.

It was easy to ignore the advances of strangers, and those of wealthy, titled men. But pushing away the man who had once been her best friend was another matter entirely. The frozen walls of her heart had to hold strong, especially now.

Seeing Paul again after so long was breaking her apart. She could never tell him the truth of what had happened. He needed to leave her be, to find another woman to be his wife. Someone who could give him the children he wanted and the life he deserved.

It was better for both of them.

Chapter Two

When they reached Eiloch Hill, Juliette walked as if in a blur. The Duke of Worthingstone had acquired a modest staff for the house, and she found herself welcomed into a room she would share with Amelia. Their housekeeper, Mrs. Larson, had accompanied them, and the matron worked alongside His Grace's servants to ensure that they had every comfort possible, though most of their clothes had been burned in the fire.

When Mrs. Larson offered to unlace her stays, Juliette refused. "In a little while." After all that had happened, she needed a few moments to clear her head. She doubted if she would sleep at all. A chill spiraled down her spine at the memory of the fire, the flames destroying everything. She was afraid of closing her eyes, of reliving the memories.

"Ye'll be more comfortable," the housekeeper insisted. "And look at your sister. The wee lass is already sleeping."

Though she would hardly consider Amelia a wee lass, Juliette was thankful that at least one of her sisters would find rest tonight.

"I'll come and fetch you when I want to be undressed," she told Mrs. Larson. "No more than an hour, I promise."

The housekeeper's gaze narrowed. "Ye're wanting to see him again, am I right? The handsome Dr. Fraser."

"No," she blurted out, startled that Mrs. Larson would think that. Her heart stammered at the thought of it. "I—I mean, he—"

Mrs. Larson crossed her arms and raised an eyebrow. "Ye can hem and haw all ye like, Miss Juliette. But we both ken that Dr. Fraser would hurl himself off a mountain if ye asked him to."

"I would never ask him to do anything for me," she said. "We're not suited at all."

Despite Juliette's protests, the housekeeper shook her head. "Give the lad a chance. He may not have a noble title, but he's got a good heart."

A title had nothing to do with her reluctance, Juliette thought.

"And he loves ye," Mrs. Larson added. "That's worth something, isn't it?"

"He doesn't," Juliette insisted. "He couldn't. We're only friends." She had to believe that. His letters had been filled with stories and funny moments during his medical studies. She would not remember the words of affection he'd written, nor the promise that one day he wanted to marry her. Friendship was all they'd ever have.

But even so, she remembered the feeling of Paul's hands upon her shoulders and the look of interest in his eyes. She'd lost herself for a moment, his gaze pushing back the years to the girl she had been.

"If ye say so." Mrs. Larson appeared unconvinced. "But ye did catch yer sister's bonnet. All of us ken that ye'll be the next to wed. Whether it's Dr. Fraser or a nobleman your mother chooses, none can say."

"No, I won't be." She didn't care what their ridiculous superstitions were. She refused to ever marry and would let no one talk her into it.

"There's a wager among the MacKinlochs. By next summer, Dr. Fraser will be yer husband. That may well be true." The smug look on the housekeeper's face was enough to push Juliette's temper over the edge.

Had Paul said something to the crofters or boasted about them? He should know better than to do such a thing.

"Perhaps ye should speak with him," Mrs. Larson suggested. "He's outside now, talking with Mr. MacKinloch."

Her first instinct was to refuse. Yet . . . what if he *had* said something to the others? She'd thought she'd made herself clear the last time, but perhaps it was time to put any thoughts of marriage firmly out of Paul Fraser's head.

She borrowed a shawl from the housekeeper and added, "I'll be back within an hour."

Mrs. Larson nodded her approval. "Be assured, I won't be telling Lady Lanfordshire about where ye've gone, if that's what you're fearing. Be careful, won't ye?" Juliette nodded, already moving outside the bedroom while the housekeeper followed. "I suppose ye'll find him if you're quick about it."

Juliette slipped down the stairs and toward the front door. Just as Mrs. Larson had said, she saw Dr. Fraser with Mr. MacKinloch. The two men were arguing, and though she couldn't hear what he was saying, there was no mistaking the anger. She frowned, wondering what their disagreement was. The two men parted, Dr. Fraser moving toward the stables while Mr. MacKinloch went to join the crofters who were setting up tents upon the duke's land.

She waited a few moments, uncertain of whether to approach. It was so late at night, and he might mistake her intentions. Behind her, she heard her mother's voice, and the door opened.

Before Beatrice could see her, Juliette fled toward the stable in the cover of darkness. For a moment, she stood at the door, calming the rapid beat of her heart. There was no reason to be apprehensive about speaking to Paul.

She found him standing beside the horses. The scent of smoke mingled with the animal odors, and she stepped inside. Paul's hair was wild, a dark tangle cropped above his ears. His coat hung open, and he'd rolled up his sleeves. At the moment, he was brushing one of the horses, as if to indulge in a mindless activity.

"Thank you for trying to put out the fire," she began, not knowing how else to begin. The words she'd rehearsed earlier, of all the reasons why he needed to walk away from their friendship, caught in her throat and would not come forth.

"I was glad to help." Paul didn't turn toward her but kept his gaze fixed upon the horses. For a long minute, the awkward moment expanded until she thought about leaving again.

"You stopped answering my letters last year," he said, finally facing her. With each step he drew closer, her guilt intensified. "You haven't written me in months. Not even when I asked you to marry me."

This was it, then. The chance she'd wanted, to discourage him from considering anything further. "It didn't seem right."

For it wasn't. No words would undo her mistakes, nor breach the distance between them. She'd paid the postage to accept every letter he'd sent . . . but she couldn't bring herself to open the more recent ones. His previous letters about medical school, and the loneliness she'd sensed in his words, had been a blade against her scarred heart. He was looking to her for friendship, and as the years had gone by, his letters had offered more. He'd bared his dreams to her, asking her to wed him when he returned.

But she was a ruined woman with another man's son. Never could she confess the truth to him. And so, it was easier to bind up the letters and put them away unread.

"I'll wait until you give me the answer I want to hear," he said solemnly.

Then he would be waiting an eternity. It would be a kindness to tell him no, to do as she'd intended, and assure him that there would never be a marriage with him.

But not tonight. It would be easier to sever the ties when she went back to London. Then, at least, she would not have to face him.

Juliette struggled to think of what to say next, and offered the only question she could: "Who do you think set the fire?" She still wondered if one of Strathland's men had somehow slipped inside their house amid the crofters.

Dr. Fraser hesitated, as if thinking about the answer. "I'm certain Strathland had a hand in it."

At the very mention of the earl, Juliette's stomach roiled. Though she'd tried to stay clear of the man, even his name made her skin crawl. Lord Strathland had constantly tried to insinuate himself with their family, and Juliette had been glad to escape him in London.

"Then there's no reason to ask why, is there? He wants us gone from Scotland so he can control the land." She made no effort to hide her distaste.

The earl had been buying up thousands of sheep, now that wool was at a premium during the war. Most of the soldiers were off fighting Napoleon's forces in Spain, and wool was in high demand for their uniforms. Lord Strathland desperately needed more grazing lands for the animals, and her family had often found his herds trespassing on their property.

"I believe so, aye." Dr. Fraser stared at her long enough for her to grow nervous, as if he could read the thoughts within her. He took a step closer, and she locked her feet in place, feeling as if the air between them had grown warmer.

Leave. Her mind uttered the warning, for if she didn't go, her willpower would crumble into dust.

"I don't know what we'll do now," she said, speaking faster. "Our debts are rising, and we've only just started to earn money with Victoria's sewing."

She hardly knew what words were escaping her mouth, for she'd grasped at any conversational topic. Yet Paul knew nothing about the sort of sewing they'd indulged in. Her sister Victoria's scandalous line of undergarments had earned far more money than they'd ever dreamed. They had called the lingerie Aphrodite's Unmentionables. Fashioned of silk and satin, they were impractical for most women, but perfectly suited to the wealthy members of the London ton who were accustomed to wearing garments only once or twice.

"She'll no' be able to sew anymore, as a duchess," Paul pointed out. "But it may be that the Duke of Worthingstone will help your family."

"I hope so." But she didn't like relying on others to solve their problems. Instead, she hoped that she and her sisters could somehow continue the business. Though Juliette loathed sewing, she did enjoy setting the prices and keeping the accounts. Tallying up the cost of supplies, the delivery fees for Mr. Sinclair, and predicting the profits were ways of filling up the lonely hours.

Perhaps she could do even more to help, if she returned to London. It was a way of helping her family, and she could make herself useful again. Especially if she never married.

She stared off into the darkness, a softness catching at her heart as she remembered her sister's face when she'd spoken her wedding vows to the duke. "It was a lovely wedding. I never thought Victoria would be the first of us to wed. But I'm glad for her."

"What of you?" he asked. "Did you enjoy your Christmas in London?" There was a sharpness to his voice, as if he'd imagined her mother parading her around to potential husbands.

"I enjoyed visiting with my aunt and her son," she confessed. *My son,* she corrected inwardly. At the memory of Matthew's round face and the way he'd attempted to stuff his fist into his mouth, she couldn't stop her smile. But when she thought of having to leave him, her throat tightened. The stolen moments with Matthew were worth the terrible cost of giving him up. And if she could never marry, she wanted to be close to him, as often as she could.

She added, "My sister Margaret loved every moment of it. She made lists of every eligible bachelor and ranked them all."

Her sister was nothing if not ambitious. Juliette met his gaze, continuing, "Though I know she's happy for Victoria, I imagine Margaret was quite chagrined that our sister found a better match than she did, without having a single Season."

"And was there a gentleman you fancied?"

She stiffened at the question, sensing the jealousy in his tone. Though she'd cooperated with her mother's wishes, attending gatherings where her aunt had introduced her to titled men, she hardly remembered any of the potential suitors. "I don't think that's any of your business."

He hung up the saddle and went to work unfastening the bridle. Without looking at her, he said, "I embarrassed you earlier today, when I caught Worthingstone's hat."

"It wasn't your fault," she began, though they both knew that was a falsehood. "But you did embarrass me, yes, with the way you were watching me." She didn't want him to be humiliated when it became clear that she would never marry him. Her face tightened, and she clasped her hands together. "You shouldn't. Others might think that—"

"That I'm in love with you?"

There was a simple truth in the words, one that devastated her. *You're not. You can't be.*

But once again, she gave no reply, unable to speak at all.

"And I'll wager I wasna the only man looking upon your bonny face."

"I'm not the woman for you, Paul," she whispered. She had to put an end to this, even if it meant hurting him. "You should turn your eyes elsewhere. I don't intend to marry anyone at all."

"Especially a Scottish rebel?" he dared.

That wasn't it at all, but she couldn't say so. Juliette lifted her shoulders in a helpless shrug. "It's dangerous, the way you ride out with the others."

"I'm a doctor. I ride many places." He took her hand in his, locking their fingers together. "And I'm no' the only one who was watching you. Ever since I returned from Edinburgh, I've seen Strathland riding near the borders of your land."

"Don't speak of him." The thought of the earl shadowing her brought a rise of fear. Juliette wrapped her arms around her waist, adding, "I don't want to even think of that man."

"He wouldna hesitate to take advantage of a young lass like yourself."

And wasn't she well aware of that? She dropped her gaze, afraid he would see the terror on her face. Paul drew closer, and she sensed the invisible tension between them, though she needed to hold her distance. "I followed you, when I could," he admitted.

"So you had someone to watch over you." A bleakness slid over her at his confession. If only he'd been there a year ago. If only she could go back and warn the innocent girl she'd been. Slowly, she pulled away, wondering if she could ever find the courage to admit the truth to him.

He released a slow breath. "I would ne'er ask for more than you're able to give, Juliette. I'll do naught except be a silent guard, when you've the need of one."

"I appreciate your friendship, Dr. Fraser." She steeled herself for what she had to say. "But find someone else for your attentions. I'm not the one for you."

And with those words, she left him standing alone.

Paul spent the night tending several crofters who'd suffered minor burn injuries when they'd tried to put out the fire. He'd mixed a healing salve and bandaged the hands of a few men before walking out to stand in front of Loch Monel. Against a clouded moon, the ripples of the water appeared like silvery fins. He stood there for nearly an hour before he heard footsteps approach.

"You're looking restless, Fraser." Cain Sinclair held out a cup. "I've brought ale. No' enough tae get drunk, but it's a start."

Aye, it was a welcome beginning. He raised his cup and offered, "Slainté."

Paul took a deep sip of the ale and then admitted, "I learned who set the fire. 'Twas Joseph MacKinloch, their footman."

"For God's sake, why?" Cain demanded.

"Strathland's men took his sister hostage. They threatened to kill her unless he set the fire. He thought they'd let her go if he did it."

"And the daft idiot believed them? Strathland canna be trusted." Cain swore and tossed back his own cup. "Where is MacKinloch now?"

"I told him no' to show his face here again. Punishing him willna bring back the house. The bloody fool."

Cain sobered, falling silent in agreement. He crossed his arms and stared out at the water. "Speaking of fools, were you daft enough to bother *her* again, Fraser?"

Paul didn't have to ask who Sinclair was talking about. Everyone knew he wanted to wed Juliette. He'd overheard the wagers on how long it would take her to say yes.

"I'll ask her as many times as I have to."

"And still, she'll say no." Sinclair drained his own cup and let it hang from his fingertips. "A man should ken when he hasn't a prayer of winning the woman he wants."

"Why should I give up?" He drank the ale, but though it quenched his thirst, it did nothing to allay the bitterness. "She just needs convincing, that's all." He shrugged, as if it were naught to worry over. But Sinclair came closer, his face serious in the moonlight.

"I shouldna be sayin' this to you. But you've been a friend, ye ken? There's a reason why she says no." He let out a slow breath, as if choosing his words carefully. Glancing down at his empty cup, he cursed and then muttered that he was wanting another drink.

Paul waited, but the longer time passed, the more Sinclair hesitated. "There's not someone else, is there?" He didn't want to think that Juliette had given her heart to another. It seemed impossible, given the way she'd accepted his casual touches in the past day. But she *had* avoided him, especially after he'd returned from Edinburgh.

He stared hard at Sinclair, not wanting to hear the reasons. And yet, he needed to understand her reluctance.

"It's no' someone else. It's because she was hurt, Fraser."

Hurt? Every tendon within him tightened with a fear he could not name. A coldness descended over him, for he suspected he would not want to hear any of this.

And yet, he needed to know. "What do you mean, *hurt*?"

The man said nothing for a time, staring out over the water. "It was over a year ago, in autumn. You were still in Edinburgh." He kept his words neutral, but with every pause, Paul's uneasiness grew. "I came out looking for my brother Jonah, who'd been fishing. When I found him, Jonah told me he'd heard a woman crying." Sinclair stared hard at him. "I followed him to the grove of trees over the rise of hills toward Ben Nevis. It's on the earl's land, north of Eiloch Hill."

The pieces of Sinclair's story started to form together, and Paul made no move to interrupt.

"When I found Miss Andrews, I thought she'd been lost or twisted an ankle," Sinclair said. "She was sitting on the ground, sobbing. Her hair was undone, and her bodice all torn up. When she saw me, she begged me no' to tell." The man's face turned violently angry, as if remembering what he'd seen.

Ice froze up the rivers of blood within him, and in his mind, Paul saw a vision of Juliette, frightened and alone. Her hair fallen around her shoulders, a wrenching terror on her face.

Her words came back to haunt him: *If it's a wife and children you want, you should look elsewhere.*

He replayed the sadness on her face when he'd spoken to her hours earlier. She'd claimed that she couldn't give him the life he wanted . . . that she didn't want to marry any man. His mind tried to put together another reason, anything else that could have happened.

But he knew. In his gut, he knew that Juliette would never have gone off on her own. Someone had taken her to an isolated place. Someone she'd trusted . . . or perhaps she'd been forced there against her will.

And that someone had hurt her.

The force of his rage, that someone would dare to harm the woman he loved, reverberated within him like a violent storm. "Who did this?" he demanded. If the man wasn't already dead, Paul had no qualms about murdering him for what he'd done. When Sinclair didn't answer, he repeated the question, grabbing the man by his shirt, letting the violence stream through him. "For God's sake, *who?*"

Sinclair's face turned grim. "She wouldna say. But I took her to your mother's house."

"My mother knew?" Though he'd seen Bridget a time or two, not a word had she spoken of Juliette.

The darkness simmering within him threatened to erupt into a violent temper. For he hadn't been there to rescue Juliette. She'd been unprotected . . . and Paul blamed himself for that. It was as if an invisible hand had reached inside and ripped him apart from the inside. Fury mingled with a drowning guilt and the need to make amends, to help her heal.

"Bridget took care of her before I brought her home," Sinclair admitted. "Your mother . . . helped fix her dress so that no one would know." His friend shot him a warning look. "Lady Lanfordshire knows naught of this, nor her other daughters. If you say one word, I'll be denying it with my last breath."

Though Paul nodded absently, his mind was reeling. "You should have told me sooner." It seemed impossible that this could have happened to the girl he loved. That anyone would have harmed her. She had suffered from this and told no one. Not even her own family. And though his instincts wanted to rage at Sinclair for never telling him of it, he knew the man had kept the secret he'd been given.

"You told me this, so I would no' push her too hard," he said dully.

"Aye. She doesna trust men. And you can understand why she's refusing to wed." Cain crossed his arms over his chest. "I won't be speaking of this again. I only told you because you should understand why she will no' let any man close to her. If it's Juliette you want, then you'll have to be patient."

Patience was the last thing on Paul's mind. He wanted vengeance against the man who had done this to her. Just imagining her terror numbed him from deep inside. She'd been alone, suffering through an attack that never should have happened.

"I escorted her to London a few days later," Sinclair continued. "She stayed with her aunt for a long time. I think she was avoiding Ballaloch."

And now that she'd returned, Juliette seemed eager to leave. It was possible that her attacker was still here.

Paul let out a slow breath, wondering what he should do now. He couldn't allow her to know that Sinclair had told him. But now, her reluctance made sense. Her innocence had been stolen from her. More than likely, he'd frightened her when he'd tried to hold her in the stable.

"I need time to think," he said to Sinclair at last. "But you've my thanks for telling me of this. I willna let on that I ken."

With that, Sinclair gave a nod and returned home, leaving Paul alone with his thoughts. He started walking toward the frozen loch in long strides, then he began to run along the edge. He could hardly see in front of him, save the reflection of the silvery ice against the moon. But he increased his pace, running hard, as if to punish himself.

His lungs burned, and still he ran. He circled the loch, hardly caring that it was past midnight. He wouldn't sleep this night. Not after what he'd learned.

When his legs began to give out, he slowed down to a walk, his breathing unsteady. His ribs felt as if someone had driven a red-hot knife into them, and he reached down for a smooth stone along the edge of the loch. He gripped the edges and hurled it hard, letting it crack against the ice.

It had been over a year since she was attacked. He understood now why Juliette had stopped answering his letters. Why she'd withdrawn from the world, claiming she would marry no man and that she had nothing left to give. A woman who had been violently hurt would want nothing to do with men.

Paul walked through the glen, letting the thoughts pour over him, replaying their moments together. She'd been afraid of him, but not to the point where she didn't want to see him. And she hadn't pulled her hands back when he'd brought them to his chest.

God help him, he couldn't say what he should do. She'd pleaded with him to go, telling him to give up. But was that truly what she wanted? To be left alone?

He couldn't abandon her. They'd been friends for years, and friends didn't walk away when they were needed. If it took years to rebuild her trust, so be it.

He'd become a doctor to heal others. But this was a deep wound, one that had battered her spirit. To win her back, he would have to woo her slowly, to bring back the friendship they'd had and make her feel safe again.

And he fully intended to find her attacker and put the son of a bitch in the ground.

Chapter Three

"What will we do?" Juliette asked quietly. Her mother was staring outside the window at the snow. From the empty look upon her face, likely she hadn't slept at all.

Beatrice took a deep breath and faced her. "You and your sisters will go to London without me. You'll stay with your aunt Charlotte for the time being." She straightened, her mouth set in a line. "I will see about repairs to the house. If it can be fixed."

Though her mother was trying to be strong, her eyes gleamed with unshed tears. Juliette moved in closer and took Beatrice's hand. "It will be all right."

"We don't have the money to rebuild," her mother confessed. "And—and it's winter. What will your father say if he returns early? I don't know how we'll manage."

"We have the sewing profits," Juliette reminded her. "The crofters were helping Victoria. Let them continue to do so, and Mr. Sinclair can sell the garments in London, as he's done before." She made no mention of the fact that they were sewing undergarments instead of dresses. Beatrice wasn't much of a seamstress, and all they needed was her permission—not her assistance. It was better if she didn't know that her daughters were sewing scandalous corsets and chemises made of silk.

"And His Grace might help us," Juliette added. Victoria's husband likely would not let them suffer. The Duke of Worthingstone appeared to be a good man who loved his new wife.

"I know he would. But I don't like relying upon others to solve our problems." Beatrice returned to her chair and picked up a sheet of paper and a pen. She dipped it into an inkwell and began writing. But when Juliette drew closer, she saw that her mother's hands were shaking.

"I don't—I don't even know what bills were paid, and whether Mr. Gilderness collected the rents in Norfolk." She rubbed her forehead, and covered her mouth with one hand. "There's just so much. The ledgers are burned, and I can't remember it all."

Juliette crossed the room and took the paper from her mother. Upon it were lists of creditors, as many as Beatrice could remember. Juliette studied the list and added a few more merchants, designating which ones had already been paid. Then she wrote amounts beside those that remained.

"I believe these are the ones you want," she said, passing the list back to her mother.

Beatrice stared at her for a moment, her brows furrowed. "How could you possibly know what was in Henry's ledgers?"

"I read them each day and changed the numbers when we added our sewing profits," she confessed. "We didn't want you to know where the extra money was coming from."

She'd expected her mother to be relieved that she had memorized the figures from the most recent accounts. Instead, Beatrice appeared upset. "Why did you feel the need to lie to me? Did you think I was so featherbrained that I wouldn't notice?"

Juliette sobered, for she hadn't thought of it in that way. "We were only trying to help."

"I knew the numbers were wrong, but I couldn't find where they'd been altered." Beatrice's tone sharpened. "Do you know how many hours I spent, trying to make them right again?"

"I'm sorry. I should have confessed the truth to you. We truly thought the extra money would be of use."

Her mother let out a sigh. "I know, darling. But I don't want to burden you with household matters when you're so young. There will be time enough for that when you're married." She stood, clasping her hands together, mustering a smile. "This is the time when you should laugh and dance . . . wear lovely frocks and flirt with handsome gentlemen."

Her mother's face grew wistful, and Juliette remembered that Beatrice had not done those things herself. She'd married an officer, because Henry Andrews was the only man to offer for her.

"You'll never find a gentleman to wed if you spend your hours buried in accounts," Beatrice insisted. "You may be good with adding sums, but it's no life for a lady."

"It has its uses," Juliette ventured. Putting on a false smile, she added, "In case a handsome rake with a penchant for gambling decides to ask for my hand."

At last, her mother's face softened. And Juliette realized that this was all a distraction for Beatrice. Finding husbands for her daughters meant that she could escape her own problems. How many years had it been since her mother had enjoyed her own life? Juliette couldn't remember the last time Beatrice had bought trinkets for herself.

Beatrice stood and brushed a lock of hair from Juliette's temple. "When you return to London, His Grace has promised to use his influence on your behalf." She reached out and took her hand, squeezing it lightly. "It was part of our agreement when he asked to wed Victoria. You'll have a Season and all the opportunities I never had."

Juliette understood, then, that although her mother wanted to maintain her pride when it came to rebuilding the house, Beatrice had no qualms about accepting help with achieving social status for her daughters.

"Promise me you'll try to find a husband," Beatrice pleaded. "And not Dr. Fraser, much as he might wish to court you." Her face flushed, as if she didn't mean to insult the man. "He's a good physician, don't mistake my meaning. But Juliette . . . he's not for you."

"Paul and I are friends," she said absently. "Nothing more."

"Then you might remind *Dr. Fraser* of that," Beatrice corrected in a subtle admonition that it was improper to call him by his first name. "He tried to pay a call on you earlier today, but I told him you were not receiving." She raised an eyebrow. "That *was* what you wanted, wasn't it?"

Her mother's assumption wasn't unfounded, from all the calls Juliette had refused in the past few weeks. But even as she shrugged in reply, a prickle of regret tumbled within her. Almost as if she wanted to see Dr. Fraser again.

She excused herself, kissing her mother's cheek before she left. Without really knowing why, she went to retrieve a woolen coat and a bonnet. She dressed herself warmly and donned boots to protect her from the snow. Outside, the air was crisp, the sun gleaming across the stark winter landscape. The mountains pierced the blue sky, while more snow blanketed the stony peaks.

Against the fence, she saw Paul waiting for her. Her heart stumbled at the sight of him, for she'd expected him to give up. He was watching her, his midnight-blue eyes holding an enigmatic expression. They were bloodshot, as if he'd not slept the night before.

Why was he here? Juliette crossed through the courtyard and saw that he'd worn a tartan today, his hands tucked inside the brown and green patterned wool. Dressed like a Highlander, he appeared less civilized than he had the night before.

"Good morning," she greeted him, her breath frosting in the air.

"And to you." His gaze passed over her, from her hair down to her boots. She clutched her coat tighter, not knowing why he'd come to see her again. "I wanted to speak to you once more, before you returned to London. Will you walk with me through the glen?"

She hesitated, glancing back at the house. Her mother was right. She shouldn't encourage him, no matter what she might feel in his presence. He'd grown so handsome over the years, but though he'd occasionally cloaked himself in the guise of a gentleman, there was something not quite tame about him.

And you like it, a sinful voice taunted her conscience.

He reached into his coat and held out a small ball of fur. "I brought you something."

When she stepped closer, she saw that it was a tiny gray and white kitten. He held it out to her, and she suddenly understood that this man was not about to play fair with her heart. He fully intended to weaken her defenses, using any means necessary.

In the early days of their letters, she had complained to him that her mother would never allow her to have a cat of her own. They were allowed in the stables, but never the house.

"You remembered," she said at last.

"Aye."

When she took the ball of fur from him, his hands brushed hers. The slight touch flared up the feelings she was trying to lock away. Being anywhere near this man was an assault upon her heart. To distract herself, she focused all her attention upon the animal.

The kitten reminded her of a white tiger, and its eyes held a seriousness, like the way Matthew had stared at her in the first minutes of his life. Her heart abruptly crumpled, and she cuddled the animal against her side. His tiny claws sank into the sleeve of her gown, but he appeared blissfully happy.

Careful, her heart warned. Paul knew her better than anyone, and it seemed that despite her warnings, he fully intended to court her. And that wasn't right.

"I shouldn't keep him," she confessed, even as the kitten nudged at her hand, letting out a tiny meow. "We're traveling back to London, and he'd be frightened without a true home."

"But you want to keep him." His gaze held steady, and when he started walking toward the glen, she found herself unable to do anything except follow. Juliette bundled the kitten beneath her coat and walked behind him.

Her brain was crying out for her to thank him and leave. Although she knew it was perfectly safe to be alone with Paul Fraser—albeit improper—she found her willpower weakening. He was handsome, but the years had weathered his face, turning him fierce. He'd always been tall, but there was a lean strength to him, and a sense that he would never let any harm come to her.

Immediately, she shut down the thought. Last night, she'd made it clear that there would not be anything more than friendship between them. Regardless of what he wanted to say to her, that could never change.

"We won't be walking too far," Paul added. "Just over by the crofters' tents."

He led her through the snow, upon a pathway trod by horses. A layer of ice had frozen on top, and he took her arm to keep her from falling. For a time, they walked together in silence, their breath frosted in the air. "The duke has promised to let them build their homes here."

"Is your mother dwelling among them?"

He nodded. "And so am I. Until our house is rebuilt."

She sobered at that. The weather was freezing cold, not at all suited for anyone to sleep in tents. "The children should sleep in the stable until we have more shelters built."

"Aye, that would be best. We'll be dividing up the land, and the building will start this morning. Soon enough, they'll be safe and warm again." His hand took hers, and the heat of his palm brought her comfort. Yet, when they stood at the top of the hill, overlooking the dozens of tents, she saw the visible signs of loss.

Her family had been displaced by the fire, just as these folk had. It was only because of her sister's marriage that they had a house to sleep in, instead of thin tents like the crofters. The frigid wind made her grasp the edges of her coat, just imagining it.

And Paul was living among them.

"No one should have to live like this," she whispered. "It's too cold to survive."

"It is," Paul agreed. "I've been tending the sick all winter. And more will die this month. Whether from starvation or cold, it's all the same." He pointed toward the rows of tents that had once held a place on her father's land. "I'll do what I can to save them."

She took his arm, leaning against him as they walked. "You're needed here."

Especially after all the uprisings. When Lord Strathland had evicted the tenants, they'd had nowhere to go. It was one thing to drive out grown men . . . but when the elderly and children were forced out into the snow, tempers were rising hotter.

"They should ne'er have been driven off their land to begin with," he insisted. "Strathland is to blame. Him and his damned sheep."

The edge in his voice held hostility, and the cold that washed over her had nothing to do with the wintery weather. "He's too powerful. None of us can stop him."

"I'll stop him, Juliette." He turned, his glare fierce. "I havena forgotten what Strathland did to my father."

Danger and vengeance simmered within his tone, and she took a step back. "If you raise a hand against Strathland, you'll only be killed."

His father's hanging had cast a pall over all of them. And although His Grace, the Duke of Worthingstone, had acquired Eiloch Hill from the earl after a gambling debt, few of the crofters were eager to live there. There were too many bad memories associated with the land.

"I'm no' a coward, Juliette. And I'll see to it that the crofters have all that they need. No man will drive them away from their homes—especially Strathland."

"What will you do?"

His gaze grew distant. "I've a few things in mind. My father's family was . . ." His voice drifted off, as if he were reconsidering his words. "That is, my uncle may have some influence."

Juliette waited for him to continue, but he offered nothing else. A frown furrowed his face, as if his thoughts had gone elsewhere. "The crofters will be fine," she reassured him. "Now that they're away from Strathland, they can rebuild their lives."

"As you will?" he prompted.

Though she knew he was referring to the fire that had destroyed their house, she focused on something else entirely: *away from Strathland.*

"Yes," she answered. She fully intended to be hundreds of miles from Lord Strathland.

Paul led her away from the crofters, and she adjusted the sleeping kitten in her arms. He saw the direction of her attention and asked, "What will you name him?"

She shrugged. "I'm not sure. Do you have any suggestions?"

A mischievous look came over his face. "My suggestions wouldna be appropriate, I fear." He guided her deeper into the woods, until they were surrounded by trees. Several of the stouter limbs held a cloak of snow.

"We had a wolfhound come to live with us once," he continued. "You remember what I named him."

"Horse." She'd nearly forgotten about the dog, after so long.

"He was the size of one. When I was a lad, I tried to ride him, but the dog didna care for it."

The thought of Paul attempting to ride the animal amused her. "I don't suppose he did."

Juliette studied the kitten and held him up. In a teasing voice, she suggested, "Should I confuse everyone and call him Dog?"

His face softened. "Or you could call him 'My Mind.'"

At her confusion, he offered, "When he goes off mousing, you could say, 'My Mind's gone wandering off' or 'I've lost My Mind.'"

She groaned at the thought. "That's terrible."

"Aye." His wicked smile warmed her, and she couldn't resist one of her own. He tucked her arm in his as they kept walking, and his face softened for the barest moment. She found herself nervous beneath his gaze. "I havena seen you smile in a long time."

The way he was looking at her now spoke of a man who didn't plan to remain only friends. Though he didn't touch her at all, he rested one hand upon a thin birch, his body leaning close to hers. Fear bolted up inside her as the bad memories came roaring back.

"I shouldn't be out walking with you." She adjusted the squirming kitten in her arms and started to turn away.

"Wait," he said. His voice held the commanding air of a man who did not intend to let her go. Then he paused and added, "Please."

He didn't understand. He seemed to believe that if he kept pursuing her, eventually she would weaken. Before she could say no, he continued. "I didna ask you here to make you feel cornered, Juliette. But there are things that I would say to you, before you leave Scotland."

She didn't want to hear any of it. Already, her skin was prickling with the knowledge that he cared for her. He wanted her, and she had nothing left to give him.

"I wish you'd stay," he said simply.

"I can't," she insisted. Though she'd returned for her sister's wedding, she needed to be back in London with her son. She could think of no greater joy than to watch Matthew grow up before her eyes. If it were possible, she'd have been his nursemaid. But then, ladies were not supposed to become servants.

The kitten had sunk its claws into her sleeve, and she gently pried it away. "You really should take the kitten back, Dr. Fraser. We don't have a home now, and I shouldn't keep him."

"An animal doesna care where you live, so long as he's loved." Paul reached over to ruffle the kitten's ears and took him from her.

"It would be too difficult right now," she admitted. And every time she saw the animal, she would think of Paul.

"He wants naught but to be close to you," Paul said, his dark blue eyes staring at her. "To sleep beside you and have you look upon him with a smile."

Blood rushed to her face, for she suspected he was no longer talking about the kitten. Before she could find the words to tell him no, he cut her off. "I remember what you said to me last night in the barn. But I also remember that we were friends once. And I'm no' wanting to lose that." His eyes locked with hers. He'd shielded all emotion from his gaze, watching her with a patience she didn't understand.

"Why?" Her palm clenched and unclenched, so afraid of what he was asking.

"Because you're worth waiting for."

The words were like salt against her wounded heart. If he knew anything about her past, he would never say such words. "I need to be back in London," she reminded him. "And I don't know if I'll ever return."

Paul's expression sobered. Then his eyes held a sudden knowledge that struck her hard. "You're running away."

"N-no. I like it in London. I lived there for most of my girlhood."

He studied her for a long moment, as if he didn't believe her. "And that's where you would be happiest?"

She gave a nod without any hesitation at all. Though it wasn't the place that drew her there. It was the sweet angel whose laugh had brightened her heart. And because there, she was safe from harm. "I don't suppose I'll see you again, will I?"

He gave the kitten back to her. "Are you wanting to?"

Color suffused her face, and she turned her gaze downward to avoid looking at him. If she let him see her eyes, he'd know the truth—that the loss of his friendship wasn't at all what she wanted. But there was no choice, was there?

"Be safe," she said quietly. She had no right to lower the walls around her heart, not when she was incapable of making him happy. It would only hurt both of them.

A thread of anger knotted inside her until she couldn't help but stare into his dark blue eyes. It wasn't fair. She wanted to go back to the beginning, to be the girl she'd once been. She wanted to be honest with Paul and confess what had happened, feeling the sanctuary of his arms around her.

But admitting the truth would change nothing. She could not let him love her, nor risk her own heart. She held on to the kitten with one hand, forcing back the urge and strengthening her resolve to say nothing. No, he wouldn't understand.

She took a deep breath and bared one truth to him. "I will miss you when I go." Before she could lose her nerve, she reached out and touched his roughened cheek.

Paul stared at the snowdrifts for a long time, his mind in turmoil. Juliette wanted to return to London. The thought of living in the crowded streets was not something he relished. He'd accepted the necessity of living in Edinburgh during his medical studies, but he'd ached for his beloved Highlands.

Here was where he belonged. Here, he was among his family and friends, and they needed him. So many had suffered from the evictions. Aside from his mother, the clan's midwife and healer, Paul was the only man with medical knowledge to help them. Left with naught but superstitions and remedies passed on by their grandmothers, the crofters often did more harm to the wounded folk than good.

A part of him believed that if he'd known how to stop the bleeding on the night of the raid, he might have saved Malcolm and the factor.

He might have saved his father, if they hadn't died.

After he'd gone to live with his uncle, Donald Fraser, in Edinburgh, he'd vowed that one day, he would become a doctor. Although it wouldn't bring back those he'd lost, Paul wanted to save the lives of others. He'd taken the knowledge passed on by his mother, intending to use it to prove he was worthy of acceptance into medical school.

But then, his uncle had revealed a secret that had ripped the foundation of his life apart.

His father had never spoken of his brothers, only saying that they were from Edinburgh originally and that he'd left to wed Bridget. Paul had never met his paternal grandfather, nor anyone from that side of the family. Not until he'd been sent away.

When his mother had forced him to leave after his father's death, he'd thought it was banishment. Now he wondered if she hadn't been trying to mend her husband's broken past. By sending Paul away, she'd given him the chance for another life. Yet, from the first moment he'd met his uncle, he had believed Donald Fraser despised him.

꙳

"So, Bridget sent you to me, did she?" His uncle Donald rubbed absently at his salt-and-pepper beard. His eyebrows tufted above his eyes as if he were a bird staring at its prey. "How old are you, boy?"

"I'll be eighteen in a few months." Paul straightened, trying to appear older. Exhaustion weighed down upon him, for he hadn't slept for more than a few minutes at a time on the journey south from Ballaloch. Most of the trip had been on a farmer's wagon, with nothing to shield him from the rain. He'd spent days miserable in cold, wet clothing.

"That would make you seventeen," Fraser corrected. "Answer the question correctly, and don't bother me with information that doesn't matter." His eyes narrowed upon him. "Your mother says they hanged your father for a crime you committed. Is it true?"

"I killed no one." Frustration and grief poured through him at the raw memory. "It was my friend Malcolm who wanted to raid."

His hands clenched into fists. "He and my father are dead because of Lord Strathland." The bemused expression on his uncle's face angered him even more. What reason did he have to smile when Paul's life had come crashing down around him?

"I suppose you think to avenge their deaths? Having all the wisdom of a lad who believes he's a man."

"Strathland will pay for what he did, aye."

Fraser studied him from head to toe. "You haven't two coppers to rub together, and you're naught but an uneducated Highlander. How could you ever be anything except dirt under the earl's feet? You're nothing and never will be."

The mockery sent Paul's fury over the edge. He grabbed Fraser's shirt and shoved him against the wall. "Don't be talking to me like that. I will bring him down. I swear it, on my life." His blood thundered through him at the taunt. He didn't care if no one believed it but him.

"If you attack him with that sort of rage, it will cost you your life." Fraser pressed him back gently, straightening his coat. "You haven't the first idea of what it takes to bring down a man of his rank." He lowered his voice, and it held an edge Paul had never guessed. "Unless you put aside your anger and learn."

The words quieted his anger, offering him a pathway of hope. "What do you mean?"

"You want him gone from Scotland, am I right?"

Paul nodded, letting out a slow breath. If the earl abandoned his property there, they could live in peace with no one to tell them how to live. "I do."

Fraser walked over to a bookshelf containing leather-bound volumes. He reached inside and pulled one out. "Killing Strathford won't make him go away. His heirs will only rise up and grow stronger. A man of his power will yield only to a greater power. And you, lad, have no power at all." His uncle handed him the book. "Can you read?"

Paul nodded, for his father had taught him since he was a lad. "Well enough."

"Good." He pointed to the shelf of books. "Your education will be the gateway to power. Learn quickly, and you can change yourself."

He might have suspected his uncle would try to fight his battles without fists. Paul didn't believe it for a moment. What good were books and learning when it came to Strathland, who could twist the law into what he wanted?

"Why should I? I could wait a few months, return, and burn his home to the ground."

"The coward's path," Fraser chided. "And what then? You'll go back to herding sheep until they bring you to trial and hang you. Just like your father."

Before Paul realized what had happened, Fraser grabbed his shirt and slammed him against the bookcase. His head knocked against the wooden shelf, and he saw stars for a moment. "And here I thought you were smarter than that." His uncle eyed him with distaste.

"I am *smart*," he gritted out, tasting blood on his lip. "But books willna avenge my father's death."

Fraser released him. "Go back to Scotland, then, if that's what you want. Kill the earl, and waste your life. I won't grieve for the loss of a brainless lad."

"I canna let it go," Paul insisted.

"Don't you understand, lad? Dying is easy. Wouldn't you rather he suffered for his sins? Would it not be a greater punishment for him to live in the same poverty he put you in?"

Paul hadn't considered that, but his uncle's words made him hesitate.

"If you were a more intelligent lad, you'd know that patience would bring a greater fall to the earl. As it is . . ." His uncle lifted his shoulders in a shrug. "You'll hide away in Edinburgh for a few months, return to Ballaloch with a loaded pistol, and end both your lives." He shook his head, his mouth curling with a dark smile. "Because you're too eager to act now, instead of learning how to truly bring down your enemy."

He wove another picture with his words: "Imagine Strathland suffering through a winter with no food. With not a coin in his pocket, debt-ridden, until his heirs inherit nothing. He'll have to sell off any unentailed land, possibly the property in Scotland. Or he'll abandon it to live in a dirt-ridden hovel in the city, bemoaning his lack of coin until he drinks himself to death. That would be a more fitting revenge. To bring him down where he belongs."

Paul's earlier rage had died down, and the image of a fallen earl was more welcome than a dead one. Strathland had never known hardship. He'd never gone to sleep hungry, the empty ache in his stomach making it impossible to rest. He'd never shivered beneath a thin coverlet or worn patched shoes in the deep winter snows. Not the way Paul had.

"What must I do?"

"Watch those who are wealthy. Learn from them, and discover their weaknesses." His uncle gestured toward his house. "I am not a poor man, though I was like you once. Did your father ever tell you about me?" There was a sudden narrowing of the man's eyes, as if he were hiding secrets.

Paul shook his head. "I ne'er knew he had brothers. He didna talk of you at all."

His uncle Donald shrugged. "Kenneth was the youngest of three brothers. We grew up in this house."

Paul was startled to hear it. He'd never guessed that there was any money at all on his father's side of the family.

"You're probably wondering why Kenneth turned his back on us. Our father threw him out when he wanted to marry your mother. He was hot-headed and lashed out, saying he'd never come back or have anything to do with us."

"Then why would my mother send me to you?" Paul asked.

"Because your mother was wiser than Kenneth. She knew that you were all that was left of us. One day, this will all come to you. If you prove yourself worthy of an inheritance."

The grandfather he'd never seen had turned out to be a viscount. Even now, the revelation stunned Paul.

Kenneth Fraser had never behaved any differently, tending sheep like the other crofters. Though Paul knew the Frasers were from Edinburgh, his father had never gone to visit his family. Now, he understood why—because his father was trying to hide his grandfather's title.

Bridget had known, and that was why his mother had sent him away, after his father had been executed. Not only to keep him safe from Strathland's men, but to reveal the truth.

"Ye'll learn to be a gentleman," Bridget had told him. *"Your father ne'er wanted that life, but you should leave Ballaloch to see the world. Donald will teach you what you need to know."*

He hadn't cared about manners or learning to be a gentleman and had told her so. But Bridget had insisted, and now he knew the reason.

A title. Wealth. Both would irrevocably change his life. Any other man would be grateful for the money, but Paul was too aware of his kinsmen who had endured freezing nights with naught but a tent and a fire to stay warm.

God above, he didn't want the title. What right did he have to hide away in Edinburgh, dining with silver and crystal, when his friends and kinsmen were here suffering? He wanted to remain the man he was, bent upon vengeance against the earl, determined to bring down Strathland's wool empire. The only reason that title had value was because it gave Paul the chance for a future with Juliette.

For so long, he'd dreamed of walking in the glen beside her. Of courting her and seeing her smile. If he let her go to London now, there was no chance for them.

Paul walked through the snow, his footsteps crunching upon the surface. All his life, he'd been a man who believed in fate. From the moment he'd laid eyes on Juliette, he'd known that she was meant to be his. And if he had to choose between following her to London or living here without her, there was no question of where he would go.

He trudged back to the rows of tents, his breath forming clouds in the winter air. Although the snowfall was lighter on this side of the glen, it was still bitterly cold. He passed by campfires and hoped that one day there would be warm houses instead of threadbare tents.

As he walked up the hillside, the grim memory of his father's death lingered. The trial had been a farce, with all of the people agreeing with whatever Lord Strathland wanted. His father had been hanged on this hill, for a murder he hadn't committed.

All to save his only son's life.

Paul stared down at the glittering snow. Never had he forgotten how his father had died. And though he'd longed to fight back, to put a bullet through the man's head, his uncle had talked sense into him. Heated revenge would only end in his own death.

Money and wealth equaled power in the earl's world. That was the way to bring down Strathland—not with midnight raids or stealing supplies, though he'd done his share of both in the past year. Paul refused to feel guilty about stealing grain to feed children who were hungry. If the earl hadn't driven them off their land, they would have had stored supplies to last them through the winter. Instead, Strathland's men had stripped the gardens, taking whatever food they'd wanted.

No, it was better to bankrupt the earl. In that case, London might well be the best solution to Paul's dilemma. He could educate himself about the wool business, learning how to bring the earl to his knees when no one would buy his fleeces. Strathland's fortune rested upon the sale of wool. Without it, he would lose everything.

Paul could make a place for himself there, perhaps as a private physician to a nobleman. In doing so, he could also be close to Juliette.

And slowly, he would win her back.

"We're leaving in a few days," Amelia told Juliette. "Mother is staying behind to see if anything can be saved from the house. We'll stay with Aunt Charlotte instead of at the town house, since Mother won't be with us."

The mention of Charlotte made Juliette's spirits lift, for she was eager to see Matthew again. Perhaps this time, her son would begin crawling. Simply the thought of his smile and belly laugh made her eager to return. It was the one bright moment in the shadows of the tragedy.

"I'm glad of it," she remarked.

"And she said we can continue our sewing." Amelia beamed at the idea, as if she'd thought of it first. Juliette didn't bother to correct her. "The crofters have continued working on the garments, and we'll take them with us to sell." Lowering her voice to a whisper, Amelia added, "Perhaps we could trade the undergarments Victoria made, in return for new gowns."

"We can't. Mr. Sinclair has to be the one to sell the garments. No one can know that we created the corsets and chemises," she chided. "It has to remain a secret."

Amelia's mood faded. "I suppose." She appeared disappointed in the need for secrecy. But then, her sister underestimated how important it was to maintain respectability.

The kitten Paul had given her, which Juliette had named Dragon, meowed, nudging her legs before he flopped down and waited for her to stroke his ears. Juliette sat upon the floor, obliging the animal. "The duke promised our mother that you and Margaret could have a Season this spring. You'll need many gowns for it," she said.

Amelia came to sit beside her on the floor. "And what about you?"

Juliette drew up her knees beneath her gown. "I've no desire for a Season at all. I'd rather remain unmarried. I'll handle the accounts for Aphrodite's Unmentionables and be contented with the work."

Her sister stared at her with dismay. "But you can't, Juliette. That would be unbearably lonely."

"I like adding sums and making money," she countered. "There's nothing lonely about it."

The lie slipped easily from her lips, and she added, "Besides, I don't need a marriage to be happy. I'll have my independence and can go as I please. Perhaps one day I'll have a home of my own and a companion when I'm old."

"Or perhaps you'd rather marry Dr. Fraser," her sister interjected. "He's quite handsome. And he did bring you a kitten."

Juliette shook her head in exasperation. "Don't be ridiculous." As if a kitten would change her mind about men. Even so, her face reddened at the mention of Paul.

Spinsterhood was good, she told herself. There was never a danger of any man touching her again.

But abruptly, Amelia stopped and stared at her for a long moment. Her sister frowned, her eyes discerning. "I don't think you're telling me the truth. I know you slipped out to see him twice already."

Clearly younger sisters made the best spies. Juliette's face flamed, but she waved a hand. "It was just a harmless infatuation when we were younger, that's all. We're friends, and I've hardly seen him in five years. We talked about nothing, really."

"No." Amelia's gaze sharpened. "It's much more than that." She studied her, as if she could see through her to the silent pain within. For a moment, fear slid over Juliette that her sister suspected more than she'd let on.

It didn't matter what her past feelings had been. What mattered was the future—one without Paul. She ignored the bittersweet pang of loss, for she'd never had him to begin with.

"My past has nothing to do with you or your own future marriage," she said brightly, steering Amelia to a different topic. "Was there a gentleman who caught your eye when we were in London for Christmas?"

"Stop trying to change the subject." Amelia picked up the kitten, which had fallen asleep. "When we were there last, you never seemed interested in any of the parties."

"Don't be silly. Even if I didn't want a husband, of course I was interested in the parties."

Lies. All lies. She'd spent every possible moment with Matthew, rocking him to sleep, shaking a rattle to make him laugh. She could have cared less about leaving her aunt's town house to be paraded about as a potential marriage candidate.

Her sister let out a sigh. "You might have been interested in the color of the drapes. But certainly none of the men." She flopped down on the bed. "If you truly do love Dr. Fraser, I don't see why you shouldn't marry him."

"I don't love him, as I said before," Juliette said. "And besides, our parents wouldn't approve. He has no title."

"Father wasn't a baron until he inherited his title over a year ago from our uncle," Amelia pointed out. "And even now, I doubt if we could attract any gentlemen at all. I'm too young, Margaret is too fastidious, and you're too melancholy. You remind me of that glum lord, the Earl of what's-his-dom."

"Castledon," Juliette corrected.

"Yes, him. The pair of you would be perfectly suited, with the way you hardly ever smile or make merry."

Had she truly been that bad? Juliette picked up a pillow and swatted her sister. "I do smile sometimes."

"Not often." Amelia snatched a larger pillow and buffeted her in return.

"Are you trying to beat me into a smile?" she teased. "When we attend parties, will you strike me with your fan if I don't smile?"

"It's not a bad idea," Amelia mused. "Though I imagine you'd be black and blue for a while."

Juliette couldn't help but laugh as her sister went on the attack, using the pillow as if it were a bludgeon. "Stop it, Amelia." Eventually, she tripped and fell upon the bed, laughing so hard she could barely catch her breath.

When was the last time they had behaved like children? She could hardly remember. But it *did* feel good to laugh, after so long.

"There now. Promise me you'll find something to make you smile. Every day," Amelia ordered.

"I promise." Juliette repinned her hair, but before they could go downstairs, her sister blocked her way.

"And promise me something else. If you do love Paul Fraser and you want him for your husband, for Heaven's sake, let the man compromise you. Then our parents will have to say yes."

Juliette was left with her mouth hanging open as her sister led the way downstairs.

"My lord, the house burned down."

Never were there more welcome words to Brandon Carlisle, the Earl of Strathland. The crofters had relocated to Eiloch Hill, and the Andrews family was left with no choice but to return to London. "Good. Make them an offer for the land."

Now was the time to take advantage of their misfortune. They had lost everything, and when he offered them a reasonable sum for the land, they would readily accept. He had no doubt of it.

"They've refused all of our offers in the past," Melford reminded him. "I doubt that will change."

"You're wrong." Brandon lifted a hand, dismissing his factor's prediction. This time, Lady Lanfordshire had no choice. He'd watched over the years as their staff had diminished, until now they had only a housekeeper and a footman. Colonel Lord Lanfordshire still had not returned from the battleground, and there was no way of knowing if the man ever would.

It irritated Brandon that he'd given them so many opportunities to end their poverty. He'd even offered to wed one of their daughters, which would allow their future children to inherit. But Lady Lanfordshire had continued to make excuses, despite the fact that their money was running out.

And Juliette had refused him.

His blood raged at the thought of it. Marriage to a man of his status was a privilege she ought to be begging him for. He wanted her, and he had a title far more important than her father's. Didn't she understand what an honor it was that he would even consider her as a wife?

Juliette had been such a fetching thing, young and innocent with the swell of womanhood upon her. At the memory, he shifted in his seat. He still relished the moment when he'd held her down, overpowering her until she was forced to accept his body inside hers. Her cries of pain had excited him, and it aroused him just to remember it.

He could have any woman of his choosing, but he wanted a quietly obedient woman. One who knew her place. One who recognized that he was worth more than a thousand Highlanders.

When Juliette had rejected his proposal, he'd had no choice but to punish her. She should have been honored to have his attentions. And after he'd compromised her, her family should have forced her to wed him.

Instead, she'd hidden herself away with her aunt's family. It was impossible to demand marriage of her when she'd simply disappeared. But now that Juliette had returned, there was time to pursue her once more.

He was the Earl of Strathland, and his fortune would only grow larger as he increased his wool empire. He could have any wife he wanted.

And he intended to have Juliette.

Brandon smiled to himself. She would quickly learn that he was not a man to give up. There were ways to ensure her agreement to a marriage, and he had little doubt that her family would agree to the match.

Especially now that they had hardly anything at all.

Chapter Four

"Are you truly making another list?" Amelia stopped her pacing to peer over Margaret's shoulder. "You've met all of these men before. Haven't you decided yet?" Personally, Amelia couldn't believe a list was even necessary. Either you liked a gentleman or you didn't. *She* knew which gentlemen she preferred, but the chance of those men remaining unwed in the next two years was unlikely. Sometimes being sixteen was unbearable. But at least it was better than being twenty and unwed, like Margaret.

Her sister dipped her pen in an inkwell and continued numbering down the page. "Some of the men had problems. For example, Viscount Lisford has been known to frequent White's on a regular basis."

"What does that have to do with anything? Most men do." Playing cards at White's was hardly a reason to drop the man to a lower rank upon the list, though Amelia secretly believed the viscount was the most handsome man she'd ever seen. Thank goodness Margaret didn't want him.

"If he plays cards frequently, then he is more likely to fall into debt. As our uncle did," she warned. "Or perhaps he is already indebted and is trying to recoup his losses. Either way, he is not a good candidate for marriage."

"I know who *you* want," Amelia said. "A foreign prince with enough money to give you a palace dipped in gold."

Her sister sighed. "No, I don't want that. But I do want a man who is polite and well-bred."

"A boring man, you mean."

"A proper man." Margaret set her pen down and eyed Amelia. "You ought to be considering the same." She smiled and added, "Remember, His Grace is going to give us all a Season, and we're to be presented at court."

Personally, Amelia had no desire to curtsy before royalty. She'd likely trip over her train and fall flat on her face. But she did want to marry well, and so she'd suffer through it.

Flopping back on the bed, she stared at the ceiling. "I suppose you're happy the house burned down. Now we have to live in London until it's rebuilt."

Margaret set down her pen. "What a horrid thing to say. Of *course* I'm upset that we lost the house. But I'll confess, I am glad that we'll be here for the new Season. And I'm grateful to His Grace, the Duke of Worthingstone, for his generosity."

"You're jealous of Victoria, too," Amelia chided. "Because she had a duke dropped on her doorstep."

"On the contrary, I'm quite pleased for her. I'm not at all jealous of her good fortune."

That was the answer her sister would continue to give, Amelia knew. "I want a husband who adores me," she pronounced. "His title doesn't matter. But if you don't want the viscount, I shall flirt with him."

"Amelia," Margaret warned, "if you're too impulsive, you could make costly mistakes. If you associate with the wrong man, your reputation will suffer."

"You're just afraid I'll marry before you will. I might," she said, unable to resist teasing her sister. "Even Juliette could. Dr. Fraser loves her and wants to marry her."

"But he's a *physician.*" Margaret shuddered. "She can't marry him."

"It's not as if she's running away with a peddler." Personally, Amelia thought Dr. Fraser was perfect for her sister.

"I worry about her," Margaret admitted. "She refuses to dance with any of the men and seems quite content to be a wallflower."

"Because she wants Dr. Fraser." Of that, Amelia was certain.

"She's changed, ever since she went away with Aunt Charlotte." Margaret stood and went to stand by the window. "But every time I ask her, she refuses to say a word of it."

"She's been pining for the doctor, ever since he left for Edinburgh. *And* he asked her to marry him in one of his letters."

"He did not!" Margaret's mouth dropped open. "How would you even know such a thing? Did you read Juliette's letters without her permission?"

"Of course I did." And she didn't feel one bit guilty over it. How else was she to know what was going on? Dropping her voice to a hushed whisper, Amelia added, "Juliette might have asked Mother for permission. And of course, she would say no."

The idea of a forbidden love fascinated her. Although she'd never played the role of matchmaker, she honestly did believe Juliette would be happiest with the doctor. He might be a rough Highlander, but he was terribly handsome.

The only problem was that it would be impossible for her sister to be with Dr. Fraser if they were separated by hundreds of miles. He needed to be here, in London, so that Juliette would see that they were meant to be together.

"*Did* she ever ask Mother for permission?" Margaret prompted.

"How should I know? I'm only guessing."

Margaret rolled her eyes with exasperation. "Because you're an insufferable busybody who eavesdrops on everyone."

"Well, not this time." An idea took root in Amelia's mind, evolving into a plan. She smiled and added to her sister, "I wonder if Juliette's been waiting to elope with him, now that he has his physician's license. Maybe *that's* why she refuses to consider anyone else."

Margaret rolled her eyes. "Don't be such a child, Amelia."

"Don't be such a spinster, Margaret."

The S-word was enough to send her sister into a fury. Margaret ran toward her, but Amelia ducked and went to snatch her sister's list off the writing desk. "The Earl of Castledon? Honestly, Margaret, he has the personality of a handkerchief."

"A handkerchief hasn't got a personality, ninny."

"Exactly."

Margaret lunged for the paper, but Amelia dodged her, running away. As she started to read the second name on the list, the door opened and Juliette entered. She was carrying their young cousin Matthew in her arms, gently bouncing him as she walked.

"What are you doing?" Juliette asked, touching the baby's hair.

"Tormenting Margaret," Amelia admitted. "I have her list."

Judging by her reddened eyes, Juliette had been crying again—and Amelia had had her fill of it. She spent all of her time playing with Aunt Charlotte's son instead of seeking a husband. If she enjoyed children that much, Amelia believed her sister ought to make a genuine effort at marrying and starting her own family. Whether her sister was grieving over Paul Fraser or crying for another reason, it was time to end it.

"I think we should have a Sisters' Meeting," Amelia announced. "Take the baby back to his nurse, Juliette, and we'll talk."

"Matthew can stay. It's not as if he's planning to tell our secrets." She kissed the baby and cuddled him closer. "That is, if you're planning to share any."

Amelia went to the bedroom door and turned the key. "All right, he can stay. I suppose he doesn't talk yet, so it's all right." She sat down on the bed and patted the space beside her. "We need to discuss men."

Her older sisters exchanged embarrassed looks, but that wasn't about to deter Amelia. "We can't all want to marry the same bachelors," she pointed out. "If we pick the same one, we cannot let it come between us."

"You choose third, Amelia," Margaret said. "I'm the eldest and therefore deserve to choose first."

"She'll choose second," Juliette corrected. "I'm not planning to choose."

Margaret shook her head. "You keep saying that. I don't believe for a moment that you want to be a spinster."

"Well, I do."

Amelia, strongly suspecting it was a lie, exchanged a look with Margaret. "What about Dr. Fraser? He loves you; anyone can see that." *And you love him back,* she almost said.

"He's a good man," Juliette admitted, "but as I said, I don't intend to marry anyone."

"Give it a chance," Margaret urged. "Aunt Charlotte and Mother are doing their best to find appropriate husbands for us. And you're not even trying."

Juliette stared at both of them. "Why must every woman marry? Does she really have to have a man to be happy?"

Amelia was shocked at the edge of anger in her sister's voice. She'd never heard Juliette this upset, but her sister stood and regarded both of them. "I've made my choices, and marriage isn't one of them. I never intend to let a man control me, nor will I ever bear children."

Margaret was staring at her sister as if she'd just announced her decision to join a convent. "But why?"

Juliette gathered her composure and spoke in a calmer voice. "One of us has to continue Aphrodite's Unmentionables, since Victoria is now a duchess. Our family needs the money more than ever, especially after the house burned down. Since Victoria can no longer run the business, I shall do so."

"The duke will take care of us now," Margaret pointed out. "There's no need to sell scandalous undergarments anymore."

"I like them," Amelia felt compelled to offer. "They're lovely and comfortable."

"They're a luxury only a few women can afford. You can't even wash them with soap or the silk will fall apart," Margaret pointed out. "Who wants a corset that can only be worn a few times? Or a chemise made of material so thin, it shows a woman's bosom if she perspires?"

Amelia glanced down at her own bosom. She wasn't daring enough to wear a chemise like *that*, but she supposed a husband might like it.

"If no one wanted them, they wouldn't be selling very well," Juliette countered. "And whether or not the two of you wish to continue, I intend to." The baby had fallen asleep in her arms, and she cuddled him close.

"And just how will you sew the garments? You can't even darn stockings," Margaret said.

"The same way we did before. I'll pay the crofters' wives to make them. They still have the patterns Victoria created." Her face was flushed, and there was a new light in her eyes that startled Amelia. It was the first time she'd noticed any excitement at all from Juliette in the past few months.

"You want this to be successful, don't you," she said. "It's important to you."

"Yes," Juliette answered. "Now, if you'll excuse me, I'm going to visit Madame Benedict's shop and find out which garments are selling the best." She stood, careful not to wake the baby.

"Wait." Amelia stopped her before she could go. "We haven't finished our discussion about husbands." She regarded both of her sisters in all seriousness. "Can I have Viscount Lisford?" Despite everything, Amelia was convinced that he would make an excellent husband.

Juliette nodded. "As long as Margaret doesn't want him first." With a wicked glint in her eyes, she added, "She *is* older than both of us."

Margaret let out a heartfelt sigh. "Only if I can have the earl."

Amelia leaned back with a satisfied smile. "If you like handkerchiefs, he's all yours."

"You have a letter," Cain Sinclair informed Paul. Holding it in one hand, he leaned across the table inside the tavern. The small room was thick with pipe smoke, and men played cards at another table. Paul set down his mug of ale and eyed Sinclair with wariness. They'd traveled south from Scotland over the past few weeks, following the Andrews girls. How on earth could there be a letter for him? No one even knew he'd come to London.

Sinclair passed it to him, and Paul studied the handwriting. "And who is this from?"

"Lady Lanfordshire." From the way the man was grinning, Paul strongly suspected Cain was lying.

"Liar. She's still in Scotland, and she wants naught to do with the likes of me."

Cain only shrugged. "Open it and see."

Paul glanced through the contents of the letter. It invited him to dwell at their London town house for a few days, until he found his own living arrangements. The girls would remain with their aunt Charlotte in the meantime. He showed the contents to Sinclair in disbelief.

"Why would Lady Lanfordshire allow me to stay in her home? And how did you get this letter?" He didn't believe for a moment that she would want him there. Especially after she'd set her sights on a titled husband for Juliette.

"It wasna written by Lady Lanfordshire. Her youngest daughter, Amelia, forged her mam's signature. She thinks you're still in Scotland and that I'll have to deliver it to you there. I got it from her when I went to sell some things on behalf of the young ladies." Sinclair grinned and tapped the note. "So long as you're gone by the time Lady Lanfordshire returns to London, there's nae harm in it. The house is empty. Take the letter to her butler, and he'll believe it."

Paul blinked at that. "But why would she do such a thing?"

Sinclair shrugged. "Could be Miss Amelia's tryin' to help you. She's given you a few days, and the servants willna know any differently."

"And when Lady Lanfordshire finds out, she'll have me hanged, drawn, and quartered. No, that wouldna be a good idea." Better to keep to his own rented hovel than to trespass where he wasn't wanted. Even if it *would* bring him closer to Juliette.

"She's a sly one, Amelia is," Cain continued. "Were I in your place, I'd take the risk. You have at least a fortnight before anyone could get here." As they continued their walk into Mayfair, he added, "And I can ensure that Miss Juliette knows you've come."

Paul wasn't certain that was a good idea. Although he had followed her here, he didn't want her to feel threatened. "Don't be saying a word," he warned. "I'll tell her myself."

Sinclair shrugged. "As you will."

Paul tucked the letter away and regarded the man. "There's something else you're no' telling me, isn't there?"

Cain drained his own glass. "They found Joseph MacKinloch's sister. Strathland's men killed her, as we thought. No one's seen MacKinloch since."

MacKinloch would not simply disappear, Paul knew. And with his sister dead, he had nothing more to lose.

"He might help us," he said to Sinclair. "He has a reason as strong as ours to bring Strathland down."

Cain poured him another tankard of ale. "And what could MacKinloch do? He's got no money, nor any family left. If he stays, he'll face trial for the fire, and lose."

"Aye." But Paul couldn't let go of the idea that the former footman could be useful in some way. "While we're here, I want you to find out what you can about the wool buyers. Find out who is buying from Strathland."

"And then what?"

"We'll meet with them and convince them to buy their wool elsewhere." Paul wasn't entirely certain how, but they had to start somewhere.

Sinclair nodded. "I'll go with you, aye. But you're the one with greater influence than me."

Paul knew he was referring to his uncle. "The title's no' mine yet." And he might not inherit at all, if his uncle ever married and had a son of his own. Though he'd given Paul a small allowance, Donald Fraser was of the mind that a man had to stand on his own feet and earn a living—which was why he'd paid for Paul to attend medical school in Edinburgh. Afterward, he'd wanted Paul to live on the estate and act as the physician for the people until he learned how to manage all of it. Instead, Paul had returned to Ballaloch. There was time enough to learn about his inheritance after his mother had a home again.

"There's no one here to say otherwise, is there?" Cain interrupted his musings. "For all they know, you *are* the viscount."

"It's a title that doesna belong to me yet."

"But you *are* his heir," Sinclair insisted. "You can see Miss Andrews, court her openly, and stay in Lady Lanfordshire's home."

Paul set aside the tankard, not at all sure that was a good idea. Although his uncle had forced him to attend social gatherings, learning the proper way to behave, Paul had never been comfortable with it. He preferred the freedom of a tartan, instead of a confining waistcoat and jacket.

"I thought you came to London for Miss Andrews," Cain said. "Or was I wrong? Were you planning to find another lass to wed?"

Paul leveled a stare at him. "She's already told me she willna wed. No' me, nor any man. Naught has changed."

"One day it might be different," Cain offered.

He shrugged, not knowing the answer. But he had a need to be near her, to learn if there was any hope at all. Time and patience were his allies now. If there was any chance that she might think of starting over with him, he would wait as long as necessary.

Sinclair tapped the letter and said, "Were I in your shoes, Fraser, I'd use the title to your advantage. You have your chance. Don't be tossing it away."

But if he attempted to infiltrate her world, it might come crashing down on him. He wasn't a viscount. He was a physician and a rebel. A man who could never entertain himself with manners and ballrooms. All of it was a lie, though Sinclair was right: It was a lie that would open doors, allowing him to be nearer to Juliette.

And perhaps that made it worth the attempt.

Winter 1808

"I've been waiting for a long time to see your bonny face, Juliette."

She spun and saw Paul following her. Snowflakes had drifted against his black hair, and his deep blue eyes drank in the sight of her. His cheeks were bristled, as if he'd not taken the time to shave on his journey.

The urge to welcome him home with an embrace came over her, but she suppressed it. They were older now, and the remnants of her childhood were gone. An invisible barrier hung between them, formed from distance and her mother's warnings about how a proper young lady should behave.

"I never thought to see you here," she said, hoping he would see the thankfulness in her face. It had been so very long, she felt awkward. Almost as if the letters they'd written to one another had been guided by other hands.

"I can only stay a few days." He moved to stand beside her, and she saw that he was wearing finer clothes than she'd seen before, possibly handed down from his uncle. His woolen topcoat was covered in snow, and he might have appeared to be a gentleman, were it not for the gloves that had holes in them.

But the warmth in his eyes, the dark longing, was enough to overwhelm her senses. I missed you, his gaze seemed to say.

"Edinburgh is so far away," she murmured, feeling as if her skin tingled with phantom sensations. As if he were touching her, using only the power of his will.

"You've no welcome for me?" he teased, reaching for her hand. He'd grown so tall, she had to crane her neck back to look at his face.

"Not here," she whispered, pulling her hand back. "Not where anyone could see." Color rushed to her cheeks, for she knew the sort of welcome he wanted. Though she wanted to fly into his arms, to feel his strength enfolding her, it was wrong.

But he listened to her, guiding her away from the thatched houses. He walked steadily at her side, using only the barest touch of his palm against her spine to lead her toward the hillside. The snow continued to fall, dusting her cheeks and nose as they trudged through the drifts. When they reached the deeper snow, Paul's fingers fingers laced with hers to keep her from falling.

The heat of his gloved palm made her heartbeat quicken. The cluster of crofters' huts was behind them now, and he helped her to the path leading atop the hillside. A grove of pine trees and leafless oaks stood to hide them from view. Here, the snow wasn't as deep, and she pushed her way past the needled branches until they were near the center of the trees. At last, Paul turned to face her, and the hunger in his eyes was unmistakable.

"You're wearing your hair up, like a lady," he remarked, reaching out to touch the brown strands beneath her bonnet. Juliette held herself motionless, her mother's rules resounding in her mind. She *should not allow him to touch her, not now. Though she was seventeen, she understood that there were reasons for keeping a gentleman at a safe distance.*

"You're a bonny lass, as ever you were before." His hand moved back as if he'd suddenly remembered that they were no longer children. "I missed you these years."

She didn't trust herself to speak, and he seemed to understand it. He was nearly a man at nineteen. And yet . . . he was still the same Paul she'd always known.

Before she could move, he pressed her back against one of the thicker trees, holding her hips and locking her eyes with his. "You've grown shorter over the years."

The laughter in his eyes warmed her, and she tipped her head back. "You're taller."

In answer to that, he lifted her up until her eyes were even with his. "Is that better?"

His familiarity made her uncomfortable, and he held her as if she weighed no more than a wisp of cloth. "Put me down, Paul," she pleaded, though she knew he was only teasing. Instead, he held her a moment longer, his strong arms wrapped around her. No longer did she feel the cold, but she was intensely aware of his body pressed close to hers. The memory of his mouth on hers lingered, and a sliver of heat moved down her spine. As he lowered her, she found herself breathless at the pressure of his body against hers.

"I brought you a gift," he said, lowering her to stand. "Took me months of saving for it."

He grimaced a moment, staring down at his hands, as if he were embarrassed by the holes in his gloves. "I apprenticed with an apothecary for a while, and then I applied to the college again. This time, I was accepted." Reaching inside his waistcoat pocket, he pulled out a ring made of silver. She saw that it was engraved with a pattern of vines and a single blossom.

He reached out for her hand and found a finger that it fit. "I wanted something to remind you of our promise. Because I can no' return again, until I've finished with my studies. And when I come back, I want you to marry me, lass."

She traced the silver with her fingertips, knowing how much this gift had cost him. There was no doubting that he'd meant what he said. Her heart swelled with a burst of joy that he loved her, and she cared for him, too. She wanted so badly to keep the ring, to run home and tell her family that Paul had asked her to wed him.

But the moment she thought of her mother's reaction, reality struck hard. Beatrice would not be happy for her at all. If she spoke a word of this, her mother would forbid her to see him again.

With the greatest reluctance, she started to remove the ring. "Paul, I—"

"Don't speak," he warned, touching her mouth with a finger. "I can see what you're thinking. But you'll keep it, and make your decision later."

She let it be, knowing she ought to remove the ring. To wear it meant giving him false hope. And yet . . . he was her forbidden secret. She didn't want to give back the ring. Instead, she wanted to keep it on a chain, wearing it hidden against her heart.

Paul took her hand again. "Come with me back to the crofters. You can help me distribute the food."

"What food?" She frowned, not understanding what he meant.

"You'll see." He gave no other explanation but led her back down the hillside. They walked toward the rows of thatched huts. Dogs barked at their approach, and Juliette held tightly to her fur-lined pelisse as the winter wind blew past the houses.

Though she'd brought bread to these people on many occasions, when she saw the children gathering at one of the homes, her mood grew more somber. Their shoes were thin, their plaids wrapped tightly about them. One of the men was passing out sacks of potatoes, turnips, and dried fish.

"Where did all of this come from?" she asked, staring at the supplies. When Paul didn't answer, she faltered.

In the barest whisper, she inquired, "They didn't steal it, did they?"

Still he made no reply. The silver ring upon her finger seemed heavier somehow, and she wondered if he had planned the raid or only participated in it.

"It's wrong," she murmured. "They shouldn't—"

"It was food stolen from them," he said, not bothering to hide the edge of anger. "Strathland doubled their rents only a few weeks ago. When they couldna pay, they had to trade in their winter stores."

She shook her head. "I don't understand. He doesn't need their food."

"No, but by taking it from them, they have no choice but to leave." His gaze hardened. "Open your eyes, Juliette. He's stealing these people blind." His expression grew taut. "And you knew it already, for you were bringing them bread."

"I had to do something," she admitted. "But it wasn't enough. It won't ever be enough. We hardly have bread ourselves."

"Then you understand." He took her hand in his, leading her to stand beside the line of children. "The food would have rotted in his storehouses otherwise. Better to make use of it, where it's needed."

Juliette took a deep breath and eyed the stolen goods. "And what if you're caught?" She traced the edge of the ring, afraid of this side of him. There was a ruthlessness here that she'd only glimpsed a few years ago. It reminded her of how deeply he hated Lord Strathland and of his vow of vengeance.

"I'll be in Edinburgh. The people can blame it on me, if they want, but they willna let Strathland know where I am. He still believes I'm here, in the north."

She met his gaze squarely, demanding, "And is this your plan for vengeance? To steal?"

Paul's mouth tightened. "I'm no' a thief, if that's what you're thinking." He drew her to stand before the doorway. "I plan to revisit upon him every hardship he's given to the clansmen and women. He should suffer in this way, knowing hunger as they do."

She didn't like the edge in his voice and turned around to face him. "And do you plan to spend the rest of your life stealing from him, taking away everything he owns that has value?" It chilled her to think that his need for revenge went this deep.

"No' my entire life," he said, drawing her back behind one of the houses, out of view. "I plan to spend most of my life with you."

With that, he took her mouth in a kiss that pushed back the edges of her childhood, reminding her that she still belonged to him. Despite all her misgivings, she melted beneath his heated mouth, knowing that there would never be anyone for her like Paul Fraser. She was numb with fear, and yet, she couldn't stop herself from kissing him back.

This man, her desperate secret that she would keep from her family.

When there were shouts from the crofters, Paul broke free of the kiss. "Stay here," he warned. "If it's Strathland or his factor, I want you nowhere close."

He pressed her back against the wall while he ventured out among the others. Juliette remained in hiding, watching as the men hurried to hide the remainder of the food. Within moments, several men arrived on horseback, and she suspected their leader was Lord Strathland's factor.

She barely heard what was going on, but the Highlanders had formed a line against the Englishmen. Juliette swallowed hard, her heart pounding within her chest. Someone was going to be hurt, and God help her, she couldn't let it be Paul.

From the side, she saw another man approaching on horseback. He wore a wool topcoat, and the horse he rode was the finest she'd ever seen. It was Lord Strathland himself. Upon his face, she saw fury, and a man who would voice orders to harm the crofters.

Without knowing why she was emerging from her hiding place, she walked away from the men, directly toward the earl. She kept her steps slow and held tightly to her pelisse, placing a false smile upon her face as she neared Lord Strathland.

Her mother's instructions came back to her, the rules of polite introduction that she was casting aside by approaching this man. But if she could spare these people from violence, it hardly mattered that there was no chaperone to introduce them.

"My lord," she greeted him, offering a slight curtsy. Explanations tangled with lies in her brain of why the crofters had sacks of food among them. "I am Juliette Andrews. I believe you know my father, Lieutenant Colonel Andrews."

Her words did have an effect on him, but not the one she'd expected. The earl's earlier anger dissipated, and his gaze fixed upon hers. Cool brown eyes studied her face, before his attention shifted down over her body.

"Miss Andrews." He nodded to her, dismounting from his horse. "Your mother would be displeased to find you so far from home this morning."

"She believes in charity to those less fortunate, as I am sure you do," she said, still clinging to the smile she didn't feel. "I brought food as gifts from my family to these people. It's part of a Christmas offering."

The earl's expression hardened, but he sent a look toward his men, nodding for them to retreat. "Have you? I am surprised that Mrs. Andrews did not arrange it herself instead of sending her young daughter to oversee the supplies."

"She was here earlier," Juliette lied. "I asked for permission to stay, to speak with some of the children." She took a deep breath and held her ground.

Again, those eyes stared at her, and she sensed a frosted anger coming from Paul. Though he didn't move, not wanting to draw attention, she sensed that he was seething.

The earl mounted his horse again, lifting his hat in farewell to her. "I've been meaning to pay a call upon your mother. Since Lieutenant Colonel Andrews is away at war, I thought I should see if Mrs. Andrews has need of my assistance, seeing as we are neighbors. When I come to the house, perhaps you will be there?"

She didn't dare tell him no. Though she didn't understand why he would want her to be a part of the conversation, she braved another smile and nodded. "If it pleases you."

"It would," he said softly. But the smile upon his face held the same hunger she'd seen in Paul's eyes. Instead of drawing her closer, it heightened her discomfort. "Merry Christmas, Miss Andrews."

With a silent command to his men, the earl withdrew. Juliette's pulse never slowed down, not even after they'd gone. A silence had fallen over the people, and they finished distributing the remaining food, all of them casting odd looks at her.

Paul crossed the throng and took her by the hand. Without a word, he led her back toward the place where he'd kept her hidden. "Why did you come out? I told you to stay behind."

"He knew what you did," she reminded him. "His men were going to hurt the MacKinlochs. I thought I could stop them from fighting." She raised her chin, lifting her gaze to his. "And I did just that."

"You have no idea what you've done," he exploded, his hand digging into the stone of the wall. "He has his eye upon you, Juliette. He wants you."

"I'm too young for that," she said, shaking her head. "He's as old as my father."

"His wife is dead, and he'll be wanting a new one. It willna be you," Paul warned.

His intensity struck her hard, and she was aghast that he was already behaving like a jealous husband. Didn't he think she had more sense than that? She would never consider letting a man like the Earl of Strathland court her.

But more than that, she didn't want Paul issuing commands. "You aren't my husband yet, Paul Fraser," she said quietly. "I have years yet before I'll make that decision." With that, she took off the silver ring and held it out to him.

The gesture cooled his temper, and he hesitated before he took it back. "I'm sorry. I just couldna stand back and watch him stare at you. I want you to be safe, Juliette."

He touched his head to hers, lowering his voice. "I'm going to be worthy of you one day, I promise you that."

She said nothing but rested her face against his heart. "Don't let's argue, Paul. You're going back to Edinburgh, soon enough."

He held her close. "I will, aye. And all I ask is that you wait for me. Don't be making any decisions until I can return. Will you no' promise me that?"

She let out a sigh and stood on her tiptoes. Gently, she kissed him, and his hands threaded into her hair, pressing her back into the shadows. It was a kiss of promises yet to be, of a man who wanted her more than any other.

Juliette awakened, her body frozen and aching. Her cheeks were wet, and she realized she'd been crying in her sleep.

She didn't know what had caused her to dream of Paul's visit, years ago. But her hand moved up to touch her lips in the memory of his kiss.

That was the day Strathland had noticed her. It had disturbed her deeply, for he was so much older . . . and the look in his eyes had been filled with lust. The more she'd refused him, the more aggressive his pursuit. He was not a man who understood the word *no*, and he'd continued to press her, even during the following year.

Her mind pushed away the harsh memories of the attack, trying to soothe her spirits with thoughts of Paul. If she'd agreed to wed him that day, her life might have been different. Perhaps Matthew would have been his son, instead of the earl's. They might have been happy together, even if they'd had to elope.

She stared up at the ceiling, thinking of her sisters' excitement about their London Season. They were eager to find a husband and become a wife. Her eldest sister, Victoria, had found her happiness with a duke.

And for Juliette, there would be nothing but columns of numbers.

Despite her desire to manage Aphrodite's Unmentionables, she couldn't help but resent the unfairness of it all.

Her eyes ached again, and she shut them, trying to tell herself that it was for the best. A slight noise alerted her to the kitten, which had crept out of his bed to come and see her. Juliette lifted Dragon up, letting the soft ball of fur snuggle against her side.

The kitten only reminded her of Paul. And despite her efforts to push him away, she couldn't deny that she missed him.

Chapter Five

Juliette reached into her reticule and pulled out a folded piece of paper. She had come with her sisters to the Duke of Worthingstone's London residence, eager to share the news that was brimming up inside her. "With the help of the crofters, we finished most of the orders." She shot a sidelong glance toward Victoria, adding, "Although Mother still thinks they were sewing gowns."

All three of her sisters were waiting expectantly as Juliette held out the paper containing the results of their sales. "I've tallied up the amounts here. Sixteen corsets, fourteen chemises, and we have orders for thirty more."

"And the money?" Victoria prompted. "Did you earn very much?"

Juliette smiled and passed her the paper. "More than enough. Over a thousand pounds."

"A thousand? But it can't be."

"It can, and it is." Juliette sat across from Victoria, pleased to give her sister the good news. It took a great effort to appear calm, when inwardly, she wanted to whoop with joy. Margaret didn't look at all pleased, but Amelia was beaming with excitement.

Victoria sat back in her chair, touching her heart. "This will change the crofters' lives. They won't have to struggle so much to survive." A hint of a smile crossed over her face at the thought. Juliette shared the sentiment. The Scottish women had worked hard, sewing well into the night to finish the garments. And they would profit, in turn, from more sales.

A glimmer of hope sparked within Juliette, for she had found a new purpose. Though she had not yet visited Madame Benedict's shop, she fully intended to investigate the sales. She would pour herself into the accounts, determining the best prices for the garments. And perhaps, if she was buried in work, she could forget the solemn eyes of the infant who had ensnared her heart. And the man who was tempting her away from spinsterhood.

"It can't continue," Margaret insisted. "If anyone found out we are behind it, Father would be humiliated. Not to mention what all of society would think of us. You might be married, Victoria, but the rest of us aren't. The men would believe we're harboring sordid thoughts." She sat down, her back ramrod straight. "It's not at all appropriate, and it's a bad influence upon Amelia. We should cease this immediately."

Margaret wouldn't know a sordid thought if it struck her between the eyes, Juliette thought. And if she knew what went on between a woman and a man in bed, she would faint in shock.

When she glanced over at Victoria, her sister appeared worried. Sewing meant the world to Toria, and it occurred to Juliette that if word got out about Aphrodite's Unmentionables, her sister's reputation could be harmed.

"Does the duke know?" she asked her quietly.

Victoria nodded. "He knew about it before Christmas. But he doesn't want me to sew anymore."

"He's right. Duchesses do not sew," Margaret agreed. "They embroider. And even then, not very often."

A flash of annoyance crossed Victoria's face. "If I want to sew, then I will. What I do in the privacy of my room is no one's concern."

Good for you, Juliette thought. Her quiet sister had a backbone, though she didn't push back often.

"I'm only trying to help," Margaret said. "You should be aware of your social position."

Amelia sent Victoria a sly look. "Don't believe her at all, Victoria. She may try to be proper, but she's wondering about what goes on during a wedding night, as much as the rest of us. Was it as exciting as I think it would be? Did he tear off your unmentionables?"

Juliette nearly choked at that. Though her sister was only teasing, a flash of fear evoked memories of that night. There was nothing at all exciting about what happened between a man and a woman. It was humiliating, and it had hurt.

Thankfully, Margaret saved them with her own retort, "She is *not* going to share such details with you."

"No, she'll only share them with the pair of you, later." Amelia sighed with dismay. "It's so unfair."

This was one moment when Juliette was grateful that Margaret had cut off Amelia's wonderings. "I, for one, believe that Victoria's wedding night can remain her own private information." She took back the slip of paper detailing the number of garments ordered and changed the subject. "Will you send any new designs back to Scotland? At the very least, the crofters' wives can sew them for you."

"I have a few sketches," Victoria said. "But I'll need to make the patterns for the women. Did the families return to Eiloch Hill, as the duke promised?"

"Yes. Dr. Fraser sent a letter that they are building their homes. The old ones were burned, so they have to start anew."

At the mention of Paul, Amelia sent her a teasing smile, as if to gauge her reaction. Juliette's face flushed, for she'd come to London fully intending to forget about Paul. But she imagined him working alongside the crofters, helping them to rebuild their lives. The memory of his dark blue eyes and the way he'd looked at her was far worse. She did miss him, though she'd hoped to forget about him while she was here.

"His Grace has sent men to help rebuild Ballaloch also," Amelia admitted. "In the spring, we should be able to return home."

Home. The word should have brought comfort, but instead it reminded her that returning to Scotland meant leaving Matthew. Right now, she felt as if she were at a crossroads, trying to decide which life to leave behind.

It was far easier to say farewell to Scotland than to leave her son. Her mother wanted her to marry, but that was an impossible notion. No man wanted a celibate marriage.

She had to focus her efforts on Aphrodite's Unmentionables and do everything in her power to ensure its success. Victoria opened her writing desk and retrieved a set of sketches she'd done. They were more modest undergarments, made from linen and the softest cotton.

"Now these are far more appropriate," Margaret pronounced. "They are sensible, and any young lady could wear them without fear of being immodest."

And they were like every other set of unmentionables. What made Aphrodite's Unmentionables unique was the fact that they were impractical for anyone but the extremely wealthy. They were well made and offered a luxury that no other garments had. The women who bought them wanted to be different, more seductive to a man.

Juliette shook her head. "These don't sell as well, I'm afraid. They may be beautiful, but the women want more revealing unmentionables."

She glanced at Toria, and her sister reddened as if she understood what she meant. But instead of fear, there was a flush of interest in her sister's face. She glanced at the bed as if she'd enjoyed the time with her husband.

"We should still make a few garments that are meant for younger women," Victoria said.

Not too many, if Juliette had anything to do with it. She would ensure that only the finest, most sensual fabrics were used. Perhaps a few could be adorned with semiprecious jewels, to make them even more unique. They could be priced even higher. Her mind began calculating the greater profits, turning over the numbers, until Margaret interrupted.

"It's getting late," she said, reaching for her bonnet. "We should return, for Aunt Charlotte will be expecting us."

Juliette put on her bonnet and gloves while Victoria rang for a footman and gave orders for a brougham to be brought for them. She hugged her sister farewell and went to join Amelia, while Margaret hung behind.

While the two of them spoke in whispers, Amelia leaned in to Juliette. "Aunt Charlotte is hosting a ball in a few days. You're coming, aren't you?"

"Perhaps." She kept her answer vague, not wanting to agree to it.

"What if . . . you found someone you fancied at the ball? Would you steal a moment away with him?" The embarrassed flush on Amelia's face sent a flare of warning through her. Was her sister plotting something? Guilt was written all over her face.

"No. And if you're considering anything like that, put the idea out of your head. You're far too young to be married."

Amelia sent her a sad smile. "And you're acting as if you're a thousand years old."

"I'm not." Juliette forced a smile she didn't feel onto her face, not wanting her sister to keep pushing.

Amelia drew her to the side. "You've been avoiding the parties, and you're becoming the way Victoria was. I thought you promised to *try* to enjoy yourself. Even if you don't want a husband." The tone in her sister's voice said she couldn't fathom why Juliette would ever feel that way.

The truth was, she *didn't* want to live a life in this way. She did want a husband and children, like any other woman. It was her sense of honesty holding her back.

"I am content to go on as I have," she said, to appease her sister.

"It shouldn't be that way," Amelia said with a sigh, hugging her.

No, it shouldn't. But what else was there?

Juliette returned the embrace, knowing that her sister was only trying to help. "We'll go to Madame Benedict's tomorrow. I need to see how the unmentionables are selling, and you should find a new gown for the ball."

Amelia beamed with happiness. But even through her sister's smile, Juliette wondered what she wasn't telling her.

⚜

Paul stepped into Colonel Lord Lanfordshire's London town house, the scent of dust coating the air. The footman took his coat while the butler led them inside.

"These arrangements are only temporary," Mr. Culpepper explained. "Once Lady Lanfordshire returns, you must acquire your own accommodations."

"Of course," Paul answered.

Each room revealed years of neglect. Most of the valuables had been sold off to pay debts, and what remained was an assorted collection of paintings, battered furniture, and worn carpet. It was clear that whatever servants remained in Colonel Lord Lanfordshire's employ had failed to maintain cleanliness.

"Lady Lanfordshire said in her letter that you finished your medical studies." The butler eyed him with the interest of a man who had his own ailments.

"I did." Paul followed the man up two flights of stairs, knowing he would be placed in the servants' quarters.

"You are a surgeon, I presume?" The butler kept his tone even, though Paul read the underlying assumption that he could do little more than amputate limbs.

"A physician and a surgeon," he corrected. He'd earned licenses for each, and he fully intended to continue practicing medicine. Though he didn't have to work, because of the allowance his uncle had sent, pride kept him from using it. This new life felt foreign to him, as if he didn't deserve to be handed a fortune.

He'd gladly hand it back, if it meant his father could live again.

The butler paused a moment, seeming to reconsider their destination. He cleared his throat and then returned down a few more stairs. "This way, Dr. Fraser."

Paul hid any reaction. Likely the man had originally intended to house him in an attic garret as a sleeping place. Instead, he was shown to a modest bedroom adjoining the nursery.

"Thank you." The room had not been aired out, nor were there fresh bed linens. Even so, he recognized the room as one that must have belonged to the daughters of Lord Lanfordshire. The rose wallpaper and gilt chairs made that evident enough. Juliette herself might have slept in this room, as a young girl.

"I will send up a scullery maid to prepare the room for you." With that, the butler left him alone.

Paul set down his belongings and went to open the window. The grim streets, the harsh odors, and the bustle of people made him yearn for the green hills of Scotland. He couldn't imagine what had brought Juliette back here. Did she truly want to live in London?

He didn't belong in a place like this, a city of strangers. He ran a hand over the roughened stubble on his cheeks. After nearly two weeks of traveling, he looked terrible. Over and over, he questioned why he was here.

Everything Juliette had done was a contradiction. With her words, she'd told him that she would never consider marriage to any man. And yet, with her actions, she'd sought him out. She'd allowed him to embrace her.

He wanted to believe that there could be something between them once more. That he could heal the invisible wounds that haunted her, those that made her believe she could not marry.

He would not press her; he would only offer his friendship. And perhaps, in time, it would grow into something more. If that meant finding his way about all the rules of London society, taking on the identity of his uncle's heir, well, he'd do whatever was necessary.

He opened up the writing desk with the intent of penning a note, when he spied a sheaf of crumpled paper scraps. They were written in Juliette's hand, and each appeared to be an unfinished letter. All were addressed to him.

The first said only: *Dear Paul*. The second note had a single sentence: *I miss you*. The third letter began with a greeting and the words: *I don't know how to say this to you*. The ink was blurred, as if she'd been crying. It was dated October of 1810, after the attack.

A rush of anger welled up inside him, along with the desire to kill the man who had done this to an innocent young woman. He was furious with himself that he hadn't been there to save her.

She had supported him, when he'd lost his father. He should have been there for her.

Paul shut the desk, resting his hands upon the wood. God help him, he didn't know what to do. If he investigated more, it would only draw attention to Juliette in a way that would hurt her. Few people knew of the attack, and he understood her need for secrecy.

It complicated his plans to win her over, but he intended to convince her that the past would not change his feelings. If anything, it made him more determined.

First, he had to make his way into her world. Physicians did not mingle with the ton—but a viscount's heir could.

"They see what they want to believe," his uncle Donald Fraser had told him, a year ago. "Become a viscount in the way you dress, in the way you speak, and in the way you behave. Tell them the lies they want to hear."

Paul stood before his uncle, wearing a fine linen shirt, buff breeches, and a black waistcoat. His jacket was bottle green, and he'd worn his hair cropped short. Although he'd agreed to wear the clothes his uncle had purchased, they felt unfamiliar, as if he were trying to be someone he wasn't.

"Stand up straighter," Donald commanded. "Behave as if you are above them all. Look bored."

Paul attempted to feign indifference, but no matter how he tried to mask himself behind the finery, he knew what he was. A poor crofter's son, trying to behave like a prince. It would never work, not in a thousand years.

"There's nae point to this," he argued. "I'll ne'er be one of them."

"Not if you keep saying nae, that's true enough. But to know your enemy, you must walk within his world. You must know what is important to him."

"Strathland's a greedy bastard who wants land and money. I willna wear clothing like this, nor walk among the gentlemen as if I'm one of them."

"You're afraid," Fraser predicted. "You're afraid they'll see past your clothes to the worthless man beneath."

"I'm no' worthless."

His uncle's face grew taut. "Then prove it. You may be my heir at the moment, but I've many years left to live. I'll not hand over an allowance to a man who can't even speak properly."

"I havena asked anything of you," Paul interrupted. "All I want is my vengeance on Strathland. Make someone else your heir."

"I'm not too old to marry and beget a son," Donald retorted, though Paul doubted if any woman would wed such a surly man. His uncle shook his head with irritation. "But if I die tomorrow, it will come to you, whether you will it or not. The estates are entailed, and damned if I'll let you squander them away. You have no appreciation of what I'm giving to you. You have so much to learn and—"

"Help me bring him down," Paul said quietly. "If becoming a viscount will help me end Strathland, I'll do what I must."

"God help us both." Donald sighed. "You cannot let your desire for vengeance control you. Even if you do kill the earl, you'll hang *for it. And then what will happen to your beloved?" He paused, as if thinking for a moment. "Oh, that's right. She'll wed a man who's worthy of her. An intelligent man who knows how to tie a cravat."*

The mention of Juliette stopped Paul cold. He had to do more, to become a man her family would be proud of. She was the reason he was attempting this façade. Juliette was his compass, guiding him toward his true purpose.

He straightened the lines of his jacket, lifting his chin. She belonged in gowns and jeweled finery. And although it felt like he was trying to put on a false face, he'd do it if it meant winning her.

"I'll learn what I need to, to become your heir," he said at last.

"If you become my heir," Donald corrected. "Finish your studies at the medical college, and make something of yourself first. The education will do you good. Afterward, you will learn how to handle the estates."

He didn't argue, for it was the chance he wanted, to live out his own dream of becoming a doctor.

"Thank you, Uncle," he said at last. For he was grateful for the schooling.

His uncle squared his shoulders. "You have a great deal to learn, and you'll have to learn it, even during your medical studies—else you'll risk embarrassing yourself." He eyed Paul as if he didn't like what he saw. "You must attend social functions and do exactly as I tell you to. You must practice behaving properly. You need to learn how to infiltrate the ranks of the upper class."

Paul had kept his word, learning everything his uncle had wanted him to. And now was his chance to put it all into practice.

He opened his bundle of clothing, staring at the black tailcoat and snowy white cravat he'd brought with him. If he behaved with enough arrogance, using the elegant clothes and presenting himself as a viscount's heir, they might believe him. He needed to prove to Juliette and to her family that he could be the right husband for her.

Even if it meant transforming himself into a different man.

Chapter Six

"**I**'ve been wanting to visit Madame Benedict's shop for *years* now."

Juliette hid her smile at Amelia's thrilled excitement. She had agreed to take her younger sister with her, but with the solemn oath that there would be no mention whatsoever of their involvement in Aphrodite's Unmentionables. A maid and a footman had also accompanied them, to help carry any parcels they might buy. Both servants kept a discreet distance from them in the shop, allowing them time together to speak.

"Do you suppose she has the corsets on display?" Amelia wondered aloud. "Or does she have them hidden in a secret part of the store?"

Juliette ignored the questions. "We're here to find out which colors and designs are selling the best. Nothing more. Promise me you won't breathe a word," she whispered in her sister's ear. "This isn't only about us. It's about Victoria's reputation as well. If anyone found out about her involvement . . ."

"They won't," Amelia promised. But her face filled with delight as she saw other women speaking with the dressmaker, while Madame Benedict held out swatches of colored silks and satins. Her sister drank in the sight of the beautifully made frocks, and when she moved closer to the other women, Juliette could tell that Amelia was eavesdropping.

She didn't fret over it, for perhaps her sister would learn something. In the meantime, her mind was fixated upon other possibilities. If her sisters each married well and she continued Aphrodite's Unmentionables on her own, the profits would continue to grow over the years. Eventually, she might amass her own fortune.

One that would allow her to live close to her son.

At the moment, Matthew was heir to an earldom. After Juliette had learned she was pregnant, she'd sought help from her aunt and uncle. Charlotte had taken her away to have the baby and afterward had returned to London, claiming the child was hers. Lord Arnsbury had embraced the idea, recognizing the boy as his heir. Matthew would never know he was illegitimate. He had parents who adored him, a fine house to live in, the promise of an education, and a title.

It should have been enough.

And yet, it was slowly killing her to watch Charlotte raise the boy as her own. Although her aunt and uncle had been childless for years, seeing Matthew grow up with another woman as his mother was worse than she'd ever imagined. Each time she visited him, Juliette couldn't repress the desire to get him back, though she knew it was futile.

Hearing her sisters talk about winning a husband, or whispering secrets in the dark about men and women, made her all the more determined never to face the same circumstances again. She would make a new life for herself, one that didn't involve men.

Madame Benedict was now revealing undergarments to the ladies, one of whom was to be married in the next few weeks. She held out a corset of soft rose silk, embroidered with green.

"Now this one, my lady, is an exquisite creation, one that will support your daughter's figure and enhance her beauty," the dressmaker began. "See how soft it is."

The young lady appeared fascinated by the material, and Amelia now made no secret of her interest. Inching her way closer, her sister said loudly, "It's the most beautiful corset I've ever seen."

"It's entirely inappropriate." The older matron dismissed it with a hand. "Show us something made of cambric or linen."

"My mother gave me one for my birthday," Amelia lied. "The silk is breathtaking against one's skin. Why, I feel as if I'm wearing nothing at all." She sighed happily, and the girl's mother appeared aghast. Before she could snap out another refusal, Amelia continued, "Of course, it was frightfully dear, and I understand if it is too much of a luxury for you to afford. I suppose I'll be very lucky if I receive another one when I am betrothed."

"There is no luxury too dear for my daughter," the matron responded in a huff. "She can have whatever she desires." Gesturing toward the rose corset, she remarked, "She is going to marry a marquess, after all. She should wear garments befitting a lady of her station."

Amelia nodded solemnly in agreement, then turned and winked at Juliette when the woman ordered three more sets of matching corsets, chemises, and petticoats. After they had left, Madame Benedict beamed at Amelia. "You are Lady Lanfordshire's daughter, are you not?" With a broad laugh, the Frenchwoman added, "Lady Everett had no intention of buying unmentionables until you hinted that she could not afford them. I must thank you for the sales, mademoiselle."

"I was only telling the truth," Amelia said, feigning innocence. "But if you would like to offer a better price on the evening gown I intend to order, that would be good of you."

Madame Benedict smiled. "We shall see." As the pair of them discussed a possible design, Juliette walked over to the window, staring at the people passing by. The shop was located in Pall Mall, near a linen draper's and a tailor's shop. She amused herself with watching the crowds, until Amelia had finished speaking with the dressmaker. Both the footman and maid joined them when they returned outside, but as they walked along the street, Juliette sensed that they were being followed.

She slowed their pace, wondering if she was only imagining it. The weather outside was fine, but before they could arrange for a hackney, someone came up behind her and pressed something into her hand.

It was a bundle of violets. Startled, she started to turn around, but a voice murmured in her ear, "Meet me at your father's house. I'll be waiting, lass."

It was the voice of Paul Fraser. The sound of his deep baritone startled her so badly, she couldn't grasp a single thing to say. Why on earth would he leave Scotland?

For you, her heart sang. *He came for you.*

Before she could say a word, he sent her a knowing look and disappeared into the crowd of people. Amelia hadn't noticed him, and neither had their footman, from the way the man's attention was rapt upon her maid.

The bundle of violets was tied up in a small piece of string. Her traitorous heart gave a slight flutter that he'd thought to find her. But why had he told her to come to her father's town house? Why wouldn't he simply pay a call upon her at Aunt Charlotte's?

Because it was unlikely that the Countess and Earl of Arnsbury would receive him.

Still, there was no one in residence at her father's house, except for a handful of servants. Perhaps that was the reason—it would grant them privacy.

"Who gave you those?" Amelia asked.

Juliette didn't answer but simply shook her head and shrugged. She wasn't certain she wanted her sister to know the truth.

"You're blushing," Amelia informed her. "Was it a secret admirer?"

"I never saw the man," Juliette lied, tucking the flowers into her reticule. But her heart fluttered within her chest at the knowledge that Paul hadn't given up on her. Though it should have exasperated her, she found herself warming to it.

"It was Dr. Fraser, wasn't it?" Amelia guessed. She beamed with delight, and Juliette stared at her.

"Now how would you think that?" A sinking suspicion grew strong within her, that her sister was matchmaking.

"I sent him a letter and asked him to come." Amelia frowned a moment, crossing her arms. "But it's too soon for him to be here. I gave it to Mr. Sinclair only a few days ago." With a shrug, she remarked, "I have no idea how he traveled so fast."

Juliette knew. It meant that Paul and Mr. Sinclair had traveled together, shadowing their journey. He'd asked her where she wanted to stay, and she'd told him London. She'd never dreamed that he would follow her.

Their footman hailed a hackney, and she and Amelia climbed aboard, their servants joining the driver. They continued along the road, toward the direction she'd seen Dr. Fraser go. Her heart beat a little faster at the thought of seeing him again.

They were not far from their parents' town house, and she spied the familiar figure approaching their home. How could Dr. Fraser think to approach the town house? Her family wasn't there, and surely he knew that. Her nerves tightened with apprehension and more than a little curiosity.

"Stop, please," she blurted out to the driver, even as her common sense warned that this was a terrible idea.

"Why are we stopping?" Amelia demanded.

"Because Dr. Fraser is walking toward our house," she answered honestly.

Her sister frowned a moment. Then she feigned a slight smile of surprise. "Why, you're right. I can't imagine why Dr. Fraser would come to Father's residence." The tone in her voice was filled with untruths, making Juliette wonder what on earth her sister was up to.

Juliette ordered their driver to take them closer. When they pulled to a stop in front of the door, she disembarked with Amelia. Then she ordered their servants to return to Aunt Charlotte's, promising to join them soon.

"Juliette, is Dr. Fraser . . . bleeding?" Amelia asked, her face blanching.

Dear God, her sister was right. Although Paul was wearing a dark coat, it hung open slightly. From her vantage point, Juliette spied a bloodstained shirt, and she hurried forward. Horror struck her at the thought of him being injured.

"Are you hurt?" she demanded, without bothering to greet him. "The blood, it's—"

"It's nothing," he said, opening the front door. "Your mother invited me to stay here while I sought employment as a physician. Won't you come inside?" He glanced behind at Amelia. "And your sister, of course."

He was staying here? She didn't at all believe her mother would do such a thing. Never in a thousand years would Beatrice invite Paul to stay in London. She was about to contradict him, but held her tongue when Amelia leaned in.

"It was my doing," she whispered. "Don't tell Mother. I wrote the letter because he needed somewhere to stay. I didn't know he was already here—Mr. Sinclair must have found him sooner than I'd thought."

The apologetic smile on Amelia's face spoke volumes. Juliette wanted to groan at her sister's interference, even as she handed her pelisse and bonnet to a footman. She greeted the butler, Mr. Culpepper, and ordered a basin of warm water and soap, as well as bandages.

"There's no need for bandages," Dr. Fraser corrected, "but a linen towel will do."

"What happened to you?" Juliette asked. When Paul removed his coat, she saw that his hands and forearms were stained with blood, as well as his shirt.

Culpepper returned with the footman, who carried in the basin and towel. "Miss Andrews, Dr. Fraser was invited to stay by Lady Lanfordshire's orders," the butler explained. "However, I am not certain she would approve of you paying a call, until she has returned. I fear that—"

"Mr. Culpepper, we are well aware of my mother's invitation. Dr. Fraser is a friend of our family, and naturally, we were concerned when we saw him covered in blood. I assure you, we wanted only to ensure that he is all right," Amelia intervened. "You may go now."

The butler clucked over his clothing, and the footman set down the basin and towel. Both retreated, but Juliette didn't doubt that they were close enough to eavesdrop.

"I spent the morning in the hospital," he told them. "The blood isna mine."

She wasn't aware she'd been holding her breath until she exhaled sharply. He washed away the blood, soaping his hands thoroughly. "Why are you here, Dr. Fraser?"

"Why do you think?" he answered quietly. Juliette glanced behind her at Amelia, but it seemed that her sister had taken the opportunity to slip away, leaving them alone.

"You don't like the city," she protested.

"No, but if this is where you're wanting to live, I'll find my way." His tone was entirely serious, making it clear that he was not giving up on her. When she stared into his dark blue eyes, she saw the steady faithfulness of a man who cared.

He rinsed his hands and regarded her. "I lost several years in courting you. I thought that before you decided to refuse me again, you should have me for a suitor before you make that decision."

Juliette clutched the bundle of violets, and the cheerful purple color evoked memories of when he'd picked wildflowers for her when she was fourteen. It seemed like a lifetime ago. Her gaze traveled to his hands, which he'd soaped and rinsed. Those hands could heal the sick . . . and she remembered the touch of his fingers against her face.

"You needn't court me," she said quietly. But seeing him again made her heart falter. How long had he been here? That he'd already begun working at the hospital suggested at least a few days.

He dried his hands with a towel and then poured more water to wash his face. Water droplets gleamed upon his chiseled face. His dark hair was ragged, half-wild with the need to be trimmed. Her eyes rested upon the exposed skin at his throat, where his shirt collar was carelessly undone.

Her skin flushed at the thought of his bare chest, and she couldn't seem to shut down her curiosity. If they were alone and she were his wife, she could almost imagine sitting in his lap, unfastening his shirt. Pressing her lips to the pulse at his throat while his hands moved through her hair.

Juliette closed her eyes for a moment, trying to erase her wayward thoughts.

"A fortnight, Juliette. Grant me that at least, for the sake of the friendship we once had."

It wasn't a wise idea, not at all. A thousand reasons why she shouldn't see him were poised at her lips. And yet, she couldn't bring herself to voice them.

You want to see him again, her heart whispered. *Because you still care.*

It was a truth she wasn't ready to face. To push the idle thoughts away, Juliette reached out to help him wash away a spot of blood he'd missed. "You shouldn't have left Scotland for me," she said gently. "Your heart is there."

"No. It isn't." Paul reached out and lifted her chin. "It's here."

The dormant feelings closed over her, despite her attempts to freeze them out. The touch of his hand against her face was a balm to her wounded spirit.

He was watching her with the eyes of a man who had no intention of walking away. The knowledge that he'd journeyed so far for her only deepened her guilt. With every moment she spent at his side, her willpower weakened.

Her mind and heart were at war, but she forced herself to speak the words that needed to be said. "Please don't ask more of me," she said. "I can't give you what you want."

"You keep asking me to leave you behind," he murmured. "But you should realize that I'll ne'er turn my back on you. No' when you really want me to stay."

The tears welled up and spilled over. He was so wrong. How would he react if he ever learned the truth?

I'll ne'er turn my back on you.

Heaven help her, she wished it were true.

He leaned forward and touched his cheek to hers. Juliette closed her eyes, unable to stop herself from indulging in the simple comfort of his touch.

"Give it a chance, Juliette," he urged. He turned, and without asking, he kissed her softly. The touch of his mouth upon hers was an offer of healing, of the happiness she'd denied herself. She was frozen against his kiss, unable to move or breathe. It was like the night she'd dreamed of him, brought back into reality. A simple kiss, an offering that pushed back the fetters of the past, offering a future she'd only imagined.

When he pulled back, he framed her face with his hands. "I'll be damned if I'll hide away in Scotland while your family tries to wed you off to someone else."

He didn't understand that she was irrevocably broken. And no matter what she'd told him, he refused to accept her decision.

The truth would drive him away. She was certain of that.

She drank in his features, trying to hold fast to this moment. If she ever laid her soul bare to him, he would no longer look upon her with anything but disgust. And she prayed he would go, before she ever had to reveal her shame.

"I must see my sister home," she told him.

Before she could pull away, he took her hands in his. "When is the next gathering you're attending?"

She frowned, not understanding why he would ask. "In a few days. My aunt Charlotte is hosting a ball to celebrate Victoria's wedding."

"I will be there."

She wondered if Paul understood what sort of event this was. It was by invitation only, and it was not the sort of party a physician would be permitted to attend. It was the sort of soirée Margaret reveled in, with society rules about what one could and could not say.

"You can't," she told him. "It's only for family and a few close friends." That wasn't quite the truth, but it was a way of making him see that he could not attend.

"I don't need an invitation to watch over you," he countered. "And I find that I'm no' wanting to sit here while other men try to convince your family that they would make a suitable husband. When we both ken that's not the truth."

She could say nothing to that. "If you try to come, they'll throw you out."

His hand reached out to her cheek, and his palm was cool from the water. Gooseflesh rose up over her skin, and she forced herself to pull back.

"Let them try."

She didn't know how he would manage such a feat. Would he disguise himself as a servant?

He let her go, escorting her and Amelia to the door. "Until I see you again," he said by way of farewell. The faint smile playing at his mouth worried her, for she didn't doubt he would try to attend.

Worse, she found herself looking forward to it, far more than she should.

There were over one hundred guests at Lady Arnsbury's gathering. Among so many people, it was an easy matter to trespass upon the premises. Especially when Paul had arrived hours later than everyone else.

With his uncle's borrowed clothing, no one cast him a second look. The black tailcoat had been fitted to his lean, taller form.

His linen shirt was crisp, and his hair was trimmed and combed back. Gold cuff links gleamed at his wrists, and he'd worn his neckcloth tied in an elaborate knot. Appearing wealthy was necessary to avoid being thrown out. That, and mimicking the behavior of the ton.

Juliette was hiding among her sisters, her hair pinned up like a crown of polished wood. Sprigs of white lilies of the valley were tucked in among her curls, and she wore a gown of the same color, adorned with green ribbons. The sight of her took his breath away.

He wanted to steal his way toward her, making it clear that he was fully capable of mingling within her circle. Though he might lack the title now, one day he'd inherit his uncle's wealth and social standing. He could rightfully present himself as the heir, which would open doors to him. This night, he wanted to slip his way past the invisible social barriers, making Juliette see that he *could* fit into her world. No longer was he an ignorant crofter's son with no hope of a future. Now, her family would have no reason at all to deny his courtship.

Paul moved inside the ballroom with an air of confidence, sending a faint smile toward one of the matrons. He'd learned long ago that the key to his success rested on rumor. A few dropped hints of wealth, the mention of a title, and before long, no one cared whether he had an invitation.

He'd learned how to read the unspoken body language of people. He knew how to discern lies and how to follow the rules of the ton. Oh, he'd made countless mistakes during the early years in Edinburgh. But the ability to blend seamlessly into a crowd was becoming easier. And now, for a few hours, he could watch over Juliette, preventing any gentlemen from offering their unwanted attentions.

Upon her face, he spied the edge of nerves, as if she was uncomfortable among the ladies. She didn't belong here, any more than he did. But he wouldn't leave until he'd stolen a few moments with her.

First, he had to reach her without drawing undue attention. He kept his posture erect as he approached an older matron. He bowed in greeting, behaving as if they'd already been introduced and he hadn't overheard her name from someone else. "It has been a long time since I've last seen you, Lady Vaughn. You are looking as lovely as ever." He was careful to hide his Scottish brogue, keeping his voice as tightly English as he could manage.

Her face revealed her confusion, and he smoothed it over. "I am Paul Fraser. The Viscount of Falsham is my uncle," he reminded her. "We were introduced last year."

She blinked a moment, then realized what he'd said. "The Scottish viscount, of course. For a moment, I wondered if you were mistaken when you said the Viscount *of* Falsham instead of the Viscount Falsham. But you're not English, are you? Of course I remember you." Her face brightened, and she added, "You're his heir, am I right?"

"I am, yes." He sent her a slight smile. "I wondered if I could convince you to help me with a small matter. Since our hostess is across the room with other guests, I thought I would approach you with a . . . favor." He nodded in Juliette's direction while offering Lady Vaughn a glass of lemonade. "I fear I am not acquainted with the ladies over there."

"And you wish to be introduced," she surmised.

"To the young lady in white with the green ribbons." He sent her a roguish smile, adding, "If it would not be too much trouble."

Lady Vaughn sent him a conspiratorial smile. "I see no harm in helping you, Mr. Fraser, since you asked so kindly." Her gaze passed over his appearance, as if assessing his future wealth.

He bowed in thanks and escorted Lady Vaughn toward the Andrews daughters, who were standing near their aunt Charlotte. He could only hope that they would not give his ruse away. Taking a deep breath, he reminded himself to appear bored, to walk as if he owned the room and everything in it.

But the moment he neared Juliette, he saw the questioning frown upon the countess's face . . . almost as if she realized Paul had not been invited. But her attention was diverted by the arrival of the Duchess of Worthingstone.

He barely overheard the introduction the matron had given to Juliette, thankful that Lady Arnsbury was too distracted by the duchess. Out of courtesy, he nodded first to Margaret, whose attention was elsewhere. She glanced at him briefly, seeming not to recognize him.

But it was Juliette's attention that he needed. She wasn't truly looking at him but was instead staring at the floor.

Look up, he wanted to command her. *See me.*

When he murmured a greeting, she kept her eyes downcast and only mumbled a response.

When the next set of dances was about to start, he asked if she would be his partner.

"I don't dance," she said apologetically, finally glancing up.

Shocked eyes met his, but he asked again, "Not even with me?"

A flush spread over her face, and she stole a look at her sisters. None were paying any attention at all, except Amelia, who was barely holding back her excitement. "I—I'll try," Juliette stammered.

Paul took her hand, guiding her toward the lines of men and women. He could almost read the thoughts scuttling through her mind as he took her hand and guided her in a half-circle.

You weren't supposed to come here. Someone will recognize you.
No one knows me.

But they will! You must leave, now, before they throw you out.

"I hardly recognized you in those clothes," she said softly. "And your accent is gone."

"Are ye missing it, then?" He exaggerated his accent. "Did ye no' ken it was me?" He sent her a teasing look, guiding her in the opposite direction. As he led her through the steps, she stared at him as if she could hardly believe what they were doing.

"You don't look like the same man," she admitted. "I cannot believe you dared to come."

"I would dare many things." His hand moved to take both of hers, and although she was shocked by his appearance here, she didn't seem displeased by it. "Though I don't ken why any of these folk say I can only dance with you once. You're the only lass I'm wanting to dance with."

Her blush deepened. "We've never danced together before. I didn't know you'd learned how." She took his hand, and when he turned her, he glimpsed a true smile, as if she was enjoying herself.

"My uncle forced me to learn," he admitted. "I thought he was daft at the time, but he said it was a useful skill." He held her hand, stepping forward as she did the same. "I'd rather take you to a *cèilidh* where I could spin you fast and hold you in my arms."

She squeezed his gloved hand in silent response. "I've never been to a *cèilidh*."

"One day, perhaps," he promised. When the music was about to end, he saw Lady Arnsbury watching them. Beneath his breath, Paul whispered, "I'll lead you back to your sisters. Then I want you to meet me in the garden."

Juliette frowned. "I can't go alone with you, and you know it."

He wasn't particularly concerned about the rules of propriety. "Grant me a moment with you. I can escort you back to your sisters afterward, if you want." He gave her his arm and led her through the crowd, noting the low buzz of gossip and rumor swirling around them. Many people wondered who he was now, and he'd drawn their eyes toward Juliette.

"My sisters will recognize you," she murmured beneath his breath. "Dr. Fraser, you must go, before Margaret tells Aunt Charlotte what you've done."

The insinuation, that he could not possibly blend in among these people, was not lost on him. "Afraid they'll throw me out, are you?" He touched her hand with his own gloved one. "They don't see a poor physician when they look at me. They see a viscount's heir." *Or at least, the heir apparent.*

"But you're not titled," she protested beneath her breath.

"Aren't I?" he murmured, allowing her to think what she would. He suspected if he told Juliette that he would one day be a viscount, it would only make her more apprehensive.

"I've known you for too long, Paul. You may be able to fool these people, but you cannot fool me."

He ignored her protest, returning her to Margaret, who was deep in conversation with another guest. "Miss Andrews."

Paul turned away quickly, before Margaret could catch a clear glimpse of him.

"Thank you for the dance." Juliette smiled. In her eyes, he saw the glint of conspiracy.

After he released Juliette's hand, he gave it a light squeeze, reminding her of what he wanted. "Until we meet again."

He moved like one of them.

Juliette saw the way Paul mingled among the guests, accepting introductions and speaking with Lady Arnsbury's friends.

He wasn't behaving at all like a poor crofter, a man who lived in a house with a straw roof and hardly any space at all. No, he had put on the manners of a viscount as if he'd been born to it.

Who was this man? He'd completely transformed from the Paul she'd known, as if he'd pulled back the edges of himself to reveal a different person. She couldn't understand how this had happened.

But more, she found herself transfixed by him. In his new clothes, he had a rakish air, handsome and mysterious. When he looked into her eyes, she could think of nothing else except the last moment his mouth had claimed hers. His kiss had not been controlling, as the earl's had been. It had coaxed her to yield, tempting her into more.

Juliette couldn't deny that she wanted to kiss him again. Her cheeks burned at the thought, and she hid her face behind her fan, keeping close to her sisters.

She was diverted from thoughts of Paul when Victoria came to greet them. The new duchess appeared painfully shy, but it was the first time she'd seen Toria venture out in public in years.

"You look beautiful," she told her sister and was rewarded with a tentative smile.

"I feel as if everyone is staring at me," Victoria admitted. "It's hard to breathe." Her husband took a few steps back, allowing them the chance to speak privately. But his eyes remained on his wife, as if to guard her.

Margaret came over and embraced Toria, smiling. "I'm so glad you came. Your gown is exquisite."

"And expensive," Amelia added. "Is it wonderful to be so wealthy? I imagine you dine on plates made of gold, don't you?"

"Hardly." Some of the color returned to Victoria's face, as if she was amused by their youngest sister's supposition. "But it *is* different as a duchess."

Her husband returned to guide her away, his palm upon his wife's spine with a protective air. After they had gone, Amelia turned back to Juliette. A mischievous gleam glowed in her eyes.

"I saw you dancing with Dr. Fraser," her younger sister exclaimed. "I never imagined he would know how to disguise himself here. What did he say?" Amelia didn't bother to wait for an answer, but whispered, "Do you need my help meeting him in secret?"

"No. I will remain here, with you and Aunt Charlotte." But while her sister continued to gush about how exciting it was that Dr. Fraser had come, Juliette found herself unable to tear her eyes from Paul.

He glanced over at her in silent response to her challenge. It was as if he was proving his own point—that he had changed a great deal since they were children. No longer was he a hot-headed rebel who could have no place in a ballroom. Instead, he'd become a polished man who would not falter from any adversary.

With an air of confidence, he crossed over to greet Lady Arnsbury, and he bowed, offering her a devilish smile. Aunt Charlotte laughed at something he said, and she no longer seemed to care that Paul hadn't been invited.

A moment later, she saw her aunt introduce him to another young lady. The miss was lovely, with curled golden hair and bright blue eyes. She blushed as the countess paired them off, sending them to dance.

Juliette clenched her fan so tightly, she nearly snapped the wood. Though she supposed Aunt Charlotte had suggested that Paul dance with the young lady, she'd never expected the flare of jealousy in her stomach. The girl was beautiful, with the flush of innocence about her. Pearls adorned her throat and hair, and she lowered her gaze demurely when Paul spoke.

He took her hand in the promenade, and when his gaze caught Juliette's, his expression was defiant. A hint of a smile played on his lips, and her gut burned as though it were coated in acid.

This is what it will feel like when you let him go, her conscience reminded her. *But you have no choice.*

The dance ended, and Paul returned the young lady to her chaperone. But his eyes turned back to Juliette. There was no apology in them, but his gaze moved toward the terrace, then back at her.

Meet me in the garden, he'd said.

She didn't dare. The thought of being alone with him, where anyone could interrupt, was unthinkable. But for a moment, she wanted to pretend that she was once again an innocent girl who had not been violated. She wanted to blot out the memories of Strathland, forcing the past to disappear.

Her heart pounded, her instincts pleading with her to give in. She had already been ruined once—what did it matter?

It matters to your sisters, her head warned. Her actions would reflect upon them. But for a single moment, she wanted to be with him.

"Amelia," she whispered to her sister. "I need your help."

Chapter Seven

Juliette kept close to Amelia's side as her sister walked with her to the terrace. The young woman's eyes sparkled with the gleam of an accomplice.

"What will happen if you're discovered with him?" Amelia whispered. "Will you have to marry him?"

Juliette stopped walking and stared. Her sister appeared entirely too intrigued by that idea.

"Don't even put that notion into your head. I won't be marrying anyone." Her face burned, and she questioned whether to turn back and abandon the idea entirely. If Amelia believed that this was a means of forcing her to wed, she shouldn't go at all. With a sigh, she admitted, "I suppose you're right. I could be discovered with him, and that wouldn't be appropriate at all."

"Don't worry about a thing," Amelia assured her. "I was only asking what would happen. I would *never* let anyone find the two of you together." Her voice held a note of dismay, as if to reassure Juliette of her loyalty.

"Thank you," she breathed. But Amelia's words made her now question the wisdom of venturing into the garden. She walked with her sister out to the terrace, and at the far end of the walled garden, she saw Paul standing beside a yew tree.

"Why did he pretend to be a viscount's heir?" Amelia asked. "Everyone is talking about him."

"To be close to me." She couldn't believe that he'd taken such a risk. And yet, he'd done nothing to reveal his true identity. It had made her blush to see everyone staring at them, the hushed murmurs about the mysterious gentleman paying attention to her.

If they only knew the truth . . .

"Be careful," Amelia pleaded. "Aunt Charlotte thinks I've taken you to the ladies' retiring room. You can stay only a few minutes."

"It will be all right." The night was cool, and Juliette began to wish she had her pelisse. She could see no one else outside. "I will meet you at the ladies' retiring room soon."

Her sister waited while Juliette crossed the small garden, moving toward the yew tree, which grew against a stone wall. The sky was dark, except for the sliver of a crescent moon peeking out from behind a cloud.

"You took a grave risk tonight," she whispered, as Paul drew her farther into the shadows. "What if you'd been discovered?"

"I'd have been tossed out on my ear," he murmured, guiding her behind the yew tree until her back rested against the wall. "But it would have been worth it to see you."

The small space closed in on her, making her nervous. She began to shiver in the frigid air, and he removed his coat, drawing it around her shoulders. Juliette could feel the lingering warmth of his body through the black fabric, and she murmured her thanks. "I don't know why I agreed to meet you, Dr. Fraser." The words spilled out, though they weren't the truth. She'd been so unnerved by the sight of him with the other young miss that she'd needed to be near him.

"Use my name, Juliette."

"Paul," she whispered, pressing her hands against his chest, as if to gain distance.

"Look at me," he commanded. His gloved hands covered hers, and his voice held her captive. "Don't be afraid."

She wasn't afraid of him—only of the demons of her past. Tremulous memories spilled over, and though he did nothing more than hold her hands against his chest, she had to calm her beating heart.

A normal woman wouldn't feel this way. She would welcome

the attentions of the man she cared about, perhaps letting him steal another kiss.

Juliette wanted to be like other women again, enjoying a stolen moment. Just being near Paul put her senses on alert, evoking desires she'd all but forgotten.

"Why did you want to see me?" she asked, trying to hide her quaking voice.

"There's something I've been wanting to give back to you. Something I tried to give you, years ago." Paul lowered one of his hands and reached into the pocket of his waistcoat. He withdrew a silver ring and held it up in the moonlight.

She stared at the band, remembering the snowy day he'd first asked her to wed him. It was the day Lord Strathland had first noticed her.

The dark fear bolted up inside, and she shook her head. "I can't accept that, Paul." The meaning of the ring was all too clear.

"It belongs to you. But I promised I would no' press you for more than you're willing to give." He held it between his thumb and forefinger. "I wanted you to know that I still have it."

"You must keep it for someone else." Someone who could give him all the things she couldn't.

"I'll keep it until you're ready to wear it yourself." The ring gleamed against the darkness, and his hand palmed her spine as he held it up. With the silver, he traced a path over her lips, drawing it downward. The gesture heightened the sensitivity of her skin, with the cool metal against her throat. Unbidden came the image of him drawing the ring over her bare skin, circling her breasts.

Gooseflesh prickled over her, and she closed her eyes, startled by the unexpected feelings. This man kindled a response she'd never imagined . . . a breathless need for human touch. Never had she expected it—not after what had been done to her. The stark yearning caught her by surprise, and when Paul put the ring away, she felt a sense of loss.

He rested both hands on the wall, on either side of her. "I'm no' wanting to think about the past," he whispered, his breath warm upon her skin. "I want you to remember what there was between us. When we used to walk together in the woods."

She couldn't speak, her heart pounding while his hands moved down to her waist. He waited infinite moments, giving her the choice of pushing him away. But she didn't move, wanting to rebuild the broken pieces of herself, overcoming her fears. Inside, she pushed away the darkness, letting herself fall into the good memories.

"I remember."

"The first time you saw me, you were in my arms," he said.

That drew an unbidden smile. "Only because I tripped over my own feet and you happened to catch me."

"It was fate," he said.

His tone had grown heated, and Juliette covered his mouth with her fingers. "Don't speak." She didn't want to hear words about how he wanted to wed her, not now.

He fell silent, leaning his head against hers. She stood in his embrace, feeling the sudden desire to flee. In his presence, her body grew warmer, heightened with an anticipation she didn't understand.

"I'm going to kiss you, Juliette," he warned.

She froze, knowing she should pull away. But before she could move, he covered her mouth with his, as if trying to awaken her from a long sleep. There was no force in it, only a reclaiming of the years lost. Her hands moved to rest upon his heart, and she found that it was beating as fast as hers.

She'd believed that this would be a kiss of healing, but instead, the heat of his mouth unraveled her senses. Her body reacted strongly, straining against the silk that imprisoned her skin. She was finding it difficult to breathe, fighting the sensations that flowed through her. The need to press close to him, to open herself, was rising higher. He was rekindling desires she'd thought were long gone. She'd believed herself incapable of feeling any physical pleasure, but when the kiss deepened, Juliette leaned in to the onslaught.

More. She wanted more from him.

Her breathing was staggered, but instinctively, she put her arms around his neck. She went numb when his mouth nipped down her jaw to the softness of her throat. When his kiss moved to the skin above her bodice, her imagination roared with thoughts of his mouth upon her bare breasts. The shocking image made her grow wet between her legs, and it was too much to bear. "Paul, no," she whispered. "We have to stop."

It was too soon for this. Despite the arousal he'd conjured within her, she was afraid to let him get closer. In his arms, it was too easy to fall beneath his spell, letting him believe that they could be together.

Or that she wanted him.

Juliette took off his coat, handing it to him. "I n-need to go back." Her teeth chattered in the cold, and she rubbed at her arms, trying to escape him. "Amelia will be waiting."

"You're afraid of me," he guessed. "There's no need."

"I'm sorry," she whispered. "I know I shouldn't have let you kiss me in that way. But you—"

You made me forget.

His embrace had awakened her to sensations she'd never dreamed of. But she couldn't say that.

Juliette stepped away from the yew tree, clenching her arms. He believed she was a virgin, a young woman he hoped to wed. Nothing would hurt him more than to discover that her innocence had been taken by another man. It wasn't fair to let him dream of a life with her. Not when she could never be a true wife to him.

She closed back the fear and pain, lifting her eyes to him. "I was wrong, Paul. I thought I could . . . let you court me. But I can't. I'm so sorry."

She picked up her skirts and ran from him, her eyes blurred with tears.

The winter air was frigid, the snow drifted in piles across their land. Beatrice Andrews was careful with her footing as she stepped outside the charred remains of their home. In her arms she carried the pieces of what had once been a mahogany desk belonging to her father. She moved without thinking, letting her thoughts drift as she cleared out the mess of wood.

The soft sound of footsteps crunching through the snow made her look up. The wood fell from her hands as she saw her husband, Henry Andrews, Colonel Lord Lanfordshire. Her hands covered her mouth as she realized no, it wasn't her imagination. But he was thinner than she'd last seen him, with a rough beard tinged gray.

His uniform was caked with mud from the road, his boots wet with snow. One arm was bandaged in a sling, and she could not tell if it was broken or wounded more deeply. His face was stoic, and he didn't move toward her—he only stared.

Her heart trembled, and her face reddened, for she didn't know what to say or do. If she ran into his arms, she might accidentally hurt him. Then, too, it had been so long since she'd seen him last. Although they had been married for over twenty years, the distance between them had gradually increased until she was hesitant to embrace him.

Finally, he walked forward until he stood before her. For a long moment, he said nothing, his eyes taking in her appearance. She was embarrassed that her clothing was in tatters, her hair in a rough tangle. What a sight she must look to him.

"Beatrice," he said. His voice was cool, holding no emotion at all. He could have been talking to a stone, not the wife he hadn't seen in three years.

"Henry." She nodded to acknowledge him, nervously wiping her hands upon the apron she was wearing. "It's been a long time." So long, she wasn't accustomed to having him here. She'd had to make so many decisions on her own, learning from her failures.

"It has," he said.

Say something else, she wanted to plead. *Let me know that you missed me. Anything.*

But he only glanced behind her at the burned roof and skeletal stone walls. "What happened to our home?"

"Someone set fire to it a few weeks ago." She lifted her chin and nodded at the crofters, who were carrying out the debris from inside. "I wrote to you, but I suppose you never got the letter. We're still in the process of rebuilding."

"And the girls?"

She softened at his mention of them. "They're fine, and all of them are staying in London. Victoria got married a few weeks ago, to the Duke of Worthingstone."

That, at least, provoked a reaction from him. Victoria hadn't left the house in five years, and yet she'd made a splendid marriage. Although Beatrice hadn't done anything to play matchmaker, she couldn't resist gloating.

"A duke? For our Victoria?" Her husband couldn't hide his shock, and at least it gave them something to discuss. She led him inside, stepping over the rubble of burned wood and stone.

"It was a shock to me, too," Beatrice admitted. "I never dreamed she would ever find a husband at all, much less a duke."

"I've missed a great deal, it seems."

His voice was rough, and she realized he was no longer talking about their daughters or the house. His eyes locked on to her, as if he couldn't believe he was seeing her again. He hadn't looked at her like that in at least ten years.

Tears sprang to her eyes, but she wouldn't allow herself to cry. "You have, yes."

She touched the front door, considering whether to lead him back outside. Perhaps he wouldn't want to see how badly the house was burned.

"There's a lot of damage inside," she said. "I've been living at Eiloch Hill for the past fortnight, but I believe the roof is sound now." She opened the door wider, deciding it was best if he knew everything. "We don't know who set the fire, but it will take months to restore the house," she admitted. "The duke has sent some men to help, but I've been trying to salvage our belongings as best I can."

Her husband spoke not a word, his attention upon the mess that had once been their home. Had he heard anything she'd said?

"Henry?" she asked, pausing at the parlor entrance. "Are you all right? Does your arm pain you?"

He shook his head. "It's nothing."

She turned around, meaning to lead him into the rest of the house, and it took him a moment before he followed. Though she spoke in a constant stream of conversation, telling him about the crofters who had offered their help to clear out the house, she sensed that he wasn't listening at all.

She broke off in mid-sentence, waiting for him to reply. He never said a word but doggedly followed her to the other side of the house and back through the kitchen to the exterior.

Seeing him again made it so hard to hold back her emotions. She wiped at her cheeks, hiding her feelings. Straightening her spine, she pulled her shawl tightly around her shoulders and turned to face him.

"We'll rebuild the house," she assured him, taking in a deep breath. "His Grace kindly offered us the use of Eiloch Hill for as long as we need it."

Henry stepped forward, and she went motionless. For a moment, both of them stood still, waiting for the other to speak.

In the end, he reached out and touched her cheek. His hand was cold against her skin, but the caress went down to her bones.

And in his eyes, she saw regret.

Two months later

Juliette was restless. Although she'd continued to see Paul at social gatherings, he'd been careful not to push beyond friendship. He would dance with her once, and the rest of the evening, he maintained a respectful distance.

But every time she saw Paul speak to another young woman or dance with her, it was like a splinter digging beneath her skin. A possessiveness dominated her mood, and she couldn't understand *why* the jealousy was taking command of her.

He'd done this on purpose. The quiet distance was slowly driving her into madness. Even being with her sisters could not distract her from the growing need to see him again.

Today, the clouds brewing in the sky mirrored her gray mood. Her sister Margaret had gone out shopping, but it was long past the time when she should have returned. Juliette paced across the room before she decided to go downstairs and peer outside the window.

Margaret was predictable, down to the last minute. She had never returned so late, not in all the time they'd been in London.

The streets were a crowded tangle of carriages and merchants, with people milling about everywhere. Juliette stared at the throng, hoping for a glimpse of her sister. Minutes later, she spied a hackney approaching their residence. It stopped, and Cain Sinclair emerged. In his arms, he carried an unconscious Margaret, her hair tangled with blood.

Panic struck Juliette like a fist, for she'd never imagined that anyone would attack her sister. *Dear God, let her be all right.* She hurried to the door, throwing it open before the footman could get there.

Within seconds, Cain Sinclair trudged up the steps, his arms gripped tightly around her sister. The man's face was grim, and Juliette feared the worst.

"What happened?" she demanded. "Is Margaret all right?"

Her sister was hanging limp against him. Someone had wrapped a makeshift bandage around her temple, but it was stained red. While it appeared that she was still breathing, that didn't diminish Juliette's fear at all.

The butler wasted no time in issuing orders to a footman, demanding fresh water and bandages.

"Miss Andrews was trying to stop the Duchess of Worthingstone from being kidnapped," Mr. Sinclair answered, following her into the drawing room. "Your sister is missing, and the servants found one of the footmen dead. Miss Andrews was lying on the pavement bleeding. She hit her head when she was thrown from the carriage."

Just the thought of it sent a cold fear trembling through Juliette. She couldn't think of why anyone would want to hurt Margaret or gentle-hearted Victoria. Especially now, when the duchess was expecting her first child.

Seeing Margaret wounded only drove the fear deeper. Though her sister's prim ways might be irritating at times, she didn't doubt that Margaret had gone down fighting for Victoria. She could only pray that the injuries weren't life-threatening. Never before had she seen her sister this pale, and she reached for Margaret's hand, feeling utterly helpless when the young woman seemed unaware of it.

Mr. Sinclair sat down on a settee, still holding her in his arms. The motion brought forth a low moan of pain from Margaret, and Juliette's worries intensified.

"She needs a doctor," she insisted.

"Go and fetch Fraser," Sinclair said quietly. "He's the only one I'd trust with your sister."

The look in his eyes made her wonder if he knew about the separation between Paul and herself. Though she'd wanted to mend the breach, she hadn't known what to say or do. But Mr. Sinclair was right—Paul was the best doctor to help Margaret, and this gave her the perfect reason to seek him out.

"All right." When the footman brought in the water and bandages, Juliette ordered him to prepare the carriage and fetch her pelisse. Though she was trying to remain calm, two of her sisters had been threatened. Margaret still hadn't opened her eyes, and Victoria was missing. Inside, her heart had gone cold with fear for both of them.

"Do they know where the duchess is now?" she asked Mr. Sinclair, while tying the ribbons of her bonnet. *Please, let someone find her.*

Sinclair shook his head. "The servants are still searching."

Juliette reached out to take her sister's hand. When she glanced over at Mr. Sinclair, his demeanor was grave. He was holding Margaret against him, as if afraid she would close her eyes and never awaken. Gone was the teasing Highlander who often liked to provoke her sister. Instead, his attention was locked on her face with worry.

"Dr. Fraser will take care of Margaret," Juliette promised. "I believe that." She swallowed hard and added, "But we need to find Victoria." The fear inside her gathered intensity at the thought of her sister's attack. She clenched her hands together to stop them from shaking. "Has His Grace returned from Scotland?"

"Not yet. The duchess was alone with the servants when she was taken."

She gripped her hands together, fearing the worst. Her sister hated going outside, and if she'd ventured out into the open, there had to be a strong reason for it. Juliette couldn't imagine the paralyzing terror the duchess must be enduring now.

But Cain Sinclair could find her. She was sure of it.

"Does anyone know where Toria was taken?" Juliette asked. "Or the reason why?"

"The servants said that Mr. Melford, Lord Strathland's factor, paid a call upon Her Grace not long ago," Sinclair admitted. "It wouldna surprise me if someone wanted to ransom her. Or use her to influence the duke."

"Then likely they'll take Victoria north, toward Ballaloch," Juliette predicted.

"Aye."

"You can find her. There aren't that many roads leading to the western Highlands." Juliette had no doubt that Mr. Sinclair could track her sister's whereabouts, particularly if Lord Strathland was behind the attack. "If they're in a carriage, they'll have to stop at the tollbooths. It will slow them down." Her gaze narrowed upon him. "But you don't have to stay to the roads if you're on horseback. You could catch up to her."

Mr. Sinclair brushed a tangled strand of Margaret's hair to one side. There was reluctance in his expression, as if he didn't want to leave. But he gave a nod. "Tell Miss Andrews where I've gone, when she awakens."

"Of course," she promised. "And I'll have Aunt Charlotte's cook prepare food for you to take. You'll have to leave quickly."

Mr. Sinclair lowered the young woman back down on the settee and grazed his hand over Margaret's cheek in a caress. Then he stood and picked up his fallen hat. "Go and fetch Fraser. He'll take good care of her."

She nodded in agreement. "Find Victoria," she pleaded. "And send word to us, as soon as you know she's safe."

He put on his hat and went to the door. "That I'll do. But would you tell her—" His words broke off as if suddenly realizing what he'd been about to say.

"I'll tell her that you were the one to save her," Juliette promised, guessing what he wanted. Although there was no chance of her sister ever desiring a Highlander instead of a lord, she would grant Sinclair that, at least.

His expression was enigmatic. "Aye. That's good then."

Her aunt arrived home at that moment, and Charlotte exclaimed at the sight of Margaret. "Help me bring her to her room," she commanded a footman. "And someone fetch a doctor."

Juliette met Sinclair's gaze, and he nodded in silent agreement. She would go after Dr. Fraser herself, despite the impropriety.

"Find Toria," she pleaded with Mr. Sinclair once more. If anyone could manage it, she trusted Sinclair. He ignored the law when it suited him, and she had every faith that he would succeed.

Paul was slowly losing his mind. Nearly a dozen times, he'd gone to the Arnsbury residence over the past few weeks, intending to talk to Juliette—only to turn back when common sense intervened. He'd pushed Juliette too soon, and nothing would change her mind. At least twenty times, he'd wanted to knock his head against the wall for stealing a kiss. She hadn't been ready for that. He should have known better. And yet, when he'd seen her soft lips by moonlight, her eyes yearning, he'd given in to impulse.

No, he couldn't pay a call. At least, not at her home. His only chance of seeing her again was in public.

He sat down at the small writing desk in the drawing room, staring at the pile of invitations. It was strange to think that the matrons of London wanted him to court their daughters. He had nothing to offer any of them—at least not yet. The title of viscount was as insubstantial as air, since his uncle was very much alive. But to them, being the heir to his uncle's fortune was good enough.

A noise from the front door caught his attention. He hardly ever had callers, except for a few folk selling their wares door to door.

Paul rose to his feet and was startled to hear Juliette's voice. "Is Dr. Fraser here?" she asked the butler. She didn't wait for an answer, but pushed her way inside her father's town house. "He's not at the hospital, is he?"

Paul stepped out from the parlor, noting her disheveled appearance and the panic in her voice. "What's happened?"

Juliette's face was pale, her bonnet ribbons undone. She hurried forward, her expression pleading. "It's my sister Margaret. She's been hurt." With her hand outstretched, she pleaded, "Come quickly."

The fear in her voice pulled him out of surprise and into action. "Get my coat and bag," he ordered the butler. Culpepper hastened to fetch them, and Paul moved forward to Juliette.

"Tell me how she was injured."

Her face was white, and she took a breath before explaining. "Victoria was kidnapped. We think it was one of Strathland's men who took her. Margaret was trying to stop him, and when she was thrown from the carriage, she hit her head."

Now this was something Paul had never expected. If Strathland had started a personal attack against the duke, it would not end well for him. "Has the duchess been found?"

"No. Mr. Sinclair went after her." Though Juliette was trying to remain strong, he could see the worry in her eyes.

"Cain will find her. Believe that." He moved closer and took her hand in his. "Do you want me to go with him to Scotland?"

She shook her head slowly. "I'd rather you stayed here." Her voice was barely a whisper, and it made him wonder if she was regretting the time spent apart. But then, before he could say anything more, she added, "I need you to look after Margaret."

Well. That answered that.

Paul ignored the twinge to his pride and let go of her hand. He began asking questions about whether Margaret was conscious and how much blood she'd lost.

"There was some blood on her head," Juliette admitted. "I—I don't know more than that." The discomfort on her face suggested that she wasn't eager to think about it. "Will you come?"

He studied her for a moment. "Why didn't you send a footman to fetch me?"

Her face went scarlet, and she shrugged. "I probably should have. I didn't think."

"I'm glad you weren't thinking," he said softly. Juliette offered him a tentative smile, and reached for his hand again.

When Mr. Culpepper returned, Paul donned his coat. With his medical bag in one hand, he followed Juliette out to the waiting landau. She let him help her into the carriage, and he sat across from her when the driver urged the horses onward.

There was no maid to chaperone them, revealing just how agitated Juliette was over what had happened to her sister. They were alone inside the landau, and he was grateful for the few private moments.

"I'll tend to Margaret, and she'll be hale again," he promised. "You needn't worry."

She nodded, but her tension wasn't diminished by the words. Paul reached out to take her gloved hand, hoping the gesture would reassure her.

Juliette squeezed it tightly between both of her palms, staring outside. "I know I shouldn't have come by myself. But you're the doctor I trust the most. I didn't stop to think."

It was clear that she would relax only when her sister was better. She didn't let go of his hand, and the longer she held it, the more Paul felt the need to say something. "Do you regret the night I kissed you in the garden?"

She didn't meet his gaze. "Sometimes."

Unfortunately, it was the answer he'd anticipated. Although he knew he was at fault for pushing her, the past two months had been filled with contradictions. One moment she shied away from him, and the next, he caught her staring at him across the ballroom. She would accept a dance with him, only to hide amid her chaperones afterward. He was weary of these games, angry at himself for being impatient, and yet he knew why she was reluctant to be courted.

Glancing outside, he saw that there were only a few minutes remaining before they arrived at Lady Arnsbury's town house. He had to speak now, while the chance was there.

"I've a question for you, Miss Andrews." He kept his tone formal, giving her every opportunity to say no.

She nodded. "Go on, then."

"Are you wanting me to go back to Ballaloch and leave you be?" He released her hands, prepared to let her go. "Or would you rather I stayed?" He met her gaze squarely, steeling himself for the answer.

"It's your choice whether you want to stay or go." She was twisting her hands again, trying to sound as if it didn't matter.

"But what is it *you* want?" He leaned forward, and the air within the carriage was charged with anticipation. For a moment, Juliette held her breath, locking eyes with his. Regret passed over her face, along with a trace of longing.

It was the longing that seized him by the throat and gave him hope.

"What I want and what I can have are two different things," she whispered. She reached out and touched his cheek. "I want you to be with a woman who will make you happy."

You would make me happy, he wanted to say. He covered her hand with his, leaning in to touch her forehead.

"Someone who will make you smile," she continued softly. "Someone who will love you."

"The way you can't?" He gripped her hand and pulled it away from his cheek.

"I never said that." Her voice was so soft, it was barely nudging a breath of air. And yet, those four words sank into his heart. "Perhaps I care enough to let you go."

"Or you're too afraid to break free of your fear," he said. "Perhaps you're afraid of being happy again. As if you don't deserve to be."

Her face colored with embarrassment, and he knew his supposition had struck true. She was living with a guilt so great, it threatened to break her. She was hiding behind her family, going through the motions of life . . . but not truly living. She had to learn that one night of violence was not a cloak of shame.

"I came to this city for you," he said quietly. "Because you said this was where you wanted to be."

"You don't belong here," she whispered. "I can see that you're unhappy."

"Aye. But it's where you are."

Her eyes flickered to the doorway. "We should go. My sister will need you."

"And what about you?" The words came out before he could stop them.

Juliette's eyes welled up. "I don't know, Paul." A tear broke free, and she admitted, "Do you want me to tell you that you mean nothing to me? It would be a lie. Shall I tell you to go back and wed someone else, while I pretend to be happy for you? That would be a lie, too."

She wrenched open the door. "There's nothing I can say except that I hold so many regrets in my heart, I'm drowning in them." With that, she stepped out of the carriage, leaving him to wonder what to do or say now.

Chapter Eight

When they arrived at Lady Arnsbury's house, Juliette led Paul up to her sister's room. She opened the door and said to her aunt, "I've brought Dr. Fraser to look at Margaret."

Her sister was awake but pale, looking as if she were about to faint. Juliette gestured for Paul to enter, while Charlotte remained behind them. Her aunt caught her arm and whispered, "I've seen that gentleman before. He was at our gathering, wasn't he?" At Juliette's nod, Charlotte added, "We need to talk about this later." The look in her aunt's eyes warned that she would not let the matter rest.

"He is a doctor and a family friend," she countered, keeping her voice low.

"And Lady Vaughn claims he's a viscount's heir. Which is it?" she whispered. "He can't be both."

"I trust him."

At that, her aunt's expression grew discerning, as if she were trying to read beneath Juliette's answer. But after a few moments, she appeared to relent.

Paul set down his bag and went to the basin to wash his hands with soap. It surprised Juliette, for none of the other doctors she'd met did that.

"An old habit," he explained, when she asked why. "My mother said that it drives out the evil spirits." The wry smile on his face said he didn't truly believe that, but she supposed there was no harm. To Margaret, he asked, "Miss Andrews, might I come and look at your wounds?"

After her sister nodded, Juliette could almost see a visible transformation in Paul's demeanor. His tone held an air of authority, and Charlotte stood back. With a pointed look toward Juliette, she said, "I'll leave you to treat my niece, then, Doctor. If you have need of us, send Juliette to me." Her aunt left the door open and retreated, leaving them alone.

Juliette wasn't afraid, for it was clear that Paul knew precisely what he was doing. From the moment he unwrapped the bandage on Margaret's temple, he spoke to her in a soothing voice. "Now then, your sister was telling me that you tried to save Victoria."

"It was Mr. Melford who took her," Margaret insisted. "I told Toria not to come any closer, but she . . . wouldn't listen." Her voice sounded distant, almost as if she'd had too much to drink. Juliette wondered why. Had someone given Margaret spirits?

"You were lucky to get out alive," Paul told her. "I understand Mr. Sinclair went after your sister."

A wide smile crossed over her sister Margaret's face at the mention of the Highlander, and she yawned. "Good. He'll find her."

From her utter lack of concern, it was becoming more apparent that Margaret was under the influence of some sort of medicine or possibly wine. As if to answer Juliette's unspoken question, she offered, "Aunt Charlotte gave me laudanum for the pain. It's quite nice."

Paul exchanged a knowing look with Juliette, and she sensed that his mood had shifted to amusement. "Yes, I suspect it is very nice indeed. You're wanting to sleep, am I right?"

Margaret yawned and nodded. "I would, yes. But not with you. That wouldn't be proper."

Juliette nearly choked at the remark. Her prim sister was loosening her tongue, and Heaven only knew what she would say.

"That's a relief to hear," Paul answered.

"And not with Mr. Sinclair, either," Margaret continued. "He's a wicked, wicked man. I don't want to ever sleep with him. Or kiss him, either. Even if he does find Victoria and bring her back."

Juliette fought to keep her mouth from dropping open. Why on earth was her sister talking about Mr. Sinclair? She thought back to the way the Highlander had held Margaret in his arms when he'd brought her here. His eyes had been locked upon the young woman, as if she meant something to him.

Had anything ever happened between them? Mr. Sinclair was a good man, yes, but he'd bent the law on more than one occasion. She couldn't imagine Margaret sparing him a second glance.

But now, she wondered.

"Mr. Sinclair has to find her," Margaret said softly, her expression turning sad again. "Toria is too frightened to travel. And now that she's going to have a baby . . . He has to help her."

"He will," Paul promised. "If there's one man I trust, it's Cain."

The mood in the room had grown somber, and he began examining the wound on Margaret's head. When she saw the blood, Juliette turned away, wincing.

Margaret inhaled sharply when he touched it. "It hurts, Dr. Fraser."

"I suppose it does at that. But I'm no' thinking it's serious, since you're able to sit up and speak with me. You may have headaches for a few days, but 'twill likely go away on its own." Juliette kept her back turned while Paul asked questions about where there was pain and if Margaret was dizzy.

"Who put the bandage on you?" he asked.

Juliette heard the sound of water being wrung out, and she guessed he was washing the wound.

"Mr. Sinclair did. I was bleeding dreadfully, you see. I hit my head when Victoria was taken."

"You were lucky no' to be hurt worse," he commented. Juliette heard him setting the basin aside, and when she risked a look, he was stitching the cut closed. After he tied off the sutures, he bandaged the wound again and said, "Are you hurting anywhere else?"

"Just a few scrapes and bruises."

"Good." He spoke to Margaret with a calm air, confident in his abilities. Juliette was startled to see him like this. It was like the night he'd stolen into Aunt Charlotte's gathering, pretending to be a gentleman. He'd slipped seamlessly into another role, and his very presence unnerved her.

Juliette could no longer think of him as a crofter's son. No, Paul Fraser had transformed into someone else entirely. Not only a physician . . . but a man who held secrets of his own.

As he treated her sister, she felt herself calming. Margaret was growing drowsy, and in time, she succumbed to the laudanum.

"I would no' have given her the sedative so soon," Paul said. "Although it doesna seem that she has suffered beyond that cut and some bruises, someone should stay with her for the night."

"I'll stay," Juliette agreed.

He started to pack up his bag, his demeanor professional. There was no trace of the man who had kissed her, almost as if it had never happened. When it occurred to her that Paul was walking out and she might not see him again, she blurted out, "Wait. A moment, if you please." She moved away from her sleeping sister and stood by the door. Thankfully, her aunt Charlotte was no longer there.

Paul stood with his bag in his hand, not moving at all. His dark blue eyes held weariness, and she couldn't find the words. He'd talked of returning to Scotland . . . and that was what she wanted, wasn't it?

No. No, it wasn't.

Although she'd pushed him away, trying to live her life alone, she'd grown accustomed to seeing him here. He was always near, like a quiet stone she could lean against for support. If he left now, he would move on with his life—she was certain of it. And she no longer wanted to stand in the shadows, watching her life go by.

She wanted to let Paul court her, to smile and spend time with him. She wanted to laugh again, to press her cheek against his heartbeat and feel his arms around her.

Time and distance hadn't changed her feelings for Paul. Instead, they'd made them stronger. And despite the protests of her conscience, she decided that the truth was better than silence.

Fumbling for something to say, she remarked, "Thank you for looking after my sister. It was good of you to come."

"You're welcome." He waited a moment longer, but when she said nothing, he started to leave.

"You did frighten me that night when you kissed me," Juliette blurted out, keeping her voice so low, he had to lean in to hear her. "Something changed between us." A ripple of anticipation swelled up inside, and she felt as if she were about to stumble off a cliff, afraid to say too much.

"It did change," he agreed, setting his bag down as he regarded her. "But I fear you're becoming like Victoria was once, lass. Hiding yourself away from the world."

His words knocked the air from her lungs as she recognized the truth of them.

"If you're wanting me to leave and ne'er bother you again, that I'll do. But if it's fear holding you back, that's another matter."

It *was* fear, along with a terrible guilt. But his accusation, that she was becoming just like her sister Victoria, held the ring of truth. She had hidden herself away in London to be near her son. Although she'd gone to balls and soirées, her heart was never in them. Was he right? Was she letting her life slip away because she felt she didn't deserve a better one?

"I can heal many wounds," Paul said, nodding back toward Margaret. "I can sew together torn skin and mend broken bones. But there are some wounds that can nae be seen. They hurt as deeply as any other. But those canna be patched with bandages or medicines."

Juliette's hand moved to touch her heart, and it was beating so fast, she couldn't calm it. He was right, though. She'd been wounded and scarred from losing Matthew. And now, she was beginning to lose herself.

"You'll have to be healing those wounds yourself, lass. The question is whether you'll run away . . . or try to start living by facing that pain."

He reached for her hand again and said, "I'll pray that your sister Victoria returns home safely."

"So will I." Her stomach was knotted with so many emotions. Fear for her sister . . . and fear that she was becoming just like her. She didn't want her life to slip away into the shadows, and she sensed that if Paul left, it would be too easy to retreat from the world.

She took his other hand in hers, wishing she'd had more courage on that night in the garden. He studied her but revealed none of his thoughts. "Thank you for looking after Margaret."

He nodded, and she glanced over and saw that her sister's eyes were closed. Now was her chance to make things right with Paul. Slowly, she took his hands and guided them to her waist. Though it wasn't exactly an embrace, it was an invitation.

She wanted to rest her cheek against his. She wanted him to say that everything would be all right with Victoria. That he would always be there for her. His palms were warm against her ribs, and his midnight-blue eyes held an enigmatic expression.

But instead of pulling her close, he let his hands fall to his sides. "Tonight is the last night I'll be staying at your father's house. I'll bid you farewell, and I hope that one day you find your own happiness." He bowed and departed, leaving her to stand alone.

This was it, then. He was leaving her. Why, then, did she feel like running after him, demanding that he stay? Inside, she was torn apart with regret.

He's right. You have been hiding away like your sister.

She'd let herself fade away, in a living death. Paul was right to leave her, for she'd given him no hope at all. He'd left his family and friends to be with her, and she'd continued to push him away during the past few months. Now that she'd reached out to him, it was too late. He'd made his choice.

A wetness spilled over her cheeks, and she was startled to be crying. She deserved this, didn't she?

Deep inside, her anger stirred, for by hiding herself away from the world, she'd allowed Lord Strathland to defeat her. Why? Why should she let his violence destroy everything she wanted? Her shoulders shook as she wept silently, gripping the edges of her gown. She hated her life, hated the woman she'd become. She was an empty shell, someone who had fallen into despair because of a single night that wasn't her fault.

She didn't want to continue the rest of her life in the shadows. It *was* cowardice, pure and simple. She was too afraid to let anyone touch her again, and instead of facing her fear, she'd retreated into a cocoon of her own making.

Paul had only spoken the truth. She *had* been hiding from her own life, trying to bury her shame. But more than that, she was afraid to ask for more. Afraid to reach for the dreams she wanted.

But if she could have even a few years of joy, would it be worth it? Did she dare to try?

"You should have kissed him," her sister remarked in a sleepy voice. "Men like kissing."

Juliette came to sit at Margaret's side. The haze of laudanum was dictating her sister's thoughts, for she knew Margaret would never say such a thing. "But that would not be proper."

"You shouldn't be a spinster, Juliette. Every woman needs a man to manage." She yawned and held on to her pillow, curling up to sleep again. "And kissing is rather nice."

Juliette's mouth softened into a smile, though she wondered who Margaret had been kissing. As she tucked in her sister, she thought of how Victoria had fought against vivid fears to step outside and live again. She'd won the heart of a duke and was now expecting her first child.

She voiced another silent prayer that Mr. Sinclair would find Victoria and get help from the duke to save her.

And in the meantime, it was time for her to break free of her imprisonment and live again.

One month later

Dear Paul,

I know I stopped answering your letters a long time ago. I believe these answers are past due.

Paul held the bundle of letters Juliette had begun sending him over the past few weeks. The first few were filled with small bits of conversation, telling him about her morning, offering news about her cat, Dragon, and asking him questions about his work at the hospital. Nothing of great importance. Sometimes she confessed to him how worried she was about her sister Victoria.

He felt like an adolescent boy, reading the letters more than once at night. But her message was clear—she didn't want him to return to Scotland. Instead, it seemed she was trying her best to move forward with her life instead of hiding behind closed doors.

He'd composed his own letter, answering her questions, and then he'd sent her a packet of cherry comfits from the apothecary shop.

The letters had kept him from returning to Scotland, for it meant there was a chance at winning her heart. And they gave him something to look forward to. He learned that her favorite color was green and that she couldn't sing at all. She loved mathematics and was terrible at sewing.

He told her that his favorite color was blue, and he was quite good at singing.

Braggart, she'd accused, claiming that she wanted to hear him before she'd believe it. And then she'd sent him a sprig of dried heather. *It's not blue, but I thought you would like it,* she'd written.

The sight of the heather made him homesick, and he wondered where she'd found it.

He wanted to see her again. An occasional dance at Lady Vaughn's ball or a glimpse of her at an assembly wasn't nearly enough. He wanted to kiss her again, to press beyond friendship.

The best letter had come only a few days ago.

Dear Paul,

I've just learned that my sister Victoria is safe. I cannot tell you how relieved I am.

In reply, he'd sent her a simple invitation. *Meet with me on the southern banks of the Serpentine. I want to hear about it.*

Juliette had agreed to come, and after an hour, he saw her strolling down the gravel pathway. She was accompanied by her sister Margaret, and the late April sunlight shone against their parasols. A maid and a footman followed them at a discreet distance while Paul stood waiting for them.

As soon as Juliette caught sight of him, she offered a tentative smile. It warmed him, and for the first time, she seemed eager to see him. He waited patiently until the pair of them drew close.

"Hello, Dr. Fraser," Juliette greeted him.

Margaret nodded and murmured her own greeting, but she was kind enough to slow her pace, walking behind them. Paul gave Juliette his arm, and she took it.

"You look well," she said.

"No' like a puir Highlander?" he teased. "I've taken to wearing my finer clothes so they willna throw me out of London."

Her face flushed, and she admitted, "They suit you. I would never have known you weren't part of the gentry."

One day I will be, he thought to himself. That is, if he remained Donald's heir. Though he hadn't minded revealing his future title to the ton, he knew Juliette didn't believe him. She believed he was taking a risk, lying to everyone. But if he ever lost the inheritance, he would feel like an even greater fool.

"Tell me what happened with the duchess," he said.

Juliette's mouth parted in a slight smile, and she said, "I learned that Mr. Sinclair and the duke saved Victoria. She's well, and so is her unborn baby." She went on to tell him all the details about the carriage accident and how the duke had ridden for hours to find her. But Paul barely heard a word of it. His eyes were locked on to her features, with her golden brown hair tucked inside a rose-colored bonnet. She wore a gown of the same color with a matching spencer.

He studied her soft mouth, and after a few moments longer, she murmured, "You're staring at me."

"I ken that, aye. You've a bonny face to look upon."

She looked down at the gravel, but she moved her hand from the crook of his arm to lace her gloved fingers in his. Though she studied the reflection on the waters of the Serpentine, she admitted, "Your face has always been handsome to me, too."

"Your sister is watching us. I can feel her glaring at me. 'Tis a wonder my coat hasn't caught afire."

"She's likely afraid that you're going to ruin me by holding my hand."

Though her words were spoken in jest, he caught the undercurrent of irony beneath them. His thumb edged at her palm, stroking it lightly. "I am weary of having naught but a single dance with you, Juliette. We used to spend hours walking through the glen."

"I remember." She glanced behind them at Margaret. "But there are no glens here."

No, but he had another idea in mind. "Find a way to leave your aunt's house tomorrow evening. There's a *cèilidh* a friend of mine is hosting. We could go together, if you're wanting to spend some time with me."

She hesitated. "I would like to, but I'm not certain how I'd manage it."

"There willna be anyone who'd ken who we are," he promised. "Wear a gown that a merchant's wife might choose. For one night, you can pretend to be a wife instead of a miss."

She seemed to think it over. Keeping her voice low, she offered, "It sounds like a place that Margaret would loathe." Then her eyes gleamed with excitement. "I can't wait."

"*What* were you thinking?"

Brandon Carlisle, the Earl of Strathland, ignored his sister's shrewish outburst. Sarah had no concept of what he'd been trying to accomplish.

"You tried to kidnap a duchess," she accused. "Why would you ever consider such a thing?"

His sister behaved as if he were a common criminal, when his actions had never been about harming the young woman. Her Grace was a bargaining piece, a pawn in a game where he intended to control the board.

He wanted the lands—not only his former property of Eiloch Hill where the duke now resided, but also the Lanfordshire estate. He intended to gain possession of the entire region, no matter what the means.

"My factor, Mr. Melford, took matters too far," he corrected, cutting her off. "As far as anyone knows, he acted of his own accord, thinking he could ransom the duchess. And he died for it."

The loss of his overseer was an annoyance, but there were other men who could take his place. For now, Brandon knew he had to lie low, in order to keep the blame firmly pointed toward the dead man. He'd left Scotland and had traveled to their family's town house in London. His original plan had failed, and it was time to reconsider his next move.

"Don't you realize that your scheming could have ruined us both?" she accused. Her voice was like shards of broken glass, irritating his mood until he wished he could be rid of her. But then, Sarah had to live somewhere, and he wasn't about to bring her into his home in Scotland. There, he was a king in his vast estate, while here, the house was a modest dwelling that boasted only a dozen rooms and four servants. It wasn't nearly enough for him.

"I believe you already ruined yourself, dear sister." Brandon took a sip of brandy, his gaze fixed upon the fire. "When you threw yourself at that earl who refused to wed you. My actions have little bearing on you."

Sarah wasn't an attractive woman, and she'd tried everything to land a husband. But although she'd been caught alone with an earl, he'd refused to offer for her. According to Sarah, the man had done nothing to compromise her, but no one would believe the story. Now, she rarely showed her face in society and hardly ever attended assemblies or balls.

That needed to change. Brandon would use her to help open doors to him, in order to get closer to Lady Lanfordshire's daughters.

"I intend to stay in London for the next few months," he informed her.

"Because you have to avoid His Grace, to keep him from killing you?" she taunted. "After the trouble you caused for his wife, I'm not surprised. You're fortunate that neither she nor her baby were harmed."

"I need to meet with the wool buyers," he continued, ignoring her comments. Despite the ongoing war against Napoleon's forces, the orders had decreased. Although he suspected it was partly due to the duke's interference, he had to do whatever was necessary to bring back the orders. He'd spent hundreds of pounds buying up more sheep, and he fully intended to profit from the wool.

"You ought to seek a wife," she suggested. "Wed an heiress, if you can find one."

Oh, he intended to seek a wife. The woman of his desires had avoided him in the past, but no longer.

"You also need to mend your relationship with the Andrews family," Sarah insisted. "If you don't, both the Duke of Worthingstone and the Countess of Arnsbury will use their influence to keep us both out of society."

Brandon drained his snifter and refilled it. "I don't care what they think of us." It was the truth. He wasn't about to lower himself by apologizing. He hadn't laid a hand upon the duchess, and soon enough, they would lay all the blame on Melford.

None of it mattered.

"Next week, Lady Rumford is hosting a ball," Sarah informed him. "There will be over five hundred guests. It's your best chance of finding a wife."

"Except for the fact that I was not invited," he reminded her. "But I believe you can change her mind, can't you, dear Sister?"

"I will try."

Regardless of whether Sarah was successful, with so many guests in attendance, surely it would be easy enough to infiltrate the premises. She reached over and took the empty glass away from him. "You are better than this, Brandon." Her voice was soothing, and he didn't doubt she was trying to manipulate him. "Don't let the Andrews family ruin our opportunities."

Our opportunities? This wasn't at all about her.

"You want to go to Lady Rumford's ball, don't you, Sister?" His mouth tightened, and he stood to pour himself another drink. "Because *you* want to find a husband."

"I wouldn't mind one." She smoothed her gown and straightened, venturing a smile. The sight of her primping was starting to annoy him. Sarah knew nothing of the struggles he'd faced to keep them from losing their fortune. His first wife, Penelope, had nearly driven him under with debt, due to her frivolous behavior. He wasn't about to let his sister spend his money on gowns and ribbons, simply to snare an unsuspecting bachelor.

His gaze passed over her worn clothing, and he shrugged. "Perhaps a potato-faced young fool might have you. If he's drunk enough."

She pretended she hadn't heard the insult, but her cheeks flamed. "I will pay a call on Lady Rumford this week and see what I can do to open the doors to you. But Brandon, truly, you must try. I know you haven't forgotten about Miss Andrews, but—"

His hand shot out and seized her wrist. "Do not mention her name to me." He didn't want to hear a word of criticism against her. "Juliette is the woman I'm going to marry."

Sarah didn't bother to hide her dismay. "I've never understood your obsession with her. She's not even beautiful."

His grip only tightened in warning until she winced with pain. "You know nothing about it." It was more than simply wanting Juliette. She belonged to him. She needed him to show her how to be a proper wife, how to mold her into the woman she was meant to be.

Sarah touched his hand. "You're hurting my wrist, Brandon."

He released her, but he didn't regret causing her pain—Sarah needed to understand that *he* would make the decisions about their futures. Her role was to open the doors to him, and see to it that he found Juliette again.

And soon enough, she would belong to him.

"Are you sure about this?" Juliette asked Paul. "What if I'm not wearing the right clothes? Are these suited to . . . where we're going?" She'd chosen a plain day dress, knowing that it would be a more casual gathering.

"It's a *cèilidh*, Juliette. It doesna matter what you wear." Paul was wearing a dark brown coat and tan breeches, though she supposed he'd have been more comfortable in a tartan.

Inwardly, she was fearful about deceiving Charlotte. Her aunt would never permit her to attend a party hosted by anyone but members of the ton. As it was, Charlotte believed that Juliette and her maid were paying calls upon a friend in town.

"And what about Nell?" she added, glancing back at her maid. "Should I bring her along?" She'd taken the young woman as a chaperone, warning her not to tell Charlotte where they were going.

"Nell is welcome to join in. She'll make merry, just as we will," he promised.

It didn't diminish her anxiety at the unknown. Yet, she was forcing herself to leave the house whenever opportunities arose. Though she might be a wallflower at heart, she was determined not to let the past control her future. Lord Strathland had taken her innocence, but he would not take away her chance at happiness.

The problem was the guilt she couldn't relinquish. For her, this was about laying the past to rest and enjoying each day to its fullest. But the more time she spent with Paul, the more she was afraid of leading him astray.

"You're looking right dour, lass. What's taken your smile away?"

"I was only thinking of—" She stopped, revising what she'd meant to say. "That is, I was wondering why you've stayed by my side for so long. Why you haven't chosen another woman to wed."

"They're made of naught but ribbons, lace, and a bit of stuffing in their heads. I'd rather have your company."

She tried to smile, venturing, "I've nothing but accounts and numbers in mine."

But Paul only smiled and took her hand, his thumb rubbing circles over her glove. He hailed a hackney cab and gave the coachman an unfamiliar address. He guided her inside the vehicle, and her maid took her place next to the driver.

Juliette sat across from Paul, and when they had traveled past a few streets, she said, "I'm surprised you haven't returned to Scotland by now."

"You've no' agreed to wed me yet," Paul answered. "I'll go, the moment you say aye and come with me."

She sobered, knowing that although she felt safe with him, she could not marry him. Not until she was brave enough to speak the truth about what had happened to her. And he might no longer want her, once he knew it.

He leaned forward, resting his hands upon his knees. "Have you no' enjoyed yourself these past few weeks?"

"I have." But it wasn't only the letters he'd sent or even the gifts. Her restlessness grew stronger as the days passed. She found herself entirely too fascinated by Paul, remembering the way he'd kissed her. She'd never expected to want a man to touch her again . . . but the lightest brush of his hand upon hers evoked a yearning.

She remembered his kiss and wondered if tonight he would steal another.

"Are you still afraid of marriage?" he asked.

"Not marriage," Juliette corrected, her face flushing with color. "Only of what comes after that." She stared out into the streets, knowing that her face was the color of a cranberry.

"Do you really think I'm the sort of man who would force you to share his bed, when you're no' wanting to?"

That made her sound as if she viewed him as a satyr. Even so, she admitted, "It's a part of marriage that all husbands expect."

His dark blue eyes flared. "If you're feeling wary, lass, I'd rather wait until you're wanting me in the same way." At the rough tone of his baritone, a secret tremble flowed through her. "What happens between us in our bedroom is for none to say but us."

"And if I—if I never wanted to?" she ventured, her voice in a whisper.

He leaned back, a cocky smile on his face. "Oh, I think you will, Juliette. Especially when I've shown you how much a woman can be pleasured with naught but my hands and mouth."

Dear God. She could almost imagine it, his hands stroking her bare skin. Her body warmed to the vision, and the air within the cab seemed heavy and fraught with possibility.

"How much farther is it?" she asked, desperately needing to change the subject.

"A mile or so, I'd wager." He had a knowing look on his face. "And I've made you uncomfortable, so I'll ask how your sisters are."

Grateful for the turn in conversation, she said, "Victoria's baby will be born in the autumn."

"I'm glad that she and the bairn are faring well."

"So am I." It was true, although she couldn't help but remember her own nightmarish experience with childbirth. She didn't envy Victoria that. "She's staying in Scotland, though I don't know why. Lord Strathland is there, and after what he did—"

"Let's not speak of him," Paul interrupted. "What's done is done, and he'll not harm your family again. The duke and all of us will see to it."

She forced herself to nod, though she didn't quite believe it. At least now, Worthingstone was there to protect her sister. And Juliette was grateful that Strathland was far away from London.

"How were you invited to this *cèilidh*?" she asked. "Are the hosts friends of yours?"

"I've been visiting the wool merchants, and several of them are Scottish, like me."

She stiffened at the mention of the wool. There was only one reason why Paul would concern himself with getting better acquainted with the merchants. "And why would you visit them? This isn't about Strathland, is it?"

He met her gaze squarely. "And what if it is?"

Juliette was afraid to think of it. She'd tried to bury all memories of the earl, but if Paul was destroying the man's income, it was a declaration of war. "What have you said to them?"

He drew her down a narrow street, stopping in front of a smaller shop. "Only what needed to be said. I told them the truth about what Strathland's been doing to the crofters. And to your family."

Juliette rubbed at her arms, feeling a chill that had nothing to do with the dreary London weather. "Have they refused to buy from him?"

He shook his head. "There's too much demand for wool. But I've convinced them to lower their orders. There are other sources of wool in Scotland. Men with no connection to Strathland."

"Like your uncle?" she suggested.

"Donald has an estate in the north, aye. But his herds are small compared to Strathland's. I only made it known that His Grace, the Duke of Worthingstone, would be quite offended if they purchased from the earl. Those who want his favor will find other sources."

"Be careful," she pleaded. "If he learns what you've done, he'll seek retribution."

"I've spoken only the truth."

"Still—" She touched the sleeve of his coat, and he took her hands. At that moment, the hackney stopped and the coachman came to open the door. Juliette knew there was nothing more to be said.

"Come, Juliette. Put aside your fear, and let's have a night to enjoy ourselves." Glancing outside at her maid, Nell, he added, "And you, lass. You might be finding a handsome gentleman, if you smile and dance."

The young maid flushed, but followed them. Juliette felt conspicuous in her gown as Paul led her inside the small pub. The few women she saw were dressed in dark woolen gowns and serviceable frocks that were more suited to servants. Already, several were eyeing her attire as if wondering why she'd come.

"I shouldn't be here," she said suddenly. "This isn't right."

"We're going below," Paul said, gripping her hand tighter. "Trust me, Juliette." He took her to a small door that opened to a narrow stairway. From the cellar came the sound of someone playing the fiddle and pipes.

It was like stepping into a different world. The men and women were lined up across from one another, spinning and whirling. The flushed faces of the women were laughing, and there were even children dancing among them. A man who looked to be eighty was whirling with a girl of sixteen, his feet moving faster than Juliette had imagined possible.

"Does this no' remind you of Ballaloch?" he said in her ear, for it was too loud to talk.

It did, except that these people were strangers. She felt herself wanting to slip into the background, to watch the young men and women. Here, there were none of the studied mannerisms and social barriers—only people laughing and enjoying themselves. In the back of the room, she saw some men and women sitting far too close to one another.

"What is this place?" she asked, standing on tiptoe to reach his ear.

"It's a gathering that you'll find far more entertaining, I hope." He pressed his palm to her spine, guiding her inside. "You've naught to fear. No' while I'm with you."

"I feel very out of place," she confessed. "Like they're staring at me."

"I'm staring at you, too," he said. "And I think you ken why." He guided her out to the line of dancers and said, "Dance with me, Juliette."

"I don't know these dances," she protested, feeling overwhelmed by the people and the music. "Really, I shouldn't."

"It's no' hard. Just hold on to me," he bade her, putting his hands on her waist and spinning her in circles. She grew dizzy from the fast movements, but when she stumbled, he lifted her up, swinging her around.

After two dances, she started to see the fun in it. The people moved with reckless abandon, struggling to keep up with the fiddler. Music filled the room, and in time, she lost sight of her self-consciousness. There was only Paul, and the way he guided her through it.

When she stumbled again, she laughed. "I feel like my feet are tied together." The steps were impossible, but she mimicked the other ladies, struggling to keep up the pace. A lad of ten asked her to dance, and she indulged him, smiling brightly while he gave her a cheeky grin.

"Me name's Rob," he told her. "Rob the butcher's son."

"I am Miss Andrews," she answered in a subtle reminder that she was far older than him.

Rob winked at her, spinning her faster. "I heard *him* call you Juliette."

"I've known Dr. Fraser for years. And I've only known you for a few minutes."

"I'd be glad if you knew me for years," the boy said with a grin.

"Leave her be, lad. She's already been claimed," Paul said, intervening to take her back again. He gave her a glass of lemonade that tasted terrible, but she sipped it anyway, for she was thirsty from the dancing. Paul brought her a chair, and they sat together, watching the dancers and listening to the music.

"Are you enjoying yourself?" he asked against her ear.

"My mother would need smelling salts if she knew I was here." She turned, and his face was far too near to hers. His midnight-blue eyes held a warmth that made her smile fade. Though he spoke not a word, she grew aware of his bristled cheeks and the heated look he sent her way. His palm moved to her hand, and his fingers laced in hers.

Her thoughts scattered like leaves on an autumn wind at the way he was staring at her. She couldn't piece together a coherent thought, nor did she protest when he stood and took her by the hand. When she glanced over at her maid, she saw that Nell was dancing with one of the older men.

She asked no questions but simply followed Paul. He led her away from the others, toward a darkened corner. "Are you enjoying yourself, *a gràdh*?"

"Yes," she whispered.

He pressed her back, and against her ear, he murmured, "I find that I'm wanting to kiss you again. If you'll allow it." His midnight-blue eyes were locked upon her, and the air was heavy with feelings she didn't understand.

"Not here," she whispered. "Anyone could see us." But even so, her heart had begun to tremble at the thought.

He glanced back at the dancing. "There's no one to see us. Look."

She realized he was right. The small corner of the room was shadowed with no light, and there was a stack of chairs that hid them from view.

Paul held out his hand, waiting for her answer. Her pulse hastened at his suggestion, and she found herself slipping beneath his spell. She wanted to kiss him again, to feel like a normal woman instead of a fallen one.

And so she put her hand in his, following him into the shadows. Gently, he pressed her back, and her heartbeat trebled.

She lifted her face to his in silent permission, and when he brought his mouth upon hers, it was not at all a demanding kiss. No, it was slow and lazy. He savored her lips, tasting her. With his mouth upon hers, she forgot about her sins and could simply be.

Although he had her trapped in his arms, she didn't feel afraid. Against her lips, Paul spoke. "I held you like this once, in the garden. But you were afraid of me then." His hands moved down to her waist, and she caught her breath at his touch. "What about now?"

She didn't know what to say to him. Her mouth was swollen from his kiss, and she wanted to lean in for another. "I'm only afraid of the way you make me feel," she admitted. When she was in his arms, she lost sight of herself. She was fighting against the darkness of the past, forcing herself to remain in place.

Paul captured her mouth again, moving to her jaw and down to her throat. Shivers spiraled through her, and she was startled at the way her breasts tightened beneath her gown.

"You're the loveliest lass I've e'er laid eyes on," he breathed. "And I'm wanting to show you what I spoke of, in the carriage. But only when you're willing."

Her thoughts tangled up within her, and a refusal caught in her throat. She knew what he was asking, and instinct roared at her to say no.

And yet . . . was this not another face of cowardice? He wanted to touch her, as a lover would. To destroy her terrible memories, leaving something better in their place. There was no fear of dishonoring herself, for not only were they hidden from view . . . but she also never intended to be with any other man. No one else would understand her in the way he did.

He'd been achingly understanding over these past few weeks and months. Most women would have had a betrothal by now. And yet, he'd never pushed her.

"If I ask you to stop, will you?" she whispered.

He gave a nod. "At any moment, lass."

She stood on tiptoe and kissed him again, bringing his hands to her waist. Against the juncture of her hips, he was hard, and she forced herself to remain motionless. The pressure of his arousal was enough to terrify her. And when she murmured, "Stop," he broke away and took a step back. Without hesitation.

She took a shuddering breath, and he stared at her. "I canna change the way you make me desire you, Juliette. But I swear, I'll stop at any moment you ask me to."

She believed him. In his eyes, there was no doubt of his longing. He craved more from her, but he had full command of himself.

For so long, she'd been tormented by her nightmares of being held against her will and being violated. Though it was entirely improper, she wanted to give something of herself to him. Even if it was nothing more than a forbidden touch.

"Kiss me again," she said softly. As he did, he held a distance between them. Likely he believed she was too timid for more. She reached for his waist and drew him against her. He broke contact with her lips, and she felt the gentle pressure of his erection against her.

He remained frozen in place, waiting to see what her response was. Though she was caught up with fear, she was more startled by the sudden warmth blooming between her legs. Her mind was rigid with visions of fear . . . but her body welcomed him.

It felt good in a way she'd never expected.

His mouth moved against her ear, and she shuddered against him, pressing close. "Careful, lass," he warned. "You're stretching my control as it is."

"But you'll stop when I ask you to."

"Aye." He inclined his head, though she sensed that with every liberty she allowed, the tighter he was wound up.

"Is it warm in here?" she asked, feeling flushed in the crowded space. Glancing over at the dancers, she realized that no one was aware of them. Not even Nell, who was supposed to chaperone her.

"Aye." His hands drifted over her shoulders and down her spine. "And growing hotter."

His mouth brushed against hers, but the heat of his breath made her wrap her arms around him. She was wearing stays, but even beneath the corset, her body arched to be nearer to him.

"I should be ashamed of myself," she whispered. "A lady would never do this."

"We're not strangers, Juliette. And one day, I hope that you'll consent to be my bride. When you're ready."

That was the reason why she was giving rein to her curiosity. Intuitively, she knew that she would never allow any other man to touch her in this way. With Paul, she felt a goodness, a sense that he honored her. And a part of her wondered if she could somehow silence the nightmares of the past by confronting her fear. That was what she wanted tonight. To learn what it should have been like to steal kisses from a man she cared about.

When she kissed him again, this time his tongue slipped inside her mouth. Desire flooded through her, and she found herself leaning in, accepting him as he thrust and withdrew.

Her breasts ached, and she embraced him, pressing herself to him. She found herself wanting more, despite the thousand voices within that cried out for her to stop.

She was walking on the edge of danger, tormenting a man who wanted her. Paul had never made any secret of that.

"Juliette," he breathed, and he pulled her hips to his, holding her close. "We can tarry only a few moments longer."

He was giving her the chance to stop, to walk away from this. And yet, she wanted him to guide her, wanted to learn more about the ways between a man and a woman.

"A little longer, then," she said.

His eyes grew hooded with desire, and his mouth was tight with unspoken need. "Slowly." He moved her to sit upon his leg. His hands moved down to her bottom, and he drew himself closer to her.

"If I could, I'd take you somewhere we could be alone." His hips were cradled against hers, and she could feel the hardness of his thigh between her legs. He balanced her weight there, and the contact embarrassed her. Not because of his touch, but by her response to him.

"I'd want to undress you, opening these buttons one by one." His hands moved down the back of her gown, touching each of them, though they remained closed. "And then I'd unlace you here." He put a slight pressure upon the back of her corset, drawing his hands down the laces. "I'd lay you down on a soft bed and taste your sweet skin."

His words were a dark caress, and slowly, he moved against her. The rigid pressure of his leg against her intimate flesh was shocking. He didn't force her, but between her legs, there was a deep ache.

"I'd worship your body," he breathed, drawing his mouth down to the skin at her neckline. "I'd spend hours learning your flesh. Finding what pleased you."

God above, his words were a sweet seduction, beckoning her to let go. She was locked into his words, unable to do anything but see the vision he'd painted.

"I'd kiss your breasts and suckle you until you grew wet." To emphasize his words, he slid against her again. "I'd make you tremble, Juliette."

"I already am," she whispered in response. All over, she was flushed and quivering, wanting him to do the things he'd spoken of. But she knew it could not go as far as he'd want it to. She could not take him inside her, letting him claim her as a husband would. Not even if she wed him in secret.

They needed to stop, for this had gone on too long. They would be caught together, and she didn't doubt that someone would see them.

Nearby, she heard a woman moan, and she glanced over to another couple in the shadows of the opposite corner. The woman was clasped against the man, and she was moving up and down. From the rhythm and the sudden gasps coming from her, Juliette sensed what they were doing. With Paul against her body, she was growing even more aroused, despite herself.

"They're too wrapped up in themselves," he countered. "They don't see us."

"Here?" she whispered. "They're not actually—"

"No. But within a few minutes more, he'll take her away." Paul's voice was strained, and while she was seated upon his thigh, he moved his hand to her ankle. Almost as soon as he predicted it, the man took the woman through a door in the back of the cellar and they disappeared.

Paul drew his hand to her calf, staring at her. "Will you let me touch you more? Or shall I stop?"

Stop, her mind begged. But she couldn't bring herself to speak the words. She *did* want more.

"I don't know what I want," she admitted.

With one hand, he moved higher, to her knee. With his hand beneath her skirts, no one could see what he was doing, and she felt a moan catch in her throat. He traced a path over her stockings, until he reached the patch of bare skin above the garters.

And then he stopped. His eyes were molten, burning with need for her. "I'm going to stop now, Juliette. But I want you to imagine my hand against your sweet flesh. You're growing wet for me, aren't you?"

She couldn't trust herself to speak, but only nodded. Her breathing was labored, and she felt her knees shaking.

"Against my fingers, I'd feel your damp curls. And then I'd slip one inside you."

A shiver of shocking need penetrated her, and her fingers dug into his shoulders. Though he didn't touch, the proximity of his hand drove her imagination wild.

"I'd touch you intimately, bathing my fingers in your wetness. Until it brought you to the edge."

His hand gripped her thigh, and it was impossible to breathe. She was fighting herself, not understanding the rush of feelings.

"Paul," she pleaded, not even knowing what it was she wanted. He seemed to understand, and in one swift motion, he took his hand out from under her skirts and began kissing her hard. She met the thrust of his tongue with her own, and the pressure of his thigh between her legs grew hotter. She moved against him, not knowing what—

"Let go, Juliette," he demanded, and with his words, he moved his leg against her. The flash of release caught her so hard, she couldn't stifle the moan that ripped free. He covered it with another kiss, and she shuddered hard as heat and a soaring tremble wracked her body. It was shattering, to the point where she lost sight of everything.

Paul looked well pleased with himself. Pressing a kiss against her temple, he murmured, "I'm taking you home now. And you'll dream of us."

"Don't shoot!"

The sound of her husband shouting in the middle of the night drew Beatrice out of her own bed. She threw open the door to Henry's room and found him thrashing in the covers, as if fighting an invisible foe.

"Henry, shh," she soothed, coming to his side. "It's all right. There's no one here."

His green eyes opened, but for a moment, he seemed unaware that he was no longer on a battlefield. She lit an oil lamp, and the soft light illuminated his haggard face. "I'm sorry I woke you, Beatrice." His voice held a hint of embarrassment, though it was not the first time the nightmares had plagued him. She'd continued to sleep away from him, claiming that it was for his own comfort.

The truth was, she'd been alone for so many years, the idea of a man sharing her bed again was . . . strange. Back when they were first married, they had often slept together. Henry would awaken in the early morning, reaching for her in the hopes of making love.

But in the past three years, she'd slept alone. She couldn't even remember the last time Henry had touched her. And although he likely expected her to share his bed again, she hardly knew the man sitting before her.

His hair was shot with gray, his eyes searching hers. A stubble of beard grew against his cheeks, and he reached out with his left hand, taking her palm in his.

"Would you . . . stay a moment?" he asked. He lay back against the pillow, patting the space beside him. She grew aware that she was wearing only a sheer nightdress, and her body had grown so wretchedly thin. Gone were the curves she'd once had.

"I'll only disturb your sleep if I stay," she said, afraid of what would happen if she dared to stay at his side.

"You don't want to be near me now, do you?" he said.

"No, that's not it at all," she lied. "It's just that you'll sleep better alone." Being near him right now made her pulse quicken, for this man was nothing like the awkward, shy officer she'd wed as a young lady. This man had known her intimately and had shared her bed for nearly twenty years before he'd left for war. But he was a stranger to her now. There were new furrows at the edges of his eyes, etched there as if marking the strain from the sight of too many horrors. To sleep beside him was akin to ignoring the years of distance and the years of feeling abandoned by him. She couldn't simply pretend it hadn't happened, returning to her place as the faithful, loving wife. They didn't know each other anymore.

"I slept alone many times during the fighting," he said. "Enough for a lifetime." He let out a slow breath. "But if you'd rather not be near me . . ."

Guilt assailed her, for he'd asked only that she lie beside him. Nothing more than that. Beatrice turned down the lamp and returned to his bed. She lay down on the left side of the bed, remaining outside the coverlet. Beside her, she could hear the sound of his steady breathing. But more, the covers were warm from the heat of his body.

A sudden resonance echoed within her, of the years past when they had been lovers. Now, she was a dried-up old woman, past forty. Hardly worthy of a husband's attention.

"How is your arm?" she asked, trying to keep her mind off their sleeping arrangement. He had taken off the cast a few weeks earlier, but she'd never asked whether he'd regained full use of his arm.

"It's healed." He lay back against the pillow, staring at the ceiling. "I hope to be able to help with the rebuilding efforts, before the men have finished."

"What about the army?" she ventured. "Will you go back?"

Will you leave me alone again, to fend for myself? Will the girls be fatherless once more?

There was a heavy silence for a time, before he answered, "No. The general didn't think I should have stayed as long as I did, after I inherited my brother's title. They told me I was better suited to handling the estates and my own affairs." He turned his head to face her. "They think I'm too old now."

"Perhaps we both are," she whispered.

His left hand reached out to take hers, and their fingers intertwined. "Our girls are grown now. Soon, we'll have grandchildren."

"We will, yes." She rolled over to face him. "I'm happy for Victoria. But I still worry about Margaret and Juliette. Margaret is getting so old now, they consider her on the shelf at one-and-twenty."

"They will find husbands, I am certain. But it won't be the Earl of Strathland—that, I assure you."

She was grateful for it. "I still believe he was responsible for the fire and Victoria's kidnapping. Even though he claims otherwise . . ." She shook her head, wishing that the man would simply disappear from their lives. Although he claimed that he was uninvolved with either incident, she didn't for a moment believe that the earl was innocent. "I want Lord Strathland to stay far away from us," Beatrice finished.

"He will. And if I ever find proof that he was guilty of hurting Victoria or arranging for the fire, he'll pay the price for it." Her husband squeezed her hand in silent promise.

"I pray that you're right."

Chapter Nine

"Juliette, I must speak with you privately," Charlotte said.

Juliette set down her pen, after scribbling the last set of numbers. Aphrodite's Unmentionables was earning a strong profit, and she was well pleased with their business. Her sister Amelia was seated across from her, studying a set of sensual designs that Victoria had suggested in her last letter. The moment their aunt stepped closer, Amelia hastily covered the sketches.

"Is everything all right, Aunt?" her sister inquired.

Charlotte nodded. "It's nothing to concern you, but I must speak to your sister. Come into my sitting room, Juliette, if you please." Without offering any further explanation, her aunt retreated from the room.

"What do you suppose she wants?" Amelia whispered. "Is it about Dr. Fraser?"

"I don't know." The mention of Paul made her blush. The forbidden touches they'd shared at the *cèilidh* had haunted her all night. She'd never known that there could be joy at the hands of a man, or such blissful satisfaction.

"Well, what else could it be?" her sister demanded. With a look of alarm, she whispered, "It's not about Aphrodite's Unmentionables, is it?"

"I doubt it." Her greatest fear was that it concerned Matthew. If it were only about Paul, Aunt Charlotte might have divulged her concerns in front of Amelia.

Though Juliette tried to calm her thoughts, she couldn't stop herself from worrying. She stood and steeled herself for whatever lay ahead. "I'll be back soon."

"And then you can tell me everything," Amelia said, with a gleam in her eyes.

Juliette made no promises, but she walked past the nursery beforehand, wanting to ensure that her son was all right. As she passed his room, she overheard the unmistakable sounds of Matthew laughing with his nurse. She stopped a moment, drinking in the sight of his light brown hair and plump cheeks. He was holding on to the edge of a low table, struggling with baby steps to move farther across the room.

Juliette couldn't resist smiling at the sight of him, wishing she could take a moment and swing him into an embrace. She supposed that there could be nothing else to be concerned about. But when she entered her aunt's sitting room, she was startled to find her uncle waiting there as well.

The earl held out a folded piece of paper. "I've had a letter from Dr. Paul Fraser, asking to pay a call upon me. I understand that he's been spending a great deal of time with you, and I suspect he intends to ask for your hand in marriage."

He already has, Juliette thought, but didn't say it.

"I have not made any decisions," she said honestly. "And if he's asked to pay a call upon you, it could be about anything."

"I cannot lend my support to this," Lord Arnsbury said with a sigh, ignoring her reaction. "You and I both know your parents hoped for a better match."

She wasn't surprised at his refusal, for her uncle viewed men by their rank. "We also know that I am unsuitable for a better match. *If* I marry, it will be to a man of my choice, regardless of whether he has a title."

"Your parents will refuse their permission."

"And that does not matter, if I wed in Scotland," she reminded them. Her shoulders tensed, and she stared at each of them. "I've earned the right to choose. And whether I wed a prince or a peddler is none of your concern." Her eyes glimmered, but she shut down the tears. "I paid the price, and I won't be sacrificed on the marital altar simply to please my family."

Charlotte exchanged a glance with her husband. "Be that as it may . . . I don't like the fact that he's lied about being a Scottish viscount's heir. I haven't exposed his story, for your sake," she added, "though I should have put a stop to it sooner."

"If you don't, then I will," Lord Arnsbury insisted. His mouth pursed in a tight line. "Juliette, you are like a daughter to us."

"I appreciate your concern," she said slowly. "But you should know . . . Paul is the only man I would consider marrying." He'd proven that she could trust him, even in the face of desire.

"I don't approve of him at all," her uncle said. "You can do better than a common physician."

"Dr. Fraser is far more than that," she argued. "He's a good man who loves me and always has, ever since I met him as a girl. If I decide to wed him, I would be proud to be his wife." Despite his rough upbringing, Paul had fought to change his way of life. He'd educated himself, and she respected him for it.

"There is no titled gentleman in London who would have me, if he knew the truth," she continued. "And both of you know the reason why. He's learning to walk in the nursery."

Lord Arnsbury had the grace to look guilty at that. "It need not ruin the rest of your life, Juliette." He rubbed at his beard, sighing. "The gift you gave to Charlotte and me is beyond price. How could I ask you to wed a poor man, when you deserve so much better?"

"As I said before, I haven't agreed to marry anyone. I still might not marry." She held her ground, though inwardly, she wondered if her memories of last night were somehow evident. Her cheeks warmed at the thought.

Her aunt exchanged another look with her husband. "There's more, Juliette. Not only about Dr. Fraser."

She waited, and from the tight expression on their faces, she knew the news could not be good.

"I've received a letter from Beatrice. It seems that the Earl of Strathland is in London. I don't know how long he's been here, but I thought you should know."

She felt as if she'd taken an invisible blow to her stomach. No, he couldn't come here. London was her sanctuary, her escape from him. Her hands twisted in her skirts, and a ringing noise resounded in her ears. "Keep him away from me, Aunt."

"I will send word to all of my friends not to receive him or invite him to any of their gatherings. He will not be welcome."

Charlotte reached out and squeezed her hands. "At a moment like this, I wish you *were* already married, my dear. For I fear he'll only pursue that which he cannot have."

Juliette straightened in her chair, knowing her aunt was right. "Are my parents still planning to stay in Scotland?"

Charlotte nodded. "Your sister Victoria has decided to remain there, until the child is born. Beatrice will want to be with her." The look of sympathy that crossed her aunt's expression suggested that she, too, was remembering Juliette's painful labor.

Silence descended as Juliette tried to determine what to do. Avoiding the earl was the best course of action, until Strathland returned to Scotland. Surely she could manage to remain invisible for a short time.

But in the meantime, Dr. Fraser needed to know about the earl's arrival. If she attended any gatherings at all, she wanted Paul shadowing her at every moment.

For she trusted him to keep her safe.

Four days later

Amelia took Juliette's arm as they stopped by a confectioner's shop. Her sister had a bright smile on her face, but although they stood and admired the rows of frosted cakes and sugared fruits, Juliette knew Amelia had another topic she wanted to discuss.

"I saw Dr. Fraser at the assembly last night," she began. "He was looking for you."

"Was he?" Although Juliette had obeyed her aunt's suggestion to avoid invitations until they knew for certain where Strathland was, she was startled to hear about Paul. "Did he dance with anyone?" She wanted to take back the words as soon as she said them. It made her sound possessive.

"Of course. *You* might have decided to be a spinster, but *he* has been invited to most of the parties this Season." Amelia changed voices, mimicking: "Why, Amelia, Mr. Fraser is so divinely handsome. And his voice! Just a hint of a Scottish accent. I could listen to him speak *all night*." Her sister rolled her eyes. "If they only knew the truth . . ."

Amelia went on to describe what Paul had worn and prattled on about the young ladies he'd danced with. A strange flare of jealousy caught Juliette's heart at the thought. Though she knew Paul was devoted to her, she didn't like the thought of young women throwing themselves at him. She wouldn't put it past them to try and compromise him, if they believed he was truly a viscount's heir.

"Why has no one discovered the truth about Dr. Fraser?" Juliette wondered aloud. "Surely someone would have exposed him by now."

"No one has questioned it at all," her sister admitted. "Either he's a very convincing liar . . . or could it be true? He did have an uncle in Edinburgh." Amelia frowned, as if considering it.

"It's not true. Paul was the son of a crofter, and his mother was the midwife. He hasn't a drop of blue blood in him."

"But I remember hearing stories about his father. Kenneth Fraser hadn't spoken to his family in years, according to Bridget. And Fraser isn't a name from the local clans—they're MacKinlochs."

Juliette smiled. "Always poking your nose into other people's gossip, aren't you, Amelia?"

"Well, how else am I to learn anything interesting? No one tells me anything."

Juliette shook her head in amusement. "It isn't true. If Paul were truly a viscount, he wouldn't have been living like that, in such a small house with his mother."

"Unless he didn't know about it," Amelia ventured. "I, for one, prefer to believe it. Can't you imagine it? The poor crofter's son turns out to be a nobleman in disguise? It would be like one of those fairy stories Mrs. Larson used to read to us." Her sister beamed and let out a dramatic sigh.

"This one isn't true," Juliette insisted. "And the longer Dr. Fraser continues the ruse, the more likely it is that he'll be thrown out." She had hoped he would stop attending the gatherings, particularly when she was remaining at home. After she'd sent him a note warning him about Strathland's impending arrival, he'd refused to hide away. Instead, he'd responded: *I'll face him when he arrives.*

She didn't like the thought of an open confrontation between the two men. She'd pleaded with him to let it go, and yet she suspected Paul was more likely to cause trouble.

They continued walking toward Madame Benedict's shop, and Juliette glanced behind to ensure that their footman was shadowing them. When they arrived, the shop was crowded with people, making it impossible to enter at first.

"There are too many orders for Aphrodite's Unmentionables," Juliette remarked beneath her breath. "I've sent them to Victoria, and Mr. Sinclair has brought back those that could be made. But the demand is too great. We'll have to raise the price again."

"Or we could hire more people," Amelia suggested. "There are many seamstresses in London."

It was possible, but not practical. Juliette shook her head. "It would be too easy for someone to trace the source. And whether or not you like the secrecy, it's necessary to protect Victoria."

"She hasn't made any new designs, has she?" Amelia stood on tiptoe to eye the women standing inside the shop.

"No. She wanted to rest during the summer." Her face softened at the thought of her sister's advancing pregnancy. Though the child would not arrive until the autumn, she prayed that all would be well with the pair of them. A sliver of fear broke through her mood when she imagined her sister's labor, but she pressed it back.

"I don't see why she couldn't draw whilst lying in bed," Amelia said. "But even so, I'm glad for the profits. And I do like visiting Madame Benedict's." She dropped her voice to a whisper. "Convincing the other women to buy our unmentionables is marvelous."

Her sister had the instincts of a gypsy trader, and the modiste delighted in their visits. As a result, Amelia had a new wardrobe that rivaled a countess's.

"We should return when it's less crowded," Juliette suggested. She was about to lead her sister farther down Bond Street when a familiar voice called out from behind them.

"Miss Andrews."

She and Amelia turned at the same time. As soon as Juliette saw the Earl of Strathland's face, her stomach twisted with nausea. She said not a word, the anger filling her from deep within. She'd hoped to never see him again. Not only for what he'd done to her, but also for all the threats toward her family.

Her hand tightened upon Amelia's hand, and she remained silent. To her annoyance, her sister answered the greeting, "Hello, Lord Strathland."

The earl smiled at them, and Juliette took a step closer to the footman. "We should go," she murmured to her sister. The last thing she wanted was to spend any time in his company.

"I hope your family is well," Lord Strathland said. "I understand they have rebuilt your home at Ballaloch."

Juliette forced herself to acknowledge the man, though she didn't want to. "Yes." She couldn't believe he had the gall to say anything to them, after all that he'd done.

She glanced back at Amelia, willing her to remain silent. Unfortunately, her sister was oblivious to the unspoken message. "You've journeyed quite a distance, Lord Strathland. How long are you intending to stay in London?"

The earl stared at Juliette. "That all depends. I came here on business affairs, but I intend to seek a bride while I'm here." His gaze lingered upon Juliette, who met his eyes with fury.

Never. She'd die before spending time in the same room with this man. The amusement in his expression only enraged her further. Did he honestly believe she would ever consider him for a husband? His arrogance had no bounds.

"I wish you good fortune, then," Amelia said. "Forgive me, but we must go now."

"I shall pay a call upon you later, then." He tipped his hat, bowing slightly.

Don't bother, Juliette wanted to reply, but didn't. What did he mean, he intended to seek a bride? The horror of it swept over her, but then, he *knew* how much she loathed him. Why he would not seek another woman's attentions was beyond her.

Amelia took her by the hand and forced her to enter Madame Benedict's shop, despite the crowd of women. The footman remained outside.

"Why would you speak to that man?" Juliette demanded of Amelia. "Have you forgotten what he did to Victoria? Or the fire?" Her lungs tightened with fear.

"Sometimes you get more information when you pretend to be an empty-headed fool," Amelia said seriously. "I wanted to know his intentions. And we wouldn't have known why he was here unless we asked."

"I don't care what his intentions are." Juliette took several deep breaths to calm her rebellious stomach. "We will not receive any calls from the earl. He is far too dangerous, and he would not hesitate to take advantage of either of us."

"But what if—"

"I know the kind of man he is, Amelia," Juliette cut her off. "And believe me when I say he is not to be trusted." She rubbed at her arms, feeling the cool spring air as if it had spiraled beneath her skin.

The knowing look in his eyes terrified her the most. Though she would never understand why he wanted her, he delighted in her discomfort. For he knew too many of her secrets, and that gave him a hidden threat. Her own parents didn't know the shame she'd suffered, and if the earl revealed what he'd done, they might try to force her into a marriage she didn't want—even if it wasn't to Lord Strathland.

She didn't doubt that the earl would revel in his power, knowing that he had a means of manipulating her into doing his will. It didn't matter what stories he told about her, for she didn't care about her own reputation. But she had to protect her sisters. Gossip whispered about her could affect them.

Worse, if she remained in hiding, others might believe what he said about her.

Her sister reached out and took her hand. "It will be all right, Juliette. There's no reason to be afraid of him."

Oh, but there was. She reached out to Amelia and squeezed her hand, as if to reassure her. It wasn't only about protecting her sisters.

She had to protect her son.

Ever since he'd learned that Strathland was in London, Paul had kept a tight watch over Juliette. Today, it had taken every ounce of his control not to move in and murder Strathland in plain sight. As soon as he'd seen the earl approaching the young women, he'd hidden himself close by during the conversation.

Although Juliette and Amelia had escaped into the modiste's shop afterward, Paul waited until he was certain Strathland was gone. He received more than his share of odd looks as he stood outside, but he would not leave until the sisters were safely home again.

Juliette was pale when she emerged from the shop with Amelia. From the sickly look on her face, Paul's suspicions sharpened. He had reasons of his own to want vengeance against Strathland—but Juliette's reaction went beyond terror.

A haze of dark rage flowed through him. Though Cain had not revealed the man who had violated Juliette, it was entirely possible that Strathland was responsible. And if it *was* him, murder was too good for the man.

Paul stepped forward. "Are you all right, lass?" he asked Juliette.

She tried to nod, but he didn't believe it at all. To the footman, he ordered, "Hire a carriage for all of us." He wasn't about to let them go home without his protection.

The servant obeyed, and Paul stood at Juliette's side, lending his own support. "I'll be fine, Dr. Fraser," she said. "You needn't go to such trouble."

"It's no trouble at all," he insisted. "And I would feel better if I escorted you back."

"I think it's an excellent idea," her sister agreed, sending him a knowing look.

Paul decided he liked Amelia Andrews a great deal. If nothing else, she was quite good at matchmaking. He sent a questioning look toward Juliette, and at last, she nodded. "Very well."

"Good. That's settled." When the carriage arrived, Paul helped the women inside and rode beside the driver while the footman returned home on foot. As they traveled, he searched the streets for a glimpse of Strathland. He didn't know how the man had found Juliette, but possibly he'd ordered a servant to watch the house. It could not be a coincidence that he'd happened upon the sisters when they were out shopping.

His mind twisted with uneasiness. If Strathland had gone to such an effort to find Juliette, there had to be a reason. And he didn't like to think of what that reason was.

The drive home was short, and after Paul paid the driver, he helped the ladies disembark. Juliette sent her sister inside, remaining outside. "Thank you for seeing us home."

He restrained himself from taking her hand in public, though he wanted to. "Will you be at Lady Rumford's gathering?"

Juliette hesitated. "I was planning to stay at home, to avoid the earl."

"And why is that?" Paul asked, watching her face closely.

Juliette turned her gaze downward, admitting, "He's always made me uncomfortable. And with the fire and Victoria's kidnapping . . . I want nothing to do with Lord Strathland."

It was a reasonable answer, but he studied her, wondering if there was more she hadn't said.

"And what about me?" he murmured, stepping closer. "Do you want naught more to do with me after what happened the other night?"

Her face flushed with color. "I—I don't know, Dr. Fraser."

The night they'd spent at the *cèilidh* was burned into his memory. He wanted so much more from her, but he sensed the invisible stone walls rising up around her feelings. Damn it all, he was growing impatient. He wanted to marry her, to lie beside her at night and hold her close. But if he pushed her now, it was likely she'd retreat again.

"I hope to see you at Lady Rumford's," he said by way of farewell, bowing as he departed. He thought about hiring a hackney but instead decided to walk. He needed to clear his head and decide what to do about Lord Strathland.

There was one clear reason for the earl's journey to London. The wool buyers had decreased their purchases, and Strathland would want to know why. No doubt he would try to sway them to his own purposes and convince them to reconsider. Between Paul's efforts and the Duke of Worthingstone's influence, the earl wouldn't get far.

Then, too, there was the question of Juliette and why Strathland had made her so uncomfortable. From the look of undisguised interest on the man's face, he intended to pursue her. Paul wasn't about to stand aside and let that happen. Juliette had endured enough without having to face a man like the earl.

His impatience stretched tighter, along with the need to protect her. If he could convince Juliette to elope with him, they could both return to Scotland and start anew. One day, it might be the life she was accustomed to, once he inherited his uncle's title and estates.

But that wouldn't happen any time soon. Although Uncle Donald had provided him with the wardrobe of a viscount and money to spend, Paul still hadn't touched any of it. It seemed wrong to take money from a family that had abandoned his father, all because Kenneth had wanted to wed a woman of a lower station. Now he was in the same straits as his mother, wanting to wed someone who was far above him.

He loathed every moment of living here in London. He didn't belong in the city, and he couldn't understand why Juliette wanted to stay here. The very air was tainted with soot, not at all like his beloved Highlands. He ached for the sight of the mountains and the clear lochs.

Paul stopped in front of the tiny flat he'd rented in London, having abandoned the town house a month ago. He paused in front of the door, wondering what he was doing. His friend Cain had advised him to behave like the viscount he would become one day. He'd worn the clothing, spoken openly about his inheritance, and attended events a physician had no right to attend.

They believed him. It amazed him that anyone would, considering he'd only learned how to behave this way in the past five years. Every moment of every day, the web tightened, making him question who he was now—a physician? A future viscount? Or a crofter's son, still trying to build a different life?

And for what? A glimpse of the woman he'd loved? Protecting her in silence, while she made up her mind whether she was willing to risk a marriage?

No. This was no life for any man. Although he'd tried to be patient, he was now behaving like a besotted young fool. He'd given her more than enough time, and he planned to return to Scotland—with or without Juliette. He wanted an answer now.

Even if it was the wrong one.

Paul unlocked the door and went inside the cold, dark space. He built a fire in the hearth and stoked the coals. As he warmed his hands, a plan took shape within his mind.

It was too late to pay a formal call upon Juliette now, but he could still see her. He knew her habits, and he knew where her room was located within her aunt's house. It would not be difficult to infiltrate the premises . . . especially with the help of a meddling younger sister.

Tonight, he decided. He would confront Juliette and determine if there was any hope at all or whether he was wasting his time.

Inside her bedroom, Juliette held her son in her arms, cooing softly to baby Matthew. He was asleep with his mouth pursed up, his warmth snuggled in the crook of her elbow. She'd taken him out of the nursery, wanting to spend a few quiet moments alone with him.

She sat back in the chair, feeling at peace. She could pretend for a few minutes that he was hers again, that he need not babble the words "Mum mum mum" to another woman. His hair had the scent of baby, and she savored the comfort of holding him in her arms.

The sound of a window opening made her rise to her feet in alarm.

"Don't be dropping the bairn," came the voice of Paul Fraser. "It's only me."

Only him? She shrank back, wondering how on earth he'd managed to climb nearly to the third floor of her aunt's town house. "You could have fallen to your death!"

He swung his other foot over the sill and closed the window tightly, then the drapes. "I don't think so, no. Amelia let me inside, and I climbed over from the balcony beside this window. 'Twas no' difficult."

She ought to tell him to leave, for it was not at all a good idea for him to be alone with her in her bedchamber. Juliette risked a glance at the door, wondering if she should say anything.

Paul only crossed his arms. "Call out, if you like. They'll only believe that I've compromised you. And we both ken where that will lead."

Embarrassment flushed over her, along with a prickling rise of anticipation. He was wrong, of course. Her aunt and uncle would not allow him to wed her, even if they *did* believe he'd compromised her.

"It's late, Dr. Fraser," she said.

"Very," he agreed. "Most of the household is asleep."

"My sister shares this room with me," she insisted. "Amelia is going to return."

"She promised to grant me time with you. She's sleeping in Margaret's room and said she would stay there until morning."

Now how on earth had he accomplished that? Her sister was an incurable romantic, but had he simply arrived at the front door and suggested it?

Paul crossed the room and stood before her. "Give the bairn back to his nurse, Juliette. I'm here for answers, and I'll leave only when I have them."

That much was clear from the dark cast to his face. There was a steely determination in his dark blue eyes, like a man who was weary of waiting on her. And yet, she wasn't ready to give him the answers she should. She'd been such a coward, trying to avoid everyone and everything.

But neither could she stand here with a sleeping baby, with a man who had no right to be in her room.

"Give me a moment," she said. "Sit down." She lifted Matthew to her shoulder and opened the door to the hallway. Silently, she took him back to the nursery, handing him over to the nurse. She took her time returning, knowing that Paul would be waiting for her.

But what could she say to him? Her heart was pounding, simply because he was here. And it was evident that he had no intention of leaving. His presence should have been a threat, and she ought to alert the servants.

Yet, she knew he would never harm her. He would not lay a hand upon her—he wanted only words. Her pulse quickened when she opened the door, closing it behind her.

"Lock it," Paul ordered, and she obeyed. Within the room, the atmosphere grew heavier, almost heated. Gone was the good-natured lad who had spent a summer with her, teaching her to fish and to find her way among the mountains. Gone, too, was the gentleman who had sent her daily letters and danced with her. Now, he stood, a fierce Highlander who would no longer be brushed aside.

Juliette didn't know what to say, and as he drew nearer, she found herself sinking into a chair, clasping her hands together.

"Look at me, Juliette," he commanded. Then he pulled up a chair across from her. "I've finished with playing games. I tried to fit into your world and did a damned fine job of it. The matrons all wanted to wed their daughters to me. But there was only one I wanted."

She forced herself to meet his gaze. In his eyes, she saw a hunger so great, it nearly undid her senses. He was angry, not only with her but with the society world surrounding her.

"You shouldn't have followed me here," she admitted sadly. It wasn't fair, asking him to give up the home he loved, when she had invisible chains that bound her to a spinster's life.

"I've waited for years, just for the sight of your bonny face again. And time and again, you push me away." He moved in to cup her cheek. "Tell me now to leave you alone. That you can no' bear to see me again, and I'll go." His hand stroked the edge of her jaw, kindling a longing she had to push back. "You willna see me again, unless you're wanting to."

Juliette held his hand against her cheek, the coldness of fear fighting against the heat he kindled. The idea of not seeing him was painful in a way she didn't understand. Words tightened in her throat, and she knew she had no choice but to reveal everything.

"Tell me I mean naught to you," he said. "Look into my eyes and say it."

"It would be a lie." Against her cheek, she felt the heat of his breath. Every part of her wanted to lean in to him, to lay down her burdens and take the comfort he offered.

"I'm returning to Scotland within a fortnight," he said. "And I'm wanting you to come with me."

She stole a glance at the door, thinking of her baby. Every moment with him had been a precious gift, to watch him grow older. "I don't know if I can leave." She'd done it before, but each day without Matthew had been its own torment.

"Then you'll have no choice but to face Strathland," he said quietly. "Without me to watch over you."

Ice slid over her nerves, for he spoke the truth. In the earl's eyes, she'd seen the obsession of a man who wanted to chase his prey. God help her, she had to avoid him at all costs. If for no other reason than to protect her son from ever learning of his true father.

"You would do that?" she asked. "Leave me to his manipulations?"

"It's you who would choose that, lass. I've offered to take you away from London. Time and again, I've asked you to wed me. What are you afraid of?"

"Myself," she whispered. It was the most honest answer she could give. "I care about you, Paul. I do. But I worry that one day you'll regret it if I say yes."

"You'll regret it if you *don't* say aye," he predicted, running his hand over the back of her neck. "Why do you no' try being my wife for a few years? Where's the harm in it?"

He wouldn't be teasing her like this if he knew the truth. She took a breath. "What if I told you . . . that I don't want to have any children? Would you still wish to marry me?"

His hand stopped moving. "I saw you with the bairn earlier, Juliette. And I'd say you do want children. Very much."

This wasn't working at all.

"What if I told you I didn't want to share your bed? What if I asked you never to touch me?"

"Like I did at the *cèilidh*?" he ventured, his voice growing rough. "You wouldna want my hands upon your skin, tempting you?"

Blood rose into her flesh, and she felt herself yielding to his words. She could say nothing at all as he kissed the softness of her neck, pulling her against the hard planes of his body.

Unbidden, her arms went around his neck, welcoming his touch. Her breath shuddered until he pulled back, his eyes holding a searing desire.

"Strathland will no' be able to touch you if you're already wed," he reminded her. "He'll have no choice but to find another woman. And from the way his wool empire is crumbling, he'll need an heiress."

She stilled at his words. It was true, what he'd said about Strathland being unable to touch her if she were married. No man could. None, save Paul.

"If you're afraid of our marriage bed, I swear to you I'll no' touch you until you want me to. You'll have your freedom to do as you please, and we'll share a home. Naught else, until you're ready."

The offer struck her speechless. Was he suggesting a celibate marriage?

She said nothing, studying his face to read beneath his words. "Why would you offer this, Paul?"

He raked a hand through his hair. "I shouldna offer it. I ken I should've left you long ago, when you told me to go." His eyes narrowed. "But Strathland took my father from me. Damned if I'll let him take someone else that I care about."

"And what about you? What about your . . . desires?" she whispered, her face flaming. "How can I ask you to wed someone like me, when you're giving up so much?"

He returned to stand before her. "Do you no' believe you could make a home for us? Could we enjoy our time as man and wife together, until you're ready for more?"

I'll never be ready for more, she thought. But his offer tempted her.

What would it be like to live with this man? She imagined sharing a home with him, seeing his face each morning. Although the vision of marriage should have made her uneasy, somehow the idea of living with Paul no longer threatened her. He might steal a kiss or touch her the way he had at the *cèilidh*. But if she asked him to stop, he would. She believed that without question.

Then, too, marriage to him offered a permanent escape from Strathland. Even if the earl did confess what he'd done, he could never force her into marriage. Not if she was already wed.

She let out a slow breath. "I need to think, Paul."

He stepped back, granting her space. "If you agree, I'll take you back to Scotland with me. We willna be needing your parents' consent, or a special license, if we elope."

Juliette didn't ask what would happen if she refused. He would return to Scotland, as he'd said. She was strongly considering saying yes, not only because of the safety it offered . . . but also because it would leave an emptiness inside her if he left. Her feelings had never dimmed over the years, although she was afraid of reaching for a life with this man. Wanting him this badly was dangerous for both of them.

And yet, being without him was far worse.

"I want your answer tomorrow night, at Lady Rumford's ball," he told her. "If you come, we'll announce our betrothal. If you're not there, I'll leave for Scotland the next day."

With that, he withdrew the silver ring from his pocket and left it on the table before disappearing into the night.

Chapter Ten

The following day, Juliette walked alongside her aunt Charlotte in the morning sunshine. She couldn't stop her smile as she drank in the sight of Matthew, happily swaddled in blankets. He was nearly a year old, and his brown eyes shone with happiness. She loved his rosy soft cheeks and his nonsensical babbling.

I can't leave him, she thought to herself.

There was no denying that her aunt adored her son. Matthew would never want for anything as long as he lived. It should have made it easier to walk away, giving him up to the woman who treasured every breath he took.

And yet, her heart bled whenever she spent time with them, knowing she could never be his mother.

"I presume you won't be attending Lady Rumford's ball tonight," her aunt commented. "As we discussed."

Juliette hesitated. "I haven't decided yet." Although Paul's offer had been on her mind all night, she did not yet know what her answer would be.

"There's nothing to decide," Charlotte retorted. "We agreed that you would remain behind doors until Strathland is gone."

She didn't know what to say, and decided the truth was easiest. "Dr. Fraser asked me to marry him last night. He wants my answer tonight at the ball."

Aunt Charlotte frowned as she passed Matthew over to Juliette to hold. "As I've told you before, I think it's highly inappropriate. You're a baron's daughter. You can do far better than a physician."

Juliette held the baby close, not surprised by her aunt's aversion. "And as I told you, it's my choice to make."

Charlotte let out a sigh. "There's something I don't understand about him. I know why your uncle and I didn't expose him, but why has no one else investigated his claim of being a viscount's heir? All of London loves a good scandal."

"Perhaps they had no way to disprove it," Juliette answered. "And he behaves like a gentleman. No one would know he *wasn't* a future viscount."

"Be that as it may, I don't think you should marry him." She adjusted Matthew's blanket and dropped her voice to a whisper. "No one knows what happened to you, and you have the chance to start again. Now that His Grace, the Duke of Worthingstone, has sponsored a Season for you, you have so many more choices."

No, she didn't, despite what Charlotte believed. "Who would marry a young woman who doesn't wish to have children? You know what happened when I went into labor. And there's only one way to prevent conception."

"There are a few elderly men who already have heirs," Charlotte suggested. "Perhaps a widower." The flush on her face suggested that she hadn't truly considered this. And Juliette had no desire to wed a man old enough to be her father.

She ignored her aunt's suggestion. "You both know that Lord Strathland will attempt to spread stories about me," she reminded her aunt. "Stories that will hurt Margaret's and Amelia's chances of finding a husband." Juliette tightened her hold on Matthew. "I won't let that happen. If marrying Dr. Fraser will prevent the earl from revealing everything, then I shall."

She said nothing of her own reasons for wanting to be with him. A marriage to Paul was a grave risk, but he wanted to make her happy. And that was worth something. Her decision was beginning to take shape, even as frightening as the future might be.

"But why this man? Why not anyone else?" Charlotte insisted.

"Because I believe him when he says he'll protect me," Juliette admitted. When she was near Paul, it felt as if no one could ever harm her. "And I've told him I won't have any children. He loves me enough that it doesn't matter."

Her aunt stopped walking, her face drawn in. "You don't know for certain that you can't have more children. It was a difficult birth, but it's possible—"

"No. I won't take the risk." Too many women died in childbirth. Juliette wasn't at all eager to be one of them.

"There are other ways to have children," her aunt reminded her. "Even if you never bear another yourself." She touched Matthew's head, and the silent message wasn't lost on Juliette. She could take care of an orphaned child, if need be. There were many, many children in need of love.

"Perhaps," Juliette agreed.

Her aunt frowned suddenly, caressing Matthew's cheek. "Before you agree to wed Dr. Fraser, you need to tell him what happened, Juliette. Not all of it . . . but enough so that he understands how you were hurt."

"And shall I tell him about Matthew?"

Charlotte shook her head. "No. He must be protected at all costs. Tell Dr. Fraser that your baby died, if you wish."

She knew her aunt was right. Before she bound Paul into marriage, he needed the chance to refuse. Likely he thought she was only scared of bedding him. He didn't know that another pregnancy could cost her life.

And yet . . . he'd offered a celibate marriage. For him to agree to such a thing meant that he really did care for her.

A fragile warmth encircled her as Juliette believed she could truly find a happiness with him. She was weary of being a victim, of feeling as if she didn't deserve the life she wanted. If Paul were by her side, she could make *him* happy. And perhaps that would be enough for both of them.

She held Matthew close, and he nestled beneath her chin, as if to burrow more deeply against her. His baby skin smelled of soap, and the downy hair was soft against her throat. Giving him up had been the hardest thing she'd ever had to do. No matter that he was conceived in a moment of terror, he was a living piece of her heart and always would be.

She met her aunt's eyes and saw the sadness within them, as if she wanted to take the baby back from Juliette's arms. In the end, Charlotte admitted, "Matthew is the greatest gift I've ever had."

Juliette kissed her son's head and closed her eyes as she embraced him. "Thank you for letting me have this time with him." She feared it might be years before she saw her son again.

They started walking back, and along the way, Charlotte said, "If a marriage to Dr. Fraser is what you want, I won't stand in your way. I'll speak to my sister and do what I can to help you. But you'll have to wed in Scotland, since you won't have your father's permission."

"It's what Paul wants," she agreed. "To return home to Ballaloch."

"But what about what *you* want?" Charlotte asked.

"I want to protect my sisters. And if that means leaving London, I shall."

"Answer me this, then," Charlotte prompted. "If Lord Strathland had not come to London, would you still agree to wed Dr. Fraser?"

She didn't know the answer to that. The more time she'd spent with Paul, the more she felt like he'd given her back her life. He'd made her realize how much she'd been hiding behind Matthew.

"Paul wants to make me happy," she assured her, avoiding a direct answer. "And I think I will be."

Her aunt led her along the gravel pathway. "If you do this, you'll be living a life of poverty. Physicians do not earn as much, and it will not be what you're accustomed to."

"I have no intention of being poor." Especially now, when she had the sewing business earning such strong profits. She intended to continue her work with Aphrodite's Unmentionables, even from Ballaloch. Although Victoria still made the design decisions, all of the accounting had fallen to Juliette. She loved the freedom of setting prices and tallying the results of their labor. Perhaps the profits would grow enough, over time, keeping her so busy that she would forget about losing Matthew.

Just as they reached the end of the path, they saw the Earl of Strathland approaching. The sight of the man made her blood freeze, and her grip tightened upon the baby.

"Don't run," Charlotte warned. "Behave as if there's nothing at all wrong."

But Juliette had to resist the urge to flee with her son. Thank God, the earl didn't know anything at all. The fervent need to protect Matthew went deeper than any fears. "Keep Lord Strathland away from me," she whispered back.

The earl had stopped his approach when his gaze narrowed upon Matthew. Juliette didn't look at him but kept her eyes focused upon the child. Her heartbeat trebled, and she prayed he wouldn't guess the truth.

At that moment, Matthew reached up to her cheek, babbling, "Mum-mum-mum." Juliette's face went scarlet, and she tried to ignore her son's chortling. Had the earl heard?

"Give him back to me, Juliette," her aunt murmured beneath her breath. "Now."

She obeyed, careful not to make eye contact with the earl as she handed him over. When she glanced up again, Strathland's eyes held the fury of a violent storm. Instead of approaching her, he kept his distance.

"Keep calm and say nothing," Charlotte ordered, holding the boy close. But against her body, he began to squirm, his face puckering as he began to whimper. The fussing grew noisier, and no matter how her aunt shifted the child to different positions, his cries worsened.

It was killing Juliette not to take her son back. She knew that at a deep level, the infant knew she was his true mother. He would quiet down if she took him into her arms. But if she dared to claim him again, it would only draw more attention. Her instinct to protect Matthew was greater than the need to comfort him.

The earl was watching them, and she could do nothing to arouse his suspicions. He departed from both of them without saying a word. Even so, she strongly suspected that he would not forget what he'd seen.

And that terrified her most of all.

After Sarah's efforts, Brandon Carlisle, the Earl of Strathland, had managed to attend Lady Rumford's soirée as his sister's escort. He had arrived early, and he'd spent the first hour dispelling rumors spread by Lady Arnsbury. He'd charmed his hostess and made it known that he was seeking a wife.

He'd dropped enough hints about his wealth that the matrons were circling like vultures, ready to offer up their young. He smiled warmly at them, enjoying their daughters' coy glances from behind their fans. He granted a few of them his attentions, while awaiting the arrival of the Countess of Arnsbury and the girls. Though he would not say anything against Lady Arnsbury, she would regret using her influence to cast aspersions upon him.

He was well aware that Juliette loathed the sight of him. It made no difference at all. He had enjoyed seeing the flash of anger on her face, followed by the fear, when he'd seen her out walking earlier today. Perhaps she'd thought he would abandon his efforts. Not at all. Brandon reveled in a game of cat and mouse. He'd given Juliette time enough to believe herself safe.

But he wasn't at all averse to spreading a bit of gossip to get what he wanted.

If he let it be known that she had given herself to him, no titled gentleman in London would have her. He had every intention of doing whatever was necessary to gain her as his wife.

The first to enter the ballroom was Miss Margaret Andrews, the eldest unwed daughter. She put on a bright smile and eyed the room with all the subtlety of a predator. Despite her dowry, her prim manner had put off most of the eligible bachelors, including himself.

Next came Miss Amelia Andrews, the youngest. Brandon crossed his arms, considering her as a possibility. Though her incessant chatter drove him mad, she could be used as leverage. Juliette would do anything to protect a family member.

A surge of satisfaction came over him when he saw that Juliette had arrived after all. She wore a demure gown of cream satin, trimmed with a sapphire ribbon. Her hair was tucked away in a simple chignon, and she wore no jewels of any kind. There was a flush in her cheeks, and she braved the room, greeting other women and smiling.

It was good to see her in a better humor than she'd presented in the past. He slid behind a small crowd of people, watching her surreptitiously. She trailed behind her sisters, but not once did she glance at the gentlemen. That pleased him, and he made his way closer to her.

When she stood with her back to him, speaking to other young women, he moved into position. He remained patient until her conversation ended and the ladies went to speak to someone else. Before Juliette could join them, he interrupted, "Might I have the pleasure of a dance, Miss Andrews?"

She spun, her face appalled. It took a moment for her to gather her thoughts, but she shook her head. "No, Lord Strathland. I would rather not."

Her refusal didn't deter him a whit. "Or I could ask your younger sister, Miss Amelia Andrews?" he suggested. "She looks as fresh and innocent as you used to be."

That earned him a reaction, and anger flashed in her eyes. "Leave Amelia alone."

"Your sister does not hold the same hatred as you," he remarked. "She would dance with any man here and not care."

"*I* care."

"Then dance with me. If you do, I promise I'll leave her alone."

She glared at him. "I'd rather dance with the devil than spend any time in your presence."

He sent her a thin smile. "I may be a devil in your eyes, Miss Andrews, but I have fond memories of you." From the way she blanched, she knew precisely what he was talking about.

Fond memories indeed, especially when he'd taken her virginity. Just thinking of holding her down aroused him more.

Lowering his voice, he added, "No one knows of your secret scandal, do they? What do you think it would do to your sisters' marital hopes if I were to let out the rumors?"

Her gaze turned murderous. "Do not dare to impugn my sisters with your malicious talk."

"Then do as I've asked, and accept a dance from me." He held out a hand, relishing the victory when she placed her gloved palm within his. "We will talk about how you're going to protect them."

He had her then. In her eyes, he could see the glimpse of fear, not for herself but for Amelia and Margaret. She held no qualms about refusing him, but she would do anything to guard her sisters.

The next dance was a country dance, and as he lined up across from her, he remarked, "You look beautiful, as always, Miss Andrews."

She gave no answer at all, but stared at the wall behind him. When he held her hand and turned her around, she whispered, "Why won't you leave me alone, Lord Strathland?"

"Because I wish to marry you." He relished the idea of having her in his bed every night, particularly if she fought him.

"I would not marry you if you were the last man on earth."

"I don't like being refused," he said. "Especially from a chit who doesn't know what she's turning down. Surely you must know how well I could provide for you. You would have everything you'd ever want. I would give you dozens of children."

Something in her expression shifted, but she masked it. "Never."

There was something beyond dislike in her words, a hatred that went bone-deep. Without another word, she left him standing there, publicly showing the room what she thought of him.

A rigid anger coursed through him that she would do something that foolish. Others were staring, and he caught whispers about them. She would regret embarrassing him like this.

He would make sure of it.

⚜

"You, sir, are no gentleman. I don't know how you thought to masquerade as a viscount's heir."

The man accusing him at Lady Rumford's ball was a fanciful dandy wearing a bright blue coat and yellow breeches. Paul met the man's sneer of superiority with no response at all, save to lift his glass of punch in silence.

Perhaps he should have been wary, afraid of being thrown out. But he'd attended so many functions in the past few months, he hardly cared anymore. The only reason he'd come to this one was to learn Juliette's answer.

There were hundreds of people here, and he had not yet spied Juliette. It made him uneasy, for he suspected what that meant.

And yet, he intended to find Lady Arnsbury and learn for certain whether she had come. If that meant wearing fine clothes and pretending to be a gentleman one last time, so be it. He started to walk away when the dandy approached again. "I know who you are, *Doctor*," he scoffed. "I saw you leaving the hospital the other day."

Paul debated whether to ignore the man, but he was drawing more attention. He placed his glass upon a tray and approached the dandy. "I don't believe we've met, sir."

The dandy reddened, and drew himself up. The top of his head nearly reached to Paul's chin. "I suggest you leave, Doctor, before I alert our hostess."

His patience snapped, and Paul leaned in closer, dropping his cultured speech. "Go ahead and tell her whate'er you wish. But you should ken that I'm a Scot. We don't take kindly to insults." His mouth spread in a thin smile, and he lowered his voice to a whisper. "If you're wanting to, we could be talking about this outside. Where your blood willna get on the floor."

The man blanched, and before he could say another word, Paul added, "I don't think you're going to say anything to Lady Rumford, am I right?" Though he smiled, he made no effort to hide his irritation.

Damned meddling fool. What did it matter about his uncle's title, especially when Paul intended to return to Scotland?

Another matron stepped forward to intervene. Though she was flustered, she sent Paul a warm smile. "I can vouch for Viscount Falsham. I was well acquainted with his uncle, Donald Fraser."

Paul went still, uncertain of who the matron was or how she knew his uncle. Why had she called him Viscount Falsham, when Donald Fraser was very much alive? But the tone of her voice held sincerity, as if she thoroughly believed Paul had inherited the title. He offered nothing to undermine her, but bowed and excused himself.

He had expected to see a glint of conspiracy in her eyes. Perhaps a sly nod and a wink, as if she now wanted him to pay attention to her daughter. Instead, she nodded to him and excused herself.

Her response unnerved him more than the dandy's accusation. He felt the stares upon his back as he went toward the doors leading outside. Before he could retreat farther, Margaret Andrews stepped forward. Her eyes flashed and her mouth tightened.

More than likely, she, too, would tell him that he was an imposter who had no right to be here.

Instead, she walked past him and gritted out, "Strathland is causing trouble for Juliette. He's spreading rumors, and people are beginning to talk. Do something." With that, she walked away.

Juliette was here? Relief flooded through him at her sister's proclamation. He finally saw her through the crowd, and as Margaret had claimed, Strathland was watching from a distance.

Vicious anger coursed through Paul at the sight of the man. He crossed through dozens of people, ignoring those who tried to speak to him. He saw Juliette standing near her aunt Charlotte, looking miserable.

Look at me, he willed silently. When her eyes finally glanced up, he nodded toward a door that led into the conservatory. It would give them a moment to speak alone.

Juliette frowned a moment but gave a discreet nod to show that she understood. Paul didn't know what rumors the earl was starting, but he knew of one certain way to end them.

By causing a few rumors himself.

Juliette waited until Paul disappeared into the conservatory before she made her way toward the room. Margaret and Amelia walked alongside her, keeping her shielded from anyone who might approach. She wasn't at all certain what Paul wanted, but he'd raised a finger to his lips, bidding her not to tell anyone.

She started to glance behind her, but Margaret ordered, "Don't look. The earl is following us."

Which explained why her skin was crawling. "I want to go home." Though she knew Paul wanted her answer, right now, she was wishing she hadn't come at all.

"We can't depart now," Margaret insisted. "We'll offend Lady Rumford if we leave too soon."

"Tell her I have a headache. Anything." She took a breath, trying to think of how to slip into the conservatory. "Perhaps, if I had a moment to myself, I would be able to endure more of this night. But please make sure Lord Strathland doesn't follow me."

"Oh, he won't," Margaret countered. "Even if I have to dance with him myself." She shuddered at the thought.

Juliette stopped walking when they reached the conservatory. "I'll slip inside. If you and Amelia could keep him away . . ."

"Consider it done." Amelia stood before the door. "I shall scream if anyone attempts to get past me."

"You can't remain here alone, Amelia," Margaret argued. "It isn't safe for you, either."

"And that's where you're wrong. Lord Strathland finds me highly annoying. If he dares to come close, I'll start chattering on about colors of ribbons. Believe me when I say he'll run to the other side of the room."

Amelia beamed at the thought, and Margaret took her arm. "I think I should stay here with you."

Grateful for her sisters' interference, Juliette turned the knob and entered the conservatory. Paul was already standing on the opposite side of the room, and she turned the key in the lock.

"I heard that Strathland was bothering you. If you wish it, I'll beat the bastard unconscious." He moved closer, but his gaze remained on the door.

"He threatened my sisters if I didn't dance with him." She rubbed her arms as if that could rid her of his memory.

"And I heard Margaret say he was threatening you."

"He was talking about me, yes." After she'd given him the cut direct, he'd begun spreading rumors about her. It had been particularly evident when the men who had previously asked her to dance had suddenly found reasons why they no longer wished to be her partner.

"It's time to end that." His voice was merciless, as if he were contemplating a fight. "He and I will be having words."

She swallowed hard, and her skin went frigid with fear. "Be careful, Paul."

He stared at the doorway for a long moment. "He needs to understand that you'll ne'er belong to him." Turning back to her, he added, "The question is whether you're wanting to belong to me."

She didn't answer yet. Although she understood that being alone with him would start enough rumors, causing others to believe that he'd compromised her, she had not yet made a decision.

"You're still afraid of me, are you no'?"

Juliette nodded, her mouth dry. "A little. But I know you would never hurt me." She was more afraid of herself and the way he made her feel when she was around him.

He stood before her and lifted a pin from her hair. A lock of hair fell against her jaw. "No, I wouldna harm you, lass."

He pulled another pin and tucked it in the pocket of his waistcoat.

"Paul, what are you doing?" The touch of his hands against her face made her grow warm, though he did nothing except free a few locks of hair.

His dark blue eyes drank in her features. "Perhaps Strathland thinks to compromise you with words."

She understood, then, what his intentions were. "And you're planning to compromise me in truth, is that it?" Her heartbeat quickened, but he caught her wrist, shaking his head.

"No. But I could make it look as if I did." With his hands, he loosened more of her hair, drawing it down about her face. "If Strathland's starting any rumors about you, our betrothal announcement will put them to rest. That is, if you'll have me as your husband."

His hands rested against her cheeks, and she held them to her skin, watching him. The ice around her heart had cracked apart. She didn't deserve a man like Paul, someone so patient.

"What is your answer?" he asked quietly.

"I've thought a great deal about your proposal," she murmured. He withdrew his hands from her face, taking her palms in his. His thumbs grazed the edge of her knuckles, offering comfort. "I will wed you," she said softly. "But if there ever comes a time when you regret it, I promise to set you free. If you find another woman to love . . ." She paused, gathering her thoughts.

Another woman to share your bed and give you children . . .

"I'll do nothing to stand in your way," she finished. "We could annul it, or I'll grant you a divorce, if need be—"

He cut off her words with his mouth. The kiss was meant to silence her, and his lips brushed upon hers as if to take away her words of protest.

She cared so much for Paul, but every time he touched her, she lost command of herself. Even now, her skin warmed with anticipation, and she found herself leaning in. His strong arms embraced her, while her breasts tightened against her gown.

When he drew back, his eyes were heated. "I won't find another woman to love, Juliette."

He reached for a fallen strand of hair and twisted it, replacing the hairpin. There was a mirror hanging on one wall, and he guided her toward it. "You'll have to help me with this hair, lass. I'm no' verra good at this."

In the reflection, she saw her swollen lips and flushed face. Even if she did fix her hair, she suspected others might guess what she'd been doing. Nonetheless, she fixed the updo until there were no strands out of place. "What will we do now?"

"You'll return to your sisters, and I'll go out another way." He pointed to another door on the opposite side of the room. "Go and stand with your uncle, Lord Arnsbury. Tell him of our betrothal and let him know that I'll be coming for you in the morning. We can announce it to the others . . . or if you're no' wanting to, we'll leave before Strathland can do any further damage. We'll marry once we've crossed the border into Scotland."

If her father found out her intentions, he'd be furious. Although Beatrice had written of the baron's return, Juliette was afraid of facing him. She remembered Henry Andrews as a stoic man who rarely took an interest in his daughters. He was often distracted and had seemed eager to go to war, rather than spend time isolated in Scotland. If he learned that she'd run away with Paul, he would ask questions she didn't want to answer. And even after they were married, she didn't doubt that her father would try to force an annulment.

"You havena said a word," Paul said, reaching out to her again. "Having second thoughts?"

No, she wasn't. She was considering whether to tell him now about being ruined. The words were poised at her mouth, ready to offer the truth. But then, such a public place was not right for giving a confession.

"I will wed you," she affirmed, though it wasn't her own thoughts that troubled her. She also worried that Strathland might guess the truth about Matthew. And if she left him behind, did that not endanger him more?

Paul touched her nape, drawing her close. Though he didn't kiss her, his finger reached along the chain she wore around her throat. Slowly he pulled it free of her gown, revealing the silver ring hanging from the end.

"You kept it."

She nodded. "But before you wed me—before we go anywhere, I need to . . . talk to you alone. There are some things you need to know, before we marry."

"We're already alone," he pointed out. "Tell me now."

Not here. Especially not if he changed his mind. The last thing she wanted was to be abandoned in a ballroom.

Paul's fingers tangled in the chain a moment, then he let it fall. "Shall I come to you tonight, then?"

"In the morning. Before you arrange for a coach to take us to Scotland." If he changed his mind, she didn't want him going to any trouble.

"Juliette, this marriage will be a good one. I promise you that."

She let out a slow breath. "I only hope you don't live to regret it."

The Earl of Strathland saw Juliette emerging from the conservatory. Although her clothing showed no signs of being in disarray, he had glimpsed a man in the shadows. The mysterious viscount whom everyone was talking about. Though he hadn't seen the man's face, many of the young ladies had been eager to dance with him.

Juliette's lips were slightly swollen, as if she'd been well-kissed. Although every strand of her hair was in place, jealousy roared through him. She dared to give him the cut in front of everyone, only to fall into the arms of another man?

Had the viscount clasped her hair when he'd kissed her? Had she let the man touch her?

Damn the slut for this. She belonged to him and no one else. Right now he wanted to seize her by the arm and drag her away, overpowering her with his body until she understood who she belonged to.

He'd mistakenly believed that she had matured in the past two years. That she would recognize how wealthy he had become and what a good husband he would be. Instead, he'd found her going off into a conservatory with a man, like a common trollop.

But then, she was only nineteen. Just a girl behaving with the impulses of a passionate nature. With the right man to discipline her, she could be the wife he wanted. He envisioned spending his days teaching her how to please him, both out of his bed and in it.

A shiver of anticipation rocked through him.

His patience had come to an end. It was time to ensure her compliance. Once he revealed Juliette's shame to her parents, they would demand that he wed her.

He stared at her across the room, remembering the way she'd held the child in her arms. The urge to claim her, to make her young body swell with *his* child, was far too tempting. To his footman he ordered, "Bring the carriage around and inform my sister that we are leaving."

Feigning a smile, he said farewell to his hostess and waited for Sarah to join him.

Within the month, he intended to have Juliette as his bride.

Chapter Eleven

Paul found Juliette waiting for him outside in her aunt's tiny garden, while the rain poured down on her umbrella. Strange that she would be out here alone, in such wretched spring weather. But then he saw that her gaze was fixed upon a row of yellow and purple crocuses just starting to emerge from the ground. He walked through the rain until he stood before her. Seeing the misery on her face, he tensed. She looked all the world like she was planning to break their agreement.

"I've come, as you asked me to." Upon one of her fingers, he glimpsed a flash of silver. She was wearing the ring he'd given her. And just like that, the air returned to his lungs. Then she must not have summoned him here to call off their engagement.

Paul moved to sit beside her, no longer caring that his clothes were getting soaked. "Tell me." He took the umbrella from her, shielding both of them.

She twisted at the band of silver. "When I've finished, you may not want to marry me anymore. But . . . it would be wrong to wed you, unless you understand what happened while you were in Edinburgh."

Though he already knew what she intended to say, he could read the fear and nervousness in her posture. He wanted to spare her this moment, but he couldn't admit that Sinclair had told him of the attack. Despite the knowledge, it was far worse seeing her struggle to tell him. He didn't want to hear it from her lips. Instead, he wanted to forget it, to bury the past that haunted her.

Juliette's face was pale, her hands clasped together. "I should have told you this long ago," she began, "but I was too afraid you would look upon me with hatred."

"Nothing you say would ever make me hate you," he offered. But from the tight expression on her face, he knew she didn't believe him. Likely she thought he would be furious with her or blame her in some way. He wouldn't. But even imagining that night brought a dark violence within him. He wanted to murder the man who had hurt her. And though he didn't know the attacker's name, his suspicions were on edge. He'd already guessed who it was . . . but he didn't truly want her to confirm the answer.

"I told you I didn't want to marry you, or any man," she said at last. "But there was a reason why. A reason I was too ashamed to say."

He waited for her to tell him of the attack. His gut clenched, his mouth somber in readiness.

Juliette took a deep breath and let it out slowly. "In May of last year, I gave birth to a son."

God above, that was the last thing he'd expected her to say. All of the tension within him stretched tighter, until Paul felt as though his body had turned to stone. Though he'd known about the rape, Sinclair had said nothing about a child. Juliette had a living reminder of the night she'd been violated. Not only had she suffered the loss of her innocence, but she'd become a mother as well.

"My family doesn't know about this. I gave him to another woman." She stared at him, her eyes holding the weariness and pain of a mother who had to let go of a child she loved.

Paul remained silent, revealing nothing at all. A numbness flowed over him at her revelation, as another piece fell into place. His mind went cold, and he could find no words to respond. It was as if the ground beneath him had vanished, leaving him to fall into a void.

"Say something, Paul," she whispered, twisting at the silver ring. Her glance flickered toward the house, and he realized now what her true reason was for wanting to be in London.

Her son was here.

His mind flashed with the memory of her holding a bairn in her arms, rocking him at night. She'd looked upon him with such love. There was no question of what had happened to her son.

"Your aunt is raising him, isn't she?"

She hesitated for a long pause, then nodded. "Charlotte took me in and made the excuse that I would be her traveling companion, since Lord Arnsbury was too busy to go with her. She took me to Norway, where I lived until I gave birth."

Her voice had gone quiet, and she covered her flushed cheeks with her palms. "I nearly died. The labor pains went on for days, and the birth didn't go well. I was out of my mind with fever, and it was a miracle I lived."

Paul let out a slow breath, knowing how many died in childbirth. He'd seen them suffer, and countless women died from hemorrhaging or childbed fever. To think of Juliette wracked with pain evoked a phantom regret that he had not been there for her.

"It's unlikely I'll ever bear another child. It would kill me," she admitted.

He revealed none of his thoughts, for he could see the vivid pain in her face. Her eyes gleamed with tears, and she said at last, "I hope you understand now why I cannot . . . ever share your bed. It's more than my fear of what happened to me. It could cost me my life."

She stared at Paul as if she expected him to look upon her with revulsion. It wasn't that. It was as if he were seeing her through a pane of glass. There was an invisible barrier there that could never be broken. And behind it was a woman hurting. A woman who believed she was unworthy of happiness.

Paul needed to know who the son of a bitch was so he could kill him. "You never gave yourself to anyone, did you?" he said slowly, trying to keep himself calm. "You were attacked."

Her face drained of color, but she nodded. "I—I went out walking alone. It was my foolishness, and there was no one to hear me cry out for help." A tear slid down her face, and she gripped her hands together. "I fought him, but . . . he was too strong."

"Who?" he demanded. The words were a razor, for he fully intended to avenge her. The man didn't deserve to live, and Paul had a mind to ensure that the bastard was incapable of being with a woman again.

Juliette remained silent for a long time. At last she said, "If I tell you, you'll try to kill him."

"You're damned right I will. Or he'll wish he was dead." He had no qualms about hurting the man who had violated Juliette. An eye for an eye . . .

But he could see the reluctance on her face. He reached up with one hand to cup her cheek. "I deserve his name, Juliette."

"What's done is done. No matter who it was, nothing can undo what happened."

She closed her eyes, covering his hand with her own. Although he was trying to remain calm, his blood was boiling. This man had stolen her innocence, and because of it, she would not willingly share herself again. The need to know burned within him.

"I want to ensure that you ne'er lay eyes on him again."

She turned in his embrace, resting her cheek against his heart. "Isn't it enough that I've told you this much?"

"No' for me." He gripped her in his arms and said, "Give me your trust, Juliette. I won't be running off like a lad of seven and ten, bent on murder."

It wasn't entirely the truth, but she didn't need to be any more afraid than she already was.

A tear rolled down her face, and he wiped it away with his thumb. Seeing her like this only fueled the rage against the man who had hurt her.

"It was Brandon Carlisle," she said softly. "The Earl of Strathland."

And there it was. The truth he'd never wanted to hear from her lips.

The moment she voiced the answer, his emotions solidified into one purpose—to kill the man who had taken so much away from those he loved. Poverty wasn't enough anymore.

He wanted the earl no longer breathing.

In her eyes, he saw the fear that she'd said too much. To comfort her, Paul tightened his arms around her, fighting to calm the storm of rage and disbelief. He focused on breathing in the scent of her hair, trying to will himself not to release the fury inside him.

A twitching anger stretched his skin tighter, winding him up like a clockwork spring, renewing his desire to bring Strathland to ruin. He could hardly hear any of the words she said, and it took an effort to breathe.

"I wanted to die that night," Juliette confessed. "I almost didn't come home. I wished he had killed me. I—I couldn't tell anyone, but your mother and Mr. Sinclair helped me." She clutched his hand, shuddering. "Strathland wanted to marry me, and I'd refused him. This was his way of punishing me, of forcing me into marriage. I knew if I stayed, he would tell my parents. So I fled Scotland to my aunt Charlotte's, leaving only a note for my mother. Mr. Sinclair helped me to reach London safely."

She poured out the rest of the story, of her shame and the pregnancy that followed. He understood that she'd done what she'd had to, to escape. But now, Strathland was threatening her again.

"If you no longer wish to marry me, I would understand," Juliette finished. "I know I'm no longer a wife any man would want. I'm ruined."

"You should have told me." He tilted her face to look at him. "I would have helped you, lass. You shouldn't have suffered through it alone."

"Please don't tell anyone of this. Only a few people know of it."

"Is that the reason you're wanting to remain in London? Because of your son?"

She nodded. "I wish I could have kept him." Her eyes lit up as she described the infant boy. "Matthew is an innocent in all this. But he's perfect. The sweetest boy I've ever seen. When he laughs—" Her voice caught in her throat, and she smiled through her tears. "It breaks my heart to see him. And yet, I need to be near him."

"Will you tell him the truth, one day?"

Her smile faded. "I can't. As my aunt's son, he will inherit the title of earl and all of their estates. If anyone knew he's illegitimate, he would have nothing."

She closed her eyes for a moment as if to blot out the pain. "You deserve children, Paul. And I can never give you that. It isn't fair to you, to take me as your wife."

"And it isna fair for you to walk away from the life you wanted, because of Strathland." His hand moved down to her shoulder. The rain had stopped, and he lowered the umbrella. Her bonnet was soaked, and he loosened the ties.

"We could be happy together, Juliette. Even without children." Though he would have loved a son or daughter with her smile, he wanted Juliette more.

"I don't believe that," she whispered. "You were meant to be a father. And I can't imagine you being happy with me in a marriage like this." She reached for his hand and tightened her gloved fingers around it. "I care enough about you to let you go."

He drew back to look into her eyes. "Do you believe that you've no right to be happy?"

Confusion clouded her face, and she didn't have an answer for him.

"What happened to you was no' your fault," he said. "You were his victim, no' his lover. And you shouldna lose out on the rest of your life because of that."

She rested her palms upon his chest, her expression shocked. It was as if she'd lived with the burial shroud of her sins for so long, she didn't know how to cast it off.

"I'd be lying if I said I didna want to share your bed," he admitted. "But there are ways a man and a woman can touch one another without risk of a babe. Or don't you remember that night at the *cèilidh*?"

She flushed at the mention of it, and Paul reached up to cup her cheek. "We'll try it, Juliette. If it means living with you, sharing a life with you, 'twill be worth it."

"I fear you'll grow to hate me one day."

Her words offended him. "I *can* control my urges," he said. "Though I might want to be with you, I ken when to stop."

She winced and nodded. "I'll be your wife in name," she agreed, "but not in body. I can't give you all that I should."

"I willna ask for more than you can give," he said. "But for now, I'll ask for a kiss."

She lifted her mouth to his, kissing him lightly. Breath and mouths mingled, and he tasted the salt of her earlier tears. But the gentle offering only flared up feelings of possession. He wanted to drive out the memories of Strathland, until she thought of nothing but him. He cupped her face in his hand, claiming more. The kiss transformed, deepening until he ached to touch her. He gave in to his desires, pulling her into his lap. But the moment he drew her against his aroused body, she froze beneath his touch.

"It's naught to be afraid of," he murmured, pulling back. "As I said before, you've no reason to fear me."

Juliette touched her fingers to her swollen lips, pushing her way off his lap. "I—I know. But please . . . I need you to go slowly."

He would. Her insistence that they could not have a physical joining between them was surely born of fear. Though he'd never force her against her wishes, he fully intended to touch her and bring her pleasure.

Surely, it couldn't be that difficult to have intimacy with Juliette, even without a true joining. He'd never made love to another woman before, despite the ribbing of his fellow class-mates at the medical college. Though he could have easily joined them at a local brothel, his sense of loyalty was stronger than the need for an hour's worth of pleasure.

It would have been a betrayal of Juliette. All these years, he'd chosen to wait, wanting her to be his first and only lover.

He didn't regret it. He'd heard enough tales about what to do on a wedding night from his friends. Many had claimed that women preferred being brought to their release without penetration. The idea of exploring Juliette's bare flesh all night, of learning what brought her pleasure, was deeply arousing. Perhaps it would be enough for both of them.

But all that mattered now was protecting her from Strathland, taking her far away from London.

No matter how long it took to gain her trust, he intended to lie with Juliette in his arms.

Even if that was all he'd ever have.

The Countess of Arnsbury was barren for nearly ten years. Every-one knows that.

Brandon paced across his home, his sister's words still ringing within his mind. He'd remarked to Sarah that he'd seen the countess and Juliette out walking with a baby the other day, and she'd responded without thinking.

Barren. Until this past year, when Juliette had come to stay with her.

The image of Juliette holding the baby was etched in his mind like a burning scar. Though logically the child belonged to Lady Arnsbury, Brandon thought back to the look of terror in Juliette's eyes. She'd clutched the baby as if she feared something would happen to the boy.

At the time, he'd dismissed her reaction as that of a woman afraid. But what if . . . it hadn't been a fear of him? What if she had been afraid for the child? Was it even possible?

He thought back to the night he'd taken her virginity and counted the months. She would have given birth to the child when she was eighteen, in May. That meant the boy would be nearly a year old, which was likely, given the child's size.

Juliette had disappeared from Scotland after he'd claimed her, staying away for almost a year. She'd traveled with her aunt Charlotte, he'd heard, and had returned to London for several months.

The more he pieced together the past, the more convinced he became that this could be *his* son. Juliette must have hidden the boy away, trying to pass him off as the Earl of Arnsbury's child. Since the countess had not borne a child in so many years of marriage, most people believed it was a happy miracle.

But Brandon suspected it was a lie.

He stared outside, wishing his driver would go faster. He needed to see the child again for himself, to discover if there were any traces of his own appearance. On that day in the park, he'd paid little attention to the boy, and now he regretted it.

He intended to confront Juliette and learn the truth. If she'd stolen his son from him, he would take the boy back. Though the child could not inherit, that didn't matter. Even a bastard son deserved to know his father.

His rush of anger suddenly dissipated when he realized that he now had a trump card that Juliette could not deny. He could threaten to expose her son unless she married him. If she refused him, Brandon would tell the world that the boy was a bastard, and he'd lose everything.

If the child truly *was* her son, she would do anything to protect him. And Brandon intended to see to it that she suffered for all the humiliations she'd given him. She would be sorry for all that she'd done.

The coach pulled up to the Arnsbury residence, and he disembarked with help from a footman. Anticipation swelled up inside him at the thought of seeing Juliette, of watching her pride diminish. She would beg for his forgiveness, he had no doubt. But he would allow her a token, by taking their son back after she'd wed him. Eventually, she would see that her place was with him.

He couldn't wait.

"Miss Andrews, you have a visitor," the butler informed her. "The Earl of Strathland has come to call."

His words struck her cold, for she'd never expected Lord Strathland to confront her here. Not this soon. Though she'd known he was angry at the ball last night, she'd expected to be gone before he could retaliate. A rush of anxiety caught her in the stomach as she wondered what he wanted.

It didn't matter. Just because he had come to call didn't mean she had to see him. She pushed back the instinctive fear, reminding herself that there were a dozen servants who would come to her aid. She was in no danger at all.

Even so, she gripped her hands together to stop them from shaking.

"Tell him I am not at home," Juliette responded.

All around her lay piles of clothing and a single trunk. She'd decided not to pack everything for her return to Scotland, since she had no need of court gowns or dresses for balls. Amelia would make better use of them. For tomorrow morning, she was leaving for Scotland with Paul.

"Forgive me, Miss Andrews, but he was most insistent. He bade me give you this, if you refused." The butler held out a small note.

Why couldn't Lord Strathland understand that she would never change her mind? No matter what he said or did, she would die before allowing him to court her. With a sigh, Juliette accepted the note and broke the seal. The six words, written in clear black ink, stood out on the paper as if they were marked in blood.

We need to discuss our son.

The room spun, and the color drained from her face. "Leave me," she ordered the butler. The man bowed, and as soon as he left the room, Juliette ran to the chamber pot and sank to her knees, retching. Her body shook with tremors so hard, she couldn't bring herself to stand.

He knows. Oh God, oh God, he knows.

She rested her cheek upon the carpet, wanting to curl up into a ball and avoid facing him. She'd been afraid of this for so long, of endangering Matthew. If she refused to see Lord Strathland, he would believe that the boy was indeed his. He'd well and truly cornered her now.

She got to her knees and held on to the bedpost as she rose to her feet. *Be strong,* her mind ordered. *Deny the truth and force him to go.* If she convinced the earl that Matthew was not hers, then Strathland had no ammunition at all.

Slowly, she went to her dressing table and began to brush her hair, pinning back any stray locks. She pinched her cheeks for color and took slow, steady breaths.

You can do this, she told herself. *You must lie for the sake of your son.*

She could only pray that her words would be convincing.

"You've been keeping secrets, haven't you, Miss Andrews?" Lord Strathland stood from his chair when she entered. Juliette nodded to the butler, who stood at the doorway just as she'd ordered him to. Although this was going to be a difficult conversation, she would never be alone with Lord Strathland. Had her aunt and uncle been present, she would have begged them to stay.

"The note you sent me was a lie," she said, tossing it onto the hearth. "I have no son, and neither do you."

Not if I can help it.

It took an effort to keep her tone even, for inwardly, she was shaking. "I was holding my aunt's son," Juliette continued. "She would not take kindly to your calling him a bastard."

"I thought you might deny it," he said smoothly. "The true question is what you would do to protect his future."

There it was—the threat she'd been expecting. Lord Strathland was a petulant man who apparently did not understand the word *no* in any form.

"Why will you not leave me alone?" she demanded. "I've told you, time and again, that I want nothing to do with you. Ever." There had to be madness within him, to think that he could coerce her to be with him again.

"Your father is going to give you Ballaloch for your dowry. And it will then come into my possession."

"No." She shook her head emphatically. "It's not mine and never will be."

"It's a useless piece of land now, with hardly anything there at all. You will ask them for it."

She said nothing about how her family had rebuilt the house, not knowing if he was even aware of that. "I want you to leave."

"I'm certain you do." He crossed the room and stood before her. "But I wanted you to know how you can keep the child safe. How to buy my silence, so that I'll never threaten him."

"I don't need to buy your silence for a lie."

"All I have to do is plant a few rumors." Strathland rested his hand upon the fireplace mantel. "I can tell them of your shame and how I compromised you. Of how you bore the child in secret."

"It's not true," she insisted.

"No man will ever have you, after I tell them of how you seduced me. My words alone could ruin not only your reputation and your sisters' . . . but also the boy's. They will question what they've heard. And when they dig for answers, how difficult do you think it will be to find the truth?"

Juliette struck him across the face, her hand leaving an imprint against his skin. The butler entered the room, and Strathland lowered his voice. "I hope you fight me like that again, when I next share your bed." He sent her a sly smile. "Wed me, and I'll leave the boy in peace. You can give me other sons."

He took a step back. "The choice is yours."

Chapter Twelve

Paul sensed that someone was following him. Ever since he'd left his residence, he'd glimpsed a black carriage with an insignia that seemed familiar somehow. Every time he glanced back, he saw it.

Was it Strathland's? He couldn't be certain, but when he hailed a hackney, he noticed that the carriage shadowed his path toward the Earl of Arnsbury's town house. The question was whether they would stop when he reached Lord Arnsbury's or continue on.

When he reached his destination, he paid the driver and looked behind him. The carriage slowed, and he caught a glimpse of an older man inside, before it drove past. Paul wasn't certain what it was about, but before he could approach the Arnsbury residence, he saw Lord Strathland walking out.

There was a gleam of smug satisfaction on the man's face, and Paul no longer cared that they were in public. The man had clearly gone to bother Juliette, and after learning what the earl had done to her, there was only the need for blood. A primal craving for vengeance roared through him, and he ran forward.

Only to be slammed against the stone façade of a nearby building.

"Don't," came the voice of Cain Sinclair.

Paul plowed his fist into Sinclair's nose. "This isna your business, Cain."

"Leave it be, Fraser. The last thing you're needing is to be brought up on assault charges against an earl. They can hang you for that."

He knew Sinclair was right. But logic wasn't enough to dim the need for blood. "He's the one who hurt her. He's going to die, and I'll be the one to send him to Hell."

"If you do, you'll go right along with him." His friend restrained him against the wall, using his strength to keep Paul from acting upon impulse.

A dark rage blazed through him, destroying any trace of mercy. There was naught but the need to bring pain to the man who had destroyed so many through his ruthless greed. "Don't be asking me to stand aside, Sinclair."

Justice was what he needed right now. He wanted to tear Strathland apart with his bare hands until the earl's blood ran in the streets. He had no intention of standing here, of watching the bastard walk away. With all his strength, he fought Sinclair, trying to wrench himself free.

"My lord Falsham!" a man's voice shouted. Without knowing why, Paul turned.

It was a mistake, for Sinclair grabbed him again and held him fast. "Sorry, lad, but I won't be letting you kill yourself."

With that, Cain bashed Paul's head against the wall behind him. Darkness dragged him under, and his last thought was that this wasn't over.

Not by half.

My lord. Are you awake?" came the voice of a man.

Paul's head felt as if someone had split it open with a dull axe. Against his cheek was a wooden floor, and he scented the stale ashes of a hearth.

"Best wake up, or I've another way of getting your attention, Fraser," Cain Sinclair added. "A bucket of water poured over your thick head."

"That's hardly necessary, lad. The puir man's been through enough without ye giving him more discomfort. Now go on, and fetch food and drink for His Lordship."

"I'm not your damned servant," Cain retorted. "Nor his. He can fetch his own whisky."

"Where am I?" Paul managed. "And who are you?" His eyes hadn't adjusted to the dim light, and the two figures blurred before him.

"I've been searching for you, these past few months," the man explained. "I am Colin Kinlark, your uncle's solicitor."

"You were following me," Paul said. "In the carriage a few hours ago."

"I was, yes," Mr. Kinlark agreed. "I regret that you were harmed, but under the circumstances, I believe Mr. Sinclair was trying to avoid further complications." He offered his hand to help him up. "If he had not intervened, you might have been brought up on charges of a felony assault."

Which would be accurate, since Paul *was* wanting to murder Strathland.

Mr. Kinlark bowed slightly. "I've brought ye to an inn, but dinna be fearing that ye'll stay here long. It was only necessary while you were—"

"Fashed in the head," Cain finished. "Lacking in brains."

"Aye." Mr. Kinlark shook his head. "Had ye fought Lord Strathland, 'twould have cost ye a great deal in bribes. Ye'd not want to lose coins due to . . . an excessive display of anger."

It brought to mind his uncle's insistence on cool-headed logic. Donald was a notorious pinchpenny. No doubt the man would be furious if Paul had given in to his instincts, thereby causing the need for excessive bribery.

"Don't be worrying, Lord Falsham. I'll be arranging for ye to stay in better quarters, now that they are aware of your rank."

Rank? He had no idea what the man was talking about. "I'm a physician," he muttered. "No' yet a lord."

"That was true several months back, to be sure. But since your uncle passed on, God rest him"—the elderly man bowed his head in respect—"ye've inherited his title."

Paul sat up, and the room swayed. "What happened? And when? He wasna so very old." He'd never dreamed of inheriting the title, not this soon. Donald Fraser was barely fifty and had seemed in perfect health.

"'Twas his heart, I fear. His servants found him dead at the breakfast table three months ago. Quite sudden."

It hardly seemed real. One moment, he was a physician with only a few sparse funds to call his own. And now there was a title . . . and lands.

"I ne'er expected this," he admitted.

"Certainly you were aware that you were next in line," Mr. Kinlark said. "You are now the Viscount of Falsham, with all the estates and incomes that accompany that title."

Paul stared at the man, still in disbelief of what he was hearing. "Exactly how much was my uncle worth?"

"He has three estates in Scotland. Edinburgh is where he holds the most property, though there's a smaller bit of land in the west, not far from Glenfinnan. And then there's the northern estate along the sea. There are no debts, for your uncle was quite frugal. He didna believe in owing money to any man. That's a good piece of luck for ye."

Paul looked over at Sinclair, whose expression was unreadable. "I don't ken why my father turned his back on his family. He lived as a crofter and told none of us."

None, save Bridget.

"He was disinherited when he chose to marry your mother. But since he was the younger son, it mattered not. Your uncle Donald inherited upon his father's passing, and now the title falls to you, as the eldest heir."

Paul drew up his knee, and his vision started to clear. "Why wasn't I told about his death sooner?"

"There was some difficulty finding you, my lord. We traveled to Ballaloch first, and only then found that you'd gone to London. But the title has been yours since the end of February."

That was why no one in London had questioned it. Likely someone had investigated Paul's claims and found them to be true. He could hardly fathom any of it. Never had he guessed that he would become the viscount so soon. In truth, the title had felt imaginary, as though it wouldn't come to him at all.

Paul let out a slow breath, realizing what this meant. He had power of his own now. A means of providing for Juliette that her father would respect, even if he didn't approve of their marriage.

Though he didn't particularly want to live in Edinburgh, at least it was in Scotland. He knew his uncle's house and the servants, after dwelling there for the past five years.

"Well, then, now that your bread's baked, you might give some over." Cain grinned. "As a high and mighty lordship, your coins'll buy a wee dram of whisky."

"I'll buy you a drink," Paul agreed. "Then I'll be paying a call upon Miss Andrews. Before I kidnap her and force her to elope with me."

The alarm upon Mr. Kinlark's face suggested that he wasn't entirely certain that Paul was teasing. "My lord, if I could but advise you—"

"She's already agreed to wed me," Paul told the man. "But I suppose I should be asking her uncle before I take her away. I am planning to borrow his coach, after all."

"Lord Falsham, you already have a coach of your own. I've brought it here, in the hopes that you'll return to Edinburgh."

Paul wondered what Juliette would think if he brought her to a fine house. Would she be glad to live in such a place? He rather liked the idea of taking his bride to a house that would be her own.

"I'll be taking Juliette with me in that coach, then." To Mr. Kinlark, he added, "And you'll find your own transportation back to Scotland. I want you to leave tonight and prepare the house for our arrival. I will bring the new Lady Falsham with me."

"But, my lord, would you not wish to have the wedding in Edinburgh? The bride's parents could be there."

"The bride's father would put a bullet through my head, if he knew my intentions." Paul shook his head and waved the man off. "No, we'll wed when we cross into Scotland and visit Edinburgh afterward. We'll stop at a few inns along the way, and if you make haste, you can prepare a proper welcome for us."

"Aye, my lord. Very good, then." He started to back away, but Cain caught Mr. Kinlark by the arm. To Paul, he said, "If tonight's your last night as an unwed man, you'll be needin' to have that whisky. We'd best get started, and *he* can pay for it."

Paul swayed to his feet, rubbing the back of his head from where Cain had knocked him senseless. "You're right, Sinclair. We should raise a toast to the bride and to my last night as an unwed man." Eyeing Mr. Kinlark, he added, "Well, you're coming then, aren't you?"

The elderly man muttered something that sounded like a prayer to Jesus for strength.

The next morning, Juliette ushered Paul into the parlor, where they could speak alone. Although her belongings were still packed upstairs, it felt as if all her plans had been uprooted.

"There's been . . . a complication," she told him. After she explained what Strathland had said, she ended with, "I can't leave London now. Not when the earl is threatening to tell the world about Matthew."

Strathland had tightened the chains around her in a way she could not escape. She saw the flash of displeasure on Paul's face and realized that he didn't understand. He didn't have any children of his own and could not possibly know what it meant.

"That's what he's wanting from you, Juliette," Paul told her quietly. "And that's precisely why you canna stay."

She started to argue with him, but he cut her off. "He's only guessing about Matthew. If you leave, he has no proof of anything."

"And if I walk away, he'll destroy Matthew's future by claiming he's a bastard. I can't let that happen."

"It's no' your responsibility."

"I'm his *mother*," she insisted. Of course it was her responsibility. Though she'd given him into the care of her aunt and uncle, she would cut off her right arm to keep him safe.

"You don't understand," she said softly. His face was impassive, but in his blue eyes, she saw frustration. To him, Matthew was nothing but a child conceived between herself and another man. No doubt Paul would be glad if he never laid eyes upon the boy. And suddenly, it was important for her to show him why she had to protect him.

She rang for a footman and asked him to bring Matthew and his nurse. When the servant was gone, she lowered her voice to a whisper. "I want you to see my son." Although it still might not make a difference, she wanted him to look at the boy. Matthew was an innocent, and nothing would ever convince her to abandon him to the mercies of a man who wanted to destroy his future.

When at last the nurse arrived, the baby was dressed in a soft cotton gown, his face rosy from sleep. Juliette took him from the nurse's arms and added, "I'll ring for you to come and get him in a few minutes."

"Lady Arnsbury will be wanting him, too, Miss Andrews." The nurse frowned, not at all approving of Juliette's interference. There was an unspoken reminder that Matthew did not belong to her.

"I'll only be a minute," she promised.

When they were alone again, she pressed a kiss to Matthew's forehead. His skin was soft, and he smelled of soap. Just holding him brought another ache to her heart. "I'm afraid for him," she admitted. "With a few words, the earl could ruin his life. And I wouldn't be here to help him."

"When will you start living your own life again, Juliette? You made the choice to give him to your aunt and uncle. He is *their* son now."

"He's the only son I'll ever have. I can't turn away from him." She fought back the tears, facing him. "If you ask me to choose between you and protecting my son, there is no choice to make."

The look in Paul's eyes sliced her heart, and though it was the truth, she hadn't meant to hurt him. She did care about Paul, so very much. If he walked away from her now, an emptiness would remain in her heart.

"I won't beg, Juliette." Paul drew closer, and his words held a cold edge. "But I'll speak the truth. If you don't walk away from the lad, Strathland will win this battle. He'll manipulate you until you've given him everything. And I'll no' be able to save you."

"How can you ask me to leave him?" She held the boy tighter, kissing her son's cheek. He babbled nonsense at her and grinned. At the sight of Matthew's first two teeth peeking out from the bottom, she didn't want to miss more of his life. "I can't go now."

"I thought you had more courage than that."

"It's not about courage," she snapped. "It's about keeping my child safe."

"He's no' yours any longer."

"He'll always be mine." Juliette couldn't hold back the tears now, and Paul crossed over to touch her shoulder. The boy was squirming to get down, and she set Matthew down by the chaise longue, letting him hold on to the edge.

"You're framing your life around his," Paul said gently. "You're a danger to Matthew, the longer you stay." The boy began to chortle as he balanced himself and tried to take a few steps. A moment later, he fell on his backside, startled at the loss of balance.

"He's an innocent," she whispered. "I don't want him to lose everything because of the earl's suspicions."

Paul helped the boy to his feet, holding on to Matthew's hands. "I'm not asking you to ne'er see him again. Only to walk away from Strathland's snares."

She said nothing to that. The rational side to her mind knew that he was speaking sense, but it was more than the need to protect Matthew. It was her shameful desire to be in his life, to be his mother, even if from an invisible distance. To give him her love, even if she could never give him a home.

Paul crossed his arms, his voice hard. "If you stay, Strathland will continue his schemes. He'll use your sisters, your family, and Matthew to twist you into obedience."

"I can't just stand aside and let the earl hurt the people I love." Even to consider it was unthinkable.

"So you'll be the sacrificial lamb, is that it?" Paul demanded. "You'll stay here, and he'll force you to marry him. He'll get everything he wants."

"I don't want him!" she exploded. "I wish to God the earl would go away and leave me alone." Furious tears spilled over, but at least he was now listening. "Do you think I want him to ever touch me again, after all that happened? I'd sooner see him dead."

Her skin crawled at the very thought of being in the same room with the earl, much less succumbing to a forced marriage. Never again.

"Then we'll leave," Paul ordered. "Come with me to Edinburgh, and we'll disappear for a time. He willna be able to find you, and he'll have no recourse but to back away."

"And what about Matthew?" The boy had begun whining, and Juliette lifted him against her shoulder, soothing him with soft words. But she already knew he was overtired and needed a morning nap. With reluctance, she rang for his nurse and gave him back to the older woman. After a few moments, his crying faded when the nurse took him upstairs.

"If you're no' there, Strathland canna accuse you of having any connection to him," Paul answered. "So long as the earl continues to acknowledge him as his heir, naught else matters."

An emptiness rose up within her at the thought.

"Strathland will realize that he was mistaken." Paul moved in close, taking her hands in his. "For no true mother would abandon her bairn." He wiped her tears away with his thumbs. "If you want him to be safe and loved, you've no choice but to let him be your uncle's heir. Give him the life you were wanting him to have."

She wept openly, so afraid he was right. If she turned away from Matthew, letting him go, Strathland's words would be meaningless air when Lord Arnsbury continued to acknowledge the boy as his son.

"What about my sisters?" she asked. "What if he tries to hurt one of them?"

" They'll stay away from him," Paul said. "Or Amelia might talk him into an early grave."

An unexpected laugh broke out, amid her tears. "I don't know if I can do this, Paul." He kissed her hand, and she stepped into his embrace, holding him tight.

"I did come here with the intent of kidnapping you," he offered. "You could claim you had no knowledge of my wicked intent."

"It's not truly kidnapping if I go willingly," she said.

"And will you go?" he asked, his voice turning serious. "If it means keeping Matthew safe?"

She didn't know. Her instincts roared at her to seclude herself in this house, doing everything in her power to shield Matthew.

But if she did, people would talk. Already she sensed that the servants were whispering about her unnatural attachment to the baby who was supposed to be her cousin. With every moment she spent at his side, she undermined the parents he deserved. Her aunt adored Matthew, as did her uncle.

"Yes," she breathed at last. "I'll go with you."

He rubbed her shoulders and regarded her. "I must speak with your uncle now, since your father is no' here." He looked at her strangely, asking, "How would you feel about living in Edinburgh, in my uncle's house?"

She shrugged. "I had thought we would return to Ballaloch . . . that we would make our home among the crofters." She'd not imagined that he would want to take her elsewhere.

His face turned serious. "That's not the life I want for you, Juliette."

"Perhaps not. But we'll make do with what we have. I don't need a grand house to be happy." It was true, though she fully planned to increase their income from the profits of Aphrodite's Unmentionables. In many ways, she rather liked the challenge of building what little funds they had together. She glanced down at the ring he'd given her.

Its worth was far greater than silver, for it would keep her forever safe from Lord Strathland.

⚑

"Lady Lanfordshire, there's another package for you," Mrs. Larson announced.

Beatrice threaded her needle, her face blushing at the news. "Set it on the table, Mrs. Larson. That will be all, thank you."

She didn't unwrap the paper, already knowing what it contained. After sending half a dozen letters to her daughters, she'd learned that they had stopped selling gowns nearly six months ago. They'd been selling unmentionables.

And not respectable white linen petticoats and chemises. No, her girls had made corsets lined in silk and satin, some of the chemises made of fabrics so sheer, a woman's skin was entirely visible.

She'd been outraged at first . . . until Mr. Sinclair had told her of the banking account sum of nearly a thousand pounds. It was a devastating amount, large enough to make a sizable difference in their debts.

It felt terribly wicked to allow her girls to conduct business in something so sinful. The garments were inappropriate for young ladies to even look at. And yet, she understood the practicality of what they had done. These chemises and corsets were selling exceptionally well because there were no others like them. They were unique.

She could hear the rustle of skirts, knowing that Mrs. Larson was dying to see the contents of the mysterious parcels that kept arriving. Beatrice had hidden most of them in the parlor, behind the drapes and in secret places. She'd wrapped them three times, so that no one could even glimpse the seductive fabric. Thus far, it didn't seem that Mr. Sinclair was aware of the contents, and for that she would be eternally grateful.

But when her husband abruptly strode into the room, his face had gone crimson. In his hand, he held a ledger containing the accounts Juliette had adjusted in the past few months.

"I should like to discuss these with you, Beatrice."

She eyed the carpet, wondering whether honesty was truly the best idea in this instance. "Is something the matter?"

He walked over to the doors and closed them, leaving them alone. His posture was erect, and he strode across the room like the soldier he'd once been.

"There are quite a few errors in the accounts. We do not have an additional thousand pounds, as the entries suggest." Henry set down the books and pursed his mouth in a line. "Such an egregious mistake would ruin us, if we went by these figures."

"There is another account in London," Beatrice said. "I assure you, we do have the funds."

Only because she'd ordered Mr. Gilderness to create the account. It was easier to deposit the profits directly in London, rather than bring the sums back here.

"And just where, may I ask, did these 'funds' come from?" The tone in his voice had grown supercilious, as if he didn't believe her. "An inheritance we knew nothing about?"

"Victoria married a duke, remember?" she said, hoping he would make an assumption and drop the matter.

But then he withdrew a folded piece of paper from his waistcoat. "Would you care to explain what Amelia is talking about when she spoke of Aphrodite's Unmentionables? Surely our daughters have nothing to do with . . . selling things."

His airs began to irritate her. *He* had been the one to leave them three years ago, while he'd traveled with the army. He'd burdened her with accounts she didn't understand, debts that had to be paid, and left them in the middle of nowhere in Scotland.

Her girls had found a means of supporting them, no matter that it was scandalous. And although she, too, had protested at first, she could not argue with the profits. Because of them, they'd been able to restore the house and furnishings without borrowing from the duke. Not only that, but she'd come to be friends with several of the crofters' wives, finding them to be amiable women with a true talent for sewing. A talent that was going to save all of them.

"The accounts are correct, and the profits of Aphrodite's Unmentionables have helped us a great deal," she said slowly. "No one knows of our family's involvement."

"Involvement in what?" he demanded.

Beatrice calmly handed him the newest package, bracing herself for his reaction. When he opened the paper, a sheer rose chemise was within it, trimmed with matching lace and ribbons.

A soft embroidered row of rosebuds adorned the edge of the neckline.

It certainly wasn't the most scandalous garment they'd made, but her husband's face turned purple. "You are *not* selling garments like these. Why, you can see right through them!"

"A thousand pounds, Henry."

"And whose idea was this, Beatrice? Yours? Or was it the Scottish refugees?" He tossed the chemise aside, adding, "It's disgraceful. I want you to have nothing more to do with this."

She picked up the chemise and folded it carefully, tying it back into the brown paper. "You may think what you wish. But the girls and I intend to continue on as we have."

The silence in the room held all the weight of twenty-four years of marriage. "You will not."

She raised herself up and looked him in the eyes. "Your wastrel brother left us with a mountain of debts while you went off to seek glory on the battlefield. I had to let most of our servants go, and I sold the sapphire bracelet you gave me."

He remained motionless, fury brewing in his eyes. But he said nothing.

"I had to fight for our very survival, *without you*, Henry. Our girls were intelligent and resourceful. Because of them, we are rebuilding our prosperity without relying upon anyone else."

"It's improper."

"Perhaps. But no one knows of our secret. And no one ever will." Before he could blister her ears again with all the reasons why she should not lift her needle, Beatrice met his gaze. "You left us on our own. And you have no right to criticize what our girls did to survive it."

Chapter Thirteen

Her wedding day was gray. Juliette stared at the ominous clouds, hoping they would lift soon. After over a week of traveling, they had reached Edinburgh, and Paul had chosen a small parish in the south for a simple wedding. During the journey, he had slept in different rooms at the inns, respecting her wish to be alone. But despite his kindness, Juliette couldn't suppress her worries over Matthew. It seemed wrong to elope when her son's future hung in the balance.

Her aunt and uncle had supported the marriage, particularly after Paul had spoken privately with Lord Arnsbury. Something had changed his mind, and she didn't know what it was. One moment, they were both upset with her decision to wed a physician . . . and the next, they were behaving as if she'd made the match of the Season. Strangely, Paul had said nothing of what had caused their change of heart. Perhaps they were simply glad she'd decided to marry and knew that he was her best hope. Charlotte had even suggested that they travel to Ballaloch, where her parents and Victoria could enjoy the wedding.

She'd refused, of course, knowing that her family would never support her marriage to a physician.

"Are you disappointed that your family is no' here?" he asked, taking her by the hand. "Would you rather I sent for them?"

She shook her head. "My mother and father would only try to talk me out of this." Squeezing his hand, she added, "But it wouldn't work."

Despite Charlotte's insistence that her parents would not be angry, Juliette wasn't about to risk it. "I was hoping for nicer weather, though." As a girl, she'd imagined herself marrying a man she loved, and wearing a beautiful gown, with flowers in her hair. There would have been dancing and feasting, with her favorite custard and cake.

As she daydreamed, the clouds broke open, the rain spattering down upon them. She couldn't resist a laugh, for it was so dismal. Lifting her face to the sky, she remarked, "I think the sky is telling us to hurry up." She hurried with Paul to the entrance of the church, lifting her skirts to avoid their being dragged in the mud.

When they were inside, Paul poured some of the water off his hat and donned it once more. "Wait here. I've a gift for you." His eyes softened as he ventured back into the rain.

After he returned from the coach, he had a brown parcel tucked beneath his coat. "I didna think you'd be wanting to wed in a traveling gown."

Juliette took the package, startled that he'd thought of it. "When did you have time to get this?" Warmth spread through her, at his gesture.

"I'm no' one for buying women's clothes, but I asked your aunt to choose something suitable. The minister's wife can help you to dress," he offered, pointing to a matron who was speaking to her husband farther inside the church. Juliette held the parcel a moment, before standing on tiptoe to kiss his cheek.

"Thank you," she whispered.

His palm rested upon her waist, and he added, "I'll always take care of you, Juliette."

Her heart softened at the thought of how he'd done so much for her. She regretted that she had not had time to do anything special for him. But then, this was only the beginning of their years together.

Slipping free of his embrace, she ventured a smile. "I'll go and change my gown." She clutched it to her breast as she went farther into the cold stone chapel, meeting the enthusiastic Mrs. MacKenzie. The woman reminded her of a sparrow with her brown hair and brown eyes, hopping about with excitement.

"Oh, my dear, we'll have ye out of these wet clothes in a wee bit," she chirped, ushering her into the sacristy. Juliette removed her bonnet, tucking a wet lock of hair up while Mrs. MacKenzie unbuttoned her. For a moment, she thought of Victoria's wedding day. Her mother and sisters had been bubbling over with excitement while Toria had been strangely quiet. Now, she thought she understood her sister's mood.

She wanted to wed Paul; truly, she did. But there was a sense that her life was about to change in a profound way.

When Mrs. MacKenzie unwrapped the gown, Juliette drew in her breath at the sight of it. Made of silk, the short-sleeved gown was a rich burgundy color. The bodice was trimmed with ribbon and pearls, befitting a baron's daughter. It was the sort of gown she might have worn had she married a duke or an earl.

"Och, but it's a bonny color with your hair." Mrs. MacKenzie sighed. "I canna wait to see it on ye." She helped raise the gown over Juliette's head, buttoning it up over her stays. There were long white gloves to accompany the garment and matching slippers. No doubt, the cost of the gown and accoutrements had been dear. But Paul had tried to give her something to make the day special. And despite the dreary weather and the unusual circumstances, she was looking forward to becoming his wife.

"There now, ye look like a proper bride," Mrs. MacKenzie pronounced. "Are ye ready?"

"I am." At least, she thought so. She was terribly nervous inside, hoping she would not let Paul down. He'd been so good to her, and she wanted this to be a strong marriage.

She followed Mrs. MacKenzie back to the chapel, where the minister awaited them. Paul stood with his hands clasped behind his back. He was staring at the stained glass windows, and as she returned from the sacristy, he turned. The expression on his face was of a man transfixed. He regarded her as if she were the answer to so many years of loneliness. And when she dared a smile, he held out his hand.

He was her best friend, and he was about to become her husband. Even as a young girl, she'd dreamed of this day.

And as the minister spoke the words binding them together, Juliette made a vow of her own.

I will try to be the wife you wanted.

Paul heard none of the words spoken by the minister. He gave his vows, but his mind was not on the ceremony—only on the night ahead. Though he would not consummate the marriage, he wondered if Juliette would ever learn to trust him. She had a slight smile on her face during the wedding, and that gave him hope.

He leaned forward to give her a kiss of peace and found that her hands were freezing. He rubbed them, and the minister gave a final blessing.

After they signed the parish register, it seemed odd to think that he'd married her at last. That this girl, whom he'd loved for so long, was now his. All because of a few vows made and ink upon paper.

He led her outside, and thankfully, the rain had stopped. Juliette stopped a moment and turned to him. Although her face still held the smile, she met his gaze and admitted, "I can't believe we're married now. It's not at all the way I thought I'd feel."

"I was thinking the same thing," he confessed. "How *are* you feeling?"

"Like I ate an entire cherry tart by myself."

It wasn't at all what he'd expected her to say. "Deliciously wicked? Or like you're about to have a stomachache?" he prompted, hoping it was the former.

"A little of both, maybe." Her voice held traces of nervousness, but she took his hands and drew them to her waist. "I'm glad of it."

He kissed her lightly, and when she returned it, his mind conjured the vision of being able to kiss her for as long as he wanted to. And aye, he was nervous, too. His instincts had served him well before, but tonight would be very different.

Juliette let him help her inside the coach, then wondered aloud, "Where is the driver?"

"I sent him ahead to prepare our room at the inn. He borrowed a horse from the minister." A trace of guilt caught him, that he still hadn't revealed the truth to Juliette about his inheritance and title. But he wanted their first night together with nothing to come between them. She would learn the truth when they reached Edinburgh.

"And you're going to drive us now?" she ventured. She rubbed at her arms, and he saw the slight rise of gooseflesh upon them. The wind had lifted from the grass and was bringing a chill with it.

"I will, aye. You can stay inside the coach and be warm for both of us."

Instead, she stepped out and approached the driver's seat. "Help me up, won't you?"

Paul reached down and boosted her up. "You want to sit beside me?"

"I did just marry you," she reminded him. "It seems like a more appropriate place to be."

Paul drew her cloak around her shoulders and brought a blanket to cover both of their laps. "I waited for this day for five years," he admitted. He'd known, from the first, that Juliette was the woman fated for him. "And I want to set your fears to rest about tonight and every night thereafter. I'll never force you into anything you don't want."

Her shoulders relaxed slightly. "I know that, Paul." She leaned her head against him, and he brought his arm around her.

Over the next hour, the afternoon drifted into evening. He drove north, bringing the coach to stop at the inn. His driver came out to greet them and took their belongings inside.

"Why do you want to live in Edinburgh?" Juliette asked. "Is it because of your uncle?"

Tell her now, his conscience urged. This was the perfect chance. And yet, he found himself not wanting to spoil the simplicity of this day. He wanted one night with her where they could simply be man and wife.

"In a manner of speaking," he hedged. "My uncle left me his house when he died. I thought we'd live there for a while." He said nothing else, letting her draw her own conclusions.

"I'm sorry to hear about his passing," she said. "You never told me of it."

"I only learned of it a short time ago." He cleared his throat, adding, "But I hope you'll be comfortable living there."

She nodded, and the innkeeper led them upstairs to their room. Inside, there was a small bed and a table pushed against one wall. Two chairs awaited them, along with a wedding supper of cheese, bread, meat, and wine. A small covered silver dish contained the surprise he'd arranged for her.

"This is lovely." She smiled at him, taking off her bonnet while he closed the door.

"And this is for you." He gestured toward the silver container, hoping she would be pleased by it.

As soon as she uncovered the dish, Juliette's eyes brightened. "Custard." She eyed it with unabashed longing.

Paul found a spoon and dipped it into the dish, offering it to her. Juliette ate it, closing her eyes as she savored the taste. His mouth went dry at the sight of her, for she looked like a woman well-pleasured.

"More?" he offered.

"Oh, yes," she said with a sigh. His skin tightened with the sudden image of Juliette naked while he licked custard from her bare skin. "Please."

He gave her the spoon, and she indulged in another bite. Heat roared through him at the sight of her, and he couldn't tear his eyes away.

"How did you ever get the money for all this?" Juliette asked, holding out a spoonful to him. "You went to a lot of trouble for me."

"I wanted you to enjoy your wedding day," he said, shrugging. "And as I said, my uncle left me an inheritance."

Now, the voice reminded him again. *Tell her everything.* But still he held his silence.

"The custard is even better than a wedding cake. It was always my favorite." She smiled, taking the spoon back. Paul leaned in to kiss her, and her lips tasted of sweet custard, with a hint of spices he could not name.

"You're distracting me from my dessert," she said against his lips. But there was a smile in her tone, as if she didn't mind. "Are you as hungry as I am?"

He nodded, but it wasn't food on his mind. He wanted his wife upon the bed. He wanted to remove the clothes from her body, kissing every inch of her.

You can't, the voice of reason interjected.

"Then eat," she said, breaking off a piece of cheese and feeding it to him. He caught her fingers and sucked at the end of one, swirling it with his tongue. It was too strong an urge to resist.

The shocked expression on her face gave rise to a blush. "Paul, I didn't mean you should nibble at my fingers. Not when there's perfectly good food," she teased.

"Is there?" He took her hand and kissed her palm, bringing it to rest on his cheek.

She went motionless. "I thought you said we wouldn't—"

"Aye. But I never said I wouldn't tempt you."

She froze, paling at his words. He reached for the bread and tore off a piece, handing it to her. "Did I hurt you when I kissed you? Or when I touched you that night at the *cèilidh*?"

"No." Her voice was the barest whisper, her eyes wide.

"Then trust that nothing I do will hurt you." He removed his coat and waistcoat until he wore only a linen shirt and breeches. She was staring at him as if she'd found herself caught in a trap of her own making. "We're married now," he reminded her. "You're going to see a lot more of me than this."

He poured a cup of wine for each of them and held it out. "Drink."

"Are you trying to get me foxed?"

"Not at all. Simply giving you something to quench your thirst." He filled a plate and offered it to her. "You could take your shoes off."

"I'm comfortable as I am."

She was putting up walls again, and he realized that they had different expectations for this marriage. "I'm not meaning to frighten you, lass. But neither am I going to behave like a man who has no wife. There are some things I'm wanting from you, even if we are no' lovers."

"What do you mean?" She eyed the door as if she were considering fleeing the room.

"I won't be having an English marriage with separate rooms." Her brow furrowed, and he continued. "You'll no' be sleeping in your own room. You'll sleep beside me, as a proper wife does."

"Oh." She eyed him as if expecting him to ask for more. "My parents shared a room, before my father went to war. I suppose that would be all right."

"What are you wanting from me?" he asked. "In this marriage, I mean."

She studied him a moment, breaking off another piece of cheese and offering it to him. "I want to put the past behind me and start over. Living with my best friend," she added.

Not to mention, he would grant her protection from the earl. But he saw in her the desire for a second chance. The hope in her eyes was strong, and he wanted to believe in it.

"And beyond that?" He drank a sip of wine and offered her a piece of cold mutton, teasing, "Surely you'll want to take all of my coins and spend them, as most women do."

She gave him an incredulous look. "I'll manage your money, but I've no need to spend it all."

"Now you're lying," he remarked. "You want to get your hands all over my—"

"No!" she blurted out. "That's not what I—"

"—accounting ledgers," he finished. When her face turned crimson, he laughed aloud. "What were you thinking I was going to say, lass?"

She threw a piece of cheese at him. "Stop teasing me." He picked up the cheese and ate it before he came to kneel beside her.

"We both know how much you adore ink and paper," he said. "And keeping accounts. I thought I'd give you all of my money to manage."

Her face softened. "You're not teasing me now, are you? You're speaking the truth?"

"Aye. If it would make you happy."

She drew her arms around him and pressed a kiss against his mouth. "It would, yes."

Her response pleased him, and now she seemed more relaxed about being with him.

"I'm going to remove your boots," Paul told her. "If you'll allow it."

Juliette lifted the hem of her gown and held out her boot. He unfastened the buttons and eased the first one off, then the second. When she was in her stockings, he pulled her foot into his lap, rubbing it softly. She leaned back, but her leg muscles tensed at his touch.

"No one has ever done this for me," she confessed.

"We've been traveling for a long time. Let me tend to you." He rubbed the insoles of her feet, using his thumbs to stroke her.

She was tensing at every touch, and though he tried to gentle his hands, she was biting her lip hard.

When he grazed the center of her foot, at last, she let out a shriek. "You're tickling me. I can't stand it."

He hadn't expected her to say that, and he let go. "It was no' my intent to torture you."

"I know." But she withdrew her feet and stood up. "I won't do the same to you. But would you like me to . . . rub your shoulders? My mother sometimes did that for my father."

He gave a nod, unbuttoning his shirt and lifting it over his head. "I would like your hands on me, very much indeed."

The air within their room felt heavier, almost heated in intensity. Juliette had never before seen Paul without a shirt, and it startled her to see the carved muscles upon his shoulders. He had a workingman's body, of one who had done his share of heavy lifting and labor.

Have courage, she told herself. Touching him gave her the power of controlling the storm of emotions gathering within. She reached out, resting her hands on either side of his neck, and found that his skin was warmer than she'd expected, smooth and hard. Her fingers found the tension there, and when she began to move her hands over him, he sucked in a breath of air.

But he didn't ask her to stop. She explored his back, finding the knots of tension by touch. As she'd seen her mother do, she used her thumbs to gently press against him, finding a way to release the pain.

"Take your hair down," he said quietly.

She moved her hands back, pulling the pins free and laying them upon the table. There was no need to ask why. He wanted intimacy with her, to know her as a husband should. And this, at least, was no threat at all.

"Do you want me to stop?"

"No. I'm wanting your hands upon me for as long as you want them there." He guided them back to his shoulders. "You could touch my neck, too."

She did, finding even more tension there. Her hair spilled over one of his shoulders, and he took the strands, lifting them to his nose. "You smell like summer, Juliette."

Gently, he guided her around to sit upon his lap. Both of his arms came around her, and he moved his mouth to hover above hers. Though he didn't kiss her, she recognized the invitation.

This time, she brought his mouth down to hers, initiating the kiss. His lips were familiar, a welcoming presence.

But somehow, there was more. As she kissed him, his hands drifted into her hair, gathering the locks and resting upon her nape. She felt his arousal beneath her, and her first instinct was to run.

He held her steady, pulling back. "I gave my word, Juliette. You've naught to fear." He kissed her temple, running his mouth along her jaw. "It's only the reaction of a man who desires you."

Paul kept his hands loosely around her, and when she started to sit up, his hardened length nestled against her. This gown was far too thin, and she recognized the familiar ache between her legs. It was just like the time when he'd touched her at the *cèilidh*. He leaned to kiss her again, and his hands moved around her waist. "Don't be afraid of my touch, Juliette."

His voice mesmerized her, his midnight-blue eyes staring into her own. "There can be pleasure between us, even if I'm no' inside you. You ken this."

When he moved again, she felt his length touching a secret place within her. She was growing wet between her legs, and her breasts were tight, the nipples forming hard nubs.

"I remember," she whispered. And yet, she couldn't stop the unwanted memories from intruding. The violence of the rape, and the way the earl had forced himself within her, overlaid this moment. She was trembling, so afraid of the feelings he'd evoked. But Paul would never hurt her. She trusted in that.

"Let me undress you," he commanded. "Let me touch you the way I'm wanting to."

Juliette didn't know what to say. Although he'd caressed her in secret that night, the idea of baring herself to Paul made her fear that he'd want to claim her with a husband's right.

"I don't know if we should," she hedged. She was nervous about letting him see her without any clothes, though she knew it was only natural. What if he demanded more of her and lost control of himself? She remembered too well how she'd forgotten herself that night at the *cèilidh*.

But a secret part of her had also delighted in his touch.

"You are in command of me, Juliette." He captured her mouth again, kissing her hard until she was breathless. "If you'll allow it, I want to bring you pleasure with my hands and my mouth."

She hesitated, tempted by a forbidden desire. The last time Paul had touched her, she'd been overwhelmed by sensation. He'd sensed what she wanted, until her body had shuddered beneath his hands.

A wicked voice inside was urging her now to surrender. She'd promised herself that she would try to be a good wife, and all he wanted was to touch her a little. Surely there could be no harm in that?

"Strathland stole your innocence and gave you naught but nightmares," Paul said. "Let me give back to you what was taken."

"What do you want from me?" she whispered.

He drew her to stand up. "I'll remove the gown, but you'll keep your chemise and petticoat on. That is, until you're ready for me to learn every part of your body."

His words painted a sensual picture, and she imagined his hands upon her. She gripped the edges of the gown, braving a courage she didn't feel.

"I don't want the memory of *him* intruding on what we have together," he said. "I want to cast out those demons this night and start anew."

The thought of standing here and submitting to his touches only heightened her anxiety. She didn't see how it could possibly make things better. Although he had never harmed her, and she *had* felt a shuddering release when he'd touched her before, somehow this night was different.

"Could I . . . touch you first?" she ventured. If their roles were reversed, *she* could be in command. The idea of exploring his shoulders and chest wasn't at all threatening. Instead, it might be a way to alleviate her own nerves.

"Aye," he said. "If it would make you feel better."

She rested her hands upon his shoulders, exploring his bare skin. She kept her touch light, and his eyes burned into hers. Then his hands moved to the buttons of her gown.

"You canna be unfastening these by yourself, Juliette."

"No. I'll need your help." She allowed him to push at the buttons while she ran her hands over his heart and down his ribs. His broad back held the strength and resilience of a man who had known hardship and overcome it. "I never thought I'd have a wedding night," she confessed.

"Especially with me?" he predicted.

"With anyone. I thought I would be a spinster until the day I died." She grew distracted when he lifted the gown away, exposing her chemise and petticoat. Though it was not one of the more daring garments, Amelia had given her a rose satin chemise and corset, trimmed with embroidery. The fabric was soft against her breasts, but when she saw the way Paul was staring at her, her body went rigid.

Then his hands moved to the back of her corset. The heat of his palms made her a little fearful, and she distracted herself by learning the texture of his skin. He asked, "May I remove this?"

She almost said no, but then, that wasn't practical. She had no maid, and the only person who could help her undress was Paul.

"Go slowly," she pleaded.

He moved her hair to the side and pressed his mouth to her throat while he loosened the ties of her stays. He freed her from the laces and lifted the corset away.

She couldn't stop herself from crossing her arms over her chemise. Though he couldn't see through the satin, her breasts were tight and aching, the points taut through the fabric.

Paul stood up and reached for her hands, gently lowering them to her sides. "You've no need to hide from me, Juliette."

Perhaps not, but shyness reigned over her at the moment.

His eyes were shielded as he moved his hands up her spine. "You take my breath away, Juliette. And always have."

"I have no breath, either," she confessed. "I feel as if I'm about to faint."

Paul led her toward the bed and guided her to sit down on the left side. Strangely, he didn't press her down, but instead sat at the foot of the bed so that their backs were against one another. "I've an idea," he said. "Look at the wall over there, and I'll simply tell you what I was wanting to do this night."

"But you won't touch me?" she whispered, lifting her gaze to the faded wallpaper.

"No' unless you ask me to."

The promise *did* make her feel better, knowing that he would slow down the pace, giving her a moment to gather her senses.

"You go first," he prompted.

"In what?"

"Tell me what you were wanting to do to me this night." He leaned back against her, and the pressure of his bare back against the silk suddenly reminded her of the days when they used to steal away to talk. They had sat on opposite sides of a tree, hidden within a small pine grove. Paul had complained about his frustration at never being able to leave Ballaloch, while she'd complained about her sisters.

"I'd want to kiss you," she began.

"No, you can imagine better than that, lass. Tell me something wicked that you're wanting to do."

He sounded so interested, she couldn't help but smile. "I'm no' a wicked lass," she mocked, using a Highlander accent.

"We'll have to be changing that, won't we? Go on, then. Tell me where you were wanting to put your hands and your mouth." His left hand reached around and took her right palm in his.

She was tempted to invent something that wasn't true. To shock him with words. But in the end, she was too embarrassed to speak. "I suppose I'd want to kiss the space over your heart. To see if your skin is as sensitive as mine."

"I'll lower your chemise and touch your breasts with my hands. Then my mouth," he countered. "I'd want to see if your nipples grew hard, and I'd want to see how they felt against my tongue."

A deep ache rose up between her legs. She imagined the sensation of his heated mouth sucking against her breasts, and she suspected she would like it.

"I would want to try it with you," she whispered. "I'd want to know if you would feel the way I do inside."

"I'll touch your ankles, then move my hands higher to take off your stockings," he said.

Just the thought of his hands so near to the aching center of her made her heartbeat quicken. Juliette reached beneath her petticoat and unfastened the garters, rolling down one stocking, then the other. The heat of her own palms echoed the visions of her imagination.

"And after that?" She almost didn't want to know the answer.

"Your turn," he prompted.

"I'd reach for your breeches and help you unfasten them," she said quietly. "I'd slide them down, over your hips."

He moved against her, and from the rustling noise, she realized that he'd done just that. Was he . . . naked? Her face went scarlet, and she was struck with curiosity, wanting so badly to know.

She gingerly moved her hand backward, toward the direction of his thigh. When she touched bare skin, she jerked back as if she'd touched hot coals. Paul laughed, turning to look at her. "Don't be afraid of me, *a chrìdhe*. I only did as you asked."

He guided her hand to touch him again. "Do what you will with me." His voice held all the sensual promise of a man who had all the time in the world.

Juliette hesitated, not knowing whether she should. But she didn't want to live in fear for the rest of her life. Strathland might have destroyed her innocence, but she didn't want to remain under that shadow any longer. Women *did* enjoy sharing a man's bed; that she knew. Her sister Victoria hadn't seemed at all displeased by her marriage to the duke. And because of it, she was going to have a baby.

Paul stroked her hair, and the touch of his hand was comforting. She wanted him to know that she did trust him.

"I didn't wed you only to escape Strathland," she confessed.

When she turned to kiss him, he responded to her, threading his hands in her hair as his tongue met hers. The kiss was a way of speaking the words she couldn't yet say.

"And I didna take you away from your son to hurt you," Paul added. "It's safer for him, though."

"I know you're right." She understood that, though she hadn't wanted to go. "But I don't want to think of that right now." She burrowed her face against his chest, listening to Paul's heartbeat.

She could feel every inch of his hard body against hers. Rather than feeling threatened by him, it felt good to be held. His hands continued their lazy, smooth strokes through her hair. As if he didn't expect anything at all from her.

Perhaps that was why she suddenly felt the urge to give him something of herself. Slowly, she stood up from the bed. "Close your eyes," she whispered. "Please."

Paul obeyed. In the dim candlelight, his skin was bathed in amber, contrasting against the white sheets.

Juliette turned her back to him and removed her petticoat first, then her chemise, placing them on the chair. When she was naked, she peeked around and saw that Paul's eyes were still closed. Although she was nervous about being without her clothes, she slipped beneath the sheet until she was covered from the neck down.

It felt sinfully wicked, even if he was her husband now.

"How long do I have to keep them closed?" he asked.

"You can open them now," she said. Her voice sounded strange to her, almost as if it were coming from another woman. What did it matter if he saw her without clothes? Now that they were married, it was an intimacy that a husband should enjoy. She had to overcome her anxiety and trust that he would not take more than she could give.

He studied her face for a moment, noting the chemise and petticoat on the chair. "You honor me," he said quietly. "And while I'm wanting to hold you now, to feel your skin against mine, I'll wait until you're ready." He remained leaning upon his side, his eyes dark with desire.

I'm not ready. I might never be ready, her heart quaked.

But that was what a coward would say. She couldn't hide from her worst fears, not if she wanted to start again.

Let him hold you, her mind coaxed. *He'll stop if you ask him to.*

She rolled away from him and drew his arm around her waist. Though she kept a distance between them, Paul brought his mouth to her shoulder. The moment he kissed her, a thousand shivers took hold over her skin.

"I'm wanting you closer. Skin to skin," he warned.

She forced herself to say nothing, to remain absolutely still. But when she felt the heat of his body pressing against her backside, she went motionless. Against him, she felt so small, his warmth enveloping her.

"Are you all right?" he murmured.

"I think so." She adjusted to the feeling of his body and the hard length of his erection pressed to her spine.

"Don't be worrying yourself, lass. I'll keep my word. But tell me if you're wanting more," he said against her skin. His breath sent a fevered shiver over her body, and she felt the aching wetness between her legs.

All over, she was growing hotter with need. She took his hands and brought his arms around her, so that his forearms crossed her breasts. Her nipples tightened, and she bit her lip against the sensation. For a moment, his hands remained in place. Then he turned her to her back, still keeping his arm over the top of her shoulders. His mouth moved over her throat, descending lower.

"Tell me if I should stop," he murmured.

His mouth drifted lower, over the top of her breasts. She could feel the warmth of his breath pulling at the strings of her inhibitions. He slowly lowered the edge of the sheet. Juliette closed her eyes, unwilling to see his reaction when he bared her breasts.

"You're perfect," he said, reaching up to cup them in his hands. The warmth of his palms against her sensitive skin was a jolt of awareness. And suddenly, it was too much, too soon.

His thumbs caressed the tips of her breasts, while his mouth moved against the curve of her throat. The touch of his hands was arousing a response that overwhelmed her, and she struggled to breathe.

She took his hands and drew them away from her breasts. "Paul, stop."

He did, though his eyes were searing with hunger. Beneath her hips, she could feel his erection, and the look on his face resembled pain.

He didn't move, nor did he speak. Juliette calmed her heartbeat, struggling to gather her composure. She watched him for a moment, thankful that he'd obeyed her without question.

"It was . . . too much," she explained, flushing. Her body was on fire, every part of her sensitive to his touch. She didn't know how far she could let him go before both of them lost their senses.

"Will you let me kiss you again?" he asked.

That, she could allow. She leaned in, wrapping her arms around his neck while he kissed her thoroughly. His tongue slid within her mouth, and she met it with a thrust of her own, trying to tell him without words that she did care. She did want him, no matter that it was dangerous. He pulled her against him, her bare breasts against his chest. His manhood was pressed against her stomach, but although it was erect, she was no longer quite as bothered by it.

As Paul devoured her mouth, she grew aware that he was rocking against her in a slow rhythm. Warmth blossomed between her legs, and she instinctively pressed herself to him, meeting him as his hips met hers.

She could feel him against her most intimate center, and the restlessness only grew. Though he didn't do anything except kiss her, the rhythmic motion evoked a delicious ache. She ought to tell him to stop.

But she was startled to realize that she didn't want him to.

"Juliette," he whispered in a husky voice. There was raw need in him, as if he were fighting for control. His mouth moved against her throat and above her breasts, drawing lower.

But he stopped at the curve above her breast. His tongue and lips tempted her, though she was afraid of her own response.

As she strained against him, he murmured against her skin, "Shall I stop again?"

She was trembling with every motion, feeling as if she were about to fall into an abyss. His heated breath warmed her skin, and without knowing why, she found herself grinding against him . . . seeking something. Her body was so hot, her lips swollen. "Not yet. I think . . . I want more."

Her hands gripped his hair, pulling him lower. She was lost in sensation, unable to pull together any clear thoughts—only that she needed him. She guided him down, until at last his mouth fastened upon her nipple.

A rush of wondrous need poured through her, and she felt an echo between her legs. He pulled gently, his tongue swirling around, and her breath caught, in shuddering gasps. Paul seemed to instinctively know what she wanted, and his palms splayed upon her bottom, lifting her against him until she arched back and pressed hard.

Between her legs, the intensity of his thrusting erupted with a violence that made her cry out, going liquid with a release like the one he'd given her at the *cèilidh*. Only this time, it was even more wondrous. She pressed hard against him, and the ecstasy continued, until her body jerked with spasms of shocking heat and pleasure.

She had gone pliant beneath him, her body feeling as if all the blood had drained away. It was more blissful than anything she'd ever experienced.

But the look in Paul's eyes was grim. He was still taut with desire, his body stiff beneath her. Although he had not found his own release, Juliette reached out to touch him. The moment her hand slid down his back, he pulled away. "I think you should go to sleep now," he said.

She didn't argue as he pulled the coverlet over her. But instead of curling up against her, he swung his legs to the side of the bed and crossed the room. A moment later, he donned his clothing.

"Where are you going?" She'd expected him to sleep beside her, since it had grown dark outside.

"I'll be back later" was all he said. After the door closed behind him, she could only wonder when he would return.

Or if he would return.

His groin felt as if someone had taken a hammer to it. Paul drained his second mug of ale, but it did nothing to diminish the raging ache. Though he didn't blame Juliette for not wanting to consummate their marriage, right now, he wanted to be inside his wife. He craved that connection, wanting to join their bodies together.

The hell with it. He wanted to erase all memories of Strathland. Inside, his blood was hot with fury, and he couldn't seem to calm it. The earl had known Juliette more intimately. *He* had claimed her virginity, and because of the violence, she had no desire to ever consummate her marriage.

It was understandable. If she believed another pregnancy would kill her, why should she want to risk being intimate with him? His body was on the edge, craving it all . . . and it could mean her death.

He ordered another mug of ale, hoping he could get drunk enough to pass out. For he couldn't go back to his wife's bed. If he slept in the same room with Juliette, he would have his hands upon her, all night long.

God help him, he'd set himself up for torture. When he'd agreed to her conditions, he'd never imagined the torment would be this great. She'd warned him that she would not share his bed. All along, she'd been clear on her wishes. But he'd underestimated how difficult it would be to keep his hands away.

"What on earth are ye doing here?" a female voice demanded. "Ye should be abovestairs with yer lady wife, tryin' to get bairns on her."

Paul ignored the innkeeper's wife, holding out his empty tankard. "Another."

"I'll no' be helping a drunkard. Get out of here, and talk to her. Be gentle, and she'll welcome ye, I've no doubt."

"Wheesht, woman." He had no longing to hear her advice on how to handle his wife. Though it was true he'd never taken a woman to bed, he'd already pleasured Juliette twice. He had five years' worth of ideas in his brain, not that it would do him any good.

"No woman wants to be alone on her wedding night, that I can tell you." She went on and on about how Juliette was likely frightened, and even offered to talk to her.

"There'll be no need for that," he said. But he was ready to go anywhere to escape her prattling.

With disgust, he stood up and tossed a few coins on the table to cover the cost of the ale. It had been over an hour since he'd left Juliette. If she were asleep, he might be able to slip back inside the room without her knowing he was there.

But when he returned, he spied a candle glowing in the darkness. It spilled over Juliette's face, like a touch of gold upon her skin.

"I was hoping you'd come back," she said gently. "Why did you leave for so long?"

"Because I had to." He sat upon the chair, far away from her. The remnants of their evening meal remained, though they'd finished the wine already. "I didn't trust myself around you."

"You stopped when I asked you to." She sat up, exposing a bare shoulder that he wanted to touch. Reminding him that everything he ever wanted lay beneath a linen sheet.

"I didn't want to stop." He turned toward the window, feeling a chill in the air. "In that moment, I was just like the earl. I wanted to thrust inside of you, no matter what words I'd vowed."

She paled, crossing her arms over her chest. It was right that she should be afraid, after what he'd just confessed. He wouldn't be surprised if she wanted him to sleep downstairs or on the floor.

But then she exhaled slowly, as if gathering courage. "You wanted to. But you didn't."

"That's nearly as bad." There was a small hearth on one end, and he bent to make a fire. The distraction of a task was needed right now.

"You were right, you know," she whispered. "I did feel good when you touched me. I wasn't as afraid as I thought I would be."

He continued building the fire until a small warmth emitted from the flames. The distance was what he needed right now. But then she asked, "Paul, come and lie beside me."

"It would no' be a good idea." Not when he was so aroused by her.

"We'll only talk," she said. "That's all."

"I'd rather talk over here."

Juliette eyed him for a moment, then shook her head. "If you won't come to me, then I'll come to you." She tugged one of the sheets and wrapped it around her, walking to him barefoot. The sight of her made him feel even more uneasy, for fear that he would lose command of his senses.

"You're hurting," she said softly. "And I don't know how to ease you."

"It will pass," he said. "There's naught to be done."

She brought her arms around him from behind, pressing her face to his back. "The last thing I wanted was to cause you pain. And I just thought I could—"

"It burns me that he took you like that," he shot out, before he could stop himself. "That he hurt you and made it so you can't ever be joined with a man again." He turned around and faced her, knowing that the words he spoke were a mistake. And yet he couldn't stop them. "He had you in a way I never will. And it's like acid in my veins."

She looked stricken at what he'd said. Tightening the sheet around her, she whispered, "I wish I had never gone walking alone that day. I should have taken Mr. MacKinloch or some-one—anyone—with me. I thought it was safe."

"It wasna your fault, Juliette. But I canna help wishing I could murder him for it."

She folded her arms across her waist. "It isn't that I don't want to be a true wife to you, Paul." Her face reddened, and her hands clenched into fists. "I believe that . . . it would have been good. And I can't imagine a better man to be a father."

He let her speak, though he was frustrated by a past he couldn't change. "Who told you that you couldna bear another child?"

"The midwife," she admitted. "I bled so much, and afterward, the fever took me. She advised me to never have a second child, or I would die." She reached up to touch his face, and her cool fingers quieted the storm of frustration within him. "I can't take that risk."

And well he knew that there was nothing that would fully pre-vent conception, save celibacy.

She was quiet for a long moment, as if considering it. "You said yourself . . . that there were other ways of being together."

But not in the way he wanted her most. Paul let out a sigh and took her hand, leading her back to bed. He removed his shirt and waistcoat, sitting beside her. "Go back to sleep."

"I'll sleep when you lie down beside me." Her voice was soft, almost inviting. It killed him not to go to her and hold her in his arms. But if he dared to set one foot inside her bed, he would want too much from her. She tempted him far more than he could endure.

Paul touched her hair and covered her up with the blanket. Without another word, he squeezed her hand and left.

A voice inside made him wonder if she'd been right . . . that he would one day regret this marriage.

Chapter Fourteen

"There are other daughters," Sarah reminded Brandon. "Miss Amelia Andrews and Miss Margaret Andrews are still unwed."

Brandon ignored her suggestion. "Amelia is only sixteen, and Margaret is nearly on the shelf at one-and-twenty. I've no wish to marry either of them."

"Then you must give up this notion of acquiring their land," Sarah said. "Let it go."

Perhaps he should. And yet, he loathed the idea of the Andrews family living so close to him. He wanted to command all of the western Highlands, increasing his fortunes tenfold. But more than that, it was a matter of pride. He was a man of means, one who ought to have half a dozen heirs running about.

Or at least one heir. He remained unconvinced about the child he'd seen and had sent inquiries to find out more about the boy. If there was any hint that the child could be of his blood, he fully intended to reveal the boy's illegitimacy and take him.

It infuriated him that Juliette had eloped with Dr. Fraser. The little bitch had ignored her opportunity to wed *him* and had instead chosen a physician with hardly two coins to his name. He couldn't imagine why. Brandon could give her everything. And she'd chosen a man who was a continual thorn in his side.

Now he knew that Fraser was the mysterious viscount who had talked to the wool buyers. He didn't believe it was possible that the man could inherit a title. The doctor had to be telling falsehoods, for he'd been born in poverty and lived in filth all his life. Lies never changed a man's blood.

Fraser mistakenly believed that he could influence the men not to buy wool from Brandon. And the Duke of Worthingstone had also joined in Fraser's efforts to bring down his empire.

It would make no difference. Wool was in high demand, due to the war and the need for uniforms. Brandon had all that was necessary, and when some of the buyers refused him, he'd arranged for the wool to be sold under a different name. If his men took the fleeces, they could lie when necessary, and gain the necessary profits. It wasn't difficult.

Let them try to end his fortune, and he would see to it that Paul Fraser was brought to ruin.

"Have you learned anything more about the Andrews daughters?" he asked. "Any sort of scandal that I could use against them?"

Sarah frowned. "I'm not certain. There is something different about their family, but I've not discovered what." She stood and walked over to the window. "Have you thought of another woman you might marry?"

"No." There was only one woman he wanted, and he'd not given up on her yet, though she had married another.

A thin smile crossed his face. Juliette hadn't gone to her marriage bed as an innocent. He wondered what Fraser would say if Brandon revealed that he'd claimed her first. Had she told her husband the truth? Perhaps a letter might do well to remedy that. But then, he didn't know where they'd gone. According to his sources, Dr. Fraser had taken Juliette away, and none could say their destination.

It didn't matter. There were ways to coax Fraser back to Ballaloch, if he wasn't there already. His mother was there, was she not? And Fraser would undoubtedly come to her aid, if she required it of him. Strathland smiled at the thought.

"Brandon, there is an assembly tonight that I wish to attend." Sarah's voice interrupted his plans.

"Go without me." He had little desire to put on airs or pretend interest in brainless debutantes.

"You're not living up to our arrangement," she argued. "We would have no invitations at all, if it weren't for me. I thought you intended to seek a bride."

"My intentions are none of your concern. Go and throw yourself at men, if that's your wish. I don't care."

"I want a good husband. One who's wealthy and kind, who—"

"Then look among the men who have one foot in the grave, Sarah. God knows, none of the younger men would take a second look at you, unless they were blind and deaf. You've got the face of a horse, and there's not a young man in London who would have you."

Her cheeks burned red, and her gaze turned icy. "You needn't be cruel."

"I'm speaking the truth, dear Sister. Throw yourself on their mercy, if that's your will. But I'm leaving for Scotland within the week. Whether you come or stay does not matter to me."

"You know how much I loathe Scotland."

"Then stay in London. Find an old woman, and be her companion. Join the ranks of the courtesans, for all I care. But I'll not stay here any longer."

Brandon waved a hand, and she obeyed the unspoken command, closing the door behind her. He didn't doubt that she'd find a way to remain in London.

While he intended to put an end to Paul Fraser's interference.

The coachman drove them down a winding path that led to a manor house atop a hillside. Juliette stared at the estate, made of gray limestone and windows that were taller than her. Smoke drifted from the chimney, making it clear that someone was there waiting for them.

"Is this your uncle's house?" she asked. "I never expected it to be like this." The house and lands were vast, with acres as far as the eye could see. She guessed the house had at least twenty rooms, if not more.

Paul let out a breath, his gaze distant. "It was his, aye."

She waited for him to explain more about it, but he said nothing. Then, too, she hadn't known about his uncle's death before yesterday.

After they disembarked from the coach, Juliette took his arm, noting the grim expression on his face. Something was weighing upon him, and she strongly suspected it had to do with her.

He hadn't returned to their bed last night. She didn't know where he'd gone, but the glassy stare on his face suggested that he hadn't slept at all. His pace slowed along the gravel pathway, and she stopped walking. "Do you want to tell me what's bothering you, or am I supposed to guess?"

He glanced at the house and then back at her. "My uncle was the Viscount of Falsham before he died a few months ago. This house now belongs to me, as does the title. Which makes you Lady Falsham."

Had he announced himself as the King of England, she couldn't have been more surprised. "Then . . . all of the rumors in London were true?" She'd never imagined it was possible. How could he have lived in such poverty all his life, only to inherit this?

"They were, aye. But I didna ken about my father's family until I left Ballaloch to study medicine." He continued walking, leading her up the stone steps.

She frowned, not knowing what to make of that. Others had told her that he was a viscount's heir, but she'd not believed them, for she'd known Paul for so many years. It felt as if he'd given her lies of omission, leading her to believe they would live in poverty. And yet, he'd never denied the stories.

A footman opened the door and offered Paul a broad smile. "Praise be, and thanks to Heaven, His Lordship is home. Come in, come in." When he spied Juliette, the man's eyes brightened. "My lady, we are glad to welcome you home."

The butler joined them in the hallway, bowing low. With a silent gesture, he ordered the footman to fetch their belongings. "You are very welcome indeed, my lady," he said.

"This is my new viscountess," Paul said. To Juliette, he introduced the older man. "This is Mr. John Fraser, the butler. If you have any needs, he will see to them."

Juliette sent Paul an amused look. Although she knew there were many Frasers in the region, it surprised her that the butler shared the same surname as her husband.

"It would be my pleasure, Lady Falsham." There was kindness in the butler's voice, along with a genuine sense of welcome. She liked him immediately.

"If you wouldn't mind, Mr. Fraser, I will need a lady's maid," Juliette asked. From the abrupt embarrassment on the man's face, she surmised that there were no suitable maids at the moment.

"My wife can serve you, my lady. Until we can hire a maid of your choosing, that is." The butler bowed and then added, "I believe you'll want to meet our housekeeper, Mrs. Maggie Fraser, this afternoon."

"How many . . . Frasers are there?" Juliette ventured.

The butler cleared his throat. "Quite a few, my lady."

"And on our staff?"

He stole a glance at Paul and stared down at the ground. "All are Frasers."

Juliette couldn't stop her smile. "Then if I'm not certain of someone's name, I simply call him Mr. Fraser or her Mrs. Fraser?"

He nodded. "That would be about the way of it, I'm afraid."

Paul took her arm and led her inside. "I will take Lady Falsham for a tour of the house. If you'll arrange for a hot meal, we'd be very grateful for it."

The butler bowed, leaving them to walk alone. Paul started to tell her about his uncle, but Juliette barely heard any of it. Instead, she opened one of the smaller doors and found that it led into a library. With Paul's hand in hers, she led him inside and locked the door.

"When did you tell my aunt and uncle of your title?" she asked, though she already suspected the truth.

"The day before I took you away," he admitted. "They decided the match was a good one, after they learned of it. Mr. Kinlark, my uncle's solicitor, gave them a list of my assets and estates."

She stared at him, several pieces beginning to fall into place. The wedding gown. The sense that he'd been hiding something from her. "And you didn't think it was worth mentioning that you have a title now?"

He rested a hand upon a bookshelf. "This life isna familiar to me, Juliette. I wanted our wedding to be simple. And last night as well."

Although there was nothing simple about it. He looked, for lack of a better word, tortured. She reached up to touch his face. "I don't know why you left me last night."

He took her hand in his and lowered it. "Let me show you the rest of the house."

It was only a means of avoiding her question. She had no desire to look through old rooms when it was clear that he was trying to distance himself. But although she relented, she wondered if there was a way she could ease him. And so, she decided to ask.

After she voiced her question, he stared at her. "What do you mean?"

"Last night, you made me feel beloved, even though we weren't lovers," she said. "Is there a way I could do that for you? Perhaps if I touched you—"

"No," he cut her off. The flash of heat in his eyes belied his words. She suspected that there was far more he wasn't telling her.

Juliette stepped in front of the door, blocking Paul's way. "We can't endure years of marriage like this."

Paul raked a hand through his hair. "I ken that. But it may be wise to have separate rooms at first."

It was a direct contradiction to his earlier assertion last night. "I thought you believed a wife and husband should share a room."

"I changed my mind."

The look in his eyes was harsh, of a man frustrated beyond words. "Surely you don't mean that."

She started to reach for him, and without warning, he pressed her back against the bookcase. "What are you wanting from me, Juliette?" he challenged. "Are you wanting me to lose control?"

His hands slid from her waist up to the sides of her breasts. "I'm no' Strathland. I won't ever claim you, for we both ken the risk." His thumbs slid over her tightened nipples, tempting her until her breath caught. "But don't be playing games with me. I have my limits, and you're pushing them."

She didn't know what to say, but her skin prickled with interest. He reminded her of a caged animal, pacing its bars. He wanted her but was determined not to take her.

And God help her, he was temptation in the flesh. He kindled a hunger in her, not only to be touched but to touch him as well.

"I don't mean to push," she whispered.

Though he was speaking good sense, to stay apart, she sensed that it would only heighten his frustration. And although she'd tried to warn him about wedding her, tried to make him stay away, he'd refused to let it go. Now that they were married, she wanted to make the best of their companionship. But without intimacy, she suspected that with each passing day, he would grow more resentful. Later, it might come between them, just as she'd suspected it would.

She couldn't let that happen. Already she'd lost her son. She didn't want to lose her husband, too.

Paul had tried to give her so much already—a gown for her wedding, a night together where he'd made her feel wonderful. Even a fine house that was nicer than the one she'd lived in for most of her life. The handsome physician had transformed into a viscount, almost like the fairy stories Margaret had read to them when they were growing up. Only Paul didn't seem happy about it. There was uneasiness in his demeanor, as if he felt unworthy of the title.

There had to be a way of making him feel comfortable in his new role. And she wanted to do whatever she could to help their marriage begin on the right note.

"You don't even ken what you do to me," he murmured, drawing his hands over her spine.

No, but she wanted to give him the same release that he'd given her. The idea of touching him intimately, of bringing him that same arousal that he'd given her, was a sense of power she'd never known. What would he do if she touched him and kissed him in the same way?

Without thinking, she drew her arms around him, bringing his body against hers. He was tense, his shoulders tight as she pressed close. "We should share one room. Not two." She raised her mouth to his and kissed him softly. With her lips open, she teased at him with her tongue, hoping to coax him out of his dark mood. He opened slightly, his mouth responding, while his hands moved to her spine. Against her hips, she felt the rise of his desire and heard the shift in his breathing.

A sudden restless yearning took hold of her as she continued kissing him, and she took his face between her hands. His cheeks were bristled from not shaving, and it reminded her of the primitive Highlander he was. Yet he was holding fast to his control, never taking command of the kiss. Beneath his mouth, she felt his silent discontent, as if he were made of stone.

"No. We won't." With that, Paul stepped around her and unlocked the door, leading the way down the hall.

It seemed her husband had no intention of being close to her again. And Juliette wondered if it was even possible to change it.

Beatrice had not owned a new gown in nearly ten years. After it arrived as a gift from Victoria for her birthday, she marveled at the yards of blue silk. She almost felt like a girl of twenty again and was eager to try it on.

"Happy birthday, Lady Lanfordshire." Mrs. Larson beamed, helping her to lift the gown over her head. "Ye'll look bonny indeed in this. Lord Lanfordshire willna be able to keep his eyes off ye."

Beatrice flushed, hoping that was the case. Over the past few weeks, Henry had immersed himself in the ledgers, uneasy about their profits from Aphrodite's Unmentionables, but still trying to unravel years' worth of financial problems. She hoped that he would put the books aside tonight, at least.

"Will Her Grace be joining ye and Lord Lanfordshire for supper tonight?" Mrs. Larson asked, as she finished buttoning up the new gown. "I could bake a cake, if it pleases my lady."

"I've invited Victoria and His Grace," Beatrice admitted. "I hope they will come, and yes, a cake would be lovely." Though Victoria's pregnancy was advancing rapidly, she was glad for her daughter's company.

Mrs. Larson helped her fix her hair, and when it was done, Beatrice stared at the woman in the looking glass. The years had left their mark on her, and although she'd begun gaining back some of the weight she'd lost, she could no longer look at herself and see a young woman. There were lines around her eyes, and her neck showed the signs of aging. She gave a sigh and turned away. Some things couldn't change.

When Henry came into their room, she forced a smile. "I haven't seen you for most of the day."

"I've been busy." He hardly glanced at her, and she waited for him to say something about the gown. Instead, he went to the writing desk and opened several drawers in search of a pen.

Her earlier happiness deflated instantly. But then, he hadn't really looked at her.

She crossed over to the desk and stood directly beside him, waiting. At last, he glanced up. His eyes passed over her updo, which Mrs. Larson had threaded with matching ribbon. Then he briefly saw the gown, but said nothing. "Was there something you wanted?"

Yes, she wanted to blurt out. *I want you to notice me. I want you to see the wife you've been married to for over twenty years, and not just the mother of your daughters.*

"Will you be joining us for supper tonight?" she asked. "Victoria and His Grace might come."

He frowned a moment. "Shouldn't she be at home, in her condition? Do you think it wise for her to travel?"

"We live a few miles from them," Beatrice pointed out. "And it's only supper."

"Why would they come?" Henry asked. "And why are you all dressed up?"

"It's my birthday today," she pointed out. Clearly he'd forgotten. "And since this gown was a gift from our daughter, I thought it only polite to wear it."

"Oh." He found the pen he'd been searching for and closed the desk. "Then I suppose I ought to join you, then."

"If it wouldn't inconvenience you." It took effort to keep the frost from her voice, as though nothing were wrong. She should have known he wouldn't remember.

Henry nodded, and a moment later, a smile came over his face. "I do have a gift for you, Beatrice, as it turns out. I suppose since it's your birthday, I might as well give it to you now. I sent for it from London." He went to the chest of drawers on the far end of their bedroom and opened the bottom drawer.

Some of her resentment dissipated. Perhaps she'd been too quick to jump to conclusions. He *had* been gone to war for years, after all. With all that he'd been through, perhaps a birthday wasn't something he thought about very much. Curiosity filled her when she saw the small brown-paper parcel.

When he gave it to her, the weight of the package surprised her. A sense of excitement filled her, as she wondered what gift he'd sent for, all the way from London. It couldn't be the sapphire bracelet, for this was too heavy, and she'd sold that, years ago. Silver, perhaps?

She untied the strings and folded back the paper only to reveal a set of three brass doorknobs, complete with locks and metal keys. It took her a moment to realize that yes, he had indeed given her doorknobs for her birthday. Not silver. Not a token of affection.

Doorknobs.

A tightness took hold in her stomach, and she couldn't find the words to say anything.

"After the fire, I thought we should protect ourselves with a set of new locks," Henry explained. "I'll have them put in, and then you'll be safe from the danger."

Beatrice set down the doorknobs, forcing the air in and out of her lungs. He truly thought it was a good gift. That was what rattled her the most. He didn't know that anything was wrong.

With extreme effort, she kept herself from breaking into tears. "Take them, if you want," she said quietly. "I wish to be alone for a while."

"Don't you . . . like them?" He rewrapped the doorknobs in the paper, staring at her as if he genuinely didn't understand why she would be upset. "They're made of solid brass, Beatrice."

"I'm sure they will be fine. Please go." Before she made a fool of herself and started weeping in front of him.

Only when the door closed behind her husband did she realize how utterly hopeless it was. She was wedded to a stranger who had been away to war so long, they didn't know each other. She let the tears fall, gripping her handkerchief in one fist.

The door opened again, and he caught her crying. "Beatrice, what is it?"

"Nothing," she sniffed, reaching for a handkerchief. She didn't want to discuss it, especially now. Her own daughter had sent her a lovely gown, remembering her fondness for the color blue. And as for her husband—she knew he hadn't remembered her birthday.

"You didn't like them, did you?" he said.

A bitter laugh caught her. "What woman would want doorknobs for her birthday, Henry?"

At his bewildered look, she shook her head. "It doesn't matter. I don't need anything. Just . . . try to remember to come to supper tonight at seven. Your daughter will want to see you."

His expression grew shielded, but he nodded. "I'll be there."

She went to sit beside the window, resting her face against one hand. Henry wasn't going to change. She'd grown old while he was gone and had become the wallpaper wife. One always there, hardly noticeable at all.

She'd simply never expected it to hurt so much.

Although they'd gone their own ways in the house, Paul could see that Juliette didn't understand why he needed the distance. He'd been an utter fool when he'd thought he could marry her and be content with not making love to her.

It wasn't as if she were walking around naked. No, she was dressed like a lady, she behaved like a lady, and he needed to stop thinking of her in that way.

But his mind would not let go of the sensation of having her bare skin against his own. She'd been so trusting, letting him have that moment. He'd wanted to spend all night exploring her body, watching her unravel before him. She was the girl he'd dreamed of marrying . . . and he wanted her to be happy.

He'd never expected that the night they'd shared together would cause such resentment in him. Not toward her, but toward the man who had hurt her.

Paul walked outside, hoping the physical exertion would give him the peace he craved. Jealousy was darkening his temper, and he needed to control it before he lashed out against the person he cared most about. Strathland had been inside her. He'd made her pregnant and given her a son she loved with all her heart. A son she'd had to give away.

Because of the violence, he couldn't destroy those memories or eradicate Strathland's presence. Every time Paul looked at his wife, he imagined her pain and fear. It broke him apart to know that he hadn't been there for her. He hadn't saved her.

And he still couldn't save her, teaching her what it was to be with a man who loved her. She would never be mother to a son or daughter of his blood.

His gut twisted with anger and the need to kill Strathland. That would have to be his purpose now. Damned if poverty was enough for the earl. Paul wanted blood.

For nearly an hour, he walked across the land, unable to accept that it now belonged to him. It felt as if he'd stolen an inheritance from a more worthy man. He didn't know the first thing about managing an estate or making sense of the ledgers.

But he knew someone who *could* make sense of them. He'd promised her the ledgers, after all.

With Juliette's help, they both might make sense of his uncle's holdings and work together to continue the profits. And when she was comfortable running the estate without him, he would turn to what mattered most.

Killing the man who had taken away everything.

There were days when being sixteen years old was a plague. Amelia knew she was lucky to even attend assemblies, but it bothered her that she was too young to speak to anyone under the age of forty.

She had her eye on Viscount Lisford. It didn't matter that he was five-and-twenty. He was dashing and kind. His manners were exquisite, and he never once made a misstep when he danced.

She sent him the brightest smile she could muster, hoping that he would see her pining from across the room. Even if she was too young now, she could marry within two years.

Two. It sounded like eternity. She'd heard of a few young women who had married at seventeen, but when she'd asked about it, Mother had promptly informed her that the women had married because they *had to*. Whatever that meant.

"Don't you think it's time you went up to bed?" Margaret asked from behind her. "It's after midnight."

"*You* aren't going to bed yet."

"No, I'm not." The serene look upon her older sister's face was irritating.

"And how is your quest for a husband progressing?" Amelia tried to keep the bitterness out of her voice, but truly, it wasn't fair that Margaret was old enough to do everything, while she had to remain pinned to Aunt Charlotte's side.

To her surprise, Margaret blushed. "There might be someone. But I came to ask you about Juliette's letter."

"She asked me to send half a dozen of the *you-know-whats* to her." Standing on tiptoe, she whispered in Margaret's ear, "She wanted the most seductive we had."

Margaret fanned herself furiously. "Well, I—I suppose Juliette *has* been married for nearly a fortnight now."

"I took some of the extra garments that Victoria sent us and had them posted to Edinburgh instead. Madame Benedict doesn't need to know about them."

"I still don't like the risk." Margaret lowered her fan, frowning. "Though I have been glad about the money."

"No one will know," Amelia promised. "Our secret is entirely safe. In the meantime, we can continue to stand on the edges of the crowd like ninnies, hoping for a man to smile at us."

Waiting around was not Amelia's strong suit. She much preferred to make decisions and act upon them.

At that moment, the object of her adoration turned and began walking straight toward them. Amelia went breathless as the Viscount Lisford crossed the room. She half expected angels to begin singing when he smiled in her direction.

"Miss Andrews, I believe the next dance is mine?" he said.

Yes. A thousand times, yes.

But with horror, Amelia realized he was speaking to Margaret. Prim and proper Margaret. Not her.

The angels suddenly began screeching off-key in her brain. *It's a dance,* she told herself. *Only a dance.*

But from the way her sister was returning Viscount Lisford's smile, she knew what *that* meant. The "someone" Margaret had spoken of was escorting her to join in a country dance.

All the happiness within her dried up into a hollow shell. Margaret had *known* how much she wanted the viscount. She'd known it, but she'd gone and smiled at him anyway. Whatever happened to her complaints that Viscount Lisford gambled at White's? And what about their Sisters' Meeting, where Margaret had been more interested in the Earl of Castledon?

Whirling around, Amelia was prepared to march away when she crashed into a gentleman standing behind her. "Oh! I'm sorry. I didn't see you there."

Good Heavens. It was the Earl of Castledon—otherwise known to her as Sir Personality-of-a-Handkerchief. He was the very last person she wanted to encounter. A quick escape was what she needed.

"I should have watched where I was going," she apologized. "I didn't see you at all."

"I was busy being a wallflower," he remarked drily. "It doesn't surprise me that you never noticed."

She took a closer look and realized that he wasn't entirely

bad-looking. A little average, but he was exceptionally tall, and his blue eyes were nice.

"Men aren't wallflowers," she said. "The term is too delicate for a man. Stoic is a better word, I think. Or aloof."

He eyed her in silent amusement. "Or I could be a wall-hedge instead of a flower. Shrubbery would be more masculine, don't you think?" From the ironic look in his eyes, she suspected he was making fun of her.

Distracted, she answered, "Yes. That's it exactly." With a glance, she saw her aunt signaling her from across the room.

Right. She wasn't supposed to be talking to men or to be seen in their presence. She hadn't made her debut, and it was inappropriate to be anywhere near an unmarried man, even if he was harmless.

But as she apologized again and excused herself, she couldn't help but cast another longing glance at the viscount of her dreams. Margaret wouldn't try to steal Viscount Lisford, would she? Her sister truly ought to be with a man like Lord Castledon. A handkerchief who was kind, well-mannered, and likely would do whatever a woman told him to.

But from her sister's blushing face, Amelia suspected that her worst fears might happen after all.

Chapter Fifteen

Juliette sat at the large mahogany desk, surrounded by ledgers. Her hands were stained with ink, and she'd spent hours deciphering Donald Fraser's handwriting. Scraps of paper lay all over the desk, figures she'd tallied regarding the estate's assets.

Her husband was not poor. Not tremendously wealthy, either, but his uncle had left him with several hundred acres of land. There was another estate, far to the north, which supposedly had sheep and acres for grazing, but it wasn't clear if that house was suitable for a residence. Then there was another estate in the northwest region. Already she'd scribbled half a dozen ideas on how to increase their profits.

She set down her pen, still awed that Paul had given her command of the estate ledgers. It had been such a comfort to immerse herself in numbers, adding the columns and sorting everything into rents paid and bills that needed to be handled. It might have been an unusual gift for a new wife, but she was grateful to have a way of spending her hours. Especially since her husband had been avoiding her.

Despite her desire for a shared bedroom, he'd given her a room of her own, two doors down from his own.

Almost as if he didn't trust himself not to open an adjoining door.

Their life had fallen into a pattern. Rising, eating meals together, and then he went to meet with the tenants, ensuring that they had everything they needed. At night, he gave her a kiss on the cheek, and then they went off to their own rooms.

It bothered her more than it should. Ever since the first night they'd shared together, she'd grown restless, realizing that she wanted more from this marriage. Her husband was keeping a respectful distance, and it irritated her. She wanted that closeness back, of being wedded to her best friend.

After she wrote to Victoria, her sister had sent a letter containing instructions that had made Juliette blush. But then, she'd wanted to know about ways of satisfying a husband. Her sister's response had been eye-opening, to say the least. Even better, a package had arrived from Amelia that Juliette believed would help to make things right with Paul.

Footsteps approached the study, and she glanced up to see her husband standing in the doorway. "Did you find everything in order?" he asked. His hair was windblown from riding, and his coat was askew. She rose from her chair and went to greet him.

"I did, yes." She kissed him on the cheek, and added, "I think I've sorted it all out. If you'd like me to go over the figures with you—"

"I'll leave it to your judgment," he said. "Just tell me what you're wanting to do, and you needn't worry." His demeanor was distracted, as if his mind were elsewhere. He was staring above her, outside the bay window.

"What is it?" she asked.

He withdrew a folded piece of paper from his coat. "I've received a letter from my mother, asking me to come back to Ballaloch."

"Is something wrong?"

"That's just it. Ne'er in my life has she written to me. It's no' her way." He held out the letter, and Juliette took it. "I've no idea if she can even hold a pencil."

"Obviously, she can, if she took the time to write to you." Juliette smoothed out the paper, studying the note. Bridget informed her son that she needed him there to help with some of the crofters who were wounded. She urged him to come quickly.

"My mothers hasna asked for my help for as long as I can remember," Paul said. "I don't think she wrote this letter. Someone else did. Someone who wants me back at Ballaloch."

And Juliette suspected she knew who that someone was—Brandon Carlisle, the Earl of Strathland. "How did he find us?"

"It's no' difficult. Not since I became the viscount." He took back the letter and replaced it in his pocket. "The question is: What is he wanting?"

"Nothing good," Juliette said. "He's angry at us and at me for wedding you."

"He canna change that." Paul took her hands and drew her into his arms. She rested her cheek against his heart, and the scent of his skin made her want to cling even tighter. But he tensed the moment she did.

"You'll stay here," he told her. "I'll go and find out what's happening."

"No. We'll go together," she insisted. She wasn't about to remain behind while he went in search of trouble.

"You're daft if you think I'm going to take you into harm's way. You'll stay, and that's that."

"Is it? And what's to stop me from following you, after you've gone?" She knew, even if he wouldn't admit it, that Strathland was foremost in Paul's mind. He fully intended to avenge what had happened to her. "You're not thinking clearly," she said softly. "You're acting on instinct instead of logic."

"I willna hide from him, Juliette. He's hurt everyone I love, and I'll no' hide away outside of Edinburgh while he threatens my family."

She stilled, realizing what he'd said. *Everyone I love.*

Did he love her, then? He'd never said it, though she'd suspected as much. The word dug into her heart, for the look in his eyes gave her the truth.

He did love her. And because of it, he was planning to walk directly into danger, to ensure that Strathland never again hurt any of them. As he'd said, he wouldn't hide.

But that was what she was doing, wasn't she? Hiding away in this house, running from the man who had taken so much.

"What will you do when you confront him, Paul?"

He stared back at her, his eyes full of hatred and frustration. "I'm going to kill him."

Her breath exhaled in a rush, for that was what she'd feared. "And when you're caught? What then?"

"I don't care what happens to me. He deserves death for what he did to you. A thousand times over. And if I'm the one to bring him to justice, it means that he canna ever hurt anyone again."

"*I* would care what happens to you." She took his hand in hers and drew it to her face. "Do you think I want to be a widow?"

He shook his head and shrugged. "I'm hardly much of a husband to you, as it is."

"You're right," she said suddenly. His gaze narrowed, as if he'd never expected her to say it. "It isn't much of a marriage. You sleep apart from me, and we only see one another at mealtimes."

"That was the marriage you wanted," he pointed out. "Or did you forget that we can no' be sharing more than that?"

"We could, if you weren't so afraid."

"It wouldna take much for me to go over the edge, Juliette." His hand curled against the back of her neck, and goose bumps rose over her skin. He wanted her badly, and she intended to ease the ache inside of him.

Juliette crossed back to the window and drew the drapes shut. "Lock the door."

The room was dark, the air charged with anticipation. She wasn't afraid of him, and knowing that their marriage would never be consummated had given her a boldness she'd never expected. He was wound up so tightly, she suspected that if she didn't find a way to satiate his desires, their lives would break apart.

Her sister had given her a few ideas. And although they were shocking, Juliette wanted to touch her husband. She wanted to see him come apart, feeling the intense pleasure that he'd given her.

"What are you wanting, Juliette?" he demanded.

"Lock it," she repeated. "I'm wanting some time with my husband. Before he goes off like a hot-tempered lad, to fight an enemy who's not worth the mud on the ground." She had his full attention, but he still hadn't locked the door. So she went and did it for him, taking the key away.

"Juliette, don't be starting something we canna finish."

She set the key down and approached him, resting her hands upon his heart. "Will you ever stop talking?"

His eyes grew hooded, and she ran her hands up his spine, watching the way his muscles tightened. It was like trying to melt a stone, and she turned around in his arms. "You left me, the first night we were together. And I never had the chance to touch you the way I wanted to."

There seemed to be a desperate hunger raging within him with every touch of her hands. When she removed his coat, he reached for the back of her gown. Juliette held her breath, hoping he would like the undergarments she'd chosen. Her sister had promised that Paul would appreciate them.

"How were you wanting to touch me?" he asked.

"The way a wife does. The way that pleases you," she said, lifting her mouth up to be kissed. His hands were rapidly unfastening the buttons, his kiss turning hotter. She stood on her tiptoes, welcoming the feeling of his hands upon her. When she loosened his shirt and lifted it over his head, her palms went to touch his bare skin. She broke the kiss and moved her lips to his chest, swirling her tongue over his skin. He tore out the pins in her hair, letting it fall to her shoulders.

"Take off the gown," he ordered, and she lifted it away. When he saw the gauzy material of her chemise and the emerald corset, he reached out to touch the silken fabric. The corset supported her breasts, but the sheer chemise revealed every curve.

"Where did you get this?" he demanded.

"From my sister."

"God bless her." He started to unlace it, but Juliette stopped him.

"Not yet." She led him over to the desk and bade him stand against it. This wasn't about her—she wanted to learn about his body and what he desired. She reached for his waist and drew her hands around him. His face was unreadable, and when she touched the first button of his trousers, his hands covered hers.

"I don't like seeing you this way," she murmured. "You're unhappy and avoiding me." Her hands were trembling on the first trouser button. She knew what her sister had told her to do, but fear held her back. She didn't know if he would want her to touch him in that way or if it would please him the way Victoria had said it would.

He held her gaze in his and opened the first button. "I'm not unhappy at all."

"Aren't you?" She opened the second button, and his hard length both intrigued her and terrified her.

"You're doing a fine job of arousing me." His mouth curved into a wicked smile. "But then, I suppose you know that."

"May I . . . touch you, then?"

"Aye." His eyes held unbridled lust as he finished helping her unbutton his trousers. He removed his drawers, standing naked before her. Instinct roared at her to be afraid, but this was different than the night she'd been violated. This man was her husband, a man who loved her. He was offering himself without any barriers at all.

And she held all the power over him.

Her hands trailed downward, to touch his hardened flesh. He was smooth and warm, a column of heat. From the moment her hand curled around him, he drew her close, inhaling sharply. She was dimly aware that he was loosening her stays, but she was too fascinated by him. Slowly, she moved her hand against his shaft and was rewarded with a bead of moisture on the tip.

"Lift up your hands," he ordered. When she obeyed, he removed the corset and swiftly stripped away the chemise. Though the room was dark, she was self-conscious of being bare before him. The last time had been safely beneath the covers.

"God above, I could kneel before you and worship," he said roughly. He didn't ask permission but bent his head and took her breast into his mouth. She shuddered at the wet heat, bending and yielding against the onslaught.

Each time he touched her, it was easier. He was kissing her with reverence, arousing the needs she'd never known were there. As he suckled her, she reached out to him again, caressing his length with her hand. He pulled her to him, so that he was cradled against her petticoat between her legs.

"Wait," she murmured. "I wanted this to be about you. I wanted to please you."

"A chrìdhe, don't you know that touching you pleases me?" His gaze turned heated. "I could do this all day. And before I leave in the morning, I'm wanting you to remember this. Remember what it was between us."

He spoke as if he didn't plan to return, and her bones went cold at the thought. "I'll remember it because you're coming back to me," she insisted.

When he didn't answer, the coldness turned to ice. "Paul, you *are* coming back."

"I might." But the tone of his voice sounded unconvinced. "But that doesna matter. You have this house, and you're wise enough to mind the accounts. You'll always be taken care of. Safe."

"You're not going to leave me a widow," she commanded. "Look at me, Paul. I don't care what Strathland did to us. If I can put it in the past, so can you."

The words struck hard, for she realized they were true. She *did* want to move forward, to erase all the shadows.

She touched his face with both hands, drawing his mouth to hers. He kissed her with fervor, his hands moving everywhere. She removed her petticoat and stockings until she stood fully naked before him.

Although the door was locked, there was a sense of danger, almost as if anyone could walk in on them. Against the far wall was a small velvet settee.

She took his hand and led him toward it. He started to guide her down, but she shook her head. "You lie down first."

He obeyed, and she ran her hands over him. Touching every hard line of muscle, learning where his skin was softer. And when her hand brushed against his erection, he gave an audible intake of breath.

She studied him, wondering what he would like. He'd enjoyed it when she'd touched him, and she did so again, exploring the hard ridge and the soft sac that hung below. His fingers dug into the velvet, but he spoke not a word.

Although he looked as if he were in pain, not once did he tell her to stop. Instead, he leaned into her touch, increasing the pressure.

She lowered her mouth to his heart, and her bare breasts pressed against him. He surged forward between them, and she thought of how wonderful his mouth had felt upon her nipples. Would he . . . want her to kiss him as well?

She moved to his nipple and licked at it, watching the way he responded. His hands slid into her hair, and he pushed her lower.

Juliette kissed at his stomach, her hands caressing his ribs and moving to his legs. Paul surrendered to her touch, letting her do as she wished, and she reveled in the complete control. He would not force her to do anything—all of it was her choice.

Lower still, and his erection brushed against her cheek. She wasn't certain if he would want her to do this, but she brushed her mouth against the side of his length.

"God above, Juliette," he gasped. "You're killing me, lass."

"Should I—should I stop?"

"I would die a happy man, just like this," he admitted. "Don't be stopping, unless you're wanting to." He reached down to touch her cheek. "I am yours to do with as you will."

She cupped him with one hand and took the head of him into her mouth. His hands clenched into fists, and a dark groan spilled from him. "Christ in Heaven, aye. That's it, love."

It startled her to realize that pleasing him was deepening her own arousal. As she took him in her mouth, she was growing wetter, imagining him inside. She was stroking him in a rhythm, tasting the salt of him as he strained against her. And when she sucked against him, he abruptly lifted her away from him and laid her flat on her back, reversing their positions.

With his hands, he lifted her knees, kissing the flat of her stomach before moving to her inner thighs. "It's my turn now, Juliette."

His turn for what?

Ohhh . . . She nearly came apart when she felt him spread her apart, his tongue tasting her intimately. The fist of pleasure gripped her hard as he nibbled and tasted. "Do you like it, lass?"

She couldn't grasp a single thought.

"You're so wet," he breathed against her. The vibration of his voice against her made her tremble. He explored her folds, licking and sucking until he found the nodule that made her cry out.

"Did I hurt you?"

"No. More of that, please," she begged, guiding his mouth to her sensitive place. As he took her higher, he invaded her with his fingers. Over and over, he pressed the rhythm, until she was shivering, so close to the edge. She reached for his erection, fisting him in her hand at the same pace.

More. She needed him to give himself to her. Despite the erotic thrill of his touch, it still wasn't enough. Keeping him tightly in her hand, she moved his hand away from her, and guided him inside.

He slid easily, with no pain. And when he was buried within her, he went motionless. "We can't do this, Juliette." He started to pull out, but she raised one leg over his waist and pulled him back. The sensation was every bit as wonderful as she'd imagined it would be. With Paul, there was no degradation. Lovemaking was a way of joining them together.

Her mind cried out that it was too grave of a risk. He could make her pregnant, and this time, a baby might end her life.

But was it any life at all, to live with a man she loved and not give him this part of her? She was his wife now, and she did love him. He was the man who had been there for her, all these years.

"I won't risk you," he said.

She locked her ankles around him, refusing to let him go. "You're going to fight Strathland, aren't you?"

He nodded, and when she moved against him, he shut his eyes, as if struggling for control.

"I don't want you to die," she whispered.

"And what do you think this is, Juliette? You said another child could kill you."

"It's a risk I'll take. Especially if you're planning to endanger your own life. If this is the last moment I'll have with you, then I want this. No matter what the price."

He opened his eyes, and the intensity of the blue mesmerized her. Inside her body, he was iron hard, his shaft fully sheathed within.

"Why?"

"Because I love you," she whispered. "And I always have." She relaxed the grip of her legs and pushed forward against him.

He pressed down upon her, using his arms to balance his weight. "There is a way . . . with less risk." He was fighting against his words, and he gritted out, "If I don't finish inside you."

"Be with me," she pleaded. "Give me this memory."

Paul was lost. He wanted Juliette so badly, the slightest motion was going to send him over the edge. Her slick heat and the tightness of her body were clenched around his shaft. He was a selfish bastard for letting things get this far.

But in her eyes, he saw the mirror of his own feelings. "I love you, Juliette." And he didn't want her to sacrifice everything for this.

She began lifting her hips to him in gentle penetrations. Sweet and innocent, she was giving so much. And when her arousal shifted higher, her breath coming in short gasps, he lost it. His body took over with instinct, and he sank inside her.

Heaven. This had to be what Heaven was. Making love to the woman he'd adored ever since the moment he'd met her. She had her eyes closed, and he couldn't resist lowering his mouth to her breast, teasing her nipple as he entered and withdrew.

"It feels good," she breathed. "So good."

Encouraged by her response, he took her nipple in deeper, shifting the rhythm of his penetration. In and out, he took her, watching to see when she pushed against him and when she hesitated.

"Faster?" he prompted, and she nodded, holding on to his hips. As he quickened the pace, her skin grew hotter. Perspiration rose upon her skin, and she moaned as he plunged inside.

She panted hard as he thrust, and when he lifted her bottom, changing the angle, she started to tremble violently. A harsh cry broke from her, and she shattered against him. White heat clenched him, and her release was all it took to make him withdraw fast, his seed spilling over her stomach.

Thank God he'd stopped in time.

He lay atop her, unable to believe what had just happened. Neither spoke, though he held her against him for long moments.

At last, he ventured, "Are you all right? I didna hurt you, did I?" He rolled to his side, searching her for a response.

"It was wonderful," she whispered. He used a handkerchief to help clean her skin, and she moved her leg atop him, snuggling close. "Just as I imagined it would be." She reached up to touch his cheek and lifted her mouth to his for a kiss.

He returned it, his hands moving over her soft skin. She was more beautiful to him than she'd ever been, with her hair tousled and her face flushed from their lovemaking.

"I love you," he said, stroking down her back to her bottom. And he'd loved every moment. She had bound him to her intimately, and it gratified him to know that Strathland had never given her this. The only joy Juliette had known in joining with a man was with *him*.

Paul kissed her throat, moving lower to her breasts. With his mouth and tongue, he nipped at each, circling until he evoked another moan from her.

"I'm wanting to touch you like this for the rest of my life," he admitted. "Explore every inch of your skin. I'll ken what pleases you and what makes you sigh."

He pressed a kiss against her shoulder, and she whispered, "You're still going back, aren't you?"

"I have to." Though it was possible that the letter truly was from his mother, he doubted it. Regardless of the outcome, he needed to ensure that Bridget was safe. And that meant leaving Juliette behind.

He stroked her again, moving his hand across her thigh. She countered by pressing her palms against his chest. "I need to go with you," she said quietly.

"No." He wouldn't bring her into the face of danger, not if Strathland was there. "I still think the letter was sent by the earl."

"Had you thought that perhaps he's trying to lure you away, so that I'm here alone?" She traced his bare skin with her hand, and her suggestion made him frown. No, he hadn't considered that. Her theory held merit, clouding his decision to leave her.

"What if I'm *not* safe here?" she continued. "If he did send the letter, he must know where we are."

Paul gave no answer, torn by the need to keep her safe, whether she stayed behind or came with him. Slowly, he sat up and helped her to get dressed before he donned his own clothing. "You're right," he said at last. "That may be his intention exactly."

"Then I should go with you. So you can keep me safe." She turned to face him, when he'd finished buttoning up her gown. "Paul, my parents are there. And so are my sister and her husband, the duke. You're not the only one who can keep me protected. And I trust them more than I'd trust being here alone."

He embraced her hard. "Do you ken what it would do to me, if aught happened to you?"

"And what if something happened to you? It's no different at all," she insisted.

But it was. He didn't care about what happened to him. Keeping *her* safe meant everything.

"Don't let your desire for revenge overshadow good sense," she warned. "You must be careful." Her hands rubbed against his back, and though his mind roared that it wasn't right, he nodded.

"All right. We'll go together. But at any sign of danger—"

"I promise I'll go to my parents or to His Grace," she vowed. "I won't do anything stupid, Paul." She reached up to touch his hair, and the gesture of affection slid down to his heart. "Besides, it's time that you met my parents as my husband."

He didn't doubt that Lord Lanfordshire would have a great deal to say in regard to their elopement. "I canna say that I'm looking forward to *that* conversation."

"I have no regrets," she whispered. "And none at all about what happened today."

He could only hope that there were no consequences, despite the care he'd taken.

Chapter Sixteen

"**M**y lord . . . the fleeces were set on fire last night. All of the barns burned to the ground. The wool—it's gone."

Gone.

The word reverberated in his skull, and Brandon could hardly believe it was true. It couldn't be.

"All of it?" he asked quietly.

His factor appeared terrified, but he nodded. "I'm afraid so. We—we have nothing to sell now."

Rage and fear roared through with a violence that made Brandon want to put his fist through glass. He knew who had done this. Without a doubt.

He stared at his factor, whose face had gone white. The man *should* be afraid. It was *his* task to keep their supplies safe from raids. Not only had the orders diminished, but now he had no means of fulfilling those he did have.

"How?" he ground out.

"It was last night . . . the fires started all at once. We think some of the MacKinlochs were involved."

"Of course they were," he growled. He'd evicted them from their homes last winter and had ordered his previous factor to burn the dwellings. It was within his right, since *he* owned the land and everything upon it. He'd allowed them to take their possessions, but that was all. Anyone who had dared to defy him and remain had paid the consequences.

And there would be consequences for this, as well. They would pay for what they'd done.

If their lives were the cost, so be it.

The journey to the northwest region of Scotland took longer than she'd expected, but Juliette didn't mind. She never tired of watching the endless green hills and glens, nor the gray lochs nestled against taller mountains. Here, she felt her spirit softening. And though she missed her son, she didn't miss London.

They had traveled within their own private coach, stopping along the way in numerous inns. She'd spent every night in her husband's arms, and no longer did she fear him in any way. Though he hadn't made love to her a second time, they had spent hours learning what pleased one another.

Yet, she couldn't help worrying that their time together was slipping away.

"You're quiet," he said to her, moving across the space to sit beside her. "What is it?"

"I'm just uneasy about returning home. It seems so strange to think of it. I sent a letter to my mother, but we might reach Ballaloch before the letter does."

"Are you afraid of what your parents will think of me?" Though he spoke the words offhandedly, she wondered if he was still sensitive about his impoverished past.

"It doesn't matter what they think. I married you, and I intend for it to stay that way." She would never be ashamed of him, no matter what anyone said.

He squeezed her hand and stared out the window of the coach. They were close to Ballaloch now, but as they continued toward her parents' land, she scented smoke in the air. It was as if the fire had happened yesterday instead of five months earlier.

"Where is it coming from?" she asked Paul.

He shook his head. "I don't ken, but I'll find out." Knocking on the ceiling of the coach, he called out for the driver to stop. He swung open the door and then helped Juliette down. The summer air was warmer than she'd expected, and she shielded her eyes against the sun.

"It's coming from the earl's land, toward the east," he said.

"What burned?" she asked. Lord Strathland had ordered the crofters' homes destroyed over a year ago, to make more grazing room for the sheep. She couldn't think of what there was left to burn.

"These fires were more recent," Paul said, turning to face the air. "Within the past few days." He turned back to her. "We should go to your parents' house and learn what's happened."

She nodded in agreement, but stopped him before he could help her back inside the coach. "Paul, your mother—"

"I'll go to her, as soon as I've seen you safely to your house. It should be finished by now, from what I've heard."

Even so, her earlier feelings of uneasiness continued to grow. It wasn't safe here. Not for her family, and certainly not for Paul and herself. He urged the driver to quicken their pace, and as they approached her father's land, the scent of smoke permeated the air, cloaking it with the scent of death.

When they reached her family's house, she was glad to see that the stone exterior had been rebuilt, and it looked much the same as it had before. The two-story home rested atop a hillside while a gravel path led toward a clearing where only a few months ago, dozens of tents had been set up. Now, all the tents were gone, since the crofters had relocated to the Duke of Worthingstone's property to build permanent homes. Although it was quiet, she heard the sound of chickens clucking and the clang of pots from Mrs. Larson's kitchen.

Paul took her hand and led her to the door. "Stay here until I return for you."

"I think you should come inside and speak with my father and mother," she said. "Before you go dashing off again."

"I feel in my bones that something bad has happened, Juliette.

I need to see that my mother is unharmed. Then I'll be meeting with His Grace to learn how the crofters were involved with these fires."

"And if something bad did happen? I don't want you caught in the midst of it." She gripped his hand tighter, as if she could force him to stay.

"I'm still a physician, Juliette. If anyone was hurt, I have to be there."

There was nothing she could say to argue with that. He had an intrinsic need to help others. Despite his new title, that would never change.

"When will you return?"

"I don't ken. But if I'm not back by tonight, sleep without me. I'll come to you when I can."

It sounded as if he had no intention at all of returning. Although they had been home only a matter of minutes, she sensed the way he'd shifted. He intended to face the danger alone, leaving her safely behind guarded walls.

"If you don't come back, I'll go out looking for you," she warned. Though he started to argue, she touched a finger to his mouth. "Promise you'll return."

"I will." Paul kissed her swiftly and ordered the driver to bring her belongings to her. Then he took one of the horses and disappeared across the glen.

But she didn't believe him.

❧

"What's happened?" Paul demanded, when he reached Bridget. His mother's gown was covered in blood, and his heart nearly stopped.

"Oh, thank God ye've come. There are so many wounded. I could use your hands, lad."

A rush of relief filled him to know that the blood wasn't hers. "Who was wounded and how?" he asked.

Bridget wiped her hands on a cloth and began assembling bandages and herbs into her basket. "The factor and Strathland's man came last night and began shooting. There's a dozen or more wounded. I've been working all night." The exhaustion on her face gave evidence to that, and Paul rolled up his sleeves.

"Did you write a letter, sending for me?" he asked.

Bridget shook her head. "No, but I'm glad ye've come."

He sobered, knowing that his instincts had been correct. Strathland had indeed wanted to lure him here.

His mother poured water into a basin and handed him a cake of lye soap. Paul scrubbed his hands, and said, "Tell me who's hurt, and I'll handle the others while you rest."

"Not yet. Only when we've seen to all of them." She took a deep breath and led him outside, her basket looped over one arm.

"Why would Strathland attack the crofters?" Paul demanded. "They're no longer living on his lands."

"Someone set fire to all of his wool stores a few days ago. He's got naught to sell now, and he took his vengeance on the innocent, to punish the guilty ones."

"Do you think they truly attacked?" Although there were many of the MacKinlochs who were hot-tempered, destroying all of Strathland's wool was an outright act of war.

"It hardly matters now," she remarked, hurrying toward one of the huts. "Strathland thinks they did."

And that was enough for murder.

Paul followed his mother, grimacing at what lay ahead. But Bridget slowed her pace before they reached the first house. "Ye wed Miss Juliette Andrews, I understand. And ye didna think to ask if _I_ would want to attend the wedding? You're my only son, and I wanted to be there."

Paul didn't think now was the best time to discuss his marriage, particularly when there were men suffering from gunshot wounds. "We wed in haste" was all he said, trying to ignore his mother's chastisement. "How many were shot?" He stepped inside the dimly lit home and found a man lying upon a bed with a bloodstained bandage around his thigh.

"Thirteen," she said. "This is Alexander MacKinloch. He was shot in his leg, and I've done what I could to stop the bleeding."

The man was in his early fifties, so far as Paul could gauge. He was lying upon a low bed, and a blanket covered most of his torso, hiding the position of the gunshot wound.

"I'm thirsty. Could I have some water?" The man's voice was tremulous, and Paul said, "We'll see about some water in a moment." Drinking anything after being shot wasn't wise at all if there were internal injuries. Paul pulled back the blanket and saw that his mother had used a tourniquet on the man's upper thigh. Even so, the bandage was stained dark red.

As soon as Paul saw the location of the wound, he knew. The bleeding wasn't going to stop. The bullet had nicked too close to the artery, and there was nothing either of them could do to save this man.

His mother sent him a silent question. He knew she'd used the tourniquet to sustain life, in the hopes that they might amputate the leg and save him. But it was far too late for that. All he could do was make the man's last moments comfortable.

"Have you a wife, Mr. MacKinloch?" he asked, reaching for his bag.

"N-no," the man said, shivering hard. "My wife died a year ago in the fires."

"Any children? Or grandchildren, perhaps? Sometimes a man can heal quicker if his family is with him." He exchanged a look at Bridget, who nodded and left the hut.

He reached inside his bag for a tiny vial containing a tincture of opium. A few drops would ease the man's pain.

At times like these, he wished there were a way to suture an artery or cauterize the wound to stop the bleeding. But the femoral artery was too deep below the flesh. The gunshot wound had blown apart all hope of saving this man. It was a miracle that he'd survived this long.

"M-most of my family left Ballaloch," Alexander admitted. "I'm s-so cold." His body began to shudder as it slipped deeper into shock.

Paul adjusted the tourniquet again, though it would do little good for this man. "Who burned Lord Strathland's wool? Have they found the one responsible for the fires?"

Alexander shook his head. "Might've been Joseph MacKinloch, Lady Lanfordshire's former footman. He's been causin' trouble, from what I've heard."

"I thought he fled to the coast." After he'd learned that the man was responsible for setting the Lanfordshire house on fire, Paul had demanded that MacKinloch leave or face trial.

Now that MacKinloch's sister was dead, it was entirely possible that Joseph had arranged for the wool to be destroyed. But he would have needed others to set so many fires.

The door opened at that moment, but instead of his mother entering, Juliette emerged in the dim light. "Mrs. Fraser thought I could help," she said. Her voice was bright and filled with encouragement. Though her gaze passed toward the bleeding man, her eyes focused upon Paul.

I'm here for you, she seemed to say. And though he didn't want to expose her to this man's pain, she appeared to have made up her own mind.

She went to sit beside Alexander and held his hand. "My husband is a doctor who studied in Edinburgh. If anyone can help you get better, it's he."

Juliette's hair was pulled up in a topknot, and her gown was the same light blue silk she'd worn earlier. She gave the man a gentle smile, and Paul didn't miss the look of gratefulness in his eyes. MacKinloch would believe anything Juliette told him, for Bridget had gone and fetched an angel of mercy.

Paul poured a few drops of the tincture of opium into a cup of water. The man's shivering increased, and Juliette rubbed his hands between her own. "There, you see, he's gone and prepared some medicine for you. You'll feel better quite soon." She took the cup from Paul and helped the man sit up to drink it. "There are some friends outside, praying for your recovery. Would you like to see them?"

"I'd rather hold the hand of a bonny lass," he admitted. "They can come in a wee bit later."

Paul met Juliette's gaze. Though both of them knew that no medicine would cure his wounds, the opium would ease his pain and make the passing easier.

"Of course," she said gently. But as his wife calmed MacKinloch and spoke soothing words to him, all Paul could think of was how devastated he would be if anything ever happened to her. He'd saved many lives over the years, and lost just as many.

She took MacKinloch's hand in hers, continuing to murmur comfort to the man. And though her words were meant to soothe him, they reminded Paul of a mother's comfort.

He'd taken that from her, stealing her away from her only son. And although he'd claimed that it was meant to protect the boy, he wondered if his own selfish reasons had intervened. He'd wanted Juliette to himself.

A woman like her was meant to be surrounded by bairns, opening her arms to them. Her voice was made to read bedtime stories and sing lullabies. But he would never father a child upon her. Not if her life was the price.

It took only a few minutes longer for MacKinloch's hands to relax their grip before he slipped into unconsciousness. When he checked the man's pulse, it was uneven and erratic. Juliette continued to hold Alexander's hand. Her green eyes met Paul's, and when Death's quiet hand took the man's final breath, she was still holding his palm.

Paul loosened the tourniquet, allowing the man to die in peace. "You didn't have to come," he said quietly, taking MacKinloch's hand away from hers and closing the man's eyes.

"I was already following you. Bridget found me and brought me here when I asked it of her." She reached out and embraced him. "There are more of them, aren't there?"

"Aye. She brought me to this man because he was closest to death. She thought I might have a way of saving him." He shook his head in regret. "No matter how many lives you save, these moments haunt you."

"You brought him comfort and peace. He died with no pain," she said. Her arms came around him, and she kissed him. The need to possess her, to take the comfort she offered, was undeniable. He gripped her hard, and he vowed that no matter how much she tempted him, he would be careful.

For he couldn't lose her. Not ever.

"Why don't you go and visit your sister?" he suggested. "I've many more men to see. I'll find you later."

She pulled back, but he let his hands trail down her neck. "We're staying with my parents," she told him. "Now that the house is rebuilt, there will be rooms enough for us."

"Or we could stay with your sister and Worthingstone." He didn't relish confronting her family after the elopement. Even with his title, there would be repercussions from their actions. The idea of sleeping under the same roof was not a welcome one. But neither could they dwell with Bridget. His mother lived in a one-room house, which was even worse.

"I've already spoken with my mother," Juliette said. "She knows of your title. That will help."

"And your father?"

She sent him a rueful smile. "That may take some time."

And well he knew it. Paul led her to the door, wiping his hands on a handkerchief. "I'll be late, so don't be waiting on me."

"Would you rather I stayed with you to help?" Though he could see that she was serious, he doubted she'd have the stomach for what he had to do.

"No. I'd rather join you when it's done."

"Then I'll wait." She reached out and touched his cheek. He touched her hand, wishing he could hold on to this moment. And when she was gone, his mother returned.

A softness edged the corners of Bridget's mouth. "I ne'er thought I'd see the day when ye'd wed the likes of Juliette Andrews. I'm happy for ye, lad."

"Why did you never tell me what happened to her?"

Bridget sobered, her gaze fixed upon Juliette until she was out of earshot. "It was her secret to tell, no' for me to say." His mother led him away and added, "I'm glad she's wedded to ye, Paul. Ye'll be the one to give her the love she needs. Perhaps a child one day."

He said nothing, uncertain of how much Bridget knew. "No. There willna be children for us."

"It could happen, lad," Bridget said. "Och, there's time yet. It's only been a few weeks since ye wed her."

Nearly a month, but he didn't correct her. She led him inside the next house, and he let himself fall into the familiar routine of treating wounds. It was kinder to agree with his mother than to make her aware that there would never be any grandchildren.

She'd barely seen her husband in three days. Though Juliette had spent the time visiting with her family, Paul had immersed himself in caring for the wounded crofters. On the occasions when she brought him a basket of food, he'd wolfed it down, kissed her, and gone back to his work.

Her father hadn't spoken a word, pretending the marriage didn't exist. Her mother had smiled brightly and chattered on, asking questions about London and Aunt Charlotte. But beneath it all, she sensed the tension between her parents.

Henry Andrews kept to himself, offering little in the way of conversation. But sometimes Juliette caught him sneaking glances at her mother. He seemed bewildered, as if he didn't know her anymore. And Beatrice seemed on edge herself, hardly speaking to him.

For that reason, Juliette had decided to pay her older sister a visit this morning. She hoped Victoria could shed light on what was happening between their parents.

When she reached the duchess's house, her sister was blossoming in the glow of pregnancy. Juliette smiled as Victoria embraced her, laughing as she turned. "Soon, I'll have to hug you sideways. I'm getting larger every day."

"You're not at all," Juliette said. Her sister had a thickened waist with a slight bump, but certainly she wasn't large. "Are you feeling all right?"

"It's wonderful," Victoria answered, a softness stealing over her face. "Sometimes when I lie down at night, I feel the baby move inside. You can't imagine what that's like."

A tightness closed up in Juliette's throat. Yes, she knew exactly what it was like. "Do you know when the baby will be born?"

"I think in November," Victoria said. She bade Juliette to sit down beside her. "And what of you? Are you enjoying your married life?" There was enough of a blush on her sister's cheeks to know that she was referring to the most recent letters she'd sent, filled with advice.

Juliette nodded. "Paul is a good husband."

"I know Amelia was quite disappointed not to see the pair of you wed. She told me so in her letter. But we're all happy for you."

Victoria reached out and rubbed her swollen middle. "Perhaps you'll have a child next year as well."

"No," Juliette answered automatically. "That is . . . I don't think so."

Her sister glanced over at her. "It only takes once, Juliette. When was the last time you had your monthly?"

Exasperated, she shook her head. "I'm not going to have a child." The one time she had made love with Paul, he had not finished within her. And since then, they had been careful not to risk it again.

"Oh, you needn't worry," Victoria said. "A child will come when he's meant to."

"Well, not now," Juliette remarked. *Or ever.*

Victoria shrugged. "Well, if you've had your woman's time since you were married, I'm sure you're right."

Juliette's smile froze, as she stopped to think about it. For she *hadn't* bled. She counted back the weeks, and she was stunned to realize that it had been over a month since her last flow. Had it been five weeks or six? Her brain tried to reorder her scattered thoughts, reminding her that there was no reason to worry. A woman could miss her monthly and it would come again in time.

But we were careful, she thought to herself. Surely it couldn't have happened. Could it?

Her sister began speaking of Aphrodite's Unmentionables, talking about the sales and ideas for new designs. But her words blurred against the panic rising within Juliette.

"Margaret doesn't like the new designs," Victoria remarked. "But I believe they will sell quite well among married women. I know His Grace likes them very much. What do you think?"

"I'm sure they will be fine," Juliette answered, though she'd not heard a word of her sister's suggestions. In fact, she remembered nothing of the drawing Victoria had shown her. It could have been a white sheet and rope, for all she knew.

Inwardly, her panic had evolved into full-fledged terror. She couldn't be pregnant. Surely there was no chance at all. The very thought sent a cold storm of fear blasting through her.

She tried to remember her symptoms when she'd been pregnant with Matthew. Almost two weeks from the time she'd missed her monthly, she'd begun waking up ill. During those first few weeks, she'd been miserable, unable to keep any food down. And whoever had come up with the idea that it was a pregnancy sickness only in the mornings was completely wrong. She'd been sick from the moment she got up until the moment she fell into bed at night to sleep. All-day sickness was what it was.

But she wasn't feeling sick right now. Only the sense that her monthly was going to start at any moment. Surely she was imagining things.

"Victoria," she interrupted. "How have you been feeling during this pregnancy? Have you been sick at all?"

"Strangely, no," her sister admitted. "Everyone told me their stories of being sick, but I wasn't. Only hungrier than usual. And"—her face reddened—"my breasts have gotten much larger."

Juliette clenched her hands together. "I suppose His Grace is happy about that."

Her sister sent her a wicked smile. "Oh, yes. It was most gratifying to have a respectable bosom with no padding, for the first time in my life. In fact, that's why I considered designing unmentionables for women who are *enceinte*. Not only do I need a different corset, but I find that I am more sensitive to the fabric." Victoria rang for a tray of food, and went on to describe her ideas for the garments. She sketched out a sample, and after a moment said, "You're really not interested in this."

"No, I am. I'm just worried."

"About your husband?"

She nodded, though it wasn't the truth. She was mostly worried that she'd confused the dates of her menses. Over and over, she reminded herself that it was too soon to tell. After all the difficulties of the past few weeks, surely it was only anxiety that was causing it.

"I'm also worried about Mother and Father," Juliette said. "They're hardly speaking to one another. Do you know if everything's all right?"

Victoria shrugged. "I don't know. Mother pretends as if all is well, but they've been apart for three years. I think they had a row when Father learned about Aphrodite's Unmentionables. Mother refused to prevent us from continuing with our business. She said if His Grace didn't mind, neither should he."

Juliette eyed her sister. "I imagine that didn't go over well." But at least it explained the tension between her parents.

The tray of tea and sandwiches arrived at last. She took one, while her sister enjoyed three, laughing at herself while she ate. "I do believe I would eat anything that wasn't still alive and fleeing from me," Victoria admitted, reaching for another sheaf of papers. "And while I'm eating the rest of your sandwiches, why don't you tell me what you think of these, Juliette?"

She looked over the remaining sketches and offered her opinion. Yet, looking at the scandalous undergarments made her think of the night Paul had made love to her for the first time. Despite being terrified, she now was no longer afraid. It had been as wonderful as she'd thought it would be. And though it was impractical, she wanted to be with him again.

"Did I embarrass you with my last letter?" her sister asked, as she put away the sketches.

"Very much," Juliette answered honestly. "I never suspected—" Her words broke off, her face crimson at this conversation. "That is, Paul and I—"

"You don't have to say anything," her sister said, her own face growing red. "I know what you mean."

She was grateful at not having to go into detail.

"Where is Dr. Fraser now?" Victoria asked. "And is he truly a viscount? Was our mother overjoyed?"

Juliette gaped at her sister. "Do you have any more questions, or can I answer now?"

Victoria patted her stomach and waved her hand. "Go on."

"Yes, my husband is a viscount. He inherited the title when his uncle died this past spring, but he's still a physician. He went to tend the wounded, and one of the men died a few days ago." She shivered, though both of them had known the inevitable. "He comes home late at night and hasn't spoken to our parents yet."

"Tell him to be careful," Victoria advised. She sobered, adding, "My husband had to return to London, since he's been neglecting his duties at the House of Lords. He doesn't know about the shootings or Lord Strathland's return." Her face turned dark, with a warning look. "And you aren't going to tell him, either."

"Toria, you shouldn't stay here," Juliette argued. "Something might happen to you and the baby."

"I'm not going anywhere," the duchess insisted, shuddering at the thought. "I've finished with traveling, and I intend to stay here in Scotland until my child is born. Parliament will be out of session by the end of the summer, and His Grace will be back long before the birth."

"But what about Lord Strathland?" Juliette asked. "Don't you think he'll be a threat to you?"

Victoria shook her head. "Not if he wants to continue selling his wool in the years to come. My husband has spoken to the buyers, along with your husband." She added, "Strathland hasn't ventured near the house or me. And he won't. He's angry at the crofters, not us."

"I still don't think it's safe," Juliette insisted. Although her sister was deeply afraid of going outside, she wished Victoria would leave Scotland.

"Ever since the shootings, I've ordered our men and some of the crofters to patrol the borders of our land. Strathland's men have trespassed a few times, but we've kept them back." Victoria's expression remained calm. Her hand moved to her swollen womb, and her face softened as if she felt a light kick. "By the time His Grace returns, I'm confident there will be no danger at all."

Juliette didn't believe that, but neither did she want to upset her sister by saying so. To change the subject, she asked, "Are you hoping for a boy or a girl?"

As she'd hoped, Victoria smiled. "It doesn't matter at all. Whether it's a boy or a girl, I can't wait to hold my baby in my arms."

The swollen ache in Juliette's heart reared up again. She didn't know if she would ever hold Matthew again. The more time she spent away from him, the more she missed him.

"You'll hold your child soon enough," she told Victoria, trying to keep the thickness of tears from her voice. "Now, if you'll forgive me, I need to return home and talk to Father about Paul. Tonight, he should be finished with all the wounded."

"Is the Colonel being difficult again?"

Juliette nodded. "At first, he tried to put us in bedrooms on opposite sides of the house, until Mother intervened. When I told him of our marriage, he was furious. He said he would annul it because I was under the age of consent."

"He can't annul the marriage," Victoria pointed out. "It's not an English marriage. Furthermore, it's been consummated."

She nodded. "I know. Mother is trying to make him see reason, but he seems appalled at the idea of me sleeping with a man, even if he is my husband."

"He still believes we're perpetually six years old," Victoria said, sighing. "When he saw me pregnant, he turned bright red and started coughing into his handkerchief. I thought he would have an apoplectic fit right there."

Juliette smiled at the thought of their father's embarrassment. "I imagine he wanted to." Rising to her feet, she thanked her sister for the refreshments. "I should go, before Paul returns home."

Before she could leave, Victoria stopped her. "Thank you for coming to see me, Juliette. I've missed you so much." With a soft smile, she added, "And I think you *are* going to have a baby. There's something different about you."

Fear choked up inside her, but Juliette tried to paste a false smile on her face. "Perhaps."

She could only pray that her sister was wrong.

Chapter Seventeen

He'd saved six of the men. Besides the one who had bled out, another crofter had died of blood poisoning. His mother had been unable to get the bullets out, but Paul felt as if he'd battled Death and won. He'd hardly slept at all in three days. And yet, his mind and body were strung so tight, his awareness was honed to an edge.

The evening had begun to wane, the golden light fading into the purple of night. He'd taken a horse this day, and it felt good to ride along the edges of the duke's land, trying to release the tension. He wished Juliette were here now so he could ride with her, taking her into the mountains so he could lay her down on the grass.

Though he'd come to her each night, she'd been asleep, her body curled inward. He hadn't touched her at all, and he'd left before dawn each morning.

Her father hadn't been pleased to learn that they'd wed. Lord Lanfordshire hadn't raged or made threats. Instead, he'd gone quiet, his disapproval a palpable thing on the rare occasion when their paths had crossed.

It wasn't about money or rank. No, despite his inheritance, the baron seemed to see past the new wealth to the crofter's son who was more comfortable as a physician than a nobleman. A viscount would never soil his hands in the way Paul had. But the title was just that to him—a word. Not a social barrier that prevented him from helping others. He didn't know if Juliette's father would ever come to accept him. Or if that even mattered anymore.

He drew his horse to a stop at Eiloch Hill, on the outskirts of the duke's residence. A large tree was dense with foliage, its thick branches casting shadows upon the ground. His father had died here, upon this hill.

So many times, Paul wished he could go back and undo the choices he'd made as a lad. One reckless night had ended all of it. Were it not for his father's sacrifice, it would have been *his* body swinging from that tree.

He dismounted and climbed up the hillside, his steps heavy with regret. When he reached the thick oak tree, he touched the rough bark with one palm. And he imagined his father's hand upon his shoulder, Kenneth speaking to him in a deep voice.

One day you'll make your mark on the world, lad. Be sure that you can look back on your life and be proud of what you've done.

He wished his father were alive today. No doubt Kenneth would smile if he knew Paul had married Juliette. His father had always liked her.

And although Kenneth had never once revealed his past, Paul understood why his father had given up so much. He'd loved his wife enough to surrender everything for her. Sometimes he'd caught his parents whispering together, even holding hands. It had given him a sense of security, knowing that he was loved and that they had loved one another.

He'd do the same for Juliette, if it were ever asked of him.

"Dr. Fraser," came a voice from behind him. Paul turned and saw five men approaching. All were armed, and one carried a rope. Though he didn't recognize any of them, their leader had an English tone in his accent.

"Lord Strathland sent us to summon you. He wants a word."

Paul said nothing, and he suspected Strathland wanted far more than a word from him. "He can come and pay a call on me in the morning. I'm staying with Lord Lanfordshire." His gaze drew in his surroundings, searching for a sign of the duke's men or a way out. No doubt the moment he made a move in any direction, they would pursue him. The question was whether they meant to kill him.

Paul supposed he ought to feel fear or a sense of urgency. Instead, his mood was pensive, as if he'd expected this.

"Lord Strathland wants to see you this evening at his house. We are your escorts," the man said. "I am his new factor, Charles Davenport."

Davenport made it sound as if Paul had been invited to tea instead of his own execution.

"You'll forgive me if I'm wanting to go home to my wife," Paul said. "But if Strathland wishes to speak to me, I don't mind returning in the morning." With an array of weapons and men to stand at his side.

"Lord Strathland wishes to see *her* as well," Davenport remarked. "We can escort both of you."

"You willna go near my wife," Paul growled, striding forward. He didn't give a damn what happened to him, but if they dared to threaten Juliette, he had no qualms about defending her.

Two of the men tried to grab him, but Paul wrenched himself away. He hauled back his fist and punched the first man. Although his knuckles connected with the man's nose, drawing blood, the other drove his fist into Paul's gut at that moment. All the air was sucked out of his lungs, and he gasped for breath.

He fought hard, but after a time, he realized that he was better off biding his time and reserving his strength. He was outnumbered, and feigning surrender might prove a more useful tactic. One man jerked his arms behind his back, while another came forward with the rope. Paul flexed his wrists, fighting against them as they bound him, trying to force the rope to be looser than they wanted.

He never saw the blow that took him from behind, dragging him into darkness.

Sunlight speared her eyes from between the drapes, and Juliette reached over to the empty side of the bed. Paul wasn't there. Though she tried to tell herself that he'd likely been tending more wounded people, she had a cold sense that something wasn't right. Even when he'd been gone for hours, he'd always come home. She would awaken from sleep to find his arms around her, and she'd welcomed the comfort of his embrace.

When she sat up, the room spun a moment, and she saw stars. Fighting off the dizziness, she reached for a dressing gown and drew open the drapes. It was far later than she'd expected, nearly eight o'clock in the morning. She turned back to Paul's pillow and saw that his coverlet was still tucked in place, the pillowcase smooth.

He hadn't come home last night.

She rang for Mrs. Larson, needing to get dressed, when suddenly, her stomach twisted with nausea. Oh God. She knew this feeling. The familiarity of it was like a physical blow, for she knew what it meant. She dropped to her knees, reaching for the chamber pot, and ended up gagging. There was nothing in her stomach, but the impulse was impossible to stop. When she was done, she rested her face upon the wooden floor.

"Miss Juliette, may I come in?" came the cheerful voice of the housekeeper.

If she lay there without moving, her stomach might not lurch again.

"Yes," she managed.

When the door swung open, Mrs. Larson hurried forward. "Oh, my poor lamb. What is it? Are ye sick?"

Juliette managed a nod, feeling as if she didn't dare lift her head.

"Well, now, let's see if we can't get ye back to bed," the housekeeper said. "Lean against me while I help you up."

Juliette did, and the room shifted beneath her feet once more. When she managed to sit upon the bed, she lowered her head to her lap, taking several deep breaths.

"It's at times like these when it's good tae be married to a doctor," Mrs. Larson pronounced. "Where is Dr. Fraser, then?"

"I don't know. He didn't come into our room last night." She kept trying to tell herself that it was nothing, but her intuition only heightened the chill of fear.

The housekeeper poured water into a basin and brought over a damp cloth. "I'll see if anyone saw him last night. He might have slept at his mother's house, if it was too late."

But Juliette didn't believe that. She needed to see him, to know if he was all right. The housekeeper gave her a cool cloth, and she wiped her face, hoping to calm the roiling fear.

"Could I get some toast to eat?" she asked. "Nothing but bread, please."

The housekeeper's face narrowed. "You're looking a wee bit peaked, Lady Falsham." A slight smile perked at her mouth. "I won't be lying. I do like calling you that. Dr. Fraser's a fine man, and now that he's a viscount . . . why, it's simply perfect." Her gaze drifted lower. "If your stomach is tossin' in the morning, I suspect it won't be long before ye have a wee bairn to look after. So soon after your wedding bodes for many children." She patted Juliette's hand. "Is it possible, do ye think?"

She gave no answer. Unfortunately, it was looking more and more likely. Right now she wanted to lie back on the bed and curl up into a ball. But if it was true and she was expecting a child, then lying down was the last thing she needed. She had to find Paul.

"If you'll help me to dress, I'll eat the toast when you've prepared it, before I go to find my husband."

"I'll see to it, my lady." Mrs. Larson helped her to don a gown over the light blue chemise and corset she'd chosen. The frock was a new one that Paul had bought for her, white with tiny blue flowers upon it. The high waist and scooped neckline clung to her body, while a blue satin ribbon was her sash. She pulled on her gloves and finished dressing, although several times, she had to stop and take deep breaths to force back the dizziness.

But when she went down to the breakfast table, she saw Cain Sinclair speaking to her mother. The grim look on the man's face confirmed her worst fears. "Where is he?" she demanded, hurrying forward.

"Strathland's men ambushed him last night. My brother Jonah saw them leaving and came to tell me."

"Is he alive?" she demanded. A roaring filled her ears, and she gripped the edge of a chair. "Tell me he's not dead." She couldn't even grasp the thought, it was so terrible. Though she'd only been wedded to Paul a short time, she'd loved him far longer than that. He couldn't die. Not like this.

The stoic expression on Cain's face was not reassuring. Her knees grew weak, and she sank into the chair, her hands shaking. "Tell me."

"I don't know what's happened, but we're going to find out. Stay here, Lady Falsham." His eyes burned into hers. "Don't interfere until we can bring him back."

She stared at him, wondering how she could possibly wait behind these walls while he went to save her husband. And then what? Strathland had crossed beyond reason and into madness. Both of them would lash out at the other until one of them was dead.

It had to end.

If Paul killed Strathland, he would be brought up on murder charges. An earl outranked a viscount, and the consequences would be severe. But she couldn't live this way any longer, running away from the man who had taken so much from her. The earl had stolen her innocence and had given her nothing but heartache. She would not allow him to harm Paul. If anyone needed to face Strathland, it was her.

"I'm not staying here," she told Cain. "I'm going with you. I've a need for my own vengeance." She hardly cared that she was risking her own life. This was about taking it back again.

"No, you won't leave," Cain argued. "He'll only use you against Fraser."

He wasn't going to listen to her. It was easier to feign her agreement than to waste time on words that meant nothing. Instead, she gave what truths she could. "Go and help Paul, then," she said. "I won't interfere with that."

And she wouldn't. She had her own purpose for paying a call upon Strathland. She trusted Mr. Sinclair to free her husband. This time, she intended to see to it that the earl understood the truth—that he no longer held any power over her or her family.

When he'd gone, her father stepped in front of her. "I know that look on your face, Juliette."

She said nothing, waiting for him to tell her all the reasons why it was wrong for her to leave. Likely, he'd try to lock her in her room, as if she was still a little girl.

"Paul is my husband," she insisted. "He's the man I love, and I'll not stand by and do nothing."

"I won't ask you to stand aside."

His words startled her, and he gestured for her to sit at the table. "But I have spent many years planning battle strategies. I wonder if you might allow a father's help in your own war."

From across the room, she caught Beatrice staring at the pair of them, her face softening. Her mother came to stand by her husband, and she touched a hand to his shoulder. "Henry, thank you."

He cleared his throat. "I know I've not been there for you, while you were growing up. I missed many things. Seeing you transform from a girl into a woman. And now a wife."

"I don't understand why Strathland won't just leave us in peace," she said. "Why he won't give up."

"There are some men who cannot accept defeat. They'll destroy everything in the hopes of acquiring what they desire most."

Her mother sat across from both of them. "I'll be the first to admit that I didn't approve of your marriage, when I first learned of it. I didn't believe Charlotte when she told me of Dr. Fraser's title, either."

Beatrice took a breath and added, "But I've seen the way he looks at you, and I believe that you both deserve to be happy."

Henry exchanged a look with his wife and nodded. "I agree with you that Strathland should leave all of us in peace. And I think I know a way to make that happen. Without killing him," he added. "The last thing we need right now is a murder trial."

Juliette leaned in. "What do you suggest?"

"You're going to die, you know." Strathland's voice was silken, as if he relished every moment of Paul's capture. "After she arrives."

Paul flexed his wrists, loosening his ropes further. He couldn't break free yet, not when there were two men guarding him from behind. "Juliette won't come. She knows better than to take that risk."

"Even to save your life?" the earl mused. "I sent word to her this morning. I think she'll be here soon enough."

Paul said nothing, studying his surroundings. There was only one door leading out of the drawing room, behind the earl. The two men on either side of him were armed with knives. He contemplated each possibility, knowing he had to disarm the two men before he could get past the earl.

"I enjoyed her, you know." Strathland's taunt resonated in the room, and Paul gripped the ropes so tightly, he envisioned them cutting off the air in the man's lungs. "She tried to fight me, but I held her down. And when I was inside her, she was wet. She wanted what I gave her."

"She never wanted you."

"She didn't want you, either," the earl said. "You were so pitiful, trying to court her with your lies. You're no viscount. You're nothing but a penniless crofter's son."

He was wrong, but Paul didn't bother to correct him. "And what does that say about you? She chose to wed a penniless crofter over an earl. It seems she didn't enjoy you after all."

Strathland's face turned purple, and he crossed the room. Pain radiated through Paul when the man's fist struck his jaw. He tasted blood in his mouth, but he forced himself to stare back at the earl.

"I had her first," Strathland insisted. "And before you die, I'm going to have her again." His smile held the promise of violence, and Paul had had enough. He fumbled with the ropes until finally his wrists were free. He kept the rope ends in his palms, awaiting the moment to strike.

"You'll never touch her again."

But before he could release his wrists from the ropes and lunge toward Strathland, the butler interrupted. "My lord, there is a caller for you."

Strathland straightened his waistcoat. "There, you see? She is here, now that I've summoned her."

Although the butler had not confirmed that Juliette was the caller, Paul wasn't about to wait around for Strathland to return. As soon as the man disappeared from the room, Paul dropped the ropes and dove toward the guard to his left. He seized the man's blade and spun out of the way when the second attacked.

There came the sound of glass shattering on the far wall, but Paul was too busy using one of the men as a shield while he fought against the other.

He shoved the man forward, and it caused the pair to topple over. On the other side of the room, a window was forced open. Cain Sinclair demanded, "Fraser, get over here!"

Paul swung his fist at the ear of one attacker, and the man crumpled. Without pausing, he hurried toward the open window, avoiding the broken glass on the carpet. He shoved the window open farther and swung his legs over the sill.

"I didna need your help," he told Sinclair. "Tell me you weren't daft enough to bring my wife with you."

"I warned her to stay. I've no idea if she listened."

Paul let out a curse, gripping the window ledge and dropping down to the ground below. "I hope to God she did." He couldn't imagine what would bring Juliette here, not after all that Strathland had done to her.

"We're not finished here," he warned Cain. "No' until I know she's safe."

"I didna think we were." Sinclair led him around the outside of the house, keeping to the walls. "There's another way in, through the kitchens."

"And how do you think we'll get inside without being seen?"

"Oh, we'll be seen. There's no doubt of that. But the kitchen maids have no love for Strathland. I think they're wanting him to get his due."

"So am I." Paul reached for the blade he'd stolen from one of Strathland's guards. He followed Cain into the kitchen, keeping the hilt in his palm. It was time to end all of this.

Juliette stood in the foyer, meeting Strathland eye to eye while her father stood behind her. His quiet presence gave her a courage she'd never expected. "Lord Strathland, I've come for my husband. I believe he is here."

"He is indeed, Mrs. Fraser." His tone was snide, as if he didn't expect her to remain a wife for much longer. "Dr. Fraser was trespassing upon my property."

"It's Lady Falsham," she corrected. "And I don't believe that's what happened at all." In fact, she knew it wasn't, but Strathland had a propensity for lies.

The earl raised his gaze to her father. "Lord Lanfordshire, was there a reason why you came?"

"To look after my daughter, of course," he said. "It would not be fitting for her to pay a call upon an unmarried gentleman without a proper escort."

Juliette sent her father a grateful look. "Now, if you will please bring my husband here, we can sort this out."

"Can we? And how will we do that? Those crofters you're protecting were responsible for my wool stores being burned."

"Just as you were responsible for our house being burned?" she countered. "Whatever happened to your wool was not our doing. You brought it upon yourself."

Strathland's face went cold. "I have evidence to the contrary. Your husband was involved in a raid that set the fires."

"It's a lie," she insisted. "We weren't even in Ballaloch when that happened."

But from the dark look in his expression, she could tell he didn't believe her. In his twisted mind, he wanted to blame Paul for all of it. "He will be brought up on charges and held accountable for my losses." His expression was cool, his countenance bitter.

"Come, Juliette," her father said. "If he will not release Lord Falsham, then we have charges of our own to press." He crossed his arms, and Juliette was grateful for his intervention. Though she didn't want to leave Paul here, it was part of her father's strategy, and she trusted him.

"You aren't going anywhere," Strathland said. "We haven't finished discussing the terms."

"You may not have finished, but I have," she countered, turning to walk back with her father. Before she moved two steps, she sensed movement behind her. She glanced over in time to see Strathland reach into his coat pocket. A pistol glinted in the light, and he pulled the trigger. Her father crumpled to the floor, blood spilling out from his leg.

She gave a cry and rushed to him, pulling out a handkerchief. Never had she expected Strathland to shoot a family member, and her rage trebled. How could he? She tried to stanch the blood with the handkerchief, but the moment she touched the wound on his left calf, her father lost consciousness. Dear God, was he going to be all right? A rush of panic roared through her. He couldn't be wounded like this. Not by Strathland's hand.

"Why would you do this?" she demanded.

"To prove a point," Strathland said calmly, loading another bullet. "That I won't allow you to control me in any way." He stretched out his hand, beckoning to her. "You're coming with me now. We're going to speak with the man who calls himself your husband."

"He *is* my husband," Juliette said, still trying to stop the bleeding. Her mind harked back to the moment when Paul had been unable to save the wounded crofter, and she prayed her father would not meet the same fate. The wound was in his calf, and she didn't think it was too bad. But the flesh was ragged and torn open by the bullet.

"You made a mistake in marrying Fraser. You belong to me and always have," the earl said calmly. "And I will no longer allow you to make your own decisions. You will do as I order, if you value the lives of those you love."

All of the pent-up rage flooded her veins. His arrogance held no bounds. "I will *never* belong to you, Lord Strathland. Never."

"You will," he insisted. "Unless you want your husband to die a painful death." His smug expression revealed his intentions. He fully intended to torment Paul until she did exactly as he commanded.

This man had pulled the strings of her life for so long, forcing her to do his will. She'd lived in the shadow of fear, losing herself and her own dreams. And suddenly, she saw the madness beneath. He thrived upon controlling others, believing it made him superior. But no longer would she play that game.

"No." She straightened, meeting his gaze fully. "I won't be used like that. You hold no power over me."

"Don't I?" He held up the loaded pistol, nodding toward her wounded father.

No. He didn't. Strangely, her fear had dissipated. Lord Strathland could indeed pull the trigger. But ending their lives would accomplish nothing.

Slowly, she took a step toward him. "You can shoot me, if that's your wish. And then you'll have nothing at all." Another step forward, until she stood with the pistol pointed directly at her heart. She held her breath, forcing herself to bluff. "I'm not afraid to die."

It wasn't true, but if he'd gone to all of this trouble to lure her here, he likely wasn't planning to kill her. At this moment, she had nothing at all to lose by confronting him. She would fight for her husband's life.

"I like the way you fight me," he said, his voice edged with lust. "I'll let all of them go, if you give yourself over to me," he said, his eyes burning with madness. "One word . . . and I'll take you away from here. We'll live somewhere far away."

He believed in that fantasy, of possessing her. There could be no reasoning with a madman. "I know that I can be . . . intimidating." His hand cupped her cheek, and his brown eyes darkened with desire. "But it's only because I am strong-willed. I'll take care of you, and you, in turn, will learn to love me. Especially when you've come to accept your place as my wife."

The look in his eyes was dangerous, and an unbidden fear took root. His hand moved down to her throat, his thumb caressing.

She said nothing, understanding that his vanity was the key to Paul's freedom. "Put the weapon down," she said softly. "You don't need it."

"No. I don't." He set the pistol down and seized her arm, dragging her to him. He gripped her shoulders tightly, and the shock of his touch reawakened a thousand nightmares through her. Juliette clenched her teeth against the fear, reminding herself that she was not alone. There were others who could help her.

"I took you once before," the earl said hotly. "You haven't the strength to fight against me."

Not then, she didn't. But she did now.

She moved her left hand behind her back, reaching toward the last button that was undone. Her palm closed over the dirk her father had given her.

In one swift motion, she brought the tip to his throat. "But I brought a weapon of my own this time."

His wife was holding a blade to Strathland's throat. Paul remained in the shadows, with Cain on the opposite side. A few feet away, he saw Juliette's father holding a handkerchief to a bleeding wound.

Instinct demanded that he rush forward and pull Juliette back before the earl could hurt her. But a sharp look from Cain held him back. No, she was in command now.

"You're too weak to kill me," Strathland said. "You won't do it."

"Won't I?" Juliette pressed against the blade, and a line of blood appeared against Strathland's throat. "Your death would free all of us."

"My sister knows about our son," he threatened. "If I die, she'll reveal that he's a bastard. What do you think will happen to him then?"

She gave an imperceptible flinch, correcting herself as she said, "I have no son."

The earl held himself motionless. "Matthew is his name, am I right? And he was born almost nine months after I took you."

Juliette's hand began to shake, and Paul saw her father sit up. He struggled to rise to his feet, holding the handkerchief to his wounded leg. His complexion was gray, but his voice was iron. "What is he talking about, Juliette?"

She pushed against the blade and faced the earl. "You might have attacked me. But I have no child and never did."

"Lady Arnsbury is barren," he argued.

"Was," she countered. "And I swear to you that the only child I've ever had is the one I'm carrying now." Her hand moved to her flat stomach, and Paul's lungs tightened. It was far too soon for that, and he wondered if she was telling a lie to taunt the earl. He hoped to God she was, for he knew the danger.

The earl moved suddenly, and the knife went flying from Juliette's hand. "The boy is mine. I know it, and I'll not let him be raised as another man's son." He backhanded her, and Juliette stumbled to the ground. Her hand automatically went to protect her stomach, and Paul moved in, unsheathing his blade. "Juliette, move away."

She obeyed without question, relief in her eyes at the sight of him.

"You and I have a score to settle," he said to the earl. He'd waited for this moment almost all his life, it seemed. Now that it was here, his focus sharpened. Strathland was an older man with a thick build. Though his enemy would lack speed, Paul knew he possessed cunning in full measure.

The earl lunged toward the pistol, but Paul threw himself at the man before he could reach the weapon. Hatred and rage coursed through him as he seized Strathland. This was what he wanted—to end the man who had caused so much harm. They grappled together, and although the earl was strong, he wasn't fast. Paul slipped free and used his legs to trip the earl, dragging him down. He didn't feel anything when he hit the floor, he was so driven by the need for vengeance.

The blade Juliette had dropped was close by. He could almost reach it . . .

But Strathland saw it first. His fist closed over the hilt, but before he could stab downward, Paul lashed out with all his strength. He struck the man's ear, then followed through with a blow to the earl's nose.

He fought with all of his strength, twisting Strathland's wrist behind him until he was forced to drop the dirk.

"You're nothing," Strathland growled. "And you'll die knowing that I had her first."

The words only fueled Paul's rage, pushing him over the edge into a sea of violence. His knuckles bled as he crushed them against the earl's face, following up with another blow to the man's gut. Although Strathland struggled to free himself, Paul held him fast.

For my father, he thought silently, as he rolled over and caught the man in a chokehold. His heated revenge transformed into icy hatred. Now was the moment he'd waited for . . . to watch as his enemy's breath left him.

For Juliette, he thought. He squeezed the life from the earl with the crook of his elbow against the man's windpipe. Strathland fought hard, his hands pulling at Paul's arm. Gradually, his body grew limp from the lack of air.

"Paul, stop," Juliette said.

He didn't want to stop. He wanted to continue cutting off the man's air until there was nothing left. "He deserves to die after what he did to you. To all of us."

"Killing him will only bring the magistrate down upon us," she said. She moved forward and touched his arm, kneeling beside him. "I won't let them hang you for murder. Let go before he's dead." Her fingers passed over his shoulder, and though he didn't want to grant any mercy at all, the quiet conviction in Juliette's eyes made him obey.

Though Strathland was unconscious now, his nose bleeding, and likely he had a few broken ribs, it didn't seem like enough. The desire to slit the man's throat or put a bullet through his brain was too strong. Seeing him touch Juliette had driven him past reason.

"I won't leave him here," Paul insisted. "He has to pay for what he's done."

"And he will. But I know a better way that he will suffer, without our laying a hand upon him." She reached out and collected the fallen knife and the pistol. Cain emerged from the shadows, and she handed him the weapons. At that moment, the two men who had held Paul captive hurried forward.

"Don't move," Cain warned. As soon as the men saw the earl's unconscious form, they raised their hands up in surrender. "Do what you will with Lord Strathland," one said. "I don't care if he dies."

The other man nodded toward the door, asking silent permission to leave. Cain stepped aside and let them go.

Paul moved toward Juliette's father and examined the gunshot wound. It wasn't too serious, and the bullet had only grazed the calf. He adjusted the makeshift bandage, intending to treat it when they brought her father back home again.

"What do you want to do with Strathland?" he asked his wife. The idea of granting the man mercy was impossible to consider.

"Take him to the most isolated place in Scotland, and strand him where there's no water," Juliette suggested. "He won't survive it."

Paul exchanged a look with her father, whose face was tight with pain. The man gave a slight nod, agreeing with his daughter. "It's a reasonable idea."

"And what if he does live?" Paul demanded. "He won't stop until he's had his vengeance upon us."

"Look at him," she said. "He has no wool to sell, and the debtors will come to take this house from him. He has nothing at all. Even if he did live, he'd spend the remainder of his days in poverty."

Though her words were logical, it wasn't enough to atone for the earl's crimes. "Why would you ever show mercy to this man?" he demanded. "After all that he's done."

"Because if he dies at your hands, the consequences are too great. I love you, and I can't let you suffer for what he's done to us. I need you to live, Paul. Especially now." She moved into his arms, holding tightly to him.

He stroked her hair and drew his hand down to her waist in silent question. Though it was far too soon to tell, he suspected she had missed her menses. If she was pregnant, then she was putting her life and the baby's life in his hands. There could be no greater task than to keep them both alive.

"We'll return to Edinburgh together. Just you and I," Juliette promised. She held out her hand, and in her eyes, he saw the longing. "I trust you to keep me safe."

"I swear to you, I'll never let anything happen to you."

She put her hand in his and met his gaze. "Promise me you won't interfere with Strathland's exile. I need you with me." She rose up on tiptoe and whispered in his ear, "And if I die in childbirth, I'll need you to be there for our child."

Chapter Eighteen

"Thank God you're back," Juliette breathed, pulling back the coverlet. It was an hour before dawn, and Paul had only just returned. He'd been gone for two days.

He'd traveled with Mr. Sinclair, taking the earl far to the north, hundreds of miles from any of the clans. They had drugged Strathland with a high dose of laudanum to keep him unconscious throughout the journey.

"It's done now. Sinclair took him a little farther and sent me back here." He stripped away his clothing and slid into bed beside her.

"I don't believe he'll survive," she admitted. "He's too accustomed to luxury. I doubt if he even knows how to find food in such an isolated place."

"Likely not." His arms slid around her, and she closed her eyes at the comfort of his hard body next to hers. She wore a nightgown, but the heat of his skin made her skin sensitive. His hands moved over her breasts, then lower to her stomach. "How long has it been since your monthly?"

"Six weeks," she whispered. "As far as I can remember." She caught his hands and rolled over to face him. "It might not be true."

His hands moved lower, to the hem of her nightgown. He raised it up, his hands moving over her bare flesh. "I think I should examine you. As your physician."

She might have smiled, if she weren't uneasy about the truth. "If I am pregnant, it must have been that time when we—"

"Shh." He pulled back the coverlet and helped her remove the nightgown. Naked, she lay against him, skin upon skin. His hands moved down her arms, to her breasts. Gently, he touched them, running his thumbs over the puckered nipples.

"They do feel different," he said. "They're thicker and slightly enlarged." He pressed his mouth to one breast, his tongue circling the nipple. She shuddered, wincing at the touch. "And more sensitive, aren't they?"

"Yes."

Paul gave the other breast the same attention, nipping at the hard nub and circling the tip. "I could taste you for hours, Juliette. But I ken these are too delicate right now."

He drew his hands lower, over her rib cage to her stomach. It was still flat, but he trailed his mouth over her skin. Upon her womb, he pressed a kiss. "I think you are pregnant. And if you carry our bairn inside you, I swear to you that I'll do everything possible to keep you safe."

She wanted that more than anything. But she didn't want to lose him. Now that they were together, with the earl gone from their lives, she felt the need to savor their marriage.

"I am afraid," she admitted. "But in spite of that, I do want this child. I've always thought you would make a good father."

"You're already a good mother, Juliette." He embraced her, and she tried to push away the fears, imagining the joy of a second baby. One she could keep forever. One who would have his father's smile.

The fear was still there, lurking. But she forced herself to dwell upon the joy instead of the uncertainty. There was time enough later to worry. For now, she wanted to enjoy this moment with Paul.

"If I am going to have a baby, then there's no harm in making love to me," she whispered to Paul, trying to pull him up.

"Aye," he promised. He parted her legs, his hand moving between them. The moment he touched her, she grew wet, and his caress made her catch her breath.

"You're sensitive here, too, aren't you?" This time, when he explored her flesh, she couldn't stop the soft moan. He delved inside her, and she shuddered against the invasion.

"Yes." She trembled against him, and when his thumb brushed the nodule of her arousal, a delicious warmth poured over her.

He continued to touch her, his hand stroking and coaxing her higher. Gently, he lowered his mouth to her nipple again, his warm breath hardening the tip. She couldn't stand it any longer and lifted one leg over his hip, guiding his length inside her.

The moment he filled her, the motion set her on edge, pushing her toward the aching release she craved. It took only a few strokes before she arched back, her nails digging into his shoulders. She squeezed him inside her, welcoming his easy thrusts as her body trembled with the unexpected fulfillment.

"That didna take long," he teased, withdrawing slightly and entering her again. "But I'm not finished with you yet."

She was quaking against him, her body welcoming his invasion. "You can do anything you wish to me."

For it didn't matter now. The damage was already done, and she fully intended to enjoy this aspect of marriage.

Over and over, he penetrated, his hands splayed over her hips as he thrust. She couldn't stop herself from shaking, the exhilaration rushing through her.

"More," she begged, and he quickened the pace, driving against her until perspiration broke over her skin.

She gripped him with both legs around his waist, and he thrust deeply, staring into her eyes as he murmured, "I love you, Juliette. And always will."

"I love you, Paul." She met his hips with her own, watching as he began to come apart, his body growing harder as his thick length merged with her flesh. She saw the moment he gave a cry, flooding her with his seed.

And she smiled, loving the feeling of his body inside hers. This was right, always meant to be.

She could only pray that these months remaining would not be their last.

Seven months later

"Have I told you how beautiful you are? Especially with ink-stained fingers?" Paul closed the door to his study, admiring his wife.

Juliette sent him a half-smile as she looked up from the desk. "I've been sorting through the accounts, and everything is in order. All the bills have been paid, as well as the taxes. I have a listing of the profits, and if you'll look—"

"I don't really care, *a chrìdhe*," he said, moving closer. "The accounts are yours to do with as you wish."

Her body was distended with the pregnancy, her hair tucked in a neat chignon. When he moved to kneel beside her, he saw that her shoes were off and her feet were swollen.

"You should look at the ledgers," she insisted. "I've done what I could to ensure that the estates are successful."

He knelt at her feet and pressed a kiss against her womb. No longer did she have the smooth curve of pregnancy; now there were sharp edges where the child's elbows or knees poked out. It would not be long now, and he didn't like the way she was anticipating the worst.

"How are you feeling?" he murmured, massaging her ankles.

"Afraid." She touched his face, pulling him up to kiss her. "I want to hold our baby in my arms. I want to be there every moment as he grows older."

"You will be fine," he promised. Not only had he been trained to deliver babies, but he'd also sent for his mother a fortnight ago. As a midwife, Bridget had seen many labors, and her practical knowledge was welcome. Then, too, he'd spoken to his colleagues at the medical college in Edinburgh, studying every case of childbirth that had gone wrong. He'd spent late nights poring over the books, learning everything he could.

"I'm glad we had this time together," she admitted. "And I pray that all will be well with our child." She reached out to take his hand, saying, "I've had a letter from Charlotte. Matthew is running around now and has begun to talk."

Though she spoke the words in a neutral tone, as if sharing news of the weather, Paul knew how much it meant to her. "After our bairn is born, I'll take you to London. You'll want to see Matthew."

Thankfully, there was no longer any threat in Juliette visiting Matthew from time to time. Although Strathland had eventually been found in the Highlands, he'd nearly starved to death. In the meantime, the unentailed property in Scotland and all the sheep were sold off to pay his massive debts. The last they'd heard of him, Strathland had gone into seclusion, and there were whispers that he'd gone mad after the experience. Months had passed, and Paul took satisfaction in knowing that the earl would never again bother them.

"I would like to see Matthew, yes," she said, but Paul could see that Juliette was distracted. A tension crossed her face, and her lips tightened.

"What is it?" he asked, noting the change in her expression.

"My back has been hurting all day. I think I'd like to go and lie down."

Her mention of back pain made him uneasy, but he would say nothing to make her afraid. "I'll help you."

He eased her up, and she sent him a rueful smile. "I wonder if I'll ever see my feet again."

"Of course you will." But as he helped her up, he saw the visible discomfort. She said nothing, but she hesitated before taking another step.

The contractions had started; he was sure of it. And she hadn't intended to tell him—at least, not yet. Each step upstairs was a struggle for her, but he led her past their bedroom, to another room he'd prepared.

"I thought you wanted me to lie down," she protested, when he opened the door.

"And so you will. But here, instead of in our room."

The bed he'd prepared was stripped of all coverings except clean sheets. He'd given her a pillow, and upon the dressing table, he'd laid out the instruments he would need. Although they had been cleaned before, he intended to boil them again to take no chances.

She sat down on the edge of the bed. "I wasn't going to tell you."

"I'm a physician, Juliette. Of course I recognize when a woman has begun her labor." He went to sit beside her, loosening her gown. His hand passed over her womb, and he felt the skin harden during another contraction. Juliette closed her eyes, her face pale.

"The contractions only just started this morning. It will be a while yet."

"We're going to remain here," he said. "This is your second child, and your labor will not be as long as the last one."

"And how many babies have you delivered?" she said, half in teasing.

"Seventeen." Most had been normal, but he'd delivered two breech children and one stillborn. He knew well enough the danger they would face together. But his greatest fear was having to perform surgery to take the bairn out. He had no desire to put Juliette under the knife, particularly with all the risks.

Her hands dug into the sheets, and she closed her eyes as another wave of pain struck. God, it made him feel so helpless. He wanted to take the agony from her, if he could. But the only medicines that would suppress the pain would also endanger the labor.

He rang for their housekeeper and ordered her to begin boiling some water. The pains were beginning to come closer together, and Juliette was struggling.

Paul began talking to her, telling her stories to set her at ease. Of how their cat Dragon had brought a live mouse into the kitchen and scared the life out of a scullery maid. He talked endlessly, but when her labor intensified, he saw that the conversation was becoming more of an irritation to her than a comfort.

"I need to examine you, to see how you're progressing," he told her. He helped her to remove her clothing and then washed his hands again.

Superstitious, perhaps, but it seemed right to do so.

Juliette's stomach was hard, and he felt the position of the child, noting where the sharp corners were. She was fighting against another contraction, and he knew it would only be a few hours longer, if that.

A knock sounded at the door, and after he covered his wife with a sheet, he ordered the housekeeper to come in. But instead of the servant, his mother stood there, a basket over one arm.

"There's my wee lamb." She smiled at Juliette and came over to give her a kiss. "It's glad I am to see ye."

"I thought I was your wee lamb," Paul remarked drily.

"Once, ye might've been, aye. But now, I've come to see my first grandchild delivered, and to help as I'm needed." Bridget poured water into the basin and washed her own hands. "I see ye started without me."

Though his mother had an air of command, Paul wasn't about to leave the room. He leaned in and kissed her cheek in welcome. "I am glad that you've come."

She nodded and went to examine Juliette. As soon as her hands passed over his wife's stomach, he saw the flicker in her eyes. She knew, as he'd guessed, that the infant was breech.

"Juliette, love, I want you to lie back," Bridget urged. "Your sweet bairn is facing the wrong way, and Paul and I are going to turn it."

His wife obeyed, but he could see the rigid terror in her face. "I was afraid this would happen."

"Every bairn has a mind of his own. And we'll fix the wee one, don't you fret. It may not be comfortable, but it can be done. Paul, come and help me."

"It will be all right," he told Juliette. "Try to relax, and we'll do what we can."

"You're going to hold your wife and help her through it while I turn the bairn," Bridget instructed.

Though Paul could do it, his mother had done it far more often, and he wasn't about to intrude upon her expertise. Juliette was fighting to breathe, perspiration upon her forehead while she held his hands.

"It hurts," she moaned. And when Bridget pressed against her womb, she cried out, shuddering as another pain wracked her. His mother continued her attempts to turn the baby, but he suspected it wasn't working.

The contractions were constant now, one coming on top of the other. Bridget met his gaze, and her sober expression confirmed what he already knew. The child could not be turned.

His eyes drifted toward his medical bag nearby, in silent question. His mother shook her head, as if to say, *It's too grave a risk.*

He knew that. But if it meant saving Juliette's life, he'd do whatever was necessary.

"Ye must stop pushing, Juliette," his mother warned. "It's too soon for that."

"It's—the only thing that helps me endure the pain," she said, her voice trembling. A cry tore from her lips as another contraction seized her. Paul had never felt so helpless in his life. Bridget continued to manipulate his wife's womb, trying once again to turn the bairn.

"P-Paul," Juliette whispered, gripping his hands so tightly, it was a wonder she hadn't broken his fingers. "I love you. I always have."

"I know, *a chrìdhe.* As I love you." He smoothed back her hair, meeting her eyes. "Hold on, and soon you'll have our wee bairn in your arms."

Her green eyes were bleak. "I was afraid this might happen. But I don't regret being with you." Tears threatened, and her voice grew hoarse. "If I die, promise me you'll take care of our baby. And tell Matthew one day . . . that I loved him."

"You'll tell him yourself," he insisted. But the surrender in her expression terrified him. She didn't believe she would live to see this child born. And if they didn't get the bairn out soon, both of them would die.

"She's ready," Bridget pronounced. "My girl, it's time for you to push now."

"H-has the baby turned?"

"No. But we'll do as ever best we can," Bridget promised.

Paul prayed to God he wouldn't have to cut in. A breech birth was dangerous enough, but surgery could claim Juliette's life in any number of ways.

The minutes stretched to over an hour, but he helped support his wife against him, holding her knees back while she pushed. Bridget was struggling, and her expression looked grave as she tried to ease the child out.

"Take her," Paul commanded. Though his mother had delivered thousands of bairns, this was his Juliette. He needed to see for himself what was wrong, or he'd never be able to live with himself.

Bridget took his place, holding on to Juliette while Paul examined his wife. Only one leg had emerged from her womb, and he didn't doubt that the tiny infant was fighting for life at this moment.

God be with us, he prayed, casting another glance toward his bag. He pushed back, feeling for the infant's leg, trying to adjust the child. His brain was screaming at him, while he recalled just how many of the infants had died in the cases he'd read.

He had to make a decision. Now, before he lost both of them.

Chapter Nineteen

Juliette was hardly aware of anything but a sea of pain. Her husband and his mother were arguing, and without warning, she felt the sharp slice of a blade. Warm blood spilled against her, but she was past the point of knowing what was happening.

The man she adored was fighting for her life and the life of their child. In the blur of agony, she saw the fear on his face. But there was nothing she could say to reassure him. Nothing except a weak "I love you, Paul."

"Stay with me," he warned. "Don't give up, Juliette. Keep trying."

She wasn't aware of anything, but her body was past exhaustion and had now slipped into a haze of defeat. Hands were pushing against her, and a moment later, she heard the faint cry of a newborn. The sound of the infant's voice slashed through her consciousness, dragging her back.

Their baby was alive. Through her tears, she managed a smile, and a moment later, Paul placed the baby on her stomach. "It's a girl."

The grateful look in his eyes was mingled with awe, as if he could not believe he was a father.

"She's a darling wee bairn." Bridget smiled. "A little bruised, but she should be fine."

Juliette reached out to touch her daughter, and a tear spilled down one cheek. "She's beautiful."

But though she marveled at the tiny life, a dizziness took hold, causing the room to dip. "You'd better take her, Paul," she murmured, closing her eyes. "I need to . . . rest now."

She felt the strength slipping away from her, while Bridget claimed the baby.

"Juliette, no. Don't give in. Look at me," Paul demanded. "I had to cut you to keep you from tearing too much. You need to deliver the afterbirth, and then I'm going to sew you up again to stop the bleeding."

"I'm tired," she whispered.

"And you can sleep all you want, later. Right now, you're going to push a little more."

"I can't."

"Aye, you can." He manipulated her womb, and she winced at the pain. "You've endured more than any other woman I know, and it's made you stronger. You can get through a little more, and then you'll hold our bairn."

She gritted her teeth as he helped her deliver the afterbirth, and soon enough, he began stitching her up. "We'll have to come up with a name. Have you any you'd like?"

"Grace," she murmured. "I always liked that name."

"Grace Fraser, she shall be," he promised. "She'll be a sweet one, won't she? She has my eyes, I think."

"All babies have blue eyes," Bridget said. "Though you can be believing that if you like. She has her mother's bonny face, too." The older woman's face held joy, and she wiped a tear away.

Juliette fought to keep her eyes open, but she endured the stitching until Bridget came to sit by her, holding the baby close, asking, "Your first birth was hard, wasn't it?"

She nodded. "The midwife told me I would never have another child. I had such a terrible fever afterward, I nearly died from it."

"But the labor," Bridget said, "was it much like this one?"

Juliette tried to think back. "It took much longer, and I kept bleeding. I don't remember much except that."

"I don't think the midwife stitched you up after," Bridget said. "It sounds as if she was naught more than a butcher." She leaned over and showed Juliette her daughter. The tiny rosebud mouth and the serious blue eyes stared back at her. "Ye did well enough in your labor, my lamb. If it's more children you're wanting, there's naught to stop you from it. A breech birth happens from time to time, but ye both are fine."

Juliette took her baby back into her arms. "We are, yes." From deep within, the sharp flare of hope broke through her. Seeing her baby daughter alive and well brought a joy that she'd never expected. This tiny new life belonged to her and Paul. Nothing would ever part them.

Her heart ached with such love, she couldn't stop the tears from spilling over.

Bridget smiled warmly. "I'll get you some healing herbs to help with the pain, and you can have some time with your husband and daughter." She departed the room, leaving them alone.

Paul washed his hands again and came to sit by her. He put his arm around Juliette, holding her and their new daughter. "I told you I would take care of you."

"You were right," she admitted. "I was so afraid, after the last time. I believed the midwife when she said I'd never have another child."

Paul touched their daughter's head, offering, "I hated seeing you in pain. I might've delivered seventeen . . . well, eighteen babies," he amended. "But it's no' the same as seeing your wife suffer."

He kissed Grace's head and then kissed Juliette's cheek. "I would have done anything to save you both."

"And you did," she whispered, pulling him back for a longer kiss. The happiness went so deep, Juliette reached for his hand. For a moment, she smiled up at him, marveling that they had endured so much together. Letting go of her son was the hardest thing she'd ever done, but she knew that Matthew was well and happy. And although her son would follow a different path, one day, he would know the truth—that she'd wanted to give him a chance at his own happiness.

She touched Grace's tiny head and looked up at Paul. "I never imagined it was possible to feel this way." Paul had been her best friend for as long as she could remember. She loved this man so much, it hurt to imagine a single moment without him.

"I did," he admitted. "From the first moment I laid eyes on you. I knew we were meant."

There was no man who understood her heart and her very soul the way he did. When she smiled through her tears, she marveled at all of her blessings. She had a husband she loved more than life itself, and a daughter who had utterly captured her heart.

"We have the rest of our lives together," she promised her husband.

And it was enough.

Excerpt from Undressed by the Earl, Book Three in the Secrets in Silk Quartet

London, 1815

Amelia Andrews had waited four excruciatingly long years to marry the Viscount Lisford. Although everyone said he was a wicked rake who gambled and took advantage of innocent women, she didn't care. He was, by far, the handsomest man she'd ever seen. His hazel eyes were mysterious, and his golden hair reminded her of a prince. This was going to be the year he finally fell in love with her, even if she had to throw herself at his feet.

Well, she could faint in front of him, anyway. Diving at a man's shoes wasn't exactly what her mother would deem ladylike.

In her mind, she envisioned reforming him, until he fell madly in love with her and—

"Planning your attack, are you?" came a voice from behind her. Amelia suppressed a groan. David Hartford, the Earl of Castledon, was here again. Sir Personality-of-a-Handkerchief, as she'd once nicknamed him.

He never danced and had never courted a single woman during these past few years since his wife died. He was just *there* all the time. Watching, like a wallflower.

"I've never understood why the ladies here are so fascinated by Viscount Lisford," he remarked. "Would you care to enlighten me?"

She shouldn't be speaking with Lord Castledon, although they'd had numerous conversations in the past year with him addressing her back. If she didn't turn around to face him, it seemed less improper.

Besides that, Lord Castledon was safe—a man she would never consider as a suitor. He wasn't so terribly old, but he'd been married and widowed. He wasn't at all dashing or exciting.

In all honesty, he was perfect for her sister Margaret.

A hard sense of frustration gathered in Amelia's stomach at the thought of her prim and proper eldest sister. There had been a time when she'd *hated* Margaret—for her sister had nearly married the man of Amelia's dreams. The viscount had cried off only days before the wedding, leaving Margaret a spinster and Amelia a shred of hope.

That had been years ago. Surely her sister would forget all about Viscount Lisford, especially if *she* had another man to wed. And Amelia strongly believed that sensible people ought to be paired together. She was not at all sensible. Impulsive, her mother had called her. Amelia preferred to think of herself as spirited.

"Viscount Lisford is quite wicked," Amelia answered honestly. "When you dance with him, you sense the danger. It's delicious."

"I'll take your word for it," he said drily.

From behind her, she sensed him stepping closer. Lord Castledon was quite tall, and even without Amelia turning around, his presence evoked a strange sense, as if he were touching her. The air between them grew warmer, and the silk of her gown made her skin more sensitive.

She stole a quick glance behind her and saw the solemn cast to his face. It didn't seem that he ever smiled, though the earl wasn't unattractive. Aside from being tall, he had black hair and shrewd blue eyes. She'd never seen him wear any color except black. And he rarely spoke to anyone, but her. She had no idea why.

"Dangerous men are nothing but trouble," he continued, moving to stand beside her. "You'd be better off choosing a more respectable man."

"That's what my mother says." Amelia opened her fan, adding, "But marriage to a man like Lord Lisford would never be dull."

"Marriage is not meant to be entertaining. It's a union of two people with a mutual respect for one another."

She eyed him with disbelief. "That sounds awful. Surely you don't mean that."

From the serious expression on his face, she realized he did. "Didn't you ever have fun with your wife?" she asked. "I don't mean to pry, but I thought you loved her."

"She was everything to me."

There was a glimpse of grief that flashed over his face before he masked it. And suddenly, her curiosity was piqued. This boring man, who all too often lurked near the wallpaper, had enjoyed a love match. Try as she would, she couldn't quite imagine him engaged in a passionate tryst. But perhaps there was more to him beneath the surface.

Amelia's heart softened. "No one will ever compare to her, will they?" She stared at him, trying to imagine a man like the earl in love with anyone.

"No." There was a heaviness in his voice. "But I made a promise to my daughter that this Season, I will find a new mother for her." His features twisted as if it was not a welcome idea.

A thought suddenly sparked within Amelia. There was nothing she loved more than matchmaking. She'd successfully paired her sister Juliette off with her husband, Paul, and now here was another chance to find a match for Lord Castledon. Her sister Margaret was nearing five-and-twenty, and after being jilted once, she might be amenable to a man like the earl.

"I have an idea," she told him, unable to keep the excitement from her voice. And oh, it was simply perfect. "We could help one another."

The sidelong look he cast at her was undeniably cynical. "And what could *you* do for me, Miss Andrews?"

"Reconnaissance," she said brightly. "You'll tell me all of your requirements in a wife, and I shall investigate your options. I know all the eligible ladies here, and I'm certain I could find the perfect woman for you."

If Margaret wouldn't suit, there were a few wallflowers who might fit his conditions.

His mouth twisted. "Indeed. And for this 'service,' what do you want from me?"

She hid her face behind her fan. "I want Viscount Lisford. You could speak to him and put in a good word for me."

He crossed his arms, staring across the room. "You're not worthy of a man like him, Miss Andrews."

Amelia felt her cheeks grow hot. "And why not? Is there something wrong with me? I know I talk too much, and most people believe I'm a featherbrain. But surely—"

She didn't finish the sentence, for she suspected what he would say. *You're too young. Too innocent.*

And that might be true, but why couldn't she set her sights on the man she wanted? Why couldn't she marry the handsomest man in London who set her pulse racing? Why should she settle for a titled gentleman with a respectable fortune, when she could have so much more?

No. She didn't need Lord Castledon's help. Not in this.

There were ways to capture a man's attention, and she was *certain* that this was her year. To the earl, she remarked, "Thank you, my lord, but I don't need your help after all. Especially if you believe I'm not worthy of the viscount." She marched in the direction of her aunt Charlotte, hoping no one would see her embarrassment.

David Hartford stared at the young woman as she took long strides away from him. Amelia Andrews was impulsive, spirited, and filled with more *joie de vivre* than anyone he'd ever met.

"No, you're not worthy of the viscount," he remarked under his breath. "You're worth far more."

AUTHOR'S NOTE

Although doctors during the Regency era were largely unaware of how infection and diseases were spread, the
Scots were a highly superstitious people. Dr. Paul Fraser would
not have known that hand-washing or boiling instruments would
kill germs, but he would have recognized that he lost fewer patients than his contemporaries. I took literary license in creating
a Scottish character who washes his hands out of superstition,
without really knowing why doing so helped his patients.

However, early physicians, such as Oliver Wendell Holmes,
wrote essays that predated the germ theory later established by
Joseph Lister. In 1843 Holmes believed that Puerperal fever in
childbirth was spread from doctor to patient; he advocated washing hands and purifying instruments.

Could other physicians have considered this, thirty-three years
sooner? It's quite possible—and I'd like to believe that my
Scottish doctor would have been an early believer.

Acknowledgments

There are some manuscripts that are more challenging to write than others. It takes a special editor with a good eye to see the forest for the trees. With special thanks to Charlotte Herscher for helping me reshape this book and for being so supportive throughout the process.

Thanks also to my agent, Helen Breitwieser, for being a listening ear and for helping me on this journey.

Most of all, thanks to Pat Willingham for always carrying bookmarks in her purse and telling perfect strangers that I write romance.

Mom, you're amazing.

About the Author

Rita® Award Finalist Michelle Willingham has published over twenty books and novellas. Currently, she lives in southeastern Virginia with her husband and children and is working on more historical romance novels. When she's not writing, Michelle enjoys baking, playing the piano, and avoiding exercise at all costs.

Visit her website at www.michellewillingham.com or interact with her on Facebook at www.facebook.com/michellewillinghamfans.